Warmaster 7: The Ivory Palace

Melissa McShane

ISBN-13 9781964545165

Cover design by Etheric Tales www.etherictales.com

Map by Matt Pivots

Pinnalore Mountains
The Repository
Finion's Gate
Branlight
Obsidian
The Welterwall
The Lonely Tor
Blighted Range
Level Sixteen
High Risk Zones
Dungeon

Chapter One

The floor of the passage created by Livia's *world door* spell squished underfoot, like walking on a rubbery bladder filled with water. Aderyn held her arms out to both sides for balance and kept her gaze fixed on the man-sized oval ahead of her. The view through the opening was dim, like the sun had almost set, and Aderyn could barely make out figures passing in front of it, shadowy and indistinct.

With a jolt, she was through, and warm, muggy air pressed in on her from all sides. Her comfortable coat was too warm now. She took a couple of involuntary steps as momentum carried her forward to Owen's side. Owen put a hand on her shoulder to steady her. "Careful."

"It was a surprise, that's all." Aderyn rested her hand atop his and watched the oval frame of *world door* shudder back into being. Isold's image appeared in the frame as if someone had painted his portrait, capturing him in motion mid-step. Beyond him, the walls of Ikharatia rose, higher than those of Finion's Gate and built of pinkish-cream colored stone blocks the width of Aderyn's arm. Aderyn didn't find them intimidating. As big and sturdy as they were, it was hard to take them seriously when they were the color of a princess's ball gown.

While she waited for the others, she Assessed the city.

Name: Ikharatia
Status: Metropolis
Government: Monarchy
Civilization level: 20

Resources: Spiritsmith x24, Spellcrafter x30, Tidecaller x28, Windwarden x29, Flamecrafter x22, Earthbreaker x29, Bonemender x25; Crafters level 20; Hospitality level 24; Food supply level 19

Ikharatia was founded centuries ago by adventurers who tired of the pursuit of experience and glory and chose to carve an outpost of civilization out of the jungle. It is the largest city on the continent and the most technologically advanced, thanks to the many Spellcrafters who make their homes here. Welcome to indoor plumbing.

This metropolis is the capital of the Southlander kingdom, which is not a thing you have in the north. The king rules over much of the land, including many large cities which are in turn ruled by dukes who owe their allegiance to the king. How stable this form of government is depends on the strength of the king and the loyalty of his dukes. Don't think this has nothing to do with you. Political entanglements will be the least of your worries soon enough.

Aderyn blinked away the Assessment and found she was staring at the gate, which stood open to receive travelers. Political entanglements? All she wanted was to complete a quest... one which all but demanded she raise an army. Political entanglements might be impossible to avoid.

World door had opened to one side of a well-trodden road, paved with stones the size and shape of those forming the wall, but gray instead of pink. At this hour, there weren't many travelers entering Ikharatia, but all of them had stopped to stare at the strangers popping into existence outside the gate. Aderyn averted her gaze. Discomfort took the place of her excitement at starting a new adventure.

"We stand out," she said to Owen. Everyone else on the road had much darker skin than she did, and none of them had Owen's blond hair.

"I guess I didn't realize what you all meant by the southern lands being isolated," Owen said. "What about *world door?* And isn't there ocean travel between here and the north?" He addressed Isold, who'd emerged from *world door* as abruptly as Aderyn had.

"Ocean travel is dangerous, because of all the monsters," Isold said, "and if you avoid the dangerous parts, the journey takes months. I don't know about *world door*, but I believe not many southern spellslingers who know it know locations in the north. In all our traveling, we've only met one Southlander in the north—remember Talandra? Still, there's plenty of adventuring available here, enough that there's no real benefit to traveling north. There's even a safe zone."

"But if the orcs invade, couldn't people retreat there? There's got to be some way to protect the noncombatants."

"That, I cannot answer," Isold said. "We have to assume nowhere is safe, because the consequences of doing otherwise are catastrophic."

"I agree." Owen chewed his lower lip in thought. "Well, there isn't anything we can do about it tonight. We'll need to find an inn and start asking questions in the morning."

Weston popped free of the portal and took two stumbling steps before he regained his balance. Even then, he did it more gracefully than Aderyn had. "This place is *hot*," he said. "Hotter than summer back home."

"It's the humidity," Owen said. "It saps your energy in a way dry heat doesn't."

"Is this what it's like where you come from?" Aderyn asked.

Owen shook his head. "The humidity is about the same, but it doesn't get nearly this hot. And it's almost evening now, so I can't imagine what it will be like at noon tomorrow."

With a snap, the final *world door* closed behind Livia. She leaned on Weston's shoulder, sagging like she was exhausted from spellslinging. "This is like being wrapped in a hot, wet blanket. I don't see how anyone lives here."

"We'll get used to it," Owen said. "And we'd better hurry. If they close the gates at sunset like northern cities do, we'll end up spending the night outside, and that's a waste of our time."

None of the Southlanders had moved in the time it took for the team to gather, not even to put distance between themselves and the foreigners. Aderyn mustered a smile for the nearest travelers as they approached the road. "Sorry," she said, though she wasn't sure what she was apologizing for.

They joined the line and rapidly neared the gate. Four armed men, all of them Staffsworn, stopped each person entering and spoke with them in low voices. "Asking their business," Weston muttered.

When it was their turn, the Staffsworn in the lead said, "Northerners. We don't see many of you here. What's your business in Ikharatia?" He sounded curious, as if he cared about the answer personally.

"Following a quest," Owen said without elaborating.

Aderyn hoped that wasn't too curt. Who knew what Southlanders considered polite? But the guard said, "Good luck to you. That's thirty gold for the entrance fee—we take northern coin."

"No exchange surcharge?" Owen asked.

The guard smiled in a friendly way. "You'll spend enough here it won't matter. Welcome to Ikharatia."

Aderyn paid, and the friends hurried through the gate and into a crowded street filled with men and women hurrying along, none of them appearing to notice the strangers. Though the sun hadn't yet set, the streets were lit by hundreds of white lanterns that cast sharp-edged shadows across the many pedestrians thronging the streets. After the emptiness of the Enchanterium, the crowds made Aderyn feel more claustrophobic even than the kobold tunnels had. "I expected to pay more, after what Grandfather said about the southern exchange rate and using gems instead of coin."

"I'll take it. We need all the good luck we can find," Owen said. "Anyone see sign of an inn? Isold?"

"My map has had no chance to expand yet. I suggest we follow the crowds." Isold waved a hand at the passing throngs. They looked like ocean currents, flowing steadily in both directions. Aderyn didn't see a difference between right or left.

"This way, then." Owen set off to the left in his usual decisive manner. Aderyn shrugged and followed him.

Ikharatia smelled deliciously of citrus and cloves and something warm and resinous Aderyn couldn't identify. She was used to northern cities smelling of whatever food was on offer, barely overriding the smell of waste or industry. These pleasant scents were more pervasive, as if they saturated the air and the stone. Aderyn inhaled deeply.

"This reminds me of places in my own world," Owen murmured, low enough for only her to hear. "The American Southwest, as far as the construction goes, but a tropical climate otherwise. All these buildings look made to keep out heat."

Buildings made of pinkish or cream-colored stone blocks lined both sides of the street. Not only were they many stories tall, those stories were taller than Aderyn was used to, twenty or twenty-five feet high. Windows too narrow for anyone to fit through came to a sharp point, paned with thick glass and shielded by heavy canopies. It was beautiful, and alien, and Aderyn's excitement rose again.

It took her a minute or so before she realized she wasn't being pressed as closely by the crowds as she should be, based on how many people filled the streets. No one stared, but she caught more than a few curious glances aimed their way. They did look strange, she admitted, though at least they weren't the only adventurers. Recalling her time in the big cities of the north, she didn't return anyone's observations. Cities had to be the same everywhere, with their citizens treasuring their privacy because they had so little of it.

Ahead, she saw a wooden sign with a mug of ale painted on it, and unexpected relief filled her. She hadn't realized how on edge the furtive glances had made her. Owen held the door for her, a peculiar custom of his world she still wasn't used to, and they entered the taproom. A cool breeze brushed Aderyn's face, bringing with it the smell of warm ale and roast chicken. Above, idly spinning blades rotated, driving the air in front of them so the movement cooled the room.

The taproom was only half full, and Owen took a seat beneath one of the spinning blades and tilted his head back. "Fans," he said. "I suppose air conditioning is too much to hope for."

"Hey there, strangers." A young woman wearing a full white apron over a halter top and knee-length trousers approached their table. "You in the mood for something cool to drink?"

"Yes, please," Aderyn said with feeling. She took off her coat and bundled it on her lap, where it still warmed her but not as much.

The woman laughed in a friendly way. "Five of the house brew, coming up."

When she was gone, Owen said, "Is anyone going to harass us for being foreigners? We're visibly different, after all."

"Maybe," Isold said. "It could be like it was in Finion's Gate—the citizens there felt justified in taking advantage of outsiders. But there's nothing we can do about that."

"That's refreshing. I wish—" Owen scowled. "Never mind. Let's just say your world is way more evolved than mine as far as race relations go, and leave it at that."

Aderyn wanted to ask what race relations were and why they upset Owen, but just then, the serving woman returned with a double handful of foaming mugs. "Here you are. New to Ikharatia, are you? You familiar with our cuisine?"

"Not at all," Isold said with a smile, "but I'm sure you can guide us."

The woman smiled back. "I like a man who's daring. We do serve northern food, but if you'll trust me, I can give you a taste of the south." With a wink, she strolled away again.

"Isold," Owen said, "for someone who doesn't do romantic talk, you are the most charming person I know."

"I like meeting new people," Isold said with a shrug. "It doesn't have to go anywhere beyond friendliness." He sounded unexpectedly stiff, and Aderyn felt awkward, like Owen had just accused Isold of making up to the server as a prelude to sex.

Owen noticed it, too. "Sorry, I didn't mean—"

"I know. I was oversensitive."

An uncomfortable silence fell, during which Aderyn listened to the conversations going on around them and wished she knew what to say. Everyone else in the room chattered about banal, everyday things, nothing worth eavesdropping over. "What are we supposed to do about the quest?" she blurted out.

"I admit I'm stumped," Weston said quickly, enough that Aderyn was sure he was as uncomfortable as she. "Convincing an army to follow us—"

"That might not be what it requires," Owen said.

Aderyn brought up her Codex and read the information on the next **[Fated One's Destiny]** quest.

[Fated One's Destiny: Crush the Horde]
An army of monstrous orcs has emerged from the Blighted Range, intent on conquering the southern human lands. Destroy their leaders and push the army back into the mountains. Recommended minimum party level for this quest is 17. Reward: [75,000 XP] plus any XP gained through actions taken to complete the quest.

"It's straightforward," she said, "except it doesn't give any hints about how to accomplish it. I mean, theoretically we don't need an army to destroy the orc leaders, just stealth and luck."

"But that won't push the army back into the high risk zone," Livia said. "I think Weston is right that we need an army of our own." She was staring into the middle distance as if she was reading her Codex, too.

"Well," Isold began.

The serving woman approached their table bearing an enormous platter balanced on one hand. With her other hand, she began setting out dishes: a stack of white ceramic plates, bowls of shredded, roasted chicken, smaller bowls filled with sauces of different colors, and a tureen of white rice. "You lay out a bed of rice," she said, pointing at the tureen, "then spread chicken over it, then spoon sauce over all that." She dropped a pile of wet cloths like thick handkerchiefs in the middle of the table. "Wash your hands thoroughly. You eat with your fingers."

Aderyn stared at her. "With our fingers? Is this a joke?"

The woman's smile broadened. "No joke. I wouldn't do that to paying customers. And only the fingers of your right hand, unless you want to look like uncouth foreigners. Enjoy!"

"Wait," Owen said. "We just arrived. What currency do you accept?"

"*Really* new." The woman nodded. "We take northern coin at this tavern, but I'll warn you the exchange rate in the south is steep unless you go to a licensed moneylender. It's still not great even there. You'll get a better price if you deal in gems."

"That's good to know. Thanks." Owen immediately scooped rice onto his plate. "Eat up. This stuff smells amazing."

"Yes, but eating with our fingers," Livia protested.

"Oh, it's not so bad." Weston sniffed a spoonful of dark brown sauce, then drizzled it over his food. He scooped up a pinch of meat and rice and conveyed it awkwardly to his mouth. "It's delicious, just messy."

Aderyn dipped a fingertip into a bright green sauce and tasted. The flavor was sharp and faintly bitter, but she liked it. Covertly observing the diners at other tables, she pinched her thumb and first two fingers together and mixed the rice, meat, and sauce together before taking a bite. The green sauce complemented the meat perfectly, though it was spicier than she was used to. She took another bite. The spicy heat intensified, burning her lips and the back of her throat. Gasping, Aderyn snatched up her mug and gulped. The ale cooled her mouth only as long as she was drinking, and when she put the mug down, the heat returned.

"That's too hot for me," she breathed out.

"Try this one. It's only a little spicy," Owen suggested, indicating a dish of brown sauce with mysterious bits suspended in it.

Aderyn swallowed and gasped again. "Owen, this is almost as bad as the first!"

"Is it?" Owen dipped a finger in the sauce and tasted it. "I guess my standards are different. I love Mexican food, the hotter the better."

"Ignore him," Weston said. He'd tried all the sauces, by the look of his plate. "*This* one isn't so strong. Talk about spices. I think my nose hairs have all burned off."

The new sauce soothed her mouth, and Aderyn dared to try a few others, finding several she could eat comfortably. They ate in silence for a while, only speaking to ask someone to pass a dish. Aderyn fell back into listening to nearby conversations. Her hearing wasn't as good as a Moonlighter's, but she heard enough to follow what people were talking about. Again, it mostly wasn't interesting, just chatting about family matters or jobs.

Then Weston stilled. "Those adventurers over there," he said. "They just said something about the army."

Aderyn managed not to turn around to stare in the direction Weston indicated. "What about it?"

"You know, that's strange," Owen said. "Nobody's mentioned a war. At all. You'd think it would be what everyone was talking about."

"If the orcs first invaded when we activated the **[Crush the Horde]** quest, it's only been a couple of days," Livia murmured. "Maybe most of them don't know."

Weston twitched. "They said something about the invasion, and why haven't the troops been mustered. And... no general."

"No general?" Aderyn spoke in a low voice. "How can they have an army with no general?"

"Hey, you're making good inroads on the food," the serving woman said, appearing as if by magic beside Livia. "Delicious, huh?"

"It's wonderful," Owen said. "I don't suppose we can impose on you further and get the name of a good inn?"

"Adventurers, huh?" The woman rattled off a list of names that had Isold nodding as the inns appeared on his system map. "You here to enlist?"

"Enlist?" Owen's innocent expression told Aderyn he'd decided to let this woman fill in the gaps in their information by pretending ignorance. "In the army?"

The woman laughed. "One of the many. Personally, I think the orc threat is exaggerated. No orcs ever leave the Blighted Range, and if they do, it's in tiny warbands easily dealt with. And none of this sounds like anything but rumor. But to hear the dukes talk, there's an army of orcs headed our way and of course each of them is the one to deal with it. Like that isn't a power grab."

"I agree, that sounds like they're in it for personal gain," Owen said. "Still, I'm not sure what benefit we'd get out of enlisting. How would we get experience?"

"I don't know how it works. I'm not an adventurer." The woman shrugged.

"You said, many armies," Aderyn said. "How does that work? Don't they need a unified leader?"

"Well, it's not as if the king can command. And all the dukes are squabbling over who should lead." The woman snorted, such a derisive sound Aderyn felt briefly sorry for the squabbling dukes.

"Why can't the king command? Is he ill?"

"He's all of five years old," the woman said. "King Monesh died last year, and his queen is regent for their son, but that means there's no precedent for this situation. Queen Devendra doesn't know how to choose a good commander general, of course."

"Why not?"

"No experience with war. She's a retired Tidecaller, and a smart lady, but that's all. I heard the dukes agreed on a way to choose, something about the military historians at the university—hey, Barant, where do things stand with the army? You re-upped yesterday, right?"

A grizzled, middle-aged man, burly and with hands that were mostly knuckle, looked up from a nearby table. "Sure, what do you want to know?"

"These visitors were asking about the army. Didn't the dukes finally come up with a leader?"

"Nah, not they." Barant wiped a hand across his mouth. "They agreed to give the choosing to the College of History, which is a stupid way to choose a military leader. Better to have the dukes duel it out."

"Dueling doesn't prove if someone has command experience, though," Aderyn said.

Barant focused on her with some effort, and Aderyn realized he was fairly drunk. "Well said, missy. You're a Warmaster. Interesting."

"So the College of History—those would be people who study wars, right?" Aderyn pressed on. "And they would know what qualities make a good general. Or did in the past."

"That's the principle, yes." Barant smiled. "Hey, maybe you should go for it!"

Aderyn blinked. "For what?"

Barant chuckled. "See, the College masters turned it back on the dukes. Me, I think they didn't like the look of any of them. So they threw it open."

Aderyn's confusion deepened. "Threw what open?"

"The contest. They'll choose a commander from anyone who

throws in. *Anyone*. Even a Warmaster!" He roared with laughter, and his friends joined in.

Aderyn sat back in her chair. "Thunderation," she said. "It couldn't be that obvious, could it?"

"I think we just found our army," Owen said.

Chapter Two

Aderyn woke early after a restless, over-warm night and lay in bed staring at the fan hanging from the ceiling. The fans she was familiar with were wedges of stiff paper, held in one hand and flapped to direct air flow toward the wielder's face. This was a five-foot-long strip of heavy fabric, a little less than a foot wide and gathered into loose folds, that swept back and forth endlessly thanks to a rope attached to a Spellcrafted device over the window. Owen had said something about it pushing the warm air down instead of letting it rise the previous night, but he'd said it as he pulled Aderyn's shirt off over her head and slid his other hand around her bare waist, pulling her close, so she hadn't paid much attention.

Now she let her eyes go unfocused, making the fan's "blade" seem doubled in its movement. So much about the south was different, not just the climate but the way people adapted to it. She'd suggested getting an early start, taking care of business before the sun grew too hot, but the innkeeper, Neeva, had laughed in a friendly way and explained that no one in Ikharatia made an early start.

"You're right about avoiding the sun, but we do it by way of staying up late, well after sunset," she'd said. "You'll find the markets and taverns open until past midnight, for example. People tend to sleep until ten or eleven in the morning."

"Where has this place been all my life!" Livia had exclaimed, ignoring Weston's groan.

Owen rolled over and raised his head. "What time is it?"

"I have no idea. The sun is well up, but I don't know what time the sun rises here. It feels early."

"If it's far enough south, the sun might always rise at the same time. And set at the same time." Owen interlaced his fingers behind his head and stared at the fan the way Aderyn had.

"How do you know all this? It's not even your world."

"The physics and geography all work the same, as far as I can tell. And that's the sort of thing we learn in school. At least, I did. Some of it I learned in college as part of becoming a history teacher. Geography and history in my world are closely linked, so when you study one you learn about the other."

Aderyn considered this. "I wish I knew more about the world. I was always so caught up in looking forward to adventuring I didn't think about studying the places I might adventure in."

"Well, your world doesn't seem to have many universities. There's the Postern Academy in Guerdon Deep, and I guess you could call the Repository a place of learning." He tilted his chin back and let out a long, thin stream of breath. "And then there's here. I almost wish we weren't here on a quest. I'd love to know more about what they teach at the Ikharatia University. It's got to be more than just military history."

"Military history is enough to make me nervous," Aderyn said. "It sounds so official. I don't know anything about it."

"You're a Warmaster. You don't have to." Owen rolled onto his side to face her.

"All right, but suppose that's not true? That man, Barant, said the military historians at the College of History are conducting some kind of test. If it's about famous battles or generals, I'm out of luck."

"I don't—" Owen paused. "This really has you worried."

Aderyn briefly wished **[Read Body Language]** hadn't given her away, because she wasn't sure her fears were justified. "We have to have an army, Owen. And almost all of that is on me. I'm worried my tactical skills won't be what they're looking for."

Owen frowned. "I'd like to reassure you that that's unlikely, but unfortunately there's historical precedent in my world for important military or government positions being filled based on who someone knows or how good their poetry is—"

"*Poetry?* Owen, you don't have to invent things to cheer me up!"

"Sadly, I did not invent any of that. So it's possible these historians believe that textbook knowledge—I mean, knowing facts and historical dates—is key to being an excellent general. But my guess is that won't be the case."

Aderyn rolled to face him. "Why is that?"

"Because they had the opportunity to pick a general from among several dukes who all want that position, all of whom are probably wealthy and powerful, and they didn't. That tells me they weren't influenced by political pressure or greed, and that makes it likely they really do want someone who can lead an army."

A chill swept over Aderyn. "That's not good. I mean, yes, it's good that they want a real leader, but it means the situation is more serious than you'd think based on the non-reaction of the average citizen. If they're willing to put good military strategy over nepotism, they're scared."

"I hadn't thought of that." Owen's eyes grew distant, like he was examining his Codex. "We're not too late, or the quest would be invalid, but we really shouldn't waste time. Barant didn't know when the test starts."

"Or we *are* too late, and the system wants us to acquire an army a different way," Aderyn pointed out.

"I'll stick with my idea, thanks."

Somewhere nearby, a carillon sounded, after which a bell rang the hour, eight distinct peals. Owen kissed Aderyn lightly and rolled out of bed. "Their leisurely morning is going to drive me nuts. I wonder if we can get something to eat this early?"

Isold had chosen the Jeweled Cuckoo Inn from the list the helpful woman had provided because it catered to the few northerners who braved the southern seas and therefore accepted northern coin. Aderyn and Owen discovered it also catered to northern dining expectations, and provided breakfast well before mid-morning. They found Weston in the taproom, eating eggs that smelled of unusual spices, using a round of flattened bread to scoop up the orange-yellow mess.

"The flatbread is an acceptable alternative to eating with your fingers, Neeva says," he told them. "I'm actually hooked on eating with my hands, but these eggs are too hot to comfortably touch."

Aderyn and Owen sat and received plates identical to Weston's. "I'm guessing Livia isn't up, but have you seen Isold?" Owen asked.

"He was up earlier even than me, and he went into the city to expand his map."

"That might not be safe," Aderyn protested. "It's a foreign city, and it's a metropolis like Finion's Gate. I—well, he won't get lost, obviously, but anything else might happen."

As she spoke, the outer door swung open, and Isold entered.

Aderyn laughed. "Never mind."

"Never mind, what?" Isold said. He sat beside her and waved a hand at the young man hovering near the door to the kitchen. "Coffee, please. I've been to the Ikharatia University in search of the College of History, and there was an unexpected crowd. It seems the draw of becoming the commander general of the united southern armies is, well, more of a draw than we expected."

A jolt shot through Aderyn, and she half-rose from her seat. "What if we're too late?"

"Calm down, Aderyn, it's fine." Isold accepted a small brass cup filled with steaming dark liquid and sipped delicately. "They're not letting anyone in yet. What's more, the winnowing has already begun. There was a sign most of the would-be generals ignored."

"A sign of what?" Owen asked.

"A literal sign, instructing anyone interested in participating in the trials to report to the Academy Hall at ten a.m. Despite this, a queue had formed outside the College of History, one of fairly long-standing as there were men eating their breakfasts with every indication that they'd been in the queue all night." Isold shook his head in mock despair. "People simply don't read anymore."

"All right. Ten. We have time." Aderyn calmed herself and scooped up more eggs. The orange-yellow color was the result of delicious tangy peppers stirred into the egg mixture, giving it a strong flavor she liked. The flatbread was soft and pliable, not crunchy, and it was easy to fold it around a mouthful of egg.

"You don't have anything to worry about," Isold said. "If this outcome is what the system intends, you need only use your Warmaster's vision and skills to prove you are the best candidate for the job. If not, we'll try something else."

"It seems so strange, though," Aderyn said. "Having these skills is one thing, but using them to lead an army—that just feels weird. Or maybe I mean it's weird that it doesn't feel *weirder*. I'm uncertain because I don't know what to expect, but I no longer feel like a fraud, presenting myself as a potential general."

"That's the right attitude. Your class is *War*master, after all." Owen squeezed her knee lightly. "Though it is curious. The contest itself, I mean. Why don't the dukes go to war over who commands? For that matter, why hasn't one of them usurped the throne? This whole situation is seriously unstable."

"I guess they..." Aderyn's voice trailed off. "You're right. Everyone's behaving so, well, civilly. It's been a long time since anyone went to war in the north, but back then the fighting was vicious. Do you suppose there's something else going on?"

"I don't know. I suspect so. But I don't know how we'd discover that." Owen wiped his mouth. "And here's Livia, who frankly looks a lot more alert than I expected."

"You people are a bad influence," Livia groused. "I was all set to sleep until noon—"

"And we would have let you," Weston said.

Livia waved that away. "But I'm so used now to being up with the sun I couldn't sleep in. And do you know what time the sun rises here? Just after six a.m.!" She groaned and accepted a small cup of coffee from the serving boy. "They don't even serve coffee in decent-sized cups here."

"You won't want anything larger," Isold warned.

Livia sipped from her tiny cup. Her eyes sprang wide open. "What in *thunder* is that stuff?"

"Coffee," Isold said blandly. "Distilled to its blackest essence."

"It's the best coffee I've ever drunk, is what it is," Livia said. "I'm afraid if I gulp it, my head will explode. I provisionally take back my grousing about the earliness of sunrise."

"Well, I'm bored," Weston said. "I say we explore the city and work our way around to the Academy Hall by ten."

"Are we all going?" Livia asked. "I thought Aderyn was on her own."

That killed Aderyn's optimism dead. All her bold words about being ready to be a general deserted her. "I don't know—"

"We'll be there to cheer her on, as much as they'll let us." Owen scooped up a final bite of eggs and popped the folded piece of flatbread into his mouth. "But I doubt it's a group effort."

"You'll do fine," Livia said. "Level sixteen Warmaster, at a young age for level sixteen anything—at the very least, you'll be a novelty."

"That's true." Aderyn straightened her spine. "Let's see what this city looks like in daylight."

In daylight, Ikharatia was hot and bright, with the sun reflecting off the many pale, towering buildings and the white bricks of the pavements and streets. It was also noisy, not just with thousands of pedestrians but with strange three-wheeled vehicles attached to tiny carriage boxes, pedaled by sweating, scantily-clad men. The vehicles made a clacking sound like a deep tick, *tuktuktuk,* as they rolled through the streets.

Many wagons trundled past, laden with goods or even people. Aderyn stared at an open-sided wagon filled with people seated on benches or clinging to poles holding up heavy canopies that sheltered them from the blazing sun. "We could ride," she said. "I've already sweated out every drop of water I drank at breakfast."

"All those wagons are full," Livia said. "We couldn't fit. But I agree that looks cooler than walking."

"We're nearly there," Isold said. He didn't look like he was sweating at all. Aderyn glared at him for daring to be comfortable in this wet, hot climate.

Somewhere in the distance, the city clock tolled the half-hour, reminding Aderyn of Obsidian. That also had a city clock tower, but otherwise Obsidian couldn't be more different from Ikharatia. She recalled how much she'd disliked that city, and her perspective shifted. Sure, this climate was uncomfortable, but at least the people weren't hostile and inclined to kill foreign adventurers.

The road they were on terminated at an arch carved of pinkish-yellow stone, covered in pictures of men and women carrying sheaves of grain. Aderyn had never seen anything like it and couldn't begin to imagine what the image symbolized. Or maybe it didn't symbolize anything, and this was where grain was stored—no, beyond the arch were more of the stone buildings, and there were no wagons laden with grain or anything else but people. Aderyn also saw the first trees she'd seen in Ikharatia, skinny tall trees lining the road past the arch. They gave the illusion of coolness in the middle of all this heat.

The people-wagon she'd observed had come to a stop ahead, and a handful of riders got off and a few others got on. Aderyn was too drained by the heat to consider hurrying to get a seat, and besides, Isold had turned off the main road and was following a narrower path, also lined with skinny trees.

It was quiet along the path, with only a few people walking ahead of them. The whole place felt empty, so unlike what Aderyn had seen so far of Ikharatia she felt disoriented. To center herself, she observed the nearest buildings. All of them were short by comparison to the rest of the city, no more than three stories tall, and the windows were wider and paned with many small glass bricks so they couldn't be opened. Ventilation would be an interesting challenge.

She began to hear a droning buzz that at first worried her, it sounded so much like a waspnettle horde, but after a few minutes it resolved into the noise of a large crowd, not angry or excited, just people talking loud enough to be heard over one another. But it was a *lot* of people, and Aderyn's anxieties flared again. So many wanting this position, and she was just one person, not even from this part of the world—

"Calm down," Owen murmured.

Aderyn swallowed. "I'm not great with crowds, that's all."

"And Isold said you wouldn't have to be. Livia, what's the time?"

Livia fished out her timepiece. "9:37, more or less. This hasn't been totally accurate since it wound all the way down in the Enchanterium."

"Close enough." Owen led the way out of the path and into a plaza big enough to fit thousands of people if they all packed in tight. Even though that wasn't the case now, there were still hundreds of men and women strolling along or entering one of the four buildings forming the sides of the plaza. The queue Isold had mentioned was immediately visible, snaking from the shortest of the buildings whose front door was a closed slab of stone, around the building's front and across the plaza all the way to the fountain that stood at its center. Aderyn glanced once at the fountain, with its marble basin and its brass trumpets spraying cool, beautiful water into the air, then followed the queue with her gaze.

"That's weird," Weston said. "No women."

Aderyn scanned the line again. "You're right. I wonder why? They can't not let women compete, because what would be the point?"

"Your world is so nice in some respects," Owen said. "Where's the Academy Hall, Isold?"

Isold took them across the plaza, skirting the fountain, to the building diagonally across from what Aderyn assumed was the College of History where the queue began. Its front door stood open, but only a few people, male or female, entered it. Inside, the temperature dropped dramatically, and Owen sighed. "Ambient cooling. What kind of magic does this?"

"No idea," Livia said. "It's probably a Windwarden thing." She looked like she felt more comfortable too.

Aderyn blinked so her vision adjusted to the dimness, also welcome after the blindingly bright sunlight reflecting off white stone outside. The entrance hall was tall and narrow, barely wide enough for others to pass the friends where they stood in the doorway. Two doors opened off the hall, to the right and the left. The few other people who entered all went to the left, ignoring Aderyn and the others.

"I guess it's the left?" she said.

Isold had crossed to the right and was examining a wall plaque. "No, it's this way," he said. The wall plaque was a black slate on which were chalked the words CANDIDATE EXAMINATION ROOM.

Aderyn's nerves tingled, this time with anticipation. She always preferred knowing what was going to happen, even if all she knew was the immediate next step. "I'll see you later."

"Wait a sec." Owen took her in his arms and kissed her deeply. "Good luck."

She kissed him back. "How bad can it possibly be?"

Chapter Three

Despite the words on the plaque, the room Aderyn entered wasn't more than a box ten feet on a side and half again as tall, empty of everything but a couple of tall stools. It was cooler even than the entrance hall, with a fan in the ceiling slowly creating a draft. A middle-aged man sat on the shorter of the two stools. He held a book open in one hand and idly stirred the contents of the basket on the taller stool with the other.

The man glanced once at Aderyn. "Here," he said, handing her a pewter coin. "Proceed to the next room. Present this when asked." He then returned to his reading and seemed to lose interest in her or anything she did. Aderyn palmed the coin without examining it and walked through the door behind the man.

She found herself in a narrow hallway that extended straight ahead for a few feet before making a sharp right-hand turn and opening into a high-ceilinged chamber a few degrees warmer than the other. Its bland, white walls contrasted with the dark, almost black finish of the floorboards, which reflected the lights from the lamps brilliantly illuminating the room. The *brrrrr* of the magic items propelling the many waving ceiling fans made a nice low hum in the background.

Aderyn focused on the rows and rows of small desks filling the space. The stools drawn up to each desk didn't match each other, which Aderyn found strange, but not strange enough to ask the slim man who approached her about it.

The man surveyed Aderyn, one swift glance from her head to the toes of her battered boots, and held out a hand. Aderyn surrendered the coin, which he squinted at and then returned to her. "Forty-two," he said, and made a note on the board he held. "Pick a desk."

There were a few other people seated at the desks, mostly men, but more than a few women. Nobody sat close to anyone else, and there didn't seem to be a pattern to where they sat, so Aderyn chose a desk at random and settled herself to wait. She set the pewter coin on the desk and prodded it to align with the wood grain as she examined it. It did have the number 42 embossed on it in an ornate writing style, the 4 curling at the bottom and the 2 making a curlicue at its lower tip. The bored man hadn't looked into the basket, so the numbers were given out at random, which meant there was no way of knowing how many candidates there would ultimately be. There might have been a hundred coins in that basket, but there weren't more than twenty people seated at the desks.

She slipped the coin into the slit pocket in her trousers, the one she almost never used now that she had the **<Purse of Great Capacity>**, and clasped her hands in front of her, resting them on the desk. More people were entering the room now and taking seats all around her. A few of them were northerners, but mostly it was dark-skinned southerners, all of whom were dressed for the climate in a way Aderyn envied: long, loose robes with no sleeves, open over thin sleeveless knee-length tunics and loose trousers, with shoes made of leather straps that left their toes and heels exposed. She was, she realized, almost the youngest person there; almost everyone was middle-aged or older, some of them much older. This made her feel more uncomfortable than being female or northern, as if there was an age requirement she was ignorant of.

A deep, chiming tone reverberated through the room, like a bell rung underwater. "Five minute warning," the slim man said.

Aderyn glanced around. Most everyone else was staring at their hands, or their coins, but a few people were watching the other candidates. Aderyn's eye was caught by the other young person, a southern man who wore his black hair long and gathered at the nape of his neck, just the way Aderyn wore hers. His eye caught Aderyn's, and he smiled. Aderyn didn't smile back. It had been the smile of someone interested in bedding her, and if he felt that way despite knowing Aderyn was married, he wasn't someone she wanted to encourage.

It occurred to her that she assumed he'd Assessed her even though she hadn't thought to Assess him or anyone else in the room. She began to bring up the Codex, then changed her mind. If "five minute warning" meant that was how much time before the test began, she wouldn't have time to Assess everyone, and even Level Assess would only tell her so much. Better to wait until most of these people were winnowed out. Unless that wasn't how it worked—and now she was getting anxious again. Aderyn calmed her breathing and reached into her pocket to rub the embossed surface of the coin. It didn't matter how things worked or what the others would do. All that mattered was how she performed, and she was the only person she had control over.

A second chime brought everyone in the room alert and sitting upright. Aderyn swiftly glanced over the desks and made a rough estimate—about fifty people. The man who'd looked at her number left the room, but returned in only a few seconds with a wooden box and a handful of charcoal pencils. He moved through the room in silence, removing a thin sheaf of paper from the box and placing it at each occupied desk along with a pencil. Aderyn waited impatiently for him to reach her and took the papers eagerly.

The top sheet of the little stack had neatly lettered instructions on it.

Write your assigned number in the top right corner of this page. Complete each entry in as much detail as you are capable of. Leave entries blank as applicable. When you are finished, hand these pages to the proctor and proceed to the next examination room.

Below that, most of the page was blank except for the words *Blight Boar*.

Enlightenment dawned. Aderyn wasn't sure how knowledge of the Monster Folio indicated ability to lead an army, and copying the information out seemed like it could become tedious, but at least this was something she felt confident in. She scribbled 42 in the indicated corner, squared up the papers in front of her, checked her Monster Folio to refresh her knowledge of blight boars, and began writing.

It didn't take as long as she'd feared, mainly because there were several monsters listed that she'd never Assessed. Unexpected guilt struck her when she reached the page labeled *Orc* and had to move past it without a response. Not knowing anything about their enemy might be a mark against her. She decided not to worry about it. It wasn't as if she could go back in time and find orcs to Assess and kill.

What did worry her was how quickly some of the other candidates handed in their pages and left the room. She told herself it didn't matter what the others did. She reminded herself that taking her time was the right approach. She even chastised herself for letting worry get to her, because if those people were done quickly, it probably meant they hadn't encountered many monsters in their adventuring careers and that could be a drawback now. But her handwriting got steadily messier as she wrote faster.

The final page simply read *Candidate's choice*. Aderyn hoped that meant she was to write about a monster they hadn't asked for and quickly listed the strengths, weaknesses, and special attacks of the deep delver. By the time she finished, only six others remained, including the young man who'd given her such a lascivious look. She resolutely didn't look at him when she gave her stack of pages to the proctor and left the room through the door opposite where she'd entered.

This hall was longer than the first, with a couple of closed doors Aderyn considered trying until she realized there was an open door farther along. No one else shared the hallway with her, and when she entered the room, she saw only another man dressed as the first proctor had been.

It wasn't a room, though; it was a long hallway lined on both sides with curtained alcoves. The curtains were a dark blue twilled fabric too heavy to twitch in the breeze that came from nowhere, keeping the hallway from being stiflingly hot. No sounds came from any of the alcoves, which might all have been empty, though in that case, where had all the other candidates gone?

The proctor beckoned to Aderyn. He examined her coin, then led her to an alcove about a third of the way down the hall. After holding the curtain back so Aderyn could enter, he walked away without saying a word, letting the curtain fall into place.

Another light breeze stirred the hair at the back of Aderyn's neck. Aderyn stared at the little desk and stool that were just like the ones in the first room. A metal contraption occupied most of the desk. It reminded Aderyn a little of something Owen called a pool table, but it rose vertically as well as horizontally and had numbered holes piercing it all the way up as well as sideways. Some of the holes had flaps blocking them, white flaps and dark blue flaps, that looked like they would spin if something passed through the hole. At the top of the... well, it sort of looked like a tower... at the top of the tower was a circular slate twice the size of Aderyn's pewter coin, on which was written the number 86.

There were a few blank sheets of paper and another charcoal pencil on the desk. Aderyn seated herself and picked up the sheet of paper already written on in peacock-blue ink.

Objective: Score as many points as possible in the time given. Time begins when you press the right-hand toggle. Activate the silver ball by pressing the first button. Activate the copper ball by pressing the fourth button.

Rules for scoring: ONE. A point is scored when the silver ball passes through the third hole after first passing through the fifth hole.

TWO. No point will be scored if the copper ball passes through the first hole unless the silver ball has not passed through any holes.

THREE...

The page was almost completely filled by peacock-blue writing. Aderyn read through the instructions. She Assessed the contraption and got only the words **Name: Ratiocinative Evaluation**. What in thunder did that mean?

She glanced at the slate. Eighty-six points, the last person had scored. She didn't think they gave candidates much time, so she'd have to be rock-solid on the scoring rules before she pressed the right-hand toggle.

She read the list again. Then she started taking notes on the blank pages. She had to turn a page over and write on the back because she'd run out of space on the front. The longer she studied the rules, the more puzzled she became. Her hand hovered briefly over the right-hand toggle. Then she gathered the pages together and left the alcove.

The hall was as silent as ever. The proctor looked up as she approached. "Excuse me," Aderyn said. "I think there's been a mistake. Something is wrong with my, um, the contraption."

"No mistakes," the proctor said. "Score as high as you can."

"That's the mistake," Aderyn said. "It's not possible to score any points under these conditions. Look, I've written it down—"

"Your number?"

"I didn't score—oh." Aderyn handed him her coin.

The proctor made a note on the board he held and gave the coin back. "Go to the end of the hall and proceed to the next challenge."

"But—" Aderyn shut up. Blushing, she hurried away. So, *that* was what the test was about. She cursed herself for taking so long to discover it was impossible. Isold or Weston would likely have figured it out immediately. At least she hadn't been so stupid as to press the toggle.

The door at the end of the hall opened stiffly, and Aderyn had to pull hard to make it move. Beyond, the hall continued a short distance and made a left-hand turn. She realized she was circling the building just as the new hall ended at an open doorway, through which she saw sunlight.

Despite the brightness of the light, the round room had no windows. Instead, the sunlight flowed through wide rectangular skylights of thin glass, set at intervals into the ceiling between more of the waving fans. Aderyn stopped just inside the door and waited for the proctor to approach. There were only three other candidates present, each of them standing before what looked like outline maps of a fictional continent. It was all Aderyn had time to observe before the proctor held out a hand and said, "Number?"

Aderyn fumbled the coin out of her pocket and handed it over. The proctor didn't return it after glancing at the number. He gestured with a jerk of his head that Aderyn should follow him. They crossed the worn parquet floor, which was deeply scuffed and scratched, to one of the outline maps. This close, Aderyn realized the outlines were grooves carved all over the flat surface, dozens of straight or curved grooves connecting to others at points along the lines.

Round wooden plaques no more than an inch in diameter were fitted into the grooves, scattered across the map. Each little plaque had a picture painted on it of some mundane object, like a bale of hay or a stack of lumber. Animals were drawn on a few of them, mostly horses, a couple of oxen.

Aderyn reflexively Assessed the board, but she had only read the words **Name: Resource Allocation Evaluation** before the proctor stopped and pressed her numbered coin into a recess sized exactly for it.

"Time begins now," he said. "Good luck."

"Wait," Aderyn said. "Are there instructions?"

"You're to figure it out on your own," the proctor said, and walked away.

Chapter Four

Aderyn closed her mouth on a useless protest. Well, if she had to figure it out on her own... She Assessed the board.

Name: Resource Allocation Evaluation

Victory condition: Bring one of each type of pictured resource to the center hub simultaneously.

Methodology: Resources move along the provided tracks. Moving one resource may affect the movement of others. Attaching a resource plaque or a carrier to a resource alters the speed of their combined movement. Secondary hubs allow for resources to cross paths.

Number of resources: Bricks (17), Wood (20), Grain (24), Water (30)

Number of carriers: Horses (7), Oxen (4)

"Huh," Aderyn said. She almost glanced at her nearest neighbor, three spaces away, before remembering this was a test and that might seem like cheating even if she was only curious. She prodded one of the bales of hay with her forefinger. It slid easily along the groove until it came up against a picture of a stack of red-brown bricks. When it touched the other plaque, Aderyn heard a quiet click. She pushed on the hay plaque again, moving it back, and it brought the brick plaque with it. Off to the other side of the board, a picture of a barrel of water moved along its track without Aderyn touching it.

Startled, Aderyn snatched her hand away. The water plaque stopped moving. Aderyn prodded it, watching the two plaques she'd just connected. They didn't move, but a horse plaque near the top of the board did.

Aderyn stepped back a pace and examined the board once more. She wasn't good at puzzles, not the way Isold was, but this didn't look like a puzzle. All the pieces were interconnected, and she just had to experiment with moving them to see which ones could be brought simultaneously to the center.

Slowly, she moved one of the oxen and observed how two other pieces shifted as a result. They were close to the center, but if she kept moving the ox, they would reach the hub well in advance of the rest of the pieces—not a good result. She moved more pieces, gradually becoming more confident when it became clear that a plaque that entered or crossed the center hub didn't invalidate the test.

Once she had moved all the pieces at least once, she set about shifting them in earnest. She discovered that only two plaques could be connected at a time, and connecting a third decoupled the first connection in favor of the new one. This made things easier. She shifted pieces swiftly, moving useless items through the lesser hubs to unlock access to the ones she wanted. She wasn't sure how she knew which ones those were, but she felt caught in the grip of her Warmaster's vision, instinct driving her on.

The more the pieces moved, the more confident she felt. She could see her chosen resources circling the center hub, moving at their own speed but in the pattern she wanted. Someone came to stand behind her, but she didn't turn around because she was so close to being done and whoever it was could wait.

Finally, she dragged a plaque of a barrel of water down along a groove and watched as three other resource plaques, one connected to an ox, plunged inward along three other grooves until all four clicked against each other in the central hub. All the grooves lit with a soft white light that made the board look like a tangle of glowing string, and the lesser hubs blinked green and gold.

"You're finished?" It was the proctor, standing behind her. He sounded surprised.

Aderyn nodded. She pried at her numbered coin, but it wouldn't come out of the recess. "It was interesting."

"Interesting." The proctor had regained control of himself and was back to sounding bored and impassive, but Aderyn hadn't forgotten how he'd reacted like she'd done something unexpected. "I suppose that's one word for it."

Aderyn surveyed the room. All the candidates who'd been there when she entered were still working at their boards, and a few new people, including the lascivious young man, had taken places among them. The realization that she'd completed the challenge faster than the others made her say, "How did I do?"

"We don't discuss the results." The proctor pressed down on her numbered coin and it popped out of the recess. He gave it to her and waved a hand at the exit. "Turn right and proceed to the next room."

Aderyn couldn't help peeking at the lascivious young man's board as she walked away. He'd made some progress, but not much. Two of his horses were well out of a position where they could boost the speed of his resources. It was too bad it would be interference with the test, because Aderyn dearly wished she could rub his nose in how superior she was at this one thing. Then she reprimanded herself for the spiteful thought. True, he'd leered at her like he wanted to see her with her clothes off, but that was no reason for her to respond in anger.

The exit hallway led to a T-junction. The hall to the left made another left-hand turn immediately, but the right-hand hallway extended some distance to an open doorway. Aderyn turned right and walked down the silent hallway. Even her footsteps were quiet, stilled by the thick carpet lining the hall.

When she reached the doorway, Aderyn smelled tobacco smoke. It was such an unexpected scent she hesitated before passing through. A man's deep voice said, "Don't dawdle, get in here." He sounded bored, whoever he was, and Aderyn stiffened, as if he'd criticized her personally. She strode through the doorway with her shoulders straight.

No windows illuminated this room, and no skylights either, but the light that came from the four lamps, one on each wall, was as clear and brilliant as daylight. Despite the brightness, Aderyn was reminded of the study in the dungeon Winter's Peril, which had been windowless and dark with oak paneling. That room had felt like a man's room, with its solid, massive desk and chairs and bookcases, and this one gave Aderyn the same sense of being surrounded by masculinity, between the heavy, well-padded chairs and the enormous oval table occupying the center of the room.

Two elderly southern men sat at the table, smoking aromatic cigars whose smoke wreathed their heads and made a haze in their immediate area. A third man, also southern but middle aged, poured himself a drink of some amber liquid from one of many decanters on a sideboard. Without turning to face Aderyn, he said, "So. A Warmaster from the north. And you believe you have any business leading a southern army?" It was the voice that had commanded her to enter.

The unexpected attack caught Aderyn off guard and stopped her before she could Assess any of them. "I—the announcement said the test was open to anyone. I assumed that was true."

"Yes, but why would a northerner care about our situation?" the thin man sitting to Aderyn's left said. He drew on his cigar and blew out a lopsided smoke ring. "We didn't believe we had to make that explicit."

"So if you're here on a whim, young lady, you ought to withdraw now," the other seated man said. He was plump but not fat, and handsome, his bearded features sculpted in sharp lines not spoiled by the extra weight he carried. He fixed Aderyn with a fierce black-eyed gaze and added, "We do not take kindly to being mocked."

Aderyn stood even straighter. "Because you're the historians who will choose a commanding general, is that why? I would think it didn't matter who you are, because nobody likes being mocked no matter their rank or position. And no, it's not a whim."

"Then explain to us why a northern girl took the exam, if not to prove a point," the first man said. He stoppered the decanter and swirled the alcohol in the bottom of his brandy glass before sipping delicately.

Since she hadn't been challenged at the door of the Academy Hall and told to leave, Aderyn had expected she'd have some time before anyone demanded she explain herself. She swallowed, wished she didn't look so uncertain, and said, "I'm here to defeat the orc army to fulfil a quest."

The thin man leaned forward, letting his cigar hover inches above his right knee. "A quest? You must be joking. There are no quests associated with the horde. That would be impossible."

"Not impossible," the plump man said. "Back in the days before the level cap—"

The thin man groaned. "And there you go bringing fanciful stories into reality."

"In the days before the level cap," the plump man persisted as if his colleague hadn't spoken, "adventurers of high level challenged the orcs in their own territory, and kings issued quests requiring armies to complete. Just because those times are gone doesn't mean they never happened."

"Musian states—" the thin man began.

"Oh, to thunderation with Musian," the plump man shouted. "You want to play dueling authorities, we'll be here all night. You should—"

"Let's not give this young woman the wrong impression of what history masters do in private," the first man said. He took a seat gracefully near Aderyn and sipped his brandy again. "A quest. What quest?"

Now Aderyn was worried. She'd never heard of anyone not believing in the level cap. Not believing it could be broken, that was one thing, but that it hadn't happened... how might someone who thought like that react to Aderyn claiming it was the Fated One quest that had brought her here? Still, lying to these men was a short-term and possibly harmful solution. "My husband is the Fated One," she said, "and our adventuring team has been pursuing a quest chain that ends with discovering what the Fated One is supposed to do to break the level cap. The current quest is to defeat the orc leaders and push the horde back into the high-risk zone."

Total silence. It was so quiet Aderyn imagined she could hear the cigars burning down and the brandy evaporating. Then the first man said, "I hope you don't think that impresses us, young lady. Even if it's true, and I'm not saying it is, we are under no obligation to give over control of our armed forces to a foreign Warmaster we know nothing about."

"I don't expect special treatment," Aderyn said. "You asked what brought me here, and I told you. I want to prove myself through passing the test you set up. Then it's you who decide who controls your army, and your choice should satisfy you, or else why bother?"

The room fell silent again. Aderyn kept her gaze fixed on the man who'd challenged her. He returned her gaze calmly, swirling the brandy in his glass once more before taking a longer sip. The plump man opened his mouth and closed it again, then settled more deeply in his chair. Aderyn's nerves began to fail her. Challenging these men, who had control over who commanded the southern armies, had been a bad idea. Now she looked young, brash, overconfident, and to the thin man, delusional. Almost she apologized and backed out of the room. But that would make her look weak, which was worse than looking young and brash.

To calm herself, she Level Assessed the three men.

Name: Tenzen

Traits: intelligent, clever, direct, honorable

Name: Druv

Class: Staffsworn (retired)

Level: 13

Name: Kash

Traits: obsessive, talkative, intelligent, optimistic

Tenzen was the brandy drinker. Druv was the thin man. Kash was the plump man. Aderyn didn't know what it meant that two of the three were non-classed. She knew not to underestimate those who'd rejected the Call, but her immediate reaction was always to believe someone in power had a class. She decided not to worry about it. Classed, non-classed, either way they held all the power.

"Tell me your name," Tenzen said abruptly.

"Aderyn." Even a non-classed person could Assess someone for their name and whether they were married. But it was still polite to let the other person introduce herself.

"Aderyn." Tenzen rolled her name over his tongue like it was fine brandy. "And you're level sixteen."

That, someone would have told him. Aderyn nodded.

"Very well." Tenzen nodded. "Return to the Academy Hall tomorrow morning at ten o'clock. Come prepared to prove yourself further."

Aderyn gaped. "I passed?"

"Don't let it go to your head," Druv said with a cynical smile. "You've passed the first round. We demand great things of the person we choose."

"Of course." Aderyn nodded politely to each man. "Thank you." She managed to keep her gait to a rapid walk as she left the room.

Not having any other options, she passed through the T-junction and followed the hall through another left turn. Eventually, she came to another open doorway, which let out on a well-lit room the size of the first one. No chairs or tables or desks filled this room; instead, dozens of men and women milled about or leaned against the windowless walls. A draft circulated from the ceiling fans, but the room was still terribly hot.

Aderyn made for the other doorway across the room, short and narrow but showing natural sunlight, but stopped when she heard Owen call her name. Her friends stood in a little huddle a short distance away and came toward her when she stopped. Owen put his arms around her and kissed her lightly. "Well?"

"I passed the first series of tests," Aderyn said. "I'm to return here tomorrow at ten for more of them."

A stranger standing nearby said, "*You* passed the tests? You're practically a child!"

Irritated, Aderyn said, "I'm twenty-one. And none of the tests had anything to do with my age."

The woman sniffed disdainfully and turned away. "I'm not sure I believe in the validity of these tests if they let someone with no life experience participate."

"I have got plenty—"

"Aderyn, don't worry about it," Owen said. "Let's go get something to eat. You were in there for hours." He hooked his arm through hers and steered her to the doorway.

Aderyn glared one last time at the woman and let herself be steered away. "I don't know what time it is. It felt like it took forever."

"It's a quarter past one," Livia said, consulting her pocket watch, "and I'm starving. But I want to know what happened!"

"I'll tell you all about it over a good meal." Now that the tension was over, Aderyn was ravenous.

Chapter Five

It was the lunch hour for all of Ikharatia, it seemed, with every inn and every tavern overflowing with loudly conversing diners. The first two places they approached had no free seats, but they managed to cram themselves around a communal table at the third tavern with only a little effort. Isold flagged down an overworked serving boy who brought them drinks, an unfamiliar citrus beverage Aderyn liked the more because it wasn't alcoholic. She felt overwhelmed enough by the morning without adding liquor to the mix.

Isold exchanged a few more words with the serving boy, who nodded and vanished into the crowd. "He will bring us meals, whatever the cook feels like preparing today. No choices."

Aderyn eyed the plates of the others at their table. She couldn't identify any food item, and even the rounds of flatbread looked different from what they'd had that morning, but it all smelled delicious. "I prefer not having to choose, given that I know nothing about southern cuisine."

"So, tell us what happened," Weston said. "I'm dying of curiosity."

"I didn't have any expectations, so I don't know how strange it was," Aderyn said. She described the experience, starting with sitting at her desk running her fingers over the embossed number 42 and watching the other candidates. When she mentioned the other young person, the man who'd leered at her, Owen said, "I hope he doesn't make it. Guys like that annoy me."

"I feel the same. I'm sure I did better than him at the final test, at least. Though I wonder—no, I should tell it in order." She went on to the first test, listing off the monsters she'd known to write about. The food arrived when she reached the deep delver, and she paused to serve herself: long-grain multicolored rice that looked like pale pink and creamy yellow confetti on her plate, with strips of marinated, broiled beef in a tangy brown sauce poured over it and topped with breaded, deep-fried chickpeas. The server set down a basket filled with those odd flatbreads and asked, "Have you had parotta before?"

"No, we just arrived yesterday," Owen said.

The server gestured at the basket. "The bread comes apart into long strings. It's tricky to manage one-handed, but don't worry, no one will judge you for using both hands. This batch is fresh out of the oven, so be careful picking it up. Enjoy!"

When the boy was gone, Isold said, "That was kind of him, especially with as busy as he is."

Weston was already poking one of the parotta rounds. "Hot, like he said." Carefully, he tore a piece from the edge. The light, fluffy bread peeled away not in a chunk, but in a long, wide strand circling the parotta's center. Weston managed to scoop up a pinch of mixed rice and meat and popped the whole messy bite into his mouth. His eyes widened. "The bread is soft and buttery. I think I could make a meal of it by itself. Though I wouldn't, because the rest of this stuff is great. Go on, try it."

Aderyn wasn't quite brave enough to eat one-handed, because the parotta, while light in texture, was just dense enough to be hard to tear without using two hands. But eventually she figured out how to handle the parotta and the beef by watching the other patrons, and she forgot about talking in favor of stuffing her face. She hadn't loved chickpeas when she had them in Finion's Gate, but they gave the meal a crunchiness she liked, and the brown sauce was spicy without being inedible.

As they all gradually cleared their plates, she said, "This is really good, though it's so different from what I'm used to. I hate to admit it, but I'm not sure we could walk into a random tavern in the north and get a meal this excellent."

"The rumor in the north about southern cuisine is that anyone wanting to set up as a purveyor of meals must go through rigorous training," Isold said. He cleaned his hand with a damp cloth from the pile on the table and added, "I'm not sure that's true, but it's possible they take food more seriously than we do."

"I'm fine with that," Owen said. "We should probably move on, free up these seats. Back to the inn? Aderyn can't be finished with her story."

They walked in silence, digesting. Now that the tension was over and she was full of delicious food, Aderyn wanted to nap the hottest part of the day away. But she wanted even more to share her experience with her friends. "The Monster Folio part was just boring—maybe not boring, exactly, but certainly straightforward. Either I knew a monster or I didn't. And I have no idea how my knowledge compared to the others. It could be I knew more than average, or maybe I was just slow in writing. I'm not exactly skilled with words."

"But there's nothing you can do about it," Livia said.

"Right. Like I said, I knew it or I didn't. It was the second test that was a surprise."

Aderyn described the strange contraption and the impossible rules. Weston snorted with laughter. "Testing your cleverness. That's interesting. And more obviously related to command."

"Testing your patience, too," Owen said. "I bet a lot of those candidates just press the toggle and bull ahead."

"That's what I thought. But it was confusing at the time. I don't have any idea how I was judged on that one. Like, do they eliminate you entirely if you don't figure out it's a trick? Or do they judge based on how long it takes for you to figure it out?" Aderyn shrugged. "I passed, so I guess it doesn't matter, but the more I think about it, the more I'm curious about what those masters learned from it all."

"What masters? You mean the ones choosing?" Livia asked. "Did you meet them?"

"Yes—but there was one more test before that. And I'm sure I nailed it." Aderyn described the final test and added, "I just knew, looking at the board, how it all had to go together. I never realized my Warmaster's vision worked like that."

They had reached the inn as Aderyn spoke, and Owen held the door for all of them. "Upstairs, because I want to hear about these masters. They must be strong personalities if they're able to dictate terms to the rulers of the south."

They gathered in Aderyn and Owen's room, sitting on chairs or the bed, with Isold leaning against the windowsill. "I don't know how strong their personalities are," Aderyn said, "but they sounded confident. And they wanted to know why I entered the contest."

"Because you're a northerner?" Livia asked.

"Yes, because they didn't see how their worries mattered to me. So I had to explain about the Fated One's quests, and one of them didn't even believe there was a time before the level cap. He argued about it with his colleague—there were three of them, Druv, Kash, and Tenzen. I think Tenzen is in charge, but that's just a guess."

"I'll take your guess over someone else's certainty any day," Owen said. "So they decided the Fated One's quest was enough reason for you to enter despite being a northerner. They didn't have a problem with you being young, or a Warmaster?"

"If they did, they didn't say anything. I mean, they knew I was level sixteen—Kash and Tenzen are non-classed, and Druv is a retired Staffsworn, but Druv didn't tell them when I was present, so somebody had to report to them about it—anyway, they didn't say a word about Warmasters being useless or how unusual it is for a Warmaster to reach such a high level. The closest they came to being dismissive was calling me 'girl,' but they were all pretty old, so I didn't mind."

"Did they say what tomorrow's tests would be?" Weston asked. "Maybe there's something you can do to be ready."

Aderyn shook her head. "They just said 'come prepared to prove yourself further.' I hope that means the tests will be more obviously related to military command. Or maybe I mean I want them to be tests that I can identify what I'm being tested on. Today was more unsettling than I realized, what with constantly worrying that I wasn't meeting their requirements and didn't know it."

Owen put his arm around her waist and hugged her. "Let it go. You passed—maybe when the testing is over, you can ask them for feedback on how you did."

Aderyn rested her head on his shoulder. "Feedback? What is that?"

"Information on your performance. Sometimes it means constructive criticism for doing something again in the future. I didn't think about that not being a word you know." Owen kissed the top of her head. "You want to rest? I mean all of us. It's too hot to go anywhere—it's almost too hot in here despite the fan."

"I want a nap," Weston said. "I can't believe I said that. Sleeping in the middle of the day, so decadent."

"Neeva informed me that it's expected that people's activity slows down from noon to three o'clock," Isold said. "If we have until ten o'clock tomorrow morning, I suggest we take the opportunity to rest."

Livia rose from her seat. "Good plan. I'll see you all in a few hours. Weston?"

When the others had left, Aderyn flopped back on the bed and again stared up at the rotating fan. "It is hot, but I feel so sluggish I don't have the energy to take my clothes off and cool down."

"I could do it for you," Owen said with a suggestive smile.

"I'm too hot for that, too, sorry."

"I was kidding. In this weather, sex feels like it would be too much work." Owen lay beside her. "Are you nervous?"

"About tomorrow? Not really. Passing the first round of tests gave me confidence, and meeting the college masters relaxed me. I mean, they're intimidating, but they're also human, and they're not total unknowns anymore." Aderyn twined her fingers with Owen's.

"That's a good attitude. You don't have enough information to plan ahead, so you might as well relax and take the day as it comes. I hope they let us watch."

"What, even if it's all boring, writing-things-down tests?"

"Maybe not that." Owen kissed her and sat up. "Strip down to your shift and drawers at least, if you're going to sleep."

Aderyn groaned, but she sat up and took her shirt off. "I don't know if the food here is good enough to compensate for the heat. I feel like I need to shed my skin, the air is so humid."

"You'll get used to it," Owen said. "Or not. Could be you'll just be miserable the whole time we're here."

"I thought you were supposed to be the optimistic one," Aderyn grumbled.

"I'm saving it up for tomorrow," Owen replied. "You're going to want it then."

Chapter Six

When they all arrived at the Academy Hall the following morning at ten 'til ten, they were stopped by a proctor. "Candidates only," he said.

"These are my companions, and my husband," Aderyn said. "Aren't they allowed to wait for me?"

"Not today," the proctor said. "You'll be finished at four o'clock this afternoon. They can return to meet you then. Rules."

"It's fine," Owen said. "We'll be back then."

Aderyn kissed him and clasped hands with each of the others in turn. "Good luck," Weston said.

"You won't need luck because you have skill," Livia said.

"I'll take both," Aderyn said. "See you later."

This time, the room with all the desks was almost empty of furniture. Just five desks and stools remained, lined up in a row facing a giant slate easily six feet across in a wooden frame. The frame was mounted on wheels so it could be moved easily. Three taller stools stood to the left of the frame. Aderyn wasn't sure, but she thought the room was cooler than it had been yesterday.

"Take a seat," the proctor said. "We will begin at precisely ten a.m."

Two of the desks were already occupied. Aderyn didn't dither about her choice of seats and what message it might send to the exam proctors; she took the desk on the far right of the row. Then she covertly Assessed the other candidates.

Name: Balraj

Traits: intelligent, analytical, conceited, cold

Balraj was an attractive middle-aged southern man with thick, curly black hair who stared straight ahead at the slate, ignoring Aderyn and the man next to him. Though he wore what Aderyn thought of as typical southern attire, his robe was a subdued dark blue over a black shirt and billowing black trousers, somber compared to the bright colors Aderyn had seen on everyone else. She didn't like the tilt of his head, his chin raised slightly in a gesture that suggested he thought he was better than everyone else. Or maybe that was her knowledge of his "conceited" trait. In any case, she immediately disliked him.

The other man openly stared at Aderyn. He was also southern, but younger than Balraj, with bad skin pitted by old acne scars and a stocky build. Still, his gaze was direct, and Aderyn liked the look of him. Her Level Assessment revealed that he was an adventurer.

Name: Janesh

∞ Aswathy

Class: Stalwart

Level: 10

He did look like a typical Stalwart. What had brought both of them here? It was tempting to make up stories for them—Balraj was impoverished nobility looking for something to command, Janesh's adventuring party had encountered the orc army and wanted muscle to back them up—but she didn't get too wrapped up in her imaginings. Probably their reasons were mundane and nothing she could guess.

She heard footsteps, but she didn't turn around. That would make her look eager, which could be a sign of weakness, and suppose they were already being judged by hidden observers? After the challenges of the previous day, Aderyn was inclined to a little paranoia. She noticed Janesh turned to stare.

The proctor invited the newcomer to sit, and the person took the desk next to Aderyn's. She sneaked a peek, and her heart sank. It was the lascivious young man. She could practically feel him leering at her. Well, she could either ignore him, or she could fight back. She turned her head slowly to stare at him, not smiling, and Level Assessed him.

Name: Ruan

Class: Swordsworn

Level: 15

She considered doing a Full Assess. More information could only help her. But Ruan smiled, a lazy smirk that wanted to undress her right there, and her irritation flowered into anger. She rolled her eyes in as dismissive a gesture as she could manage and turned away, fixing her gaze on the blank slate. Giving him her apparent attention for the time it would take to do a Full Assess would make him believe she was interested in him, and there was no way she would give that impression.

Another person's entrance distracted her, and she glanced secretly at the man who sat at the last desk, the one at the other end of the row. He was elderly, with silver hair and a neatly-trimmed silver beard, but he moved as easily as a much younger man and sat with his back perfectly straight and his head held high. Unlike Balraj, his pose didn't annoy Aderyn. She Assessed him quickly.

Name: Varoun

∞ Sudha

Class: Moonlighter (retired)

Level: 14

A retired Moonlighter? Aderyn had assumed anyone interested in commanding an army would have a martial class, but Moonlighters were clever, sideways thinkers, and that could make them good at seeing military patterns and analyzing enemy movements. And depending on Varoun's adventuring experience, he might know a lot about fighting orcs. He would be a strong opponent.

Silence fell, interrupted only by the rising and falling hum of the ceiling fans. Aderyn clasped her hands together so she wouldn't fidget. She felt Ruan's presence next to her as an oppressive weight, though she didn't know if he was still staring. Why didn't they start already? Any test the history masters came up with had to be better than sitting and waiting for the worst.

As she thought this, the chime rang out, and Tenzen entered the room through the door beyond the slate, followed by Druv and Kash.

They were dressed identically in cream-colored robes and trousers with bright blue sashes crossing their chests diagonally. Embroidered patches attached to the sashes at the shoulder were the only difference between their attire. Tenzen's bore an image of a cat with large, tufted ears, stitched in gold thread, while Druv and Kash each had smaller images in silver thread of a coiled serpent and a thick-bodied lizard respectively.

The three men lined up in front of the slate. Before any of them could speak, Balraj shot to his feet and said, "I object to that one's presence here." He pointed at Aderyn. "No northerner should command our army. Her inclusion calls into question the legitimacy of this contest. I demand she be expelled."

Tenzen regarded Balraj in steady silence for a few seconds. Druv and Kash didn't react, making it impossible for Aderyn to tell how they felt about Balraj's exclamation. Her heart pounded hard enough to hurt, and she wanted to leap from her seat to challenge the obnoxious man. She gripped her hands tighter to control her impulses.

Finally, Tenzen said, "Your objection is noted and dismissed. We did not restrict this test in any way other than by the challenges we set the candidates. Northern or southern, young or old, male or female—"

"This is to spite me, isn't it?" Balraj spat. "You're taunting me because I chose to leave the college. We all know my skills are superior, so what's the point of this show?"

"Superior," Kash muttered irritably. "Be grateful you made it to the second round of tests."

"Enough of this," Tenzen said. "Are you saying you're not willing to abide by our judgment, Balraj? Because all the dukes agreed." He inclined his head at Janesh, who smiled cheerfully.

"I'm saying I don't believe a northerner ought to be eligible. She lacks the right allegiances." Balraj glared at Aderyn. "And she's too young."

"Munesh was nineteen when he defeated the orc armies at Brandur Pass," Druv said. He alone didn't sound annoyed with Balraj. "There is ample precedent. As I'm sure you know."

"Balraj, it's your choice. Either play by the rules, or withdraw." Tenzen's calm demeanor eased Aderyn's fears that she was about to be thrown out of the Academy Hall.

Balraj glared at Tenzen for a few seconds longer. Tenzen remained impassive. Finally, Balraj muttered an oath beneath his breath and sat heavily on his stool. He refused to look anyone in the eye.

"If there are no other objections?" Tenzen swept the line of desks with his gaze. Aderyn sat up straight and tried to look alert and interested, though her hands still shook from nerves and she had to continue to clasp them tightly to make the shaking stop.

When no one else responded, Tenzen nodded and turned to Kash, who stepped forward and cleared his throat. "The five of you alone among the contenders have passed the initial battery of tests. You have qualified to advance to the second level. My advice is that you not let this go to your heads. Some of you only barely passed the assessments—and no, we're not going to say who. From this point on, you're all starting from zero."

Aderyn's heart rate sped up. He couldn't mean *her*, could he? She'd been confident about the final test, but maybe she'd made a mistake somewhere and they'd noticed. Or it was the second test, where she'd taken so long to realize the truth. Or maybe they didn't believe she'd fought a deep delver! She hoped her dismay wasn't visible, because it was bad enough she doubted herself—if the other candidates thought she was the weak one, they might be able to use it against her.

"We will begin by testing your historical knowledge," Kash continued. "Answer Master Druv's questions as they are directed at you. Speaking out of turn will be a mark against you. Understood?"

Aderyn nodded, hoping the despair filling her wasn't obvious. Historical knowledge? She knew almost nothing of history, and none of her knowledge was about battles or wars aside from the things everyone knew. They weren't going to restrict their questions to those.

Druv took Kash's place in front of the slate, and Kash and Tenzen sat on the tall stools beside it. Standing, Druv was taller than Aderyn had realized from yesterday's encounter, and he looked even thinner than he had then. He clasped his hands behind his back and waited, though Aderyn didn't know for what. To make them all tense and nervous, probably.

Abruptly, Druv said, "Janesh. Who won the Battle of Binyan Hill?"

"The human army led by Munesh," Janesh said with no hesitation.

"Varoun. When surrounded by goblin hordes at Santarus, what was Olfen's tactic for breaking the line?"

Varoun cleared his throat. "He used Earthbreakers to build a redoubt that divided the goblins on their weak side, then sent a line of riders to hold the redoubt while his forces escaped the trap."

Druv nodded. "Ruan. What was the result of the city of Branlight attacking Stonehaven?"

Ruan shrugged. "I have no idea. I don't know anything about northern battles."

Aderyn sat up straighter. This question, she knew the answer to!

Druv noticed her alertness. "Then let's give the northerner an easy question. Aderyn?"

"Branlight nearly destroyed Stonehaven, and the citizens of Stonehaven relocated into the mountains and founded Finion's Gate." Aderyn's nerves made her jumpy, but she thought she'd sounded calm.

"Balraj," Druv said, "give two main consequences of the war between Adhiraj and Khantak."

"The consequences are well-known," Balraj said. "First and most obvious, Khantak was destroyed, its citizens scattered. But a second result of the war meant Adhiraj's duke was well positioned to take the kingship. In the fighting that followed—"

"That's enough, thank you." Druv didn't sound annoyed the way Aderyn thought Kash would have. "Aderyn, continue Mas—Balraj's explanation. What forces ultimately came to battle over the claim to the throne?"

Aderyn considered her options. She was certain she wasn't going to get lucky with her questions again. So she could either go on failing to answer each new question, or... "I don't know," she said, facing Druv fearlessly. "I'm sorry, but I've never studied the history of warfare. I only know about Branlight because I was in Finion's Gate a few weeks ago and it's a well-known story."

"Then you admit to ignorance about the central issue of this contest?" Balraj declared.

"Shut up, Balraj," Kash said.

"Let's not be rude," Druv said. "Balraj, you are not administering these tests. Please keep your comments to yourself." To Aderyn, he said,

"You realize this puts you at a disadvantage. Not knowing what battles have been fought to which end limits your abilities as a general."

"I don't want to sound dismissive, because I'm sure you're right that's important, but how much of a limit is my ignorance, really?" Aderyn wasn't sure where that had come from, but it felt right, so she forged ahead. "It's like studying swordsmanship. My father is a Swordsworn who teaches fighting, and he encourages his students to study all these fancy moves and how to counter them. But he also says winning is what matters, and if it comes to a fight between someone who's studied and someone who has experience, there's nothing to say the one will have an advantage over the other."

"So, you're saying this test is unimportant," Druv said.

"Please don't put words in my mouth. I'm saying that it shouldn't disqualify me if I don't know historical battles. I'd like to be tested on my skills." A tiny voice at the back of her skull was shrieking at Aderyn to stop, stop now before he kicks us out! But she was riding the wave of her confidence like those people in Owen's world who surfed the ocean waves. She understood now why people did that, if the rush was anything like what she felt now.

Druv watched her, his eyes narrowed. "We will not be dictated to."

"I'm not! I'm asking you to consider my point. That's all."

"Let's continue," Tenzen said. "No more questions for Aderyn."

"You might as well exclude me, too," Ruan said. He propped one elbow on his desk and rested his chin in his hand. "I'm not really the academic sort. Never did study history."

Druv threw up his hands and turned away. He had a low-voiced conversation with the other masters Aderyn wished she was a Moonlighter to eavesdrop on, though if she were a Moonlighter, she wouldn't be there.

When Druv turned around, he looked far calmer than Aderyn had expected. "Aderyn and Ruan agree to take a penalty for failing to participate in this test?"

Aderyn's heart sank. It was too reasonable for her to counter, even though she felt her reasoning was correct. She nodded. Ruan waved his other hand carelessly, like this was all too boring for words. Aderyn wished she knew why the Swordsworn was even here.

"Then we will continue." Druv went back to asking questions, leaving Aderyn feeling conspicuous and awkward about being left out even though she'd agreed to it. Failing before she'd even started! Maybe it was just a penalty—they hadn't kicked her out—but that could mean anything. And she was sure now she'd alienated Druv.

Well, there was no point behaving as if she'd already been eliminated. She'd just have to work extra hard to overcome the penalty. And it wasn't about the Fated One quest anymore. They clearly believed she and Ruan were the same, even though Ruan obviously thought the challenge was beneath him and Aderyn wasn't a smug git like him. She was going to win this challenge and prove to the masters that abstract knowledge wasn't the essential they believed it was. And she was going to leave Ruan in her dust.

Chapter Seven

The questioning went on for a few hours, by the end of which time Aderyn was starving. If they didn't offer food, wasn't that like expecting them to perform at a disadvantage, since hunger made you short-tempered and unable to focus? She wished she could say with certainty that the masters cared about their physical well-being.

But when the chime rang again, interrupting Druv in the middle of a question, the masters waited for Varoun to finish answering, then left the room by the door they'd entered through without another word. Aderyn incautiously caught Ruan's eye, but he didn't leer or smirk; he looked as uncertain as she felt.

The other door opened, and a proctor appeared. "Follow me for your midday meal," he said, and left as swiftly as he'd arrived. Aderyn rose from her stool and hurried after him, not caring if her eagerness was something the others might use against her. But Janesh beat her to the door, and Ruan wasn't far behind. Only Balraj loitered, Aderyn thought to put even more of a separation between himself and the others.

The proctor led them to a small room furnished with three round tables and a lot of backless chairs. Five places were laid at one of the tables, surrounding platters and baskets of food. Aderyn waited for Ruan to seat himself, then took a chair that put her out of his direct line of sight. It was childish, probably, but sitting next to him had left her disinclined to have more contact with him than she had to.

She ended up between Varoun and Janesh, both of whom served themselves before offering the plates to her. At least that much of good table manners was the same between north and south; she didn't know what she'd have done if they'd deferred to her, given that she still wasn't familiar with southern cuisine. As it was, she observed the way they spread rice on their plates before scooping dollops of various meaty sauces across the rice layer, and when it was her turn, she mimicked them, hoping she wouldn't get anything too spicy for her to bear.

The baskets contained parotta, and Aderyn mentally thanked the server who'd explained how to eat it. She still needed both hands to tear hers apart, but once it was in shreds, she easily scooped up the rice mixture and ate one-handed. She couldn't say it was entirely delicious, because despite her care there were a few sauces she had to covertly push aside, but mostly it was an excellent meal.

They ate in silence, with Janesh helping himself to rice and sauce twice, until most of the food was gone. Then Janesh said, "There's no reason we shouldn't get to know one another, you know. All this silence, it's murder on the digestion."

"I see no reason to pretend we're all friendly," Balraj said. "Only one of us can triumph, and I intend it to be me. The rest of you might as well not bother."

"Thunderation, Balraj, what crawled up your ass and died?" Janesh laughed. "You may be famed for your knowledge of history, but you're sitting next to one of the great generals in living memory—you see, I recognize your name, sir."

"As I recognize yours," Varoun said. "What brings one of the dukes of the Southlands to compete for command of the unified armies? I would think you have power enough."

Aderyn gaped. Janesh, a duke? "Wouldn't they just give you command, my lord?" she asked.

"Just Janesh, since we're all equals here, whatever Balraj thinks of it," Janesh said. "With the king being too young to command, and the queen regent not being a military woman, there was no consensus on who should take charge. You won't know this, but the Southlander kingdom is more fragile a thing than it looks to outsiders. I'm not willing to sacrifice my autonomy to another, and I say I'm as good a commander as anyone, but my fellow dukes see only a grab for power."

"Which it is," Balraj said.

Janesh shrugged. "Call it what you want. The point is, we all agreed to this choosing, but none of us agreed to give up trying for the brass ring. I'm not surprised the Duke of Adhiraj didn't pass the first round of tests. Simla is too brash and too impetuous a thinker to be good at command. And Kanan... well, he's working by proxy, isn't he?" He tilted his head at Ruan and raised his eyebrows in invitation.

Ruan shrugged. "The Duke of Tielana sees potential and makes use of it. He's a powerful sponsor."

"Then the rumors are true," Varoun said. "You're the Fated One."

Aderyn coughed as she inhaled a morsel of food down the wrong pipe. "Sorry," she said when she could speak again. "You're the Fated One?"

"In the flesh," Ruan said with a mocking smile. "Didn't think you'd be this close to greatness, eh?"

"Um, no." Aderyn weighed her options. Reveal her true reason for being there, or lie and risk being scorned when they all found out? "You mean, you're *a* Fated One. There are hundreds all over the world."

Ruan's smile grew. "But how many of those know what quests are required of the true Fated One? I assure you, I'm the real thing."

Aderyn's instincts took over. "That is interesting, and I agree the true Fated One follows a path. I know this because, as it happens, my husband is the Fated One and we're here because of that quest chain."

Ruan's eyes widened. Then he burst out laughing so loudly the sound echoed off the walls. "You're joking. What are the odds two Fated Ones would end up in the same place?"

"If we're both following the same quest, very good odds, actually." Aderyn suppressed her anger. Maybe Ruan really was just amused at the coincidence, but it sure as thunder felt like he was laughing at her. "Are you here because of the orc army?"

"I'd rather not share my quest, sorry. Suppose they interfere with each other?" Ruan picked up his glass of water and sipped. "So you shouldn't either."

"I… guess that makes sense." It didn't, really, but Aderyn didn't like the idea of sharing any information with this fellow. "Then why do you want to command the army, if not for a Fated One quest?"

"It's a challenge, right? And I love challenges." Ruan gazed at her with a direct look that said clearly he saw Aderyn as another challenge to be overcome. She chose to ignore his blatant come-on.

"The Fated One has a quest that requires his wife to command an army?" Janesh sounded skeptical. "Isn't that a lot of responsibility to put on someone else? What's the point of being the Fated One if you don't take direct action?"

"Ruan is right, I shouldn't share the details," Aderyn said, "but we have an adventuring team, and all of us work together to support the Fated One. That's part of the prophecies."

"Interesting," Varoun said. "Then, if that's true, who supports you, Ruan?"

"Oh, Ruan's situation is unusual," Janesh said. "You don't have more in your team than your brother, right?"

"My brother is my partner," Ruan said. "It's how the Warmaster class works."

Again, Aderyn felt like she'd been struck in the gut by Owen's legendary fastball. "But—a Warmaster? How did you figure it out?"

"It was simple, really." Ruan shrugged again. "One or two battles together proved that his skills supported mine."

"I'm sorry, this is just too much," Aderyn said. "You're brothers—did you get the Call and wait around for him, or vice versa, or—"

"*Twin* brothers," Ruan said. "We got the Call within minutes of each other. I don't know if that's how it works for all twins, but for us, pairing up was an obvious choice."

"That's astonishing." Aderyn forgot she disliked Ruan and his sexually aggressive leers. "We should meet, he and I—I've never met another Warmaster as high a level as this."

"We'll see. Suveer isn't much for talking to people." Ruan smiled again. "Though he could make an exception for someone as lovely as you."

Varoun cleared his throat. Janesh looked uncomfortable. Aderyn hadn't thought Ruan would come right up to the line of what was acceptable behavior toward a married woman, and her dislike returned. How dare he flirt overtly enough to make these other men uncomfortable? "That's a nice compliment I'm sure my husband would agree with," she said. "But I'm serious about wanting to talk to—Suveer, was it? Another Warmaster—"

The door opened. The proctor said, "If you're finished, please follow me to the next examination room."

Aderyn pushed back her seat and rose to follow Janesh. The excitement of possibly meeting another high-level Warmaster made more tests seem like nothing by comparison. She needed to focus. Winning was why she was here. Everything else could wait.

The proctor led them to the long hallway lined with curtained alcoves. This time, palm-sized slates with their names chalked on them marked five of the alcoves, spaced widely enough apart there was no chance of hearing anything from a neighboring cubicle. "Take your places and wait for instructions," the proctor said.

Aderyn found the alcove marked with her name and slipped past the curtain. The contraption she remembered was gone. In its place was a square table, larger than she could circle with her arms, with two-inch-high sides making a shallow box. Aderyn stepped closer, fascinated. The box was full of fine, pale sand in drifts like a very precise wind had shifted the tiny dunes without scattering the sand on the floor. She almost felt she could see patterns. **[Improved Assess 3]** gave her no additional information, not even a name.

The curtain twitched aside, and Kash entered. He carried a box the size of a large folio and a sheet of paper. He set the box on a ledge along the back wall that looked like it was meant for just that purpose and consulted the paper with his head down. "Aderyn," he said, but contemplatively, not as if he was addressing her.

"Sir?" Aderyn asked when he didn't immediately continue.

"Should I assume you are ignorant of strategic notation?"

Aderyn blushed. "I've never learned it, no."

"And yet you're here. No historical knowledge, no language of tactics... by all rights we should send you packing."

"I passed the tests," Aderyn said.

"Which is why you are still here." Kash fell silent again. Aderyn waited. Finally, the history master shook his head and folded the paper away into his robe. He picked up the box and began removing carved finger-length pegs from its depths.

"I ought to set up your test and force you to work out the details," he said as he placed peg after peg into the sandbox. "But that would not accurately assess your skill. So I will show you how to lay out a basic strategic diagram before beginning your test."

Aderyn looked at the box instead of Kash. The pegs were more like roughly-shaped human figures painted green or yellow, standing in groups with their bases wedged into the sand. Their arrangement at first looked random, but when she tilted her head to look at the display from a different angle, it came into focus: two tiny armies poised to attack each other.

"There are standards," Kash said, "basic conventions agreed on over centuries of warfare. Yellow is the color of the defender, and green the color of the attacker. In more simplified displays, triangles denote defenders and circles, attackers. Strategic diagrams are intended to show the rough disposition of forces at a moment in time for the sake of evaluating tactics."

Aderyn nodded understanding. "And here, the defenders have the advantage."

Kash paused. "What makes you say that?"

Aderyn gestured, pointing at three places. "They control the high ground—oh. Maybe that's coincidence, and the layout is random, in which case it's not meant to be actual terrain."

"No, you're correct." Kash reached into the box again and pulled out some wooden blocks larger than the green and yellow figures. He set the blocks down in a pattern and rearranged the figures. "Who has advantage now?"

"The attackers. It's a two-pronged attack, and there are too few defenders to counter. The attackers will overrun those blocks with a hard push."

"Indeed." Kash handed the box to Aderyn. "Show me how to rearrange or add forces to give the defenders the advantage."

Aderyn searched the box for more yellow figures. They were roughly molded, but up close, the carving suggested a face, and each had the outline of a tiny sword sheathed at his hip. She set out her defenders, glancing once at Kash to see what he thought. The history master remained impassive. Finally, he said, "That is mostly correct. You failed to account for the second prong of the attack breaking free to circle around, overwhelming the defenders on this side."

"Oh." Aderyn surveyed the small battlefield. "You're right."

Kash rearranged the blocks and removed all the yellow defenders. He took the box from her and pulled out more figures. These were of pewter rather than wood, more finely modeled and painted realistically. Each of them bore a flat disk atop its head, marked with the traditional symbols of adventuring classes: staff, sword, fist, crescent moon. Kash arranged these four figures in front of the pile of blocks he'd made, surrounded them with a handful of green pegs, and said, "This level ten adventuring party was ambushed by seven level nine and ten Assassins. Show how you would deploy the adventurers to defeat their enemy."

Aderyn's confidence swelled. *This*, she could do easily. She switched the Staffsworn and Swifthands' positions and moved the Moonlighter in a wide arc to put her behind the Assassins. "The Moonlighter and the Assassins both have **[Hide in Plain Sight]** at their levels, but you implied it was an ambush the adventurers are aware of, which suggests the Assassins have revealed themselves. The Swordsworn, Swifthands, and Staffsworn can force the Assassins through this choke point here, while the Moonlighter picks off stragglers from behind."

"And if the Assassins have crossbows?"

"Then the adventurers had better hope their affairs are in order. Charging an enemy who's shooting at you is a fast way to get dead." Aderyn narrowed her eyes. "The Swifthands could manage it if he were a little higher level. Get up close, make it impossible for them to shoot without hitting their friends."

"Hmm." Kash again set the box on the ledge. Then, without another word, he left the room.

Chapter Eight

Aderyn stared at the curtain as it flapped shut. She was sure she was right in her analysis, so what was that about? Her nerves returned full force. She'd guessed wrong—her answers had been partly instinct, but it all looked so obvious—or maybe she'd guessed *right* and she was too accurate. Maybe Kash thought she'd cheated, though how that was possible, she had no idea.

She played with the figures, marching them around the sandbox and setting up imaginary conflicts, until the curtain swung aside again, admitting not only Kash, but Tenzen as well. Tenzen eyed Aderyn speculatively. "She passed?"

"She passed," Kash replied.

Aderyn's relief was short-lived. Tenzen immediately followed this up with, "I'm not sure what you want me to do. If she cheated, she will be expelled immediately."

"I did not cheat!" Aderyn exclaimed. "I'm a Warmaster. A tactician. This is what I do, see weaknesses and vulnerabilities. None of you seemed surprised that a Warmaster could be a high level, so I figured you knew what I'm capable of."

"I see no way you could have cheated," Kash said. "I gave you several different assessments, all of which would have required different methods of cheating, and it's unlikely anyone could be that well prepared for the possibilities, two of which I made up on the spot."

"Then why—"

"I want a second opinion," Kash said. "Call it security."

Tenzen gathered the figures and blocks and used a small hoe and rake to smooth out the sand. He laid out a new diagram. "Show me how the attackers can triumph."

Suppressing a groan, Aderyn pointed out the weaknesses in the defense and shifted a few figures. Tenzen tapped a finger against his lips. Then he held the box out to Aderyn. "Your turn. Set up a scenario for me to analyze."

Aderyn thought back to their battle against the deep delver. She chose pewter figures from the box, Swordsworn, Moonlighter, Earthbreaker, and Herald—there was no Warmaster miniature, which annoyed her. She piled blocks in the center and positioned the figures the way her team had been situated, even though the deep delver had been more dangerous than any human.

Tenzen tapped the head of an attacker. "Interesting. Based on experience, or imagination?"

"Experience. Mostly."

"Interesting," Tenzen repeated. After another few seconds, he said, "This is a solid offense, but it falls apart if any one point is defeated. It's really more the province of a war game than a simple tactical exercise."

"Oh." Aderyn felt stupid. Of course the deep delver battle had moved too fast for the outcome to be obvious at the start.

Tenzen ignored her. "I wouldn't worry about it," he told Kash. "This is just one of many tests. If it's a fluke, we'll know soon enough."

"A fluke?" Aderyn said, outraged again.

"You're dismissed for the day," Tenzen said. "Return here at ten o'clock tomorrow morning for further assessment." He and Kash left the cubicle, and Aderyn heard their voices growing quiet with distance: "...not sure what..." "...a chance..." "...not much time left..."

Aderyn concentrated on her breathing until it was slow and regular. Then she left the curtained alcove and went in search of the exit.

The big room where she'd met Owen and the others the previous day was empty. It was too bad there was no Assessment that told you the time, because she suspected she'd finished early. The light outside didn't look like late afternoon light, though this was a foreign land and light probably looked different than it did in the north at this hour. Still, her downhearted feeling intensified at not finding her friends waiting for her.

There was a wide double door that led directly outside in addition to the smaller door leading to the candidates' entrance. Aderyn pushed the big door open and stood in the doorway, watching the plaza. It bustled with activity, so it had to be after three or everyone would be indoors napping. What a great tradition, afternoon naps. This climate was perfect for them.

She wandered over to the fountain. Wooden benches surrounded it, most of them empty. Aderyn sat and let the cool mist spray her face. She closed her eyes and ran back through the afternoon's activities in memory. She'd done all right for someone who didn't know the conventions of how to diagram a military scenario. It wasn't as if there were a lot of wars these days. The orc invasion was the first she'd heard about in her lifetime, maybe in her parents' lifetime.

That got her thinking about the College of History. Why would they have scholars who specialized in an archaic form of conflict? And Varoun, he was a famous general—what wars had there been for him to lead an army in? Of course, he was very old, so that could be something from well before her time.

Someone sat next to her. "Finished early, too, huh?" Ruan said. "It's my good fortune that gives me more time with you."

His tone wasn't seductive, but his words irked her anyway. She resolved to match him in politeness until he came close to the line, at which point she was going to knock him back. "I'm curious about your adventuring history, Ruan. I think your brother and I might be the highest-level Warmasters in the world."

"It's nothing special. We fought monsters, did quests. Typical adventuring." Ruan leaned forward, clasping his hands on his knees. "Is your partner as powerful a fighter as I think?"

"Of course. You both get boosts from your Warmaster partner." This was probably a mistake, but she couldn't bear being this close to another Warmaster like her and not taking advantage of it. "Maybe we could have dinner sometime, my team and you and your brother? I really would love to meet him."

"I'm sure we could arrange something." He put his hand on Aderyn's knee. "Or it could be just the two of us."

Aderyn grabbed his hand and thrust it away. "That's it," she said. "That's as much as I'm willing to put up with. I don't know why you think I'm available for your flirting, whether women in the south like those attentions when they're married to someone else, but I'm not like that. Don't touch me again."

"Hey, I didn't mean anything." Ruan laughed. "Most women like the attention from a Fated One—but if you're married to—"

"That's right. Think about that. I'm married. Give your attentions to any of the single women who will fall all over you." Aderyn rose. "I'll see you tomorrow." She managed not to add *unless I can avoid it.*

She walked in a random direction, only caring about getting away from Ruan, so she was startled when Owen called her name from behind her. She hurried to join her team and flung her arms around Owen's neck. "I'm so glad to see you."

"So am I, but you're not normally this demonstrative—did something happen?"

She shook her head. "It's been a long day. Lots of testing, and I almost failed before I began because they had this stupid test about historical battles—"

"I was afraid of that," Owen said. He kissed her so sweetly she relaxed a bit. "But you passed?"

"No. They let me take a penalty, I don't know what that means exactly, and I didn't have to participate. But then they thought I cheated in the afternoon test, and I'm so mad about it!"

"You should be mad," Livia said. "I bet you were too good, and they were suspicious."

"More or less." Aderyn described the sandbox test. "It was easy enough, so maybe I didn't act like it was difficult? I don't know. Oh! But one of the candidates has a Warmaster partner—level fifteen, even!"

"You mean that bastard who came onto you," Owen said. "He's partnered with a Warmaster?"

"His twin brother. I wanted us to meet, have dinner or something, but then Ruan made a pass at me again and I got so angry I forgot."

"He made a pass at you?" Owen's smile disappeared. "Do I need to do something about him?"

"I smacked him down. I don't think he'll try again. It's all right, Owen, I can handle it."

Owen still looked angry. "If he doesn't take the hint, I'll give him a stronger one. You shouldn't have to put up with that."

More of Aderyn's tension eased. She didn't know why Owen was so intent on defending her, but she liked it. If this was more of his world's traditions, maybe some of them were worth adopting. "Thank you. It won't come to that, but—thank you."

"So you made it through another day," Weston said. "How long will this take? Because we've been hearing rumors of orc attacks, and people are starting to talk war."

"And they are quite vocal about the need for someone to command the army," Isold said. "Many of them have their favorites for the role, and only some of them are aware of the testing to choose the commander."

"Let's get something to eat," Aderyn said, "and you can tell me about these favorites."

"It's way too early for dinner, at least by southern standards," Livia said.

Aderyn groaned. "A snack, then. I'm starving. And maybe some of that citrus beverage. But really I'm ready to sit with friends and not think about tactics."

"Consider it done," Owen said.

ADERYN WAS THE FIRST TO ARRIVE AT THE ACADEMY HALL the next morning. The giant slate and desks had all been removed. Two small square tables with two chairs pulled up to each had been placed at random near the center of the large room. One table was covered by a red satin tablecloth that was long enough to pool on the floor. The other looked the same except for the tablecloth being deep sapphire blue.

Aderyn wandered over to the blue table. Her heart sank. A square gameboard of varnished honey ash, seventeen inches on a side, sat precisely at the center of the table. Piles of flattened glass pebbles, white and black, were heaped separately on either side of the table. Lines burned into the board made a grid seventeen squares by seventeen squares. She knew the number without counting just as she knew the dimensions without measuring. How in thunder had they landed on her personal nemesis for the next test? All right, a game couldn't be a nemesis, but this one certainly tried. Was it just her, or did the room feel warmer than usual?

She turned at the sound of footsteps to see Balraj enter. Today he dressed all in shades of brown, somber as always. He approached the tables, and his lips curved in a calculating smile. "The game of Wall," he said. "I am an expert, of course. I look forward to proving myself."

Aderyn said nothing. She didn't consider herself an expert, given that she'd played hundreds of games of Wall against her grandmother and won barely a handful of them.

Varoun and Janesh entered together, trailed by Ruan, who sauntered as if he had all the time in the world. "Hey, I know this game," he said. "My brother and I play it often."

"And I suppose you're a master," Varoun said. Aderyn had observed his disdain for Ruan, and it gave her a sense of fellow feeling with the elderly general.

Ruan shrugged. "I can hold my own."

The far door opened, and the history masters emerged. "We will assign your seats," Druv said. "You will play one another—four games each, four opponents. Each round, one of you will sit out. You may use this time to observe the opposition."

Kash read from a sheet of paper. "First round. Janesh versus Varoun, Aderyn versus Balraj, Ruan to sit out."

Aderyn drew out a chair and sat at the blue table. Balraj lowered himself gracefully into his seat, like a drab brown bird alighting on a branch. "You may take the first move," he said.

"First player is chosen at random," Tenzen said. He palmed two stones and held them behind his back before presenting his closed fists to Aderyn. Aderyn tapped his left fist, and Tenzen revealed the white pebble. "Balraj, you may begin."

Balraj selected a black pebble with overly formal delicacy and placed it at the intersection of two lines. Aderyn placed her first white pebble immediately. She wasn't going to sabotage herself, she would play to the best of her abilities, but she couldn't bring herself to be anything but discouraged about her prospects.

They played for a while, typical opening moves. Balraj took some territory that Aderyn recaptured. It wasn't until Balraj set a stone down with more than necessary force that Aderyn looked at him. His eyes were fixed on the board, and his thunderously angry expression surprised her into hesitating. Immediately, Balraj transferred his furious gaze to her. "You think you're so clever," he snarled.

"I—what?" Aderyn surveyed the board. To her surprise, she was within a few moves of winning. She placed her next stone, transforming three of the black stones to white. Balraj muttered something and shoved away from the table. "Don't you want to finish?" Aderyn asked.

"I'm not going to play out this mockery of a game. You were toying with me." Balraj stood, shoving his chair farther.

"I was just playing the game, Balraj." Aderyn's excitement at nearly having won died in the face of her opponent's anger. "And you're the one cheapening the experience. I haven't won yet."

"Don't act so naïve. You're the winner. I just accept inevitability." Balraj stalked over to the red table and loomed over Varoun and Janesh's game.

Aderyn turned to Tenzen. "Um... what now?"

"A forfeit is not the same as a loss," Tenzen said. He scrutinized the board. "But Balraj is correct that two moves would win Aderyn the game. I declare a victory for Aderyn."

Aderyn's heart beat faster, like she'd won a race instead of a quiet game of Wall. Balraj must not be much of a player, and her other opponents would be far more difficult to beat, if she even could beat them. But—she'd won! And at a game she would have sworn she was terrible at. Well, everyone could get lucky once.

Chapter Nine

Her next match was against Janesh. He played intently, leaning over the board and making his decisions for building his walls swiftly, but it took only a few moves for Aderyn to realize it was all bluff. Despite his seriousness, he played erratically, making odd choices and giving up territory unnecessarily. Aderyn won more quickly than she had against Balraj. Janesh saluted her when the game was over, saying, "I'm terrible at Wall, I know."

"You're not as terrible as I am," Aderyn said.

Janesh laughed. "You won, Aderyn. How can you call yourself terrible? I'd suspect you of false modesty if I didn't judge you far too straightforward a thinker for that."

"But I never win at Wall." Aderyn listened to herself and felt stupid. She'd won twice, so why did she still think she sucked at it, in Owen's words? And yet—all those games against her grandmother, all those losses. If you couldn't beat your aging grandmother at a basic board game, how could you call yourself a winner?

"Guess you can't say that anymore." Janesh nodded and excused himself. Aderyn remained in her seat. How strange a readjustment of her perceptions it was to see herself as a winner of this game. If it was her Warmaster's vision that was doing it, it was happening at a level she wasn't aware of, because by now she knew how it felt to be swept along by those instincts. This was different.

Ruan dropped into the chair opposite her. "My turn," he said with a grin. "I won't go easy on you."

"I like a challenge," Aderyn replied. Her odd mood vanished, replaced by a keen desire to not just defeat Ruan, but to pound him into the floorboards.

Ruan's play style was slow, almost hesitant. He paused so long over his moves Aderyn almost called one of the history masters to make him speed it up. But he was a better, more intelligent player than either Balraj or Janesh despite the slowness, and Aderyn found herself caught up in the game, planning her strategy.

When she placed a final stone that converted four of Ruan's white ones to black, Ruan sat back and groaned. "Of course you would have to be a master of Wall," he said. "Just my luck. I guess I don't have enough skill on my side." He sounded amused, but there was a dark look in his eye Aderyn didn't like.

"I've really never done this well before, I swear," she said. Instantly she felt like a fool. That was the sort of thing simpering maidens said, or card sharps looking to fleece an ignorant mark.

"That doesn't make it better, you faking innocence," Ruan said. He rose and walked away.

Aderyn got up and walked in the other direction, stretching her legs. Ruan was a bastard, but that didn't mean she had to taunt him, even unintentionally. She thought back over her three games. The memory of playing against Gran superimposed itself over them. Every tactic she'd used, she'd learned from desperately trying to find a way to beat Gran. Maybe she was wrong about her grandmother's skills.

"Aderyn and Varoun, take your seats," Druv said.

Aderyn joined Varoun at the blue-topped table. The elderly general regarded her closely. "So, you don't win at Wall."

"I never have before. I always used to lose, any time I played. This is new."

"If I were Balraj, I would accuse you of cheating," Varoun said in a low voice, arching his eyebrows in sardonic humor. Aderyn giggled.

"But you know it's almost impossible to cheat at Wall, unless you have some mental link to a more proficient player."

Aderyn considered **[Bonded Mind]** and tried to imagine using it to cheat. Maybe at a higher skill level, but... no. "That would be unlikely."

Varoun tapped Tenzen's outstretched hand and accepted the white stone he revealed. "Your move first, young lady."

It only took three moves for Aderyn to realize she was playing against a master. Varoun played confidently, placing stones with little hesitation and waiting patiently if Aderyn chose to take a moment to analyze her move. It took ten moves for her to realize she was holding her own against him. Vaguely, she was aware of others gathered around their table, watching, but most of her attention remained on the game.

They played for what seemed an eternity, territory passing back and forth, the board shifting from primarily white to mostly black and back again. Aderyn felt herself caught in memory again, no longer sitting in the over-warm Academy Hall, but back in her grandmother's sitting room, sweating over the Wall board, cringing beneath Gran's criticisms as she took apart Aderyn's play and analyzed it after yet another loss.

With that, she saw the hole in Varoun's defenses. She heard Gran say *It looks strong, but the right play will bring that wall down.* She placed her stone.

Varoun immediately reached out to place another stone. Then he froze. "What did you do?"

"That's my move," Aderyn said, hoping she sounded confident and not brash.

Varoun stared at her. He returned his stone to his pile. "Who taught you that move?"

"My grandmother."

Varoun closed his eyes briefly. Then he gestured at the board. "I could continue, but we both know who will win. I concede."

Aderyn let out a breath. "Thank you for a challenging game, sir."

"It's been decades since I had an opponent who could play me to a draw, let alone defeat me." Varoun sighed as Aderyn had. "And she married someone else. Your grandmother is Ellowyn, isn't she?"

"You knew her?"

"We adventured together, long ago. I wanted her to stay with me, but Savion swept her off her feet—I suppose it's too much to expect a Moonlighter to compete with a Herald." Varoun smiled, a reflective expression. "Is she happy?"

"She was, sir. She and my grandfather passed away a few years ago. Influenza."

"Oh." Varoun blinked. "You'd think it wouldn't hit me, fifty year old memories, but..." He sat up straighter. "Don't think this means I'll give up in your favor. You're still inexperienced, and I believe I am the best person to command the armies."

"I understand. And I won't give up either." Impulsively, Aderyn extended her hand to Varoun, who shook it firmly.

Tenzen cleared his throat. "We will break for a meal, and the final test will be this afternoon. We will make our decision this evening."

Aderyn's limbs shook, as if she'd done something strenuous instead of playing an emotionally charged game, but by the time she walked to the dining room, she felt energized. It would be nice to have some sense of where she stood—she'd won every game of Wall, and she thought she'd done well at the sandbox game, but there was that penalty from the history test hanging over her, and she didn't know whether their results from the initial testing mattered. And the masters all knew she lacked experience and a basic grasp of tactical notation... oh, there was no point in fretting over things she couldn't control. Even so, she only picked at her food, nerves killing her appetite, and when the proctor summoned them to the final test, she followed him eagerly.

Unexpectedly, the proctor led them outside and across the plaza to the great arched university entrance. There, one of the covered people-carrying wagons waited. The proctor waved at them to board, and Aderyn hesitated only briefly before climbing into the wagon after Varoun.

Wooden benches circled the wagon's interior, with another long bench bisecting it. Aderyn sat near the driver's seat, not close to any of her rivals, but then none of the others seemed interested in getting near one another, either. The wagon smoothly shifted into motion, made a wide U-turn, and trundled eastward down the street.

Aderyn watched the people they passed, pedestrians, pedicab drivers, other wagon riders, a few mounted horsemen, without waving or drawing attention to herself. Only a few gave her more than a single glance. Cities were like that everywhere, she realized—all those people, so absorbed in their own business they didn't have time to worry about anyone else's. She liked the anonymity.

After about five minutes, she began examining the buildings they neared, curious about their destination. They'd left what she guessed was the city center behind, because the pale stone buildings were shorter now and less overwhelming, and there were fewer people on the street. Maybe it would be that single-story edifice with the row of glass windows circling it. Or possibly the single tall building, decorated on the outside with thin brass cutouts of flying birds.

But the wagon rounded a corner into an alley barely wide enough to fit it, and moments later it emerged into a secluded courtyard that was even hotter than the main street had been. Aderyn, sweating profusely, climbed down and hurried after the others. It didn't occur to her that Varoun hadn't needed to be told where to go, and that Balraj and Janesh had been similarly confident, until they were through a door into blessed cool darkness. Varoun kept walking, so Aderyn did too. If he didn't actually know where they should go, at least she could justify following him, with how confidently he moved.

The room they came to reminded Aderyn of the auditorium back in Far Haven, where the town would gather on important occasions when the weather was too bad for outdoor assembly. It had a high, rounded ceiling and a raised dais that ran the width of one end of the room. Five small groups of men and women dressed plainly in clothes suitable for the southern climate stood on the dais. All of them became alert when Aderyn and the other candidates appeared.

None of the history masters were present. Aderyn took the opportunity to Level Assess the groups. At first, they seemed a muddle of adventurers of varying classes, but Aderyn realized after a moment's analysis that the groups were more orderly than that: each group had a spellslinger, three people with martial classes, and a rogue of some type. All of them were level seven. There were no duplicates among the spellslingers—five groups, five types of magical specialization. There was no way this had happened at random.

A door at the back of the dais opened, and the three history masters entered. "For your final challenge," Tenzen said, "you will command a small force of fighters armed with non-lethal weapons. You will be given a map and sent to a location from which you will need to find your objective, a fortress on a low hill. Capture that fortress and hold it until sundown. Points will be awarded for well-executed strategy, eliminating opponents, and clever tactics, as well as capturing the objective and controlling it the longest. We will be observing using *clairvoyance.* Any questions?"

"May we assume traditional wargames rules?" Varoun asked.

"Traditional rules apply. You may trap or misdirect your enemies any way you choose, and you may eliminate an enemy with one solid hit to the chest or back, or two strikes to different limbs. Strikes to the head are not allowed. Causing injury, accidentally or intentionally, will result in a penalty to your team."

"Are there forbidden tactics?" Ruan asked.

"None except what I've already outlined," Tenzen said. "All other tactics are allowed."

Ruan grinned like this was the best news he'd had all day.

"You will be assigned teams at random," Kash said. He held up a bag that clinked like ceramic chips knocking against each other. "After assignment, you have five minutes to meet your team and develop an initial strategy. Then *world door* will send you to your starting location."

Aderyn was the last to choose. She reached into the offered bag and pulled out a thick disc of orange ceramic. "Orange team," Kash said, and pointed. Aderyn hadn't noticed in her flurry of Assessments that each team member wore a colored armband, blue, green, red, orange, or yellow.

She joined the group wearing orange armbands. "Wait a minute," she said when the taller of the two women started to speak to her. With great care, she again Assessed the other teams, noting which of her rivals had which resources. Then she turned to her own group. "Thanks for your patience. Have any of you done anything like this before?"

Two of the men nodded.

"Well, I haven't, so I need a little advice. What's common practice? I mean, are there strategies people tend to use frequently?"

The two men looked at each other. "Sometimes teams spend too much time sabotaging the enemy, and it costs them the game," the bearded man said. "But you're the one who's supposed to come up with strategy."

"Two of our enemies I judge to be straightforward thinkers, and one of those is a traditionalist. I'm trying to get a sense for what they might consider good strategy." Aderyn looked at each team member in turn. "I'm Aderyn, and I'm a level sixteen Warmaster. And I intend to win this challenge."

"A Warmaster?" the taller woman said skeptically.

Aderyn Assessed her again. "Arya, you're a Tidecaller, level seven. You specialized in water spells versus diversifying into ice—that makes sense, this place would melt any ice in seconds. Your **[Elemental Blast]** is at second tier, so you can do a water spray blast as well as a wave deluge, but I don't know what that is in practice. You'll probably get a chance to show us. You also have the skills **[Cloudburst]** and **[Thunderstorm]**. Any questions?"

Arya's stunned expression faded. "Is that what a level sixteen Warmaster can do? That's amazing."

"Thanks. Now, we're not going to waste any more time with me proving myself over and over again, are we?" Aderyn glanced over her shoulder. "And we're also not going to talk strategy where Varoun can hear us, because a Moonlighter has an excellent range of hearing. Instead, we're going to use our time in you telling me what the terrain and climate around here are like. And then we're going to get a good start on winning."

Chapter Ten

Stepping through *world door* from the cool, dry room where she'd received her instructions into a tiny forested clearing felt like being slapped in the face by a wet, mushy sponge. Sweat immediately prickled beneath Aderyn's hair and under her arms. This was going to be her biggest disadvantage, not being acclimated to the south. She pulled the leather lace tying her hair free and swept her hair into a higher ponytail, which was all she could do to cool herself. Her ordinary clothes might be over-warm, but at least she hadn't changed into the billowing southern robes. This was the wrong terrain for those.

By the sun's position, she guessed they had about five hours to sundown, if Owen was right about the sun setting at the same time every day. She surveyed the clearing while she waited for her team to pass through *world door*. The trees weren't anything like their northern kin; they had thick boles with rough, striated bark and heavy limbs sagging under the weight of fat-lobed leaves, glossy and dark green. Everything looked plump with water, as if the trees and leaves and even the wide-bladed grasses underfoot had drunk deep at the nearest river. The smell was extraordinary, rich and lush and fertile. Aderyn recalled what Livia had once said of volcanic soil growing anything planted in it. She could easily imagine the same here.

"Right," she said when the last team member appeared. "Who has the map?"

The Spider, Devash, stepped forward. He carried a waterproof scroll case from which he removed their map. "I'll need to climb a tree to fix our location."

Aderyn took the map and case to free Devash's hands. The little man scrambled up the nearest tree faster than Aderyn could have, and she was an expert tree climber. Soon he disappeared into the branches, and she and the others followed his progress by the sound of thrashing leaves. After a few seconds, the noise stopped, and Aderyn waited patiently for Devash to look around.

Finally, the man returned and accepted the map. "I saw the hill. It's a mile and a half northwest of here, a straight course. But I saw something else. Movement off to the west. One of the other teams is close to us."

"Did you see who? What color?"

Devash shook his head. "They were on the move, that's all I know."

Aderyn considered this. If they could follow whoever it was closely enough, they might be able to eliminate the team before it even came to occupying territory. On the other hand, striking too soon could give away *their* position and put them on the defensive. "Let's talk first," she said.

She surveyed her team, not Assessing them again, but recalling what she'd learned. The bearded, long-haired Sanjit was a Staffsworn, gangly and loose-limbed except when wielding his staff. He'd volunteered the information that he'd participated in two other war games and was good at finding his way, "almost as good as a Pathseer," he'd said, in a way that told Aderyn Staffsworn had not been his desired class. Sanjit would be an advantage.

Arya, the Tidecaller, might not be an advantage; her attention had drifted constantly when they were discussing options, and Aderyn wasn't sure the woman knew what was going on. With luck, she was a good enough spellslinger it didn't matter.

Devash, the Spider, was short and stocky with a shock of thick black hair that stood on end, not at all physically what Aderyn expected a Spider to look like, but she'd already seen how good a climber he was and decided not to make assumptions. Gendan, the other Staffsworn, couldn't be more physically different than Devash; Gendan was taller even than Sanjit and balding. But all three men handled the odd weapons they'd all been given, wrist-thick short staffs with fist-sized pillows at one end, with casual competence.

The fifth team member, Prita, was a Swordsworn who held her short staff like it was a sword instead. She listened to Aderyn intently without saying much, but Aderyn had a feeling Prita had more to contribute than it appeared. When she did speak, it was always a question that was to the point and insightful. Aderyn resolved to make sure Prita had a role to play.

"Balraj has no practical experience, just a lot of book learning," she said. "If he listens to his team, they might make up for that, but knowing him, he won't think anyone else has anything to teach him. We'll need to watch out for him, because he could get lucky, but my guess is he'll head straight for the fortress and make himself someone else's problem.

"Varoun, on the other hand, has a *lot* of experience, and I'd bet on him having run through many war games in his past. If we can't take the fortress before he does, we'll be at a serious disadvantage." Aderyn bit her lip in thought. "He's going to evaluate the territory first, and I'm sure someone will get to the fortress before he does."

"You mean, us?" Sanjit asked.

"Maybe. We're going to evaluate the territory, too. But that's all right. If Ruan or Janesh gets there first, I'm confident we can take them. Ruan's proud and inexperienced, but he got this far, so we shouldn't underestimate him. Same with Janesh, who acts easygoing but has a core of ruthlessness I'm not sure he realizes I've observed."

Aderyn broke a skinny branch off a nearby tree and sketched in the damp earth. "Janesh and Balraj are going to try to be the first to the fortress. Ruan, on the other hand, is going to focus on eliminating the rest of us. He doesn't realize that's a good way to lose. There are lots of ways to score points, but holding territory is the least resource-intensive. Better than going head to head against an opponent who might kill you."

"Does that mean we need to avoid him, or take him out first?" Prita asked.

"Good question." Aderyn considered. "We'll watch for him, and if we get the opportunity, eliminate his soldiers. But that shouldn't be our priority. Sanjit, will you plot us a path to the fortress?"

Sanjit stiffened into alert attention. "Yes, commander. Everyone pay attention to the undergrowth. There are trapper vines that will entangle anyone who steps on them, and they let out a shriek when they do, so we'll draw attention to ourselves."

"Oh!" Arya exclaimed. "That reminds me. I have a spell called *loose bonds* that helps free someone from another's hold, or ropes, or vines like those. But it can't do anything about shrieking."

"That's still plenty of help," Aderyn said. "Let's move out."

She dipped the end of her staff in the sack of chalk dust hanging at her right hip, coating the soft tip liberally with the orange stuff. Smacking something, or someone, would leave a livid mark in her team's color. One strike to the body, two to different arms or legs, was a "kill." Aderyn hoped not to use the weapon. She wasn't averse to fighting, and if she was being totally honest with herself, she would love to eliminate Ruan, but fighting was a distraction from her goal. She couldn't predict what the history masters would consider clever tactics, but holding the fortress was a definite win.

She let Sanjit take the lead, but followed close behind him, watching for signs of trouble. The undergrowth was sparse for the moment, but Aderyn didn't count on that staying true. A lot could change in a mile and a half. The oppressive heat weighed on her, slowing her pace until she made herself walk faster. Her heavy breathing sounded harsh and loud in the still air.

Around her, the others moved as quietly as Moonlighters, their breathing light and their footsteps lighter. When this was all over, Aderyn hoped she'd have time to talk to her team. She had so many questions. Were they all actual soldiers? Why had they been chosen for this test? Who did *they* think ought to command the army?

Distantly, a shriek that rose up and down like a klaxon drifted toward them. Aderyn grinned. "Sounds like someone stepped on a trapper vine. I hope it's Ruan."

She took another step, and the hairs on the back of her neck rose with a familiar prickle. She grabbed Sanjit's arm to bring him to a stop. "Ambush," she whispered.

Sanjit frowned. "I don't see anything."

"I know. Everyone back up." She remained at the front of the group, scanning the terrain until she saw it—a deeper shadow about thirty feet ahead, man-shaped and crouching near a suspiciously clear patch of ground. Aderyn gestured for her team to go right. This time, she led the way, creeping slowly around the trees until she could see the back of the person waiting to attack them. Red armband. Ruan's team. She Assessed the person and discovered she was a Moonlighter named Sadyaha. That she wasn't a martial class didn't make her less dangerous.

Aderyn considered her team's abilities. Then she pulled Devash aside and whispered instructions. Devash nodded and crept toward Sadyaha, his gait smooth and sinuous as a snake. Sadyaha showed no sign that she knew he was approaching. Again like a snake, Devash struck, covering the woman's mouth so she didn't cry out when he thwacked her between the shoulder blades with his stick. Sadyaha jerked once, then sagged as she realized she was out.

Devash bent to put his mouth near his victim's ear. Sadyaha listened, shook her head, and tossed her stick on the ground. Devash released her, and she sat with her back against a nearby tree, looking defeated. Devash hurried back to join Aderyn. "She won't alert her team," he whispered, "but she also wouldn't tell me where any of them are."

"Reasonable," Aderyn replied. "But based on that encounter, I already know Ruan's spread them out, searching for enemies to kill. That makes them easier to avoid, but we should go quickly anyway. If Janesh is nearly at the fortress, we don't have much time."

As if someone had overheard her, a horn sounded, three short blasts followed by a deeper, longer note. Aderyn scowled. "I think I jinxed myself. Someone's taken the fortress. Let's move."

The undergrowth thickened as they ran, gradually becoming round bushes whose leaves trembled with their passing. Aderyn eventually motioned to the others to slow. Those trapper vines would ruin her strategy if they stumbled on them, drawing Ruan, at least, to where the vines' screaming led. Better to let Janesh hold the fortress a few minutes longer, though every delay screwed her nerves closer to the breaking point.

She saw the ghostly image of a stick dipped in red chalk aimed at her chest and instinctively ducked and rolled backward, shouting, "Watch out!"

More shouting filled the air, and suddenly several people wearing red armbands rushed her team. Rolling had put her out of their reach, and she rose to her feet and plunged forward, leading with her weapon so when she reached the enemy, she struck Ruan on the arm.

Ruan cursed and swung heavily at Aderyn, who dodged easily. She didn't kid herself that she was that much better than he; a Swordsworn with a Warmaster partner had high weapons skills that might translate to fighting with these ungainly sticks. She'd need to beat him quickly. Fortunately, **[See It Coming]** worked against anyone. She aimed a blow at his chest that he deflected. "You realize you're wasting time, right? You should be trying to capture the fortress."

"Nice try, but getting rid of the opposition first benefits me later," Ruan said. He swung at her arm and converted the strike at the last moment into something aimed at her head. Again, she dodged.

"Head shots are illegal," Aderyn said.

Ruan shrugged. "Accidents happen. You can't prove anything."

"Don't need to," Aderyn said. "You won't land a blow on me." With those words, she darted to one side, thrusting at his other arm, and when he moved to block, she tossed her staff to her other hand and swatted his chest. Ruan froze, staring down at the orange splotch.

Aderyn stepped back, calming her breathing. "Got you," she said.

Ruan's gaze shifted to her. "Did you." Then, with a snarl, he reversed his staff and swung its heavy wooden end at her, aiming for her unprotected face.

Chapter Eleven

Aderyn gasped and dropped, letting the staff pass harmlessly over her head. Another horn blast shattered the air, sending a flock of brightly colored birds shrieking away with fear. "*Drop your staff,*" a voice said, reverberating so the echoes made the words almost unintelligible. "*Ruan, you have been eliminated for attacking another candidate with potentially harmful force. Stand together with your team for retrieval.*"

Aderyn stared up at Ruan, who still looked furious. He hadn't dropped the staff, and although Aderyn was sure **[See It Coming]** would protect her from another blow, she felt bad about saying or doing something to provoke him. "Eliminated" sounded awful enough if it was just the war game he'd lost, but suppose the voice meant eliminated from the contest entirely?

Finally, Ruan lowered the staff and then let it fall from his hand. Breathing heavily, he turned away from Aderyn and walked to where his four other teammates waited. Aderyn didn't see Sadyaha among them and hoped she wouldn't be left alone in the forest.

A hand came into Aderyn's field of vision, and she let Prita help her stand. "We should go," Prita said. "No point standing around waiting for that thundering loser to be retrieved."

Aderyn cast one last glance at Ruan, who wasn't looking at anyone. Then she signaled to her team to head out.

After they'd gone another twenty very sweaty yards, Aderyn sent Devash into the trees again to establish their position. She silently cursed the heavy tree growth that obscured the sky and made the horizon invisible. Devash, returning, said, "Another quarter mile to the fortress. I didn't see any movement between here and there, but there's definitely a team occupying the fortress."

"What's the terrain between here and there?"

"Many trees, enough that I couldn't see the ground beneath. There's a clearer section off to the east that would be easier going." Devash spread out the map and pointed, using his finger to mark a path.

"That would be a great place to lay a trap, too, if I was clever like Varoun," Aderyn said.

"Maybe," Gendan said. "It's not like Varoun—" He stopped, looking furtive.

"What is it?" Aderyn asked.

Gendan shook his head. "I shouldn't talk bad about my superiors, is all."

"Gendan, right now Varoun is just another enemy. I know he's a famous general, but if you know something we can use against him, I want to hear it." Aderyn glanced at the others. They all bore variations on Gendan's sheepish look except Arya, who was staring at the leafy branches above.

"It's just that General Varoun, he lost some key battles there at the end of his career," Gendan said. "He's still a great commander, I'm sure! But I wonder. Because if it were me, I think I'd doubt myself."

"Or he's got something to prove, and he'll be doubly careful," Sanjit murmured.

"All right," Aderyn said, "that's good information. Varoun might be careless because he wants to redeem himself, or he might be unusually cautious. That makes him unpredictable, and we need to stay clear of him. I don't know how many of you know Moonlighters, but my friend Weston is really good at misdirection and traps, and Varoun has had a lot more years to get even better at those if he wanted to."

She thought for a moment. "My guess is that he won't bother

setting traps until he's captured the fortress, because that slows him down. Which means it just got extra urgent that we beat him there."

Arya spoke, somewhat dreamily. "I have *clairvoyance*. I can see who's at the fortress and whether they've prepared any surprises for us."

Aderyn concealed her startlement that Arya had been paying enough attention to contribute. "That's ideal. Gendan, Devash, scout ahead, oh, a hundred yards to either side of us on an angle, understand? You want your search paths to overlap a bit. Watch for ambushes. We're going to avoid the open terrain even though it's faster going—Varoun might not lay any traps, but Balraj is still out there, and though I judge him to be a traditional thinker, traps are traditional."

Gendan and Devash nodded and slipped away into the undergrowth. Aderyn turned to Arya. "You ready?"

Arya chanted a few nonsense words. Her eyes filmed over with an ice-blue tint. She was facing away from the direction of the fortress, but she immediately said, "It's the green team. They're spread out around the perimeter, watching all four approaches."

"Janesh," Aderyn said. "Tell me what the fortress looks like."

"It's not actually a fortress," Arya said. "It's just a handful of walls set up in a square. No roof, no doors, just gaps between the walls at the corners. Some holes cut in the wood for windows, so a team could crouch inside and have some cover."

"Is there any approach more, um, approachable than the others?"

"Two sides are completely open, with no cover. They have a gentler, longer slope to the summit. One has trees growing almost all the way to the top. The fourth side has mostly low shrubs and grasses, and it's the steepest." Arya blinked slowly. "They don't seem to have set any traps, though if they're good enough, I might not see them. That's funny."

"What's funny?"

"None of them are armed. All their sticks are missing. No, I see them. They're piled in front of one of the soldiers, the one watching the fourth approach."

Aderyn frowned. "Can you describe the soldier?"

"Male, very short hair, almost pale enough to be a northerner."

Aderyn had made note of that soldier for that characteristic—and for his class. "He's a Deadeye. They're planning on him attacking any assailants at a distance, because at his level he's got both **[Thrown Weapon]** and **[Precise Shot]**. We either need to take him out, or make a different approach."

Rustling in the undergrowth preceded the appearance of Gendan and Devash. "No sign of enemies," Devash said. Gendan nodded agreement.

"Arya, which side of the hill will we face if we keep going in this direction?" Aderyn asked.

Arya blinked again. Now her eyes were back to their normal brown. "The one the Deadeye is watching."

"Steep, with low growth, and a Deadeye armed with six thrown weapons guarding it," Aderyn mused. "Interesting."

"So should we circle around to another side? The heavy tree growth could conceal us," Sanjit said.

"That's half the plan," Aderyn said. "We're going to give them a surprise."

ADERYN STOOD CONCEALED AT THE TREE LINE, COUNTING under her breath. From where she stood, she couldn't see the fortress, just the base of the hill, but that was good because if she could see them, they might be able to see her. She'd see plenty once she started her ascent.

She'd left the rest of her team hidden at the base of the wooded hillside before making her way to her present position. Not for the first time, she wished **[Bonded Mind]** worked on someone other than Owen. If anything happened to the others, like an enemy coming upon them unawares, she'd be completely ignorant. There wasn't anything she could do about it, so she pushed the worry aside.

She reached five hundred in her count and stepped forward, out of the sheltering growth. She couldn't time this attack exactly with **[Secret Message]**, because she had to be within sight of the person she sent the message to, so they were left with counting. If they'd gotten it right... but, again, not something she could do anything about. If they'd gotten it wrong, they'd lose their advantage and have to start over. Not the worst outcome.

She strolled across the ten yards of relatively open space to where the slope began and sped up slightly as she began her ascent. In this heat, she might exhaust herself before she reached the top if she tried running. The slope was steep enough to slow her almost immediately, and with the scrub and low bushes covering it, she couldn't make a direct ascent. Once the Deadeye saw her, that wouldn't matter.

She'd made it up the hill a good twenty feet before that happened, which cheered her with the idea that maybe Janesh's people were all as inattentive as the Deadeye. The Deadeye jerked upright when he spotted her. She was too far away to see his expression, but she imagined him grinning in anticipation of making an easy kill.

The first missile came in slow, flying in a lazy arc that showed just how little the Deadeye thought of Aderyn's chances of evading. Aderyn almost didn't need **[See It Coming]** to know to step to the side so it sailed harmlessly past. She kept moving upward.

The next stick flew faster, but Aderyn dropped into a crouch and it missed her by a foot. Rising, she ran to the right and then zagged to the left, pretending nervousness. Again the Deadeye threw a missile, and again she wasn't there when it landed. Half his weapons gone.

Two sticks flew in rapid succession, forcing Aderyn to drop again. If this had been a Deadeye of twice his level, she probably couldn't have avoided both. Something to remember for the future, when she was in a real fight.

No more missiles came. Aderyn was nearly at the top. Now she focused on the Deadeye, who'd kept hold of the final stick and was brandishing it awkwardly at her. His wide eyes and shaking hand told her he was seriously unnerved. Aderyn grinned. She pushed herself into a run for the last ten steps and struck.

The man shouted a belated warning, but Aderyn swept his stick aside and slammed bodily into him, knocking him back a few paces. Before he could recover, she smacked him solidly in the chest with the orange-coated tip of her weapon, leaving a bright smudge and sending up a puff of chalk dust he choked on. "On the ground," Aderyn commanded. "You're dead."

"You can't kill all of us before we subdue you, Aderyn," Janesh said. He and the rest of the team advanced out of the fortress, moving to surround her. "I suggest you surrender."

"Funny, I was about to tell you the same thing," Aderyn said. She gestured with her stick. "Look around."

"That's an amusing bluff," Janesh said. "I'm not sure what you think you can pull off by distracting us, no matter how good you were at avoiding Maruk's shots, but—"

"Fine," Aderyn said. "I don't have any problems attacking from the rear." She watched as her soldiers advanced silently around the far side of the fortress. "It's war. Winning is what matters." She signaled, and as if they'd rehearsed it a hundred times, her soldiers pounced, hitting each of Janesh's soldiers solidly in the back.

Janesh, startled, half-turned to see what had happened. Aderyn closed the distance between them and struck his shoulder. "One more hit and you're dead," she said. "I was hoping you'd surrender instead. One commander to another."

Janesh stared at the livid orange blotch on his dark shirt. "Well, shit," he said. Then he grinned. "That was clever. I thought for sure we had control of the high ground. How *did* you avoid getting hit?"

"Warmaster skill. I'll tell you the details later. For now, how about we get the 'bodies' settled for retrieval? You might as well be comfortable while I wait for Varoun to assault this position."

"Hmm. You're sure about that? Balraj is still out there."

Aderyn nodded. "My judgment is that Balraj will attempt some direct assaults we can easily repel, assuming Varoun doesn't take him out first. Varoun is the dangerous one."

Janesh regarded her closely for long enough she started to squirm inside, though she managed to maintain a calm demeanor. "You're something else," he said. "I get the feeling there's no honor lost in being defeated by you, no matter your age and nationality."

"Thank you," Aderyn said, and meant it.

Chapter Twelve

Aderyn ran a hand down the edge of one of the "fortress" walls. They really were just slabs of planed lumber with posts at each side, surprisingly well made for something so impermanent. The posts extended below the wall so they could impale the ground and keep the wall upright and steady. As Arya had described, the walls didn't meet at the corners, leaving gaps just wide enough for a person to sidle through. If Aderyn looked at the construction a different way, her perspective shifted, and she saw it as a giant sculpture rather than a building. Very odd.

"We have about two hours before sunset," she told her team. "Varoun will know soon, if he doesn't already, that we've taken the fortress. He won't want us to gain more points than him, assuming he can capture and hold this place, so he'll have to plan his assault for as soon as possible. We just have to hold out for two hours. Are you ready?"

Everyone nodded. Sanjit and Prita looked fierce, like they were prepared to wrestle Varoun personally to keep him from winning. Devash and Gendan stood nearer the back of their group, and at first Aderyn thought they were distracted, but she realized they were simply paying attention to their surroundings the way good scouts did. Arya *was* distracted, her eyes focused past Aderyn, but Aderyn expected this and had a plan to make Arya useful.

"All right," she said. "Let's make this place more defensible. The obvious place for an assault is the forest, where Varoun's people will have cover, but we shouldn't neglect the other approaches. Arya, can you do anything about making these easier slopes difficult terrain? Maybe **[Cloudburst]** or **[Thunderstorm]**? A localized rainstorm would be a great deterrent." Given the heat and humidity, Aderyn would almost have welcomed a cloudburst centered on her, soaking and cooling her.

"Those only last a few minutes each," Arya said in her distant way. She surveyed the slope adjacent to the one Aderyn had climbed. "But I can turn it into a field of mud, some of it, at least."

"That sounds great. How much ground can you affect?"

Arya shrugged. "Up to two hundred square yards, in any shape. So it could be narrow and long, or wide and short."

"Then..." Aderyn paced the edge of the hill where it began to slope. The steep side curved away to become a shallow ascent after about twenty feet. "Start at this point and extend the field as far around the hill as you can in both directions, but don't make it reach the flat ground at the base—let's give them twenty or thirty feet of clear terrain before they run into trouble. Can you see what I mean?"

Arya nodded. She raised one hand as if waving to some distant friend and chanted a few words that almost made sense. At first, nothing happened. Then the earth shifted, rippling like it sat atop a liquid layer that was in motion. The ground fractured, cracks spidering across its surface and revealing thick brown mud beneath. Gradually, the earth dissolved into the mud until all that was left was a smooth brown surface that occasionally let out a *blart* of gas and the pop of a mud bubble.

"It looks solid enough to walk on," Gendan said.

"That's part of the trick," Arya said. "Anyone stepping into it will be able to go a couple of paces before they're stuck. Not permanently, I don't have that spell, but enough to make the going slow. If we had archers, we could easily shoot down anyone in the *mud field*."

"If this wasn't a war game, you mean," Devash said.

"Right," Arya replied. "If it wasn't a war game."

Aderyn cleared her throat. "All right. We'll still need to watch that approach, but that's a good defense, Arya. Will you keep an eye out here, and be prepared to slow an assault down? The rest of you, come with me."

She led the others a short distance to where the forest began. The trees only came to about halfway up the hill, but that was more than enough. "Varoun will likely try the same thing we did—use this cover for a frontal assault and make his strike at the other side. He's a Moonlighter, so I don't anticipate him bulling ahead into the mud without some reconnaissance. I don't want to underestimate him, but at the same time, whoever he sends this way is a good candidate for us to eliminate. So the rest of you, you'll guard these two approaches."

She paused for a moment, then added, "Prita, I'm putting you in command of the others for now. Use your best judgment about what tactics to use."

Prita saluted her with her short staff, stopping before she tapped the chalky tip to her forehead.

Aderyn slipped inside the fortress. It was hotter between the walls, which blocked the light breeze that was otherwise Aderyn's only comfort. Janesh sat with his back against the far wall. He'd refused transport via *world door* when his "dead" soldiers were retrieved, casually ignoring the Flamecrafter's dismay at this breach of protocol. "Being a duke ought to have some privileges, or else what's the point?" he'd said. "And I want to see how this plays out."

Now he asked, "How are things going? I take it you haven't seen Varoun or Balraj yet."

Aderyn shook her head. "I really do think Balraj is out of the running. Varoun needed to narrow the field, and Balraj is no match for an old Moonlighter."

"You seem confident of that."

"I have a Moonlighter companion. He's already a sneaky bastard, and I can only imagine how clever he'll be in forty or fifty years." Aderyn crouched on her haunches beside Janesh. "Any chance you'd be willing to share information about Varoun? His military specialties, or his favorite tactics?"

"As a captured enemy commander, I ought to make you interrogate me," Janesh said with a grin. "Torture would not be out of place. But, having been defeated, I feel no loyalty toward our shared enemy. And I'd like to see you defeat Varoun. He's smart, driven, and someone I personally respect quite a lot, but... call it affection for the underdog. If that's what you are."

"Do you think I am?" Aderyn asked, startled.

"At first glance, sure. You're young and inexperienced, you're a foreigner, and you don't appreciate tradition. But you've more than made up for those shortcomings so far. So, maybe not. Compared to Varoun, maybe so." Janesh leaned back against the wall, which gave a little beneath his weight.

"Well, I intend to win." Aderyn rose and looked down at Janesh. "So, what can you tell me?"

"I can't think of much that will help you in this situation. Varoun is a master of misdirection, but most of his specific strategies are meant for a much bigger battlefield than this." Janesh gestured to encompass the entire hill. "Think about what the most obvious plan of attack is, then prepare for the opposite. Don't bother laying traps, because he has an uncanny knack for spotting them."

"I guessed."

Janesh grimaced. "He also is willing to risk his troops for the sake of the greater objective, and by that I mean risks no one else would take. It's what ruined him, in the end—he inadvertently sent a lot of soldiers to their deaths and lost the battle anyway. People were willing to see his strategy as a tragic necessity so long as he was winning."

"He deliberately allowed his people to be killed?" The thought chilled Aderyn to the marrow. For the first time, she considered the darker side of command. "I'm not sure I could do that."

"Not deliberately. More like taking a calculated risk that didn't pay off. It's all about command style, isn't it? And he won a lot of battles. Granted, that was thirty years ago, during the last war when Ikharatia was attacked by Durga. And his efforts kept that city from devastating the kingdom, so the king and the people were willing to forgive a lot. Just not to the extent of wanting him to go on commanding. That's a lot of years, so maybe they've forgotten." Janesh tilted his head to look up at her.

"Maybe," Aderyn said. "Thanks, Janesh."

"Thank me when you've won," Janesh said with another grin.

Aderyn returned outside and circled the fortress, surveying the land. Nothing moved except a couple of birds flying in large circles to the north, big birds by how they were visible at this distance. They didn't look like carrion eaters, though Aderyn didn't know much about birds and she could be wrong.

She ended up next to Arya, who was seated near where the slope began. "I get dizzy if I stand still too long," the Tidecaller said before Aderyn could protest. She didn't sound defensive, just matter of fact. Aderyn decided Arya could yell a warning from a sitting position as well as from standing and didn't make an issue of it.

"Nothing strange?" she asked.

"There doesn't seem to be anyone out here except us," Arya replied. "I'm sure it's an illusion, not the magical kind."

"I don't suppose you can use *clairvoyance* to see through those trees?"

Arya shook her head. "It doesn't work like that. You have to pick a spot and cast the spell so you can see it. It can't make the trees invisible."

"Too bad." Aderyn scanned the distant tree line, then walked back to where the other soldiers waited. Prita had spread everyone but Sanjit out to cover the sight lines, with herself in motion between them. It was a good tactic, and Aderyn said so. Prita nodded in acknowledgement, but she didn't relax her vigilance.

Time passed. Aderyn continued to pace, staying nearer Arya than the others. She trusted the woman's dedication, but not so much her attention span. But the forest continued still and quiet except for the noise of the birds cawing and cooing and sometimes shrieking at one another. Aderyn guessed they only fell silent when they were eating, or when someone disturbed them. That was something she'd forgotten, that the birds could alert them to the blue army's presence. She was glad nothing had happened to draw attention to this lapse.

Devash suddenly said, "Don't anyone react, but I saw movement in the trees. The kind of movement that means someone's trying to stay hidden. We should pretend we haven't seen them."

Prita didn't stop in her circuit. "Who is it? Blue or yellow?"

"Can't tell. Too much shadow." Devash yawned and idly scratched his nose. "What do we do, commander?"

Aderyn approached the three men. "Take a rest," she told Gendan and Sanjit, speaking loudly. "There's nothing coming, and we'll call you if that changes."

Gendan and Sanjit nodded and entered the fortress. In a quieter voice, Aderyn told them, "Use the fortress as cover and move to opposite sides. Stay alert for a rush attack." She returned to pacing, secretly straining to see what Devash had. On her second pass, she caught movement, and saw a flash of a blue armband. Now, what did Varoun have in mind?

Shouts filled the air, and enemy soldiers broke from cover at the tree line and ran up the gentle slope toward them. "Ready to defend!" Aderyn shouted. There were three soldiers, which meant—

"It's a feint!" she screamed. "Watch the—"

A clap of thunder from the cloudless sky drowned out her words. "We're under attack!" Sanjit roared from behind.

Aderyn raced around the fortress, not wanting to slow to dodge between the irregularly arranged walls. She reached Arya at the same time Sanjit did. Gray clouds bulging with rain gathered over the *mud field*, and a deluge poured down over two figures running toward them atop the mud. They moved fast and seemed unimpeded by the mucky ground or the torrential rain. Neither had silver hair. That left Varoun unaccounted for, which filled her with dread.

"**[Mud to Earth]**," Aderyn muttered. She'd been stupid not to remember the Earthbreaker had that skill. Then a shock of fear shot through her. She hadn't heard herself speak.

"Arya!" she exclaimed. Again, her words were silent. Arya's lips moved, and no sound came out. The Tidecaller's body was rigid with concentration as she moved the **[Thunderstorm]** to keep pace with the running figures.

Someone grabbed her arm and dragged her away from Arya. Sanjit shouted over the noise of the storm, "They cast *silence* on her. She can't cast spells because she can't speak."

Aderyn swore. "All right. We meet the attack as it comes. Don't approach them—you'll be caught in the storm, and I bet that Earthbreaker can use **[Earth to Mud]** on selected places to mire you."

She ran back to the others, who'd broken formation and run to meet the three blue soldiers. Aderyn swore again. What was it her mother always said—no plan survived three seconds past encountering the enemy? Well, it was up to her soldiers' fighting abilities now, and she would have to stop Varoun.

The **[Thunderstorm]** was fading, and the two soldiers had nearly reached the top. It was the blue army's Earthbreaker and Stalwart, two women who were both powerfully built. Sanjit held his stick at the ready, poised to attack. Arya had backed away until she pressed against the fortress wall. Aderyn wished she knew the limits of the *silence* spell. She'd seen it extended beyond the victim, but how far, she couldn't tell, and there wasn't time to experiment.

"Where's your commander?" Aderyn demanded as the two came within earshot. Both were drenched, and both looked too exhausted to give anyone a fight.

Neither spoke. Aderyn madly reviewed the skills of a level fourteen Moonlighter. **[Stealth], [Dirty Fighting], [Hide in Plain Sight]**—

She spun around in time for Varoun's staff to thwack her in the center of her chest, leaving a bright blue smudge. Varoun was breathing heavily like he'd made the difficult ascent up the same slope she had. "You underestimated me," he said.

"I guess I did," Aderyn said. Behind her, she heard a scuffle as Sanjit fought the two women. "You haven't won yet."

"Traditional wargames rules," Varoun said. "Take out the commander, and you capture the fortress. I suppose you didn't know."

He didn't sound like he was making fun of her, so Aderyn didn't snarl a cutting reply. "I didn't. Sanjit—oh, if I'm dead I can't give orders."

She turned around. Both the Earthbreaker and the Stalwart bore half a dozen orange chalk marks over their bodies, and Sanjit, breathing as heavily as Varoun, lowered his staff. "Sorry, commander. I'll go see what happened to the others and tell them we've been overrun."

When Aderyn returned to her opponent, Janesh had joined him. Varoun said, "That was an impressive attack on this position. How did you avoid getting hit going up that awful slope?"

"You saw that?"

Varoun gestured at the Earthbreaker. "*Clairvoyance.* Terina said you dodged every missile."

"It's a Warmaster skill."

"A terrifying skill," Janesh said. "I'm sure poor Maruk is still shaking." He smiled as he spoke.

Aderyn grimaced. "I was stupid to forget about *your* skills, given that my companion is a Moonlighter and I know what he's capable of."

"There are a lot of moving parts in a battle. Forgetting some of them happens. Though that's no excuse, as I'm sure you're aware." Varoun extended his hand. "For my part, I was slow to implement my plan, and you held this position too long. I won't earn any extra points for its capture."

Aderyn clasped his hand. "Thank you, sir. You're a formidable adversary."

"As are you." Varoun eyed the sky. "Is Ruan still out there?"

"No. We killed all of his army. And Janesh's."

"To my shame," Janesh said, his smile widening.

"And I eliminated Balraj," Varoun said. His smile was thin and malicious, making Aderyn wonder for the first time if there was bad blood between them. Aside from a couple of snide remarks, Aderyn hadn't noticed Varoun paying any special attention to the former history master, but maybe that meant they disliked each other enough to stay well apart.

"With all the armies but one neutralized, the game is over, though it's not yet dusk," Varoun continued. "We should wait for retrieval. I for one will be glad to return for a cool drink and a hot meal."

"And the determination of the winner," Janesh reminded him. "Not just of the war game, but of the contest as a whole."

Varoun and Aderyn exchanged glances. Aderyn was suddenly

certain the choice was down to one of the two of them. And she wasn't at all sure who the winner would be.

Chapter Thirteen

Several castings of *world door* later, Aderyn stepped through into the auditorium where she'd met her army to find it empty except for Druv and Kash. Disappointed, she walked forward to salute them. "I'd hoped to speak to my team," she said. "Find out what they thought of our battles."

"Ordinarily after a war game, the victors and the defeated participate in discussions analyzing their performance," Druv said. "For use in future battles. In this case, it's unnecessary, as that was not the point of this challenge."

"I see." She glanced over her shoulder as Janesh emerged from his *world door*. "May I ask what happens next?"

"You're dismissed until tomorrow morning at ten," Kash said. "Return to the Academy Hall at that time for our decision."

From what they'd said, Aderyn had expected the decision to be announced now. Waiting that long to know her fate was going to screw all her nerves to the breaking point, but there wasn't any point in saying that. Aderyn nodded politely and left the auditorium.

She hadn't taken five steps down the darkened hall before she realized she didn't know how to get back to the Academy Hall, let alone her inn.

"Come with me, and I'll summon you a pedicab," Janesh said from behind her. "Kash and Druv have lived in Ikharatia all their lives, and I'm sure it doesn't occur to them that not everyone is familiar with the city."

"Thanks." Aderyn followed him to the tiny, sweltering courtyard that was still hot even now that the sun had gone down. Lanterns imperfectly lit the small space, but they shed enough light for Aderyn and Janesh to find their way back to the street. There, Janesh waved down one of those strange three-wheeled vehicles pedaled by a wiry old man wearing very little clothing. Aderyn was instantly jealous. It was cooler on the street than in the courtyard, but not by much.

Janesh held back the canvas flap that served as a door and ushered Aderyn inside. "Tell him the name of your inn. All these pedicab drivers know the city better than the king."

"Speaking of royalty, how does a duke know about pedicabs? I would think you'd be too important to ride in anything but a private carriage," Aderyn asked.

"Misspent youth," Janesh said. "Maybe someday I'll tell you about it. Good night, Aderyn, and good luck."

"Good luck to you, too."

"Oh, I think we both know it's you who's going to need it." Janesh dropped the canvas. Through the open front of the cab, Aderyn saw him stroll away down the street.

"Miss?" the pedicab driver said in a creaky, whistling voice.

"Oh. The Jeweled Cuckoo Inn, please."

With a grunt, the driver put the pedicab in motion, and Aderyn settled back for the ride. The *tuktuktuk* sound grew higher pitched the faster they went until it was more of a *ticktickticck*. Whatever caused the noise, she didn't care, because its monotony soothed her. The breeze generated by their movement cooled her sweaty body, though it couldn't do anything about her dirty and no doubt smelly clothes.

She watched what she could see of the city drift past. The canvas sides concealed her from view, giving her an anonymity she enjoyed, though she didn't know why. It wasn't as if people stared or called names because she was a northerner. All right, they did stare a bit, but it wasn't as overwhelming as, say, a high society party in which everyone knew she was an unusually high level Warmaster and wanted to talk to her.

The motion and sound and the darkness inside the cab lulled her so she was half awake when the driver came to a stop and said, "That's seventeen copper for the ride, miss."

Aderyn jerked out of her doze and dug in her purse for the fare, sorting past northern coin for southern. As she handed it over, the driver said, "Don't see a lot of northerners around, even in the metropolis. You here because of the war?"

"You could say that," Aderyn said, and made her escape. In the distance, the clock bell rang the half-hour. Six-thirty, or seven-thirty? She'd completely lost track of time.

Nobody was in the taproom but Neeva's serving staff, busily readying the room for the dinner rush. That didn't clear up Aderyn's confusion, because the dinner service didn't start until eight. She trod the stairs to the third floor and walked heavily to her room. Owen wasn't there. Disappointment made her even wearier. She'd wanted to talk to him about the day's experiences, and now it occurred to her that maybe he and the others were waiting at the Academy Hall for her. The idea of yet another trip across the city made her want to lie down and cry. Well, she would lie down for a few minutes, at least, and gather the energy to go in search of her husband.

The sound of the door opening woke her, and she jerked upright. "Owen!"

"So you are here," Owen said. "I'm relieved. They only told us the candidates wouldn't return to the Academy Hall tonight, not where you were or what you were doing, and we had to hope that meant you'd return to the inn." He sat beside her and put his arms around her. "Not to be rude, but you smell like someone who's spent the day in a sauna wearing all her clothes."

"What's a sauna?"

"It's a steam bath. It opens your pores or something, I don't really know. But you're supposed to be mostly naked for it."

"Oh. Well, you're not far wrong."

Weston poked his head around the edge of the open door. "You found her! Good. Let's eat."

"Neeva won't serve food until the proper hour, remember?" Livia said. "And we don't want to offend her because this is a really nice inn I don't want to be kicked out of. Aderyn, you look like five miles of bad road. What did they do to you?"

"Come in, and I'll tell you—where's Isold?"

"Isold is right here," Isold said, following Weston into the room. "I take it there's a good story in all this."

"A story, at least. It was an interesting day. I found out Varoun knew my grandmother, and that she was a master of Wall—Owen, that's a strategy game—and I thought I was terrible at it, but it turns out that's because I only ever played against her." Aderyn leaned against Owen, then remembered her smelly condition and sat up straight. "I won every game today. It felt amazing."

"Secret master of Wall, huh?" Livia said. "I should introduce you to my father. He thinks he's pretty good at the game, and it would be so very sweet to see him lose."

"Your family dynamic is weird," Owen said. "What else happened?"

Aderyn recounted the war game in detail, lingering over her descriptions of her strategy and how Varoun had outsmarted her. "I really should have given more thought to his skills," she said.

"Moonlighters have a lot of skills," Weston said. "I have trouble remembering everything I can do, and I use them all the time."

"I'm concerned about that bastard Ruan attacking you," Owen said. "They can't possibly consider him for commander anymore. First he comes onto you, then he tries to smash your face in... that all sounds deeply unhinged."

"I agree, and like I said, I don't know if eliminated meant from the game or from the entire contest." Aderyn gripped Owen's hand in reassurance. "You can't watch over me every second, you know."

"I have a right as a protective male to be unhappy about that fact," Owen said with a smile.

"So, do you have any sense for how things stand?" Isold asked.

"None. Well, that's not true. I think it's down to me and Varoun. Balraj was eliminated quickly this afternoon, and I really think that aside from his book learning, he doesn't have what it takes. Ruan—we talked about him already. And Janesh is coming to the realization that he doesn't want it, I think. That's just my instinct, but it feels right. So even if they choose him, I think he'd turn them down."

"And Varoun is a strong challenger," Owen said.

"What do we do if they don't pick Aderyn?" Livia asked.

Owen frowned. "We still have to complete the quest. I guess we could fall back on the plan to use stealth and cunning to eliminate the orc leaders, and hope that demoralizes their army enough that it retreats."

"That's not so much a plan as it is a hope for the future, given that we know nothing about the army or its leaders," Aderyn said. "You're right, I know, but can we just hope everything works out in my favor, and worry about the alternative later?"

"Absolutely," Owen said. "And now I'm going to insist you use the bath house with its wonderful shower. Who knew all I had to do to get some indoor plumbing was travel south?"

THE WALK TO THE ACADEMY HALL THE FOLLOWING morning felt longer than usual. Aderyn watched two wagons loaded with people pass them and considered finding one that wasn't quite so full. They had to be empty at some point in the journey, right? But stopping to hunt for one would only make the trip longer, and now that the moment had come, she wanted the whole thing to be over. Anticipation made her tense, and not in a fun way.

"You're more worried than I expected," Owen said. "You know it's not the end if they don't choose you. We have options."

"I know. But I want to win. I never knew how much I liked winning until yesterday, and now I can't think of anything else." Aderyn clasped his hand and twined her fingers with his for comfort. "But I can't force them to choose my way, so I should relax and take whatever comes as it comes."

"That's a good attitude even if it's going to be difficult for you to achieve." Owen squeezed her hand lightly.

At the Academy Hall, a proctor waited just inside the door. "You may all enter," he said, rather grandly, Aderyn thought. "Go to the left and wait in the receiving room."

Relieved, Aderyn did as she was told. Having Owen and the others with her eased her mind. She didn't know if she could bear keeping the news to herself for even a short time, good or bad.

The receiving room was the large one her friends had met her in the first day of testing. It had been hot then despite the ceiling fans, but it was cooler now that it wasn't packed with people. Only a handful of men and women waited there now, including Balraj, Varoun, and Ruan. Balraj stood next to two other men dressed as somberly as he, but younger by a decade or so. A lovely older woman and a middle aged man and woman accompanied Varoun. Aderyn Assessed the elderly woman out of curiosity.

Name: Sudha
∞ Varoun
Class: Swifthands (retired)
Level: 13

Remembering that Varoun was married cheered her. She was glad he hadn't remained single out of some romantic nonsense about Aderyn's grandmother spurning him. She liked to think of him as having children, and grandchildren—he seemed the type to want that.

Ruan stood alone, just far enough from the others to emphasize his solitude. He deliberately didn't look at Aderyn when she turned her gaze on him. His dismissal of her struck her with a pang of unexpected sadness. She didn't like him, but she didn't think they had to be enemies. And he hadn't brought his brother. Disappointment took the place of sadness. With Ruan's hostility, it might be impossible for her ever to meet Suveer.

Movement at the door drew her attention, and she smiled at Janesh, who was also alone. Janesh approached her, saying, "Good morning. Is this your adventuring team?"

"Yes, this is Owen, and Isold, Livia, and Weston. Everyone, this is Janesh—I mean Duke Janesh of Shantos."

"Still just Janesh. I don't insist on formality with my peers." Janesh nodded politely to each of them. "Weston the Moonlighter, right? I didn't expect you to be so big."

"No one does," Weston said.

"And I'll bet you use that to your advantage." Janesh turned to Owen. "It's good to meet you. Your wife is a formidable opponent. I admit I wanted to see the man who was a match for her."

Owen chuckled. "I hope I'm a fit partner for her."

"Yes, I'd forgotten. Warmaster and Swordsworn. Does it always have to be a Swordsworn, or is it coincidence that the only two Warmasters I've ever met have been partnered with that class?"

"Coincidence, we think," Owen said. "Though we've met one other Warmaster, and her partner was also Swordsworn, so we could be wrong."

"Did your wife not want to come?" Aderyn asked, daring what might be a personal question.

"Aswathy is expecting our third child, and she finds the heat especially oppressive at this late stage of her pregnancy. But I'd like you to meet her eventually. I made her come here when we first heard about orc raids—Shantos is nearer the Blighted Range than any of the other cities —and she has a keen interest in seeing the orcs defeated, if only so she can return to her home."

"I'd like to meet her, too," Aderyn said.

The other door opened, and the three history masters entered. Their impassive expressions filled Aderyn with unnatural dread. It wasn't like this wasn't how they always looked when they were delivering instructions, but she'd hoped they would be happy about finally choosing a commander, or maybe relieved.

Tenzen positioned himself where he could see everyone easily, with Druv and Kash behind him, and cleared his throat. "Each of you performed well in different ways, and each of you exhibited weaknesses. We will not divulge the specifics, as we believe you are each worthy of respect and that dwelling on shortcomings is unnecessarily critical. However, the one we choose must show competence in several key fields of military knowledge and ability, not just one or two."

He looked at Aderyn, and her heart beat once so hard it jolted her painfully. "Aderyn," he said. "Your lack of historical knowledge and basic military standards is a drawback. On the other hand, you demonstrated a breadth of experience with regard to monster knowledge, your strategic understanding as demonstrated in every challenge is exceptional, and no one has ever completed the resource allocation evaluation as rapidly as you. We consider you an excellent candidate for military command."

Aderyn suppressed a wide, silly smile. She hoped she looked keenly alert and worthy of command.

"However," Tenzen continued, "Varoun's grasp of military strategy is equally impressive, and with the addition of his extensive experience in the field and memory for past battles, we consider him the logical choice. General Varoun, command of the unified army is yours."

It felt like a punch to the gut. Now Aderyn was grateful for how she'd schooled her expression. She wasn't on the verge of crying, that would be ridiculous, but disappointment coursed through her, and she didn't want anyone to know how their first words had raised her hopes.

Varoun inclined his head respectfully first to Tenzen, then to Druv and Kash in turn. "Thank you for your confidence in me. I'll do my best to ensure it's warranted."

Balraj let out a harrumph of annoyance and strode out of the room without a word, followed hastily by his companions. Janesh clapped Varoun on the shoulder. "Congratulations. It was a good choice."

"But not the best?" Varoun arched one eyebrow meaningfully.

Janesh shrugged. "It's not my decision."

"No," Varoun said, "it is not."

He approached Aderyn with his hand outstretched. Aderyn clasped it reflexively. She was still stunned at how things had turned out. No command. No army.

Varoun held onto her hand when she would have withdrawn. "Your skills are remarkable," he said. "I admit I didn't know how this would go."

"Not remarkable enough, I guess." Aderyn summoned a smile and hoped she didn't sound bitter. It was true, Varoun would be an excellent general, and when she looked at the situation objectively, it mattered more that the orcs were stopped than that she fulfil the quest.

"I disagree." Varoun wasn't smiling. "A great general needs the support of others. I have need of a second in command. I can't imagine anyone I would rather have in that position than you. Will you accept?"

Stunned again, Aderyn said, "But I—well—" She looked over her shoulder at Owen, hoping for guidance—she couldn't commit the others without their agreement. Owen nodded once. "I accept."

"Thank you." Varoun released her. "I hope our success will fulfil your quest as well as save the kingdom. I may not be convinced about the Fated One's destiny, but if it matters to you, I'm willing to keep an open mind."

"I promise I won't put my needs above the army's, if it comes to that." Aderyn didn't know where that had come from. They needed to complete the quest—the Fated One and his destiny were important to the world. And yet there was the reality that the orcs would slaughter everyone in their path whether or not Aderyn participated, and wasn't human life more important than any quest?

"You'll meet with the king and the queen regent later today, to take formal command," Tenzen told Varoun. "Then you'll be informed of the current situation and the disposition of the armies. The rest is up to you."

"I understand." Varoun again turned to Aderyn. "Any questions?"

"None, and a million," Aderyn said.

Varoun chuckled. "Welcome to the army."

Chapter Fourteen

They talked a while longer, and Aderyn thanked the history masters for their work. They looked pleased for once. "I'm glad it's over," Kash said. "We need to take action against the orcs. More of them leave the Blighted Range every day, and reports say they are unusually coordinated in their attacks."

"Then why—no," Varoun said. "Time for specifics when I can see everything laid out. Aderyn, may I introduce my wife, Sudha, and our son Mansur and daughter Shri?"

The lovely elderly woman bowed. "Varoun could talk of nothing last night but the young woman who beat him at Wall," she said with an impish smile. Varoun smiled as well, though with some embarrassment. "And Ellowyn's granddaughter. I never met her, but her reputation as a Swordsworn made her well-remembered in Ikharatia."

Aderyn refrained from asking if Sudha knew Varoun had wanted to marry Ellowyn first. "We never knew about it. She didn't talk much about her adventuring days, her or Gran'fa. But I know she sparred with my father—her son, also a Swordsworn—and I remember her correcting his stance sometimes, back when I was little." She laughed. "I'm afraid I always thought she was bossy."

"She was quite the leader, back in the day," Varoun said. "And I'd call her bossy, too. In the best way. She kept our team alive more than once because she refused to back down."

"It's so strange, and so interesting, to hear about that side of her." Aderyn gestured to her friends. "This is my husband, Owen, and our companions Isold, Livia, and Weston."

"Remarkable," Mansur said. He was the most attractive man Aderyn had seen in the Southlands yet, with a charming smile, and he spoke with confidence as he addressed them. "It's good to meet all of you. How will the rest of you participate in the war?"

"I don't know." Aderyn looked to Varoun for an answer.

"That will depend on the state of the armies," Varoun said. "And the resistance I will no doubt meet from the dukes, regardless of their agreement to honor the choice of the history masters. We'll discuss it this evening, yes?"

Aderyn nodded. "We'll meet you at the palace at four."

They exchanged more farewells, and Aderyn turned away and almost ran into Ruan. She jerked back a step. "Sorry."

"No, I'm sorry. That was inappropriate, me hovering right there." To her surprise, Ruan didn't sound angry. He also didn't have that seductive note to his words that had irritated Aderyn. "I wanted to apologize for losing my temper during the war game. I should never have attacked you. Forgive me?" He extended a hand, smiling in a friendly way.

Aderyn hesitated. She wished for the thousandth time **[Read Body Language]** worked on people other than Owen. She dearly wanted to know if Ruan was sincere, because her instincts told her this was a sham. But she couldn't figure out how, or what he expected to gain by pretending friendliness. She decided to go along with him for the moment and shook his hand. "I understand. Things happen when you're in the heat of battle, even if it's a fake battle."

"Exactly." Ruan nodded politely to the others. "I was thinking about what you said, about wanting to meet Suveer. We will both be at the palace tonight, and I can introduce you."

"I'd love that! Though I'm not sure I'll have much time for conversation."

"I understand. We really ought to have dinner together sometime, if your schedule permits. It sounds like you're going to be busy."

Aderyn's excitement surged. "Oh, but I want to make time for that! We'll figure something out."

"Then it's settled. Let me know when you're available, and we'll get together." Ruan bowed to Aderyn and left the room.

"I don't like it," Owen said once he was gone. "I think he's faking."

"So do I, but I don't know what he'd gain. It's not like he has any influence over the army or anything else by being friends with its commanders." Aderyn let out a deep breath. "Let's go. I want to rest before we meet royalty."

"I can't believe it worked out this way," Livia said as they strolled through the paths of the university. "How sure are we that this will put us in a position to fulfil the quest?"

"Sure enough," Aderyn said. "We can't push back the orc horde on our own, so we'd be working at a remove no matter what level of command we have. And, second in command—that's a lot of responsibility."

"The thing that worries me is defeating the orc leaders," Isold said. "We know nothing about who they are, or how many of them must be killed to count as defeating them, or even whether or not we need to be personally responsible for that part of the quest requirements."

"There's no point worrying about all that yet," Owen said. "After this meeting tonight, Varoun will learn how things stand with the army, and we'll know more. Maybe new information will change the quest text."

Aderyn stopped. "Let's look now."

She brought up the Codex and focused on the **[Fated One's Destiny: Crush the Horde]** quest. Disappointingly, it looked exactly as it had the last three times she'd read it. "Owen was right," she said.

"I love hearing those words," Owen said.

"So, what positions do we have in the army?" Weston said. "Or are we mercenary adventurers with no official role?"

"Generals in history always have staffs," Owen said. "I mean, groups of people who support them, not lengths of wood. Aderyn will need that. But I'm not sure we should be them. And we're not mercenaries, either."

"From what I hear of who enlists in the army, we are adventurer soldiers," Isold said. "Acting under the direction of the army's leaders. Aderyn, you're in charge of the team now."

"Isold!" Aderyn swatted him on the arm, laughing.

"All right, that was a joke, but only mostly. I don't anticipate us behaving any differently than we do in a monster fight, and you tell us what to do then." Isold began walking again. "The difference now is that your direction will be put to a broader use."

"All right, but don't anyone call me the leader, got it? We have a leader." Aderyn hooked her arm around Owen's elbow and tugged him along.

"I don't mind giving way to you for now," Owen said. "In fact, I'm looking forward to seeing you command troops. I'll buy you riding boots and a Japanese kimono and you can Douglas MacArthur your way through the enemy line."

"Is he a general?"

"He was one of the best. And one of the most eccentric." Owen pulled Aderyn closer.

"Well, you can tell me about some of his battles. I might as well start learning military history, even if it's not my world's."

"We'll see what I can remember," Owen said.

Sleeping through the hottest part of the day appealed to Aderyn, but she rarely felt tired enough to take advantage of the tradition. After the morning's tension and excitement, though, she fell asleep after lunch and slept for two solid hours. When she woke, it was to a sense of panic. In her sleep, she'd dreamed of meeting Queen Devendra and the dukes dressed in her heavy, travel-stained coat and her worn leather boots, and everyone had laughed when her back was turned and fell silent when she looked at them, exactly as if their laughter switched on and off like a <**Matchlighter**>.

She was alone in the room. More panic set in. The others hadn't been able to wake her and had gone to the palace without her. They'd gone exploring and were lost. Or maybe it was too late, and she'd missed the meeting—no, the sun was too high in the sky.

The door opened. "Sleep well?" Owen asked. His arms were full of bundles of brightly colored fabric.

"No, I had a terrible dream I'm having trouble shaking." Aderyn rose and kissed him deeply, and a little of her disorientation slipped away.

"Well, Isold and I went shopping. We figured we all might need nice clothes if we're meeting royalty." Owen dumped his armful on the bed. "Isold charmed a shopkeeper into helping us. Got us a good price, too, based on her reaction—though for all I know about comparative values here, she cheated us."

"He charmed her. Was it the kind of charming that results in spending the night together?"

Owen paused. "Actually, no. Isold didn't say or do anything suggestive, and we left without making any promises. Weird. She was pretty, too."

Aderyn raised her eyebrows. "Was she, now."

Owen grabbed her around the waist and pulled her close. "I know you're joking, because you're never the least bit jealous, but in case you need a reminder of who holds my heart..."

His lips met hers, and they kissed passionately, gradually sinking onto the bed as they drew even closer together. Finally, Aderyn broke away from his embrace, breathing heavily. "I should pretend to be jealous more often."

"I love that you know I'd never look seriously at anyone but you." Owen dragged a length of turquoise cloth from beneath his leg. "And now we're crushing our finery. Let me show you how to wear this. It's not complicated, but the fit isn't like our northern clothing."

The clothing was what Aderyn considered typical southern garb, but in very fine silk rather than the cotton or linen she'd seen on others. The trousers were more like leggings, loose and baggy and too long. Owen said they were meant to be like that, and demonstrated how to let the pants legs bunch up around the ankles. Aderyn tied the waist drawstring and tucked the dangling ends inside the leggings.

Next came a sleeveless tunic with a wide neck that slipped over her head. The hem came to the knee, and the sides were slit to the waist so she could move freely. After that, Owen helped her into a floor-length robe, also sleeveless, that hung open from neck to hem, revealing the tunic and leggings. It was comfortably cool, surprising Aderyn because she'd been expecting to sweat under those layers.

The entire ensemble was as gaudy as a flower garden: bright turquoise tunic embroidered with gold thread and a hundred sparkling pink gems the size of pinheads, leggings in a darker shade of turquoise, and the robe. Aderyn had been skeptical of matching turquoise with such a vivid shade of pink, but it worked. The robe was pale pink at the shoulders and grew gradually darker until it was deep rose at the hem. "A sword belt will look stupid with this," she said.

"No weapons," Owen said. "We got a message about where to go and what not to do. Nobody but their guards goes armed in the royal family's presence."

"Just as well. I'm vain enough to care about how I'd look with my sword dragging down my robe."

She admired herself in the wall mirror, wishing it was long enough for her to see all of herself at once, while Owen dressed in clothes whose colors complemented her outfit. His green tunic and darker green robe made them look like blooming flowers, and she said so. Owen laughed. "I hope that's good. I'm not sure I want people thinking 'rose garden' when they look at us."

"We look wonderful. And you are incredibly handsome. Good thing you're safely married, because I'm not sure I could keep a straight face while the women in the palace drop subtle and not-so-subtle hints about the reception you'd get from them."

"That's a relief. Some guys I know love the attention of a dozen women at a time, but that always seemed like it would be uncomfortable." Owen extended his hand. "Shall we go?"

Aderyn took his hand, twitched her robe so it fell more comfortably, and let him lead her out of the room.

Chapter Fifteen

Weston and Livia were waiting for them in the narrow entrance. Neeva called it the foyer, a word totally alien to Aderyn. The two were resplendent in golden yellow, scarlet, and violet, though Weston kept hitching at the neck of his robe. "It itches."

"Ignore the itching, and it will fade," Livia said.

"I'm pretty sure I don't have that kind of mental command over my body, thanks."

"Where's Isold?" Aderyn asked, cutting off the incipient argument.

"Upstairs still, I assume," Livia said. "I'm worried about him. He hasn't flirted with anyone since we got here."

"You don't suppose... no. He's not going to find southerners any less attractive than northerners." Owen looked at the staircase like he expected Isold to appear.

"Of course not. Why, is there something different about southerners?" Aderyn asked. "Maybe they're not as open to affairs?"

"That's not—never mind. It's a difference between our worlds, that's all." Owen cleared his throat. "Here he comes now."

"I'm sorry to delay us," Isold said. He wore a deep red robe and white trousers, and his tunic was cut from patterned cloth in those colors, embroidered all over with gold leaves. "I'm embarrassed to admit I dithered over my choice of clothing. I never knew I was so fashion conscious."

"Want to make a good impression on the ladies, right?" Weston said, elbowing him.

Isold's smile looked strained. "Of course."

Aderyn watched him as they all left the inn and climbed into a wagon Owen had arranged to take them and only them to the palace. Isold was definitely acting out of character if he wasn't enthusiastic about the prospect of new romantic encounters. She couldn't imagine what had changed in the last ten or so days since they'd left Finion's Gate. Maybe he was coming down with an illness. Aderyn hated that this explanation cheered her, because she didn't want her friend to be sick, but illness was something you got over, and if Isold's problem was something emotional, that might not be anything his friends could fix.

The wagon was finer in appearance and construction than the people-movers Aderyn had seen on the streets, with a colorful canopy in a geometric pattern rather than the dull and dingy white common to the other wagons. The seats weren't as rough or splintery as the one that had taken her to the war game, either. "Do our fares cost a lot?" she asked Owen, thinking of how inexpensive the pedicab ride had been.

"I rented the wagon for the evening, so yes and no," Owen said. "Neeva helped me bargain, but I don't think anyone would have cheated me regardless. Southerners like to bargain, but they aren't inclined to take advantage of the visibly foreign. Surprising, but welcome. Not at all like Finion's Gate."

Ahead, an enormous turreted building loomed. The palace wasn't beautiful, being made of many different types of stone where various ells and towers had been added to the main building, but its sheer size intimidated Aderyn. She reminded herself she was unlikely to need to find her way through it alone.

A low wall surrounded the palace grounds, just a token about four feet high, and the wagon driver steered them through an iron gate flung wide open. Aderyn caught the eye of one of the guards on duty and smiled reflexively. He didn't smile back, but Aderyn wasn't offended; she remembered Owen's stories of that place in his world where the guards weren't allowed to react no matter what tourists did. "Tourists" had been another odd concept. Aderyn couldn't imagine traveling to places just to look at them.

A wooded garden occupied the space between the wall and the palace, filling the air with the scents of flowers and resinous trees. There wasn't time to admire it before the wagon came to a stop at the front door and Aderyn and the others climbed down. Like the gate, the door was wide open, and two armed guards wearing dark gray and pale gold surcoats over their armor examined each of the friends before letting them inside.

Aderyn Assessed them in turn and discovered they were both level ten Swifthands, so the weapons were redundant. "Do you suppose they think we're a threat to the king and queen?" she whispered to Owen after they'd passed through the door.

"We could be," Owen replied. "I couldn't tell if that Assessment of theirs was a show to remind us to behave ourselves, or if they were looking for actual threats. We could do damage even without our weapons."

"Let's not think that way," Aderyn said. "We're here to plan a war. That's violence enough for one evening."

They passed through rooms filled with ornate tables and chairs, vibrant rugs even more colorful than their clothes were, tapestries and paintings depicting the prettier varieties of monsters, and brilliantly lit light fixtures dripping with crystals that sparkled in the light of the **<Everburning Candles>** they bore. Each room led directly to the next, without connecting halls, and Aderyn thought of beads strung in a long line and whether the unusual construction would give the inhabitants much privacy.

After a few minutes, Aderyn began to hear murmurs of conversation, and shortly they passed from a room painted and furnished all in shades of white and cream into an enormous chamber that glowed with gilded moldings and decorations adorning the walls. People dressed in the same kind of gaudy clothing Aderyn wore filled the room, mostly gathered into little knots of five or six attendees. Aderyn's clothes suddenly felt over warm, and she didn't think it was the warmer temperature that did it.

She turned her attention on the dais near the far wall to distract herself. The gilded white thrones at its center were unoccupied, and no one stood very close to them except two guards dressed in the same surcoats she'd seen before. Two more doors, both closed and guarded by a single man each, faced the dais on either side.

"Come on, Aderyn, we can't hover in the doorway. There's Janesh." Owen hooked Aderyn's arm over his and drew her farther into the room. She didn't see Janesh at first, but eventually she picked him out of the crowd. He stood with his arm around a heavily pregnant woman and was speaking with great animation to another man, this one shorter and younger than he.

Aderyn's attention was drawn to the second man. He was almost as good looking as Mansur, though not at all the type she was usually attracted to, what with his height and his beard, and he held himself like the tallest, handsomest man in the room. What was it about confidence that made people more attractive than their physical attributes alone?

"I don't see how it matters," the man was saying to Janesh as they approached. His gaze fell on Aderyn, and he surveyed her from head to toe, not in the way of someone interested in sleeping with her, but as if he'd been told about her and was comparing reality to that report. Aderyn, flustered, Assessed him.

Name: Kanan

Traits: determined, self-centered, driven, generous

So, this was the Duke of Tielana who was Ruan's sponsor. Aderyn kept her expression placid. He might be angry with her for usurping Ruan's place, and if there was going to be a fight, she didn't want to be the one responsible for starting it.

Instead, the duke smiled broadly and extended a hand. "You must be Aderyn. Ruan has told me of your accomplishments. I should hate you for taking what Ruan might have had, but what matters is that we win this war, no?"

"I—yes, that's true, sir," Aderyn said. She clasped his hand. It was firm, with smooth skin that bore no calluses from hard work, and yet she felt it would be a mistake to believe him indolent. "I hoped there would be no hard feelings."

"You say 'my lord' or 'my lady' when addressing nobility," Kanan said with an amused smile Aderyn didn't feel insulted by. "And I ought to call you General, if we're being polite."

That made Aderyn extremely uncomfortable. "If that's correct, then yes. I thought Varoun was the general."

Kanan laughed and released her. "You are his second in command, and what else should we call you? Don't worry, general, no one cares about missteps here. We save our offense for genuine rudeness."

Aderyn smiled to conceal her growing unease. Kanan seemed nice enough, but Aderyn was sure nobles didn't stay in power by being nice. Her Assessment of his traits warned her that this was someone to watch. "My lord, this is my husband, Owen, and our companions Weston, Livia, and Isold."

"Northern adventurers, so unexpected," Kanan said. "You didn't take the sea route, did you? Very dangerous, that."

"I can cast *scry* and *world door*," Livia said.

"Of course. Janesh, you didn't say our new general had such interesting friends." Kanan smiled at Livia, and Aderyn had no trouble reading *that* interaction. Beside her, Weston shifted his weight, but said nothing.

"I'm not your social secretary, Kanan," Janesh said, mildly but with a hint of steel in his words. "All of you, may I introduce my wife, Aswathy."

Aswathy smiled, a slightly pained expression, but then she rested a hand on her belly and Aderyn realized the pregnant woman was just uncomfortably overwarm. "So good to meet you. I wish I could greet you properly, but this war has driven me from my home."

"Temporarily," Janesh said, his voice strained enough to tell Aderyn this was a sore subject. She couldn't blame Aswathy for being resentful, but she was entirely on Janesh's side about leaving a woman close to giving birth in a city that could be attacked by orcs.

"I hope we will make it possible for you to return soon," Aderyn said.

"Thank you. Pardon me, but you are young for such a great responsibility as second in command to General Varoun. Such a dramatic contrast, as he is old and experienced." Aswathy didn't sound critical, but Aderyn felt the sting of her words anyway. She remembered Varoun saying he was going to face resistance from the dukes about his appointment; now she realized she would be in for the same thing, if for different reasons.

"A Warmaster is a tactician," she said, "and those skills make up for my lack of direct experience leading troops. And I may be the highest-level Warmaster in the world, so what I'm capable of is dramatic."

"The Warmaster Suveer is level fifteen. Does that make him a challenge to you, if he's nearly as high a level?" Aswathy asked.

"No, it makes him an ally I'd like to get to know. I don't suppose he's here?"

"Ruan and Suveer haven't arrived yet, no," Kanan said. "Excuse me. I hate to leave such an interesting conversation, but I see someone I should speak to." He gave one last meaningful smile at Livia and walked away.

Janesh let out a deep breath of relief. "That man makes my ulcer flare."

"You don't have an ulcer, dearest," Aswathy said.

"Then he's going to give me one if I have to spend much time in his company. I'll be grateful when this war is over and I can leave the capital." Janesh sighed again. "And there I go anticipating an easy victory."

"We've never fought orcs. Are they powerful?" Owen asked.

Janesh's expression became inward turned as he apparently consulted his Monster Folio. "Very powerful. They range from level ten to level eighteen depending on their age and experience, the adults are skilled with many weapon types, including bows—they're deadly at range—and they have a resilience that matches a Stalwart's. But what makes them particularly dangerous is how they work together."

"Meaning they use strategy instead of attacking singly and at random?"

Janesh nodded. "Until recently, all we ever saw of them were warbands of maybe ten or twelve at a time, but those warbands could devastate small settlements with ease and then disappear into the wilderness so well it took high-level Pathseers to find them. No one knows why they decided to change tactics two weeks ago, but if orc warbands are bad, I can only imagine what their army is like."

Aderyn didn't want to meet his gaze. But Owen said, "Two weeks ago? Not one?"

"Yes, two. That was when the first settlement was attacked, and those who went expecting to destroy a few orcs came back terrified with reports of a whole army on the borders of the Blighted Range. Why?"

"We just... thought it was later than that. It's not important." Owen's shoulders sagged in relief imperceptible to anything but **[Read Body Language]**. Aderyn understood. If their quest had triggered the orc advance, that meant they were partially responsible, and the system was sort of a bastard for compelling a monster army to attack innocents for the sake of the Fated One quest. But two weeks meant the orcs had left the high risk zone well before their team had even left Finion's Gate. Relief that the system wasn't heartless filled her. The recent changes to the system's messages to her made her feel like it was almost a friend.

"At any rate, it's not a good idea to assume we'll walk all over them just because we have an army and hundreds of adventurers," Janesh went on. "But I've fought orcs. Kanan hasn't. His perspective is different."

Horns sounded, playing an intricate three-part harmony, and Janesh turned. "That's the queen," he said. "And young King Colan."

Aderyn glanced around, but she didn't see anyone who stood out. She couldn't even see the horn players. Then the fanfare sounded again, and everyone in the room turned to face the door, backing away to leave an imaginary aisle from the door to the dais. Aderyn found herself on the edge of that aisle as even Janesh took a few steps back. Nervous, and feeling horribly conspicuous, Aderyn tried to back up, but her friends formed a solid mass behind her.

Four young women dressed all in gray, their robes covered in embroidered silver flowers, entered the chamber. Each carried a shallow basket containing something different: a bunch of purple grapes, a spindle trailing iridescent black thread, a round of parotta, and, oddly, a red brick. They paced down the aisle, not reacting to Aderyn's presence, and arranged themselves on both sides of the dais.

Two soldiers in the gray and gold surcoats, each bearing a long and menacing halberd, followed the young women. They were followed by another woman, this one dressed all in white and wearing the most elaborate diamond necklace Aderyn had ever seen. Her skin was unusually dark for a southerner, but it glowed as if she was lit from within. She held the hand of a small boy also dressed in a white, cut-down version of the robes the adults wore.

As she proceeded down the aisle, everyone she passed bowed low, so Aderyn mimicked them. When she rose, she let out a squeak, because the woman had stopped right in front of her and was regarding her with large brown eyes.

"We welcome you," Queen Devendra said. "I hope you are not a mistake."

Chapter Sixteen

Aderyn gaped, caught off guard by the queen's directness. "The history masters made their choice, and Varoun chose me," she stammered. Swallowing, she said in a steadier voice, "If I'm a mistake, then you have a bigger problem, because you're entrusting the army to the man who made that mistake. But I don't think that's true."

"Well spoken." Devendra regarded her closely, probably Assessing her. "I didn't think a northern adventurer cared what happens in the Southlands."

Aderyn hesitated, conscious of how everyone in the room was listening to this conversation. "We came because of a quest, true, but being here has made me aware of how your plight is intertwined with our cause. I've promised not to abandon my position in the army for the sake of my personal quest."

"How honorable of you." It didn't sound mocking, but Aderyn was sure Devendra wasn't convinced of Aderyn's sincerity. "And your husband claims to be the Fated One. You know we already have one of those." A ripple of laughter ran through the room.

Aderyn maintained her steady eye contact with the queen. "There are hundreds of Fated Ones throughout the world, but only we are pursuing the quest that reveals what the true Fated One must do to break the level cap. Though I understand Ruan is on the same path."

"And you don't find that a challenge?"

"It doesn't need to be. The system wants the true Fated One to prove himself, and if that's Owen, he'll succeed regardless of anyone else. And if it's Ruan, the same thing is true. All either of us can do is pursue the quest chain we're given to the best of our abilities."

The queen tilted her head, which gave her a quizzical look. "But won't you interfere with each other's actions, trying to complete the quest first?"

"No, they're different quests. I'd be happy to tell you all about it, some time when it won't bore everyone who's listening now." Aderyn risked a self-deprecating smile.

"How fascinating." Devendra laughed, which was the cue for the southerners to laugh as well. To Aderyn, the courtiers' laughter sounded insincere, but she couldn't tell if the queen thought so too. "Very well. I want to speak with you further, tomorrow perhaps. Colan, don't stare."

The boy king's eyes were fixed on Aderyn's face, and his mouth hung slightly open as if he found her startling. She smiled politely, and the king ducked his head and stood closer to his mother.

"The king has never seen a northerner before," Devendra explained. "He doesn't mean any disrespect. Colan, come with me." She inclined her head to Aderyn and proceeded down the invisible aisle to the dais, where she helped Colan settle on the larger of the thrones. His short legs dangled, but he surveyed the room with a bright, alert expression.

Devendra seated herself next to her son and settled her white robes around her. That was the cue for everyone to return to the conversations they'd been having. Mostly everyone; Aderyn, still watching the dais, observed a steady flow of people moving casually in the king and queen's direction, intent on having a few words with them. Well, probably not with Colan. Aderyn didn't know anything about nobility, but she recognized power when she saw it, and Devendra had power. The boy might actually grow up to be a good king, with her influence.

"That was interesting," Janesh said. "I wonder where she got her information from. I haven't spoken to her all week."

"Is she close to Ruan?" Owen asked.

Janesh shot him a narrow-eyed look. "You're not suggesting anything inappropriate, are you? The queen would never have an illicit liaison, not even with someone as handsome and charming as Ruan."

"No, I meant, she talked like he wasn't a stranger, so I wondered if they were friends. I imagine a queen regent can't show intimate partiality without political repercussions. Though I wouldn't put it past Ruan to have tried something." Owen looked irritated, the way he had when he'd learned Ruan had come on to Aderyn.

"Surprisingly, he hasn't, though you're right he's left a swath of broken hearts through the ladies of the court." Janesh looked irritated, too. "The queen regent must have talked to the history masters. I know they communicated their decision to the court almost the moment they made it."

"That makes sense," Aderyn said. "She'd want to know who is entrusted with her country's defense."

"Which includes you." Janesh made a show of surveying the room. "People are waiting for me to walk away so they can casually descend upon you like locusts on a field of grain."

Aderyn grimaced. "I expected that, but I was hoping..." She let her words trail off. She wasn't going to be a coward and let her dislike of crowds stop her from doing what she'd agreed to, even if she hadn't actually agreed to be pestered. "Never mind. Thanks, Janesh. It was good to meet you, Aswathy."

"Good fortune, Aderyn," Aswathy said, with a look that said she sympathized with Aderyn's plight, and the two walked away.

"Let's find something to drink," Weston said. "Something cool. I doubt they're serving food, given how early it is."

"I know you eat like every meal is your last one, but you seem unusually hungry since we got here," Livia said.

"It's the heat," Weston said. "And the humidity. Feels like I'm working twice as hard to do anything. And it takes a lot of food to fuel this physique." He slapped a hand against his broad chest for emphasis.

His words lightened Aderyn's heart. "If we move around, maybe people won't follow us. Look at how they're drifting in the queen's direction. They're practically sidling."

She hooked her hand around the crook of Owen's elbow and tugged.

"I see someone with a tray. That's like in Raynir's house back in Finion's Gate, right? Now I'm really glad I have at least a little preparation."

The five of them strolled in the direction of the serving woman with the tray. She wore gray billowing trousers and a fitted pale gold sleeveless shirt that matched the guards' surcoats and presented her tray as they approached. The rose-pink liquid in the glasses turned out to be another citrus drink, this one bubbly. Aderyn liked it even better than the first.

She saw the trio of women approaching in enough time to compose herself. The possibility that they'd demand to know her credentials for commanding an army seemed low, but she reminded herself that it was a bad idea to assume someone wasn't interested in current events just because she dressed in frivolous colors.

The three women didn't sidle up to Aderyn, instead approaching almost aggressively, making Aderyn even more nervous. But when they neared, the one in front said to Owen, "Are you really the Fated One? What about Ruan?"

"Oh," Owen said, sounding taken aback. "I am the Fated One, yes, or rather one of many. Anyone can declare they're the Fated One, but unlike them, my friends and I are on the real quest to discover the Fated One's destiny. I can't speak for Ruan."

"He's a bastard," the tallest woman said. "He tells people what they want to hear, and he's so smooth they believe it. I don't think he's the Fated One at all."

"That's right. And you're married," the third woman said. She was the prettiest of the three, though all were lovely. "You would never make promises to a woman and then not keep them."

"I definitely would not. This is my wife, Aderyn," Owen said. Aderyn suppressed a laugh at how clearly he wanted to divert the conversation.

All three focused on Aderyn. "You're the northerner who will command under General Varoun," the beautiful woman said. "How did you manage that? I thought the history masters would choose someone older."

"Didn't you listen, Volena?" the first woman said. "She's a Warmaster. I guess that class is more useful than we thought."

"Warmasters need a partner to develop their skills," Aderyn said. She'd gotten used to everyone she encountered here knowing Warmasters weren't useless, and the woman's words unexpectedly stung. "Don't you know how Suveer and Ruan work together?"

"Oh, Suveer," Volena said, her lips drawing down in a frown. "He's... well, he's not a bad sort. He's just not... not..."

"He's sort of a nonentity," the first woman said flatly. "Nobody knows much about him beyond the fact that his and Ruan's partnership has given each of them absurdly high skill ranks in some things. As if anyone can prove it. It's not like we can see skill ranks."

Aderyn Assessed the trio as the woman spoke, feeling this put her back on balance.

Name: Priyana
Class: Spiritsmith
Level: 6

NAME: TAMAYA
Traits: clever, direct, self-absorbed, romantic

NAME: VOLENA
Class: Herald
Level: 8

"In fact, a Warmaster can see skill ranks," Isold said. "No doubt Ruan and Suveer are as high in ranking as they claim."

"Except there weren't any other Warmasters around until now, and Ruan could have said anything he liked," Tamaya said.

"That's true," Volena said. She smiled at Isold. "Hello, fellow Herald."

"My name is Isold," Isold said. "I assume you've all been the recipients of Ruan's charm?"

"Bastard," Tamaya said again. "I wish he'd leave, but he's got his feet solidly under Duke Kanan's table, so what would be the point of abandoning all that luxury?"

"We heard the duke is his sponsor," Isold said. "What exactly does that entail?"

"Oh, the duke hosts him at his mansion, and he pays for his upkeep. And Suveer's," Priyana added almost as an afterthought.

"How fortunate for them. The duke is generous—or is it a business arrangement?"

Aderyn had no idea where Isold was going with this, but she controlled an impatient question. Better not to disrupt his plan, whatever it was.

"Well, Duke Kanan did want Ruan to command the army," Volena said. "He put a lot of effort into promoting his interests. I don't know what he'll do now. Maybe he'll kick Ruan out." The idea seemed to satisfy her.

"I'm sure the duke has other plans," Priyana said. "Ruan is still a skilled Swordsworn, and he did make it to the final five candidates. Aderyn, what do you think?"

Despite the women's clear dislike for Ruan, Aderyn felt awkward declaring she felt the same, like she would be stabbing him in the back. He *had* asked for her forgiveness, even if she wasn't sure how sincere he was. "He's good at tactics for small forces," she said, remembering the ambush Ruan had engineered. If not for **[Sense Ambush]**, she might have walked into it, so it had been effective. "Possibly General Varoun will have a use for him."

"I'm curious," Isold said. "Would Ruan as commander general have benefited Duke Kanan in some way? Because I'm having trouble imagining why the duke would support Ruan so lavishly if he didn't expect something in return."

"I don't know, and frankly I don't care," Tamaya said, "if I can be blunt."

"Don't be rude, Tamaya," Volena said. She smiled at Isold again, this time coquettishly. "Duke Kanan has influence over Ruan, true, but he's committed to the safety of our country and he would never use that influence for personal gain. Besides, Tielana is the largest of the dukedoms—he already has power and influence on his own."

"I see," Isold said. "I appreciate your insight. Now, if you'll excuse me, I see someone I should speak with." He bowed politely to each of the women and left the group. Volena watched him go with some disappointment. Aderyn concealed her dismay. She'd never known Isold to pass up an opportunity to make a romantic connection, and Volena was clearly interested. And she knew full well Isold didn't know a single person in this gathering they hadn't both been introduced to.

Quickly, to distract the women so they wouldn't see Isold wandering aimlessly instead of talking to someone, she said, "I'd really like to meet Suveer. I don't suppose you've seen him?"

"Oh, Suveer." Priyana echoed Volena's earlier comment, down to her dismissive tone. "He's boring. Really, we can introduce you to many more interesting people."

"That would be nice, but—"

Tamaya sucked in an angry breath. "Ruan is here," she said. "Bastard."

Aderyn followed the direction of Tamaya's gaze. Ruan, looking very good in blue and gold, stood posed like a handsome statue for others to admire, but Aderyn's attention was all for the man next to him—someone who looked remarkably like Ruan. "Excuse me," she said, not thinking it might be rude, and set off to talk to Suveer.

Chapter Seventeen

She hadn't gone two steps before she changed her mind. She wanted desperately to talk to Suveer, but suppose he had different skills than she had? Or different paired skills? Maybe that was ridiculous—it wasn't as if different Swordsworn, for example, had skills that varied with their adventuring experiences—but now was the time to Assess him, a Full Assess, before getting into a conversation. And more information was always better.

Name: Suveer

Class: Warmaster

Level: 15

Skills: Bluff (8), Climb (6), Conversation (6), Intimidate (7), Sense Truth (9), Survival (12), Swim (11), Knowledge: Monsters (15), Knowledge: World Lore (7)

Class Skills: Improved Assess 3 (10), Awareness (12), Knowledge: Geography (9), Spot (16), Discern Weakness (24), Dodge (12), Improvised Distraction (17), Outflank (22), Draw Fire (15), Keep Pace (19), Amplify Voice (10), See It Coming (9), Read Body Language (12), Basic Map Access (5), Compel (2), Spot Weakness (3), Secret Message (12), Bonded Mind (13), Sense Ambush (0)

Stunned, Aderyn repeated her Assessment. Nothing changed. It didn't make sense. All his paired skill ranks, and a few others, were as high as hers, sometimes higher. The rest were much too low. Only ten ranks in **[Improved Assess 3]**? His everyman skills were just as bad. Aderyn had seen unnaturally low skill ranks before, in Jessemia. There, Jessemia had taken bad advice and had only worked on developing a couple of her skills, resulting in an imbalance. But surely a Warmaster who'd made it as high as level fifteen, a Warmaster with a partner, wouldn't have that problem?

"Aderyn," Owen said. "Is something wrong?"

"I don't know. Give me a minute." Aderyn turned Assess on Ruan. Maybe something about the way they'd adventured meant the brothers both had that weird disparity in skill ranks.

Name: Ruan

Class: Swordsworn

Level: 15

<u>Skills</u>: Assess (12), Awareness (15), Climb (12), Conversation (14), Sense Truth (13), Spot (12), Survival (6), Swim (11)

<u>Class Skills</u>: Superior Weapon Proficiency (26), Advanced Armor Proficiency (20), Knowledge: Monsters (11), Exploit Weakness (24), Dodge (15), Parry (16), Improved Bluff (15), Outflank (22), Trip (7), Keep Pace (19), Disarm (6), Intimidate (12), Charge (6), Two-Weapon Fighting (9), Read Body Language (12), Basic Map Access (5), Overrun (5), Shatter Confidence (3), Bonded Mind (13), Weapon Mastery (greatsword)

"He's normal," she murmured. "What in thunder is going on?"

"Aderyn? Don't you want to meet Suveer?" Owen sounded curious but not concerned.

Aderyn took Owen's arm and steered him away from the group. When they were out of earshot, she said, "Something's wrong. Suveer's skill ranks aren't what they should be. He looks like Jessemia did when we first met her—some much too low, and in his case a few that are higher than mine. But Ruan's ranks are normal for a Swordsworn with a Warmaster partner—they look like yours."

"Weird," Owen said. "Why would Suveer have not practiced skills when Ruan has?"

"I don't know, but I want to find out." Aderyn took hold of Owen's arm and pulled him along with her. For once, she felt **[Keep Pace]** was working on Owen rather than her.

She examined Suveer as she approached, not Assessing him, but curious about his appearance. The closer she got, the less he looked like his twin brother. They were clearly identical twins, with the same facial features and the same build, but Suveer wore his black hair cut short and he dressed haphazardly, as if he wore an ordinary shirt and trousers rather than the same kind of finery as everyone else.

Even his demeanor was different. Suveer stood with his shoulders slightly hunched and his head bowed so he couldn't meet anyone's eyes, even when he spoke as he was doing now, responding to some question of Ruan's. If not for their physical resemblance, Aderyn would have sworn he and the confident Ruan weren't related.

As she and Owen drew near, Ruan turned to face her, which put him between her and Suveer. "Aderyn," he said. "How are you?"

"Fine. It's—everyone's been so nice," Aderyn said as if she'd talked to a hundred nice people so far. "It's good to see you again. And this must be Suveer."

Suveer twitched at the mention of his name, but didn't look up. Ruan said, "Yes, this is my brother. Suveer, this is Aderyn, the Warmaster I told you about."

"Another Warmaster," Suveer said. His voice was clear but drab, like he found it difficult to say even those simple words. "I didn't know there were any others at our level."

"Me neither," Aderyn said. "I—" She laughed. "I have so many questions I don't know where to start. How did you figure it out? Owen and I—oh, this is my husband and partner, Owen—"

"It's good to meet you, Suveer," Owen said.

Suveer didn't react. Aderyn plunged ahead. "Owen and I only found out how the class works by accident. Is that how it was for you? Ruan said it didn't take many battles for you to discover the skill boosts."

"That's right." Suveer finally raised his head, and Aderyn held back a gasp as the motion revealed a long scar that ran from above his left eye across a sunken eyelid to the top of his cheekbone. Now Aderyn sympathized with his desire to keep his head down. She didn't think it made him any less handsome—and sharing Ruan's features, he couldn't help but be handsome—but people did tend to stare.

"The paired skills are remarkable, aren't they?" Ruan said to Aderyn. "And I appreciate the boost to my weapons skill. I don't know what I'd do without my partner." He clapped Suveer on the shoulder, and Suveer finally smiled, a tiny, weak smile that told Aderyn he didn't like being on display any more than she did. Aderyn's curiosity rose again. Maybe Suveer was one of those people who didn't know how to talk to strangers, or maybe something else was going on.

"I would really like to talk about our class, Suveer, just the two of us where we won't bore the others," she began. "Could we meet—"

At the same time, Ruan looked past her and said, "Oh, there's Varoun—General Varoun, I should say. The ceremony is about to start. I'm sorry, you were saying something, Aderyn?"

Aderyn looked around, distracted. At that moment, the horns sounded a fanfare different from the first. Quickly, she said, "I was asking Suveer if he wanted to meet for dinner sometime."

"Yes, dinner. I'll send a messenger when I've arranged something. The Jeweled Cuckoo Inn, right?" Ruan put a hand on Suveer's shoulder and steered him away without waiting for her answer. Again, Aderyn was caught up in the movement of the crowd, and within seconds the brothers were lost to view.

"That's not what I meant," Aderyn said to no one. *That* had been even more suspicious than the irregular skill ranks. All her instincts said Ruan didn't want her alone with Suveer, though she had no idea what he thought she could accomplish with a private conversation.

"He doesn't want you to talk to his brother privately," Owen murmured. "What's up with that?"

"That's how I feel." Another fanfare sounded, and she scowled. "It will have to wait. I want to see the ceremony."

She pushed past people until she again had a clear view of the room. Unlike before, she didn't care if this made her conspicuous; this ceremony investing Varoun with command of the army mattered indirectly to her, and she didn't want to miss it. Owen, close behind her, put a hand on her shoulder to stop her walking into the open. "There he is," he said.

As before, the crowds divided to leave a space from the door to the dais, a space wide enough for three people to walk side by side. Varoun stood alone at the head of it, perfectly still. Unlike every other attendee, he wore a steel-studded leather cuirass and reinforced vambraces as well as steel-toed boots. It wasn't full armor, but it clearly conveyed the message that Varoun was a military man who took his new office seriously. Aderyn instantly felt underdressed, though if she'd been meant to wear armor, someone would have said.

Varoun paused at the door long enough for the crowd's restless movement to still. Then he strode toward the dais and its occupants, his hand occasionally drifting to his right hip as if resting on an invisible sword. Aderyn had seen he was left handed during their game of Wall, but his movements still looked odd, backwards. She would bet he used that backward-appearing movement to his advantage when he fought.

When he reached the foot of the dais, Varoun bowed to the king and then to the queen regent. Then he dropped to one knee and lowered his head. "My king, I am at your service."

Colan looked at his mother. Devendra leaned over and whispered in his ear. Colan slid down from the throne. "General," he said in his child's high-pitched voice, "will you serve the Southlands and defend it from all enemies?"

"I will, my king," Varoun said.

Again Colan looked to his mother for help. Devendra gestured at a nearby guard, who bore a narrow wooden box. The guard handed the box to Colan, carefully not touching him, which Aderyn found odd. Colan opened the box and removed a sleek black wand. He shifted it a few times from hand to hand, looking for a graceful way to hold it, and in the end handed it somewhat awkwardly to Varoun, who didn't react except to slide the wand into a loop at his waist that looked made for that purpose.

Devendra rose to her feet and said, "We accept your fealty and thank you for your service, General Varoun. The armies of the Southland are yours to command."

"My king, my queen, I am honored at your trust." Varoun waited for them to seat themselves, then rose from his kneeling position and bowed again. The crowd surged into motion, most of them hurrying forward to congratulate Varoun. Aderyn stood still and let them buffet her. For the moment, they'd forgotten her, but she didn't kid herself that that moment would last.

Once the crush wasn't quite so great, she wandered through the room, her hand joined with Owen's to keep him close. Everyone else she knew had vanished. She and Owen didn't speak—even with most of the people clustered on the far side of the room, the noise was great enough they'd have to raise their voices or possibly shout. A cool draft Aderyn welcomed blew in from the antechamber. She flapped her hand in front of her face, hoping it would act like a fan.

"Not a climate you're accustomed to?" Varoun said from behind her, making her squeak and turn around fast. "I'm sorry I startled you."

"It's impossible to make out individual footsteps in this din," Owen said.

"I didn't expect you to escape your admirers so quickly." Aderyn felt another cool draft and sighed happily. "And yes. Sometimes our summers get this hot, but it's a dry heat."

"Ellowyn and Savion used to complain about the weather here, too," Varoun said. "I suppose it's something one might need to be born to."

"It beats winter in the north," Owen said. "Snowstorms can be deadly."

"Now, *that* I never could imagine, weather cold enough for water to freeze," Varoun said. "And now that we've gotten the small talk out of the way, why don't you let me introduce you to the people who aren't likely to criticize my strategy or attack Aderyn verbally for being young, northern, or female."

"Why would they care if I'm female?" Aderyn asked.

"About fifty years ago, there was a movement among parts of Southlander society to restrict women's participation in a number of dangerous fields." Varoun strolled through the crowds, carefully not making eye contact with anyone. "This was after an outbreak of disease that disproportionately affected women, reducing their numbers dramatically. Many felt it was irresponsible of society to encourage the remaining women to risk themselves, and that turned into a general feeling that women *couldn't* do certain activities. Foolish, but it made sense to some."

"I guess I understand, though I'm glad most people no longer believe that. They don't, right?"

"Some of that older generation does, yes. I'm afraid you'll face their criticism."

"I can handle criticism."

"What about you? I don't understand how anyone can criticize a strategy you haven't developed," Owen said.

Varoun chuckled. "So many Southlander nobles believe they have insight into how war should be conducted they won't stop their grousing even when they have nothing to grouse about. I did say there would be those reluctant to accept the history masters' decision, even backed by the king and the queen regent as it is. Officially, the king chose me on their recommendation, but I'm sure you realize it was his mother's decision."

"I think the king has a very able regent," Owen said.

"The king has a regent who is adamant that he be allowed to grow up before he's burdened with the rule of a kingdom. And a regent who defends him and his younger sister fiercely against the sycophants and the self-interested who would warp the children's development to their own ends."

"The queen wants to meet with me tomorrow, to talk about the Fated One quest, but I'm sure it will be more than that," Aderyn said. "Can you give me any advice?"

"Be honest, be forthright, and answer only the questions she asks directly," Varoun said. "Queen Devendra has a knack for making people want to fill up her silences, giving away more than they should. She's not evil, and I doubt she wants to manipulate you, but you should be wary nonetheless."

"I will. Thank you."

"Ah, I see Lord Vitra," Varoun said. "We'll stay for an hour or so, deflecting impertinences, and then it will be time to make our escape." His sardonic tone made Aderyn laugh. "Yes, laugh now," he said, "because that escape will take us to where we will lay plans for this country's defense, and I am certain none of us will want to laugh then."

He spoke lightly, not criticizing, but Aderyn felt a chill down her spine even so. As she followed Varoun toward a tall, stately gentlemen who watched their approach with interest, an idle thought struck her—the realization she'd never told Ruan the name of their inn.

She trusted Varoun's word, but it felt like much longer than an hour that he propelled her and Owen through the throne room, speaking briefly to men and women before detaching the three of them from the conversation and moving on. It wasn't quite as bad as Varoun had suggested; few people challenged him, even fewer challenged her, but those few spoke loudly and with much heat about their inadequacies.

Varoun interrupted these tirades only once, when the woman came to the verge of criticizing Devendra for choosing anyone so unsuited to command as Aderyn. "Queen Devendra's decision is final," he said, "and I daresay your passion for the topic has overwhelmed your good sense, since there are many here who would like to see you brought low when your words reach the queen's ears." The woman's mouth snapped shut, and a moment later she excused herself.

"What would the queen do to her?" Aderyn whispered, fascinated.

"Nothing," Varoun replied. "But that woman would find herself socially ruined, if only because everyone at the court constantly searches for ways to promote themselves by crushing others. They'd talk about what other criticisms she might make, and tell stories of how Devendra never allows her into her presence anymore—never mind that Devendra pays no attention to her now—and in the end everyone would know that woman was unreliable and faithless as if she'd betrayed them personally."

Aderyn shuddered. "That's awful. I don't see why anyone wants to be part of the court, if that's how they behave."

"Because the advantages of being at the top are tremendous," Owen said. "Money, fame, influence... that's all worth the risks. Those same rumors can be turned to someone's benefit if they know how to control the court."

"You're right." Varoun eyed Owen. "You've been here before?"

"Um, no, I just read a lot." Owen shrugged. "Look, that man waved at you. Should we talk to him?"

Varoun rolled his eyes. "Definitely not. He knows only one story and it's tremendously boring, which doesn't stop him telling it every time we meet. I think it's time we made our escape."

Chapter Eighteen

They exited via the door to the right of the dais, where the guard surveyed them briefly and then let them pass. The hall beyond was narrow and dark by comparison to the brilliantly lit throne room, with a high ceiling and wood paneling that smelled the way Ikharatia had on their arrival before the scent faded from awareness. It wasn't overwhelming, but Aderyn sneezed once anyway.

She and Owen trailed Varoun—there wasn't room to walk three abreast—until they reached another door, this one unguarded. Varoun paused before opening the door. "I don't know what to tell you," he said to Aderyn. "Some of these men will resent you for having a position they aspired to. Depending on who is present, you may face prejudice due to being a northerner. I can't predict what behavior they'll respond well to. So I can only recommend you be direct and forthright and slow to take offense."

"Because some of that prejudice might be on purpose to get me to react angrily?" Aderyn said.

"You have it exactly. Will it help to know I judge you more intelligent than half my commanding officers?"

Aderyn laughed. "Sadly, yes."

"Cling to that, and we will make these men respect us." Varoun nodded once and pushed the door open.

They interrupted a loud argument that cut off when they entered. Aderyn took in her surroundings quickly—round room, round table at the center of the room, sandbox set up to display a battle scenario at the center of the table. Chairs surrounded the table, but none of them were occupied by the six or seven men present. She had an impression of another door and many paintings depicting scenes of war, nothing she recognized, which made sense as she knew almost nothing about history, southern or northern.

Before she had time to Assess those present, every man in the room straightened to attention with a rustle of motion that amused Aderyn, it reminded her so much of children rushing to line up for a treat. Varoun silently regarded the men standing like statues before him. "Thank you, I'm satisfied," he said, and everyone unfroze, though they didn't go back to their earlier, relaxed positions.

"General Varoun," said a portly man nearest them. He, like the others, wore a gray uniform with a gold sash tied diagonally across his chest, but a silver medal hanging from a violet ribbon around his neck made him stand out. "Welcome."

"Thank you, General Ananyi," Varoun said, clasping the man's outstretched hand. "I appreciate the king's trust in me, and I vow it will not be misplaced." He gestured to Aderyn to come forward. "This is Aderyn, my second in command, and her husband, Owen."

The murmuring started again. Ananyi frowned. "I thought the rumor that you'd chosen a stranger to assist in command was, well, just that. And she's young, and—" He apparently changed his mind about his next words. "I think you owe us an explanation."

"I realize some of you expected to fill that role," Varoun said. "I mean no slight on any of you. You all agree we should use every resource to the fullest, I know, and Aderyn represents that. She excelled at every test the history masters gave her, she nearly outscored me in a war game, and she defeated me at Wall." He smiled, the faintest twist of his lips, and added, "Some of you will remember her grandmother, Ellowyn."

The murmuring grew louder. A man standing next to Ananyi said,

"That's impressive, but she has no experience. We need someone who knows what he's doing." He was younger than the others and more fit, and he held his head proudly, as if he was the one he referred to as knowing what he was doing. Aderyn wished she could Assess him, but she didn't dare miss anything he or the others might say.

"Your objection is noted, Ishan." Varoun didn't sound as if he cared about Ishan's objection. "I repeat—Aderyn is fully qualified, and she has my complete approval. So if you feel like challenging me for your personal aggrandizement, go ahead. It will do you no good."

Ishan moved forward until he was face to face with Aderyn. His gaze was keen and clear and fixed intently on her. "You've been gone a long time, Varoun," he said, though his attention remained on Aderyn. "You may not remember the demands of the military. Women aren't fit to command—look around, and see if I'm not right."

Aderyn had already noticed she was the only woman in the room. "Just because you don't choose women commanders doesn't mean they can't," she said, keeping her voice calm. "That's nothing but a failure of imagination on your part."

Ishan drew in a sharp, startled breath. "Are you challenging my authority?"

"According to General Varoun, I'm the one with authority. And I satisfied the history masters as well."

"Academics," Ishan snorted. "They can't be expected to understand the realities of being in the field."

"Colonel Ishan, you are out of line," Ananyi said. His bold words didn't match his tone of voice, which was tinged with weariness. Aderyn had the sense this was what the argument had been about, because Ananyi sounded like someone who'd gone the rounds with Ishan before.

"Then you're going back on your word?" Varoun said, as calmly as Aderyn. "Because you agreed to abide by their decision. I was their decision, and I chose Aderyn."

"Who brings her husband along to this meeting," another man said. "That doesn't look confident to me."

"Then you—" Owen began angrily.

Aderyn held out a hand to stop him stepping forward. "I'm a Warmaster, and Owen is my partner as well as my husband," she said. "He and I work together. And he'd be the first to tell you I don't need his permission for anything."

"A Warmaster," Ananyi said. "And one of high level, like that Suveer fellow. You're more assertive than he, I hope."

"From what I've seen, yes, though I'm sure Suveer is skilled." Aderyn wished she hadn't given in to her impulse to defend Suveer, especially with a lie. It was a distraction from the conversation at best and connected her unfavorably with the diffident Warmaster at worst. "At any rate, it's my skills that matter, don't you think?"

"Just because Varoun has fond memories of Ellowyn is no reason to accept a woman as second in command—" Ishan began.

Varoun swiftly grabbed Ishan by the collar and shoved him into the table so the younger man was bent backward over its shining expanse. It was not the act of an old man; Aderyn hadn't been inclined to discount Varoun due to his age, but this convinced her he could still give someone a good fight.

"That's enough," Varoun said, still in that level voice. "I was willing to leave you your pride, but I'll say now in public that you were never going to command beside me. You're arrogant and self-absorbed and you've traded on your military successes for years, demanding favors and special treatment because you think you're irreplaceable. You are not. And you've just made it clear that I don't have your respect, which means I have no need of you. Get out. Your command will be assigned to another."

Ishan's eyes were wide, and he scrabbled at the table with his fingertips as if trying to find his balance. "You wouldn't dare."

"I believe I just did." Varoun released him with another shove, making Ishan cry out in pain as the edge of the table ground into his hips. "And the same goes for the rest of you. I don't expect you to agree with me on everything, I don't expect you to stay silent if I make a mistake, but by thunder you will respect me as your commander or you can follow Ishan out that door."

Ishan glared at Varoun, who stared coolly back. Then, rubbing his hip, he limped through the door at the back of the room.

No one spoke for a few moments. Then one of the men, a short, heavily bearded individual in his late twenties, said, "Dramatic. Are we allowed to ask for more details about our new commander's qualifications, or will that incur your wrath as well?"

He spoke in a drawling, lazy voice, and Aderyn expected Varoun to challenge him, but the general laughed and said, "Are you willing to face the same inquiry, Chandar?"

"You know what I'm capable of, Varoun," Chandar replied, "which I suppose is a good answer to my question. All right. Call it curiosity rather than a challenge. I'd like to know the things she brings to the fight."

Varoun nodded at Aderyn. Aderyn Skill Assessed Chandar, swiftly reading through the list and ranks and skill alerts. "You're a level twelve Pathseer, and while you're skilled with weapons, what makes you dangerous is **[Dirty Fighting]**. You'll have **[Improvised Weapon]** in a couple of levels, which will make you even more deadly in a skirmish. You started as a scout and worked your way up in command, based on how high your **[Tracking]**, **[Hide]**, and **[Camouflage]** skills are. And you have specialized knowledge about orcs and ogres. Are you sure you're a general? Because—I'm sorry, I don't mean to be rude, it's just that it seems like a waste for you not to fight with a team."

Chandar's amused expression gradually gave way to stunned astonishment. "Thunderation," he breathed. "Who told you I was a scout, back in the day?"

"No one. It's all in your skills." Aderyn hoped she didn't look smug, but she did love surprising people who underestimated her.

"Well." Chandar regained control of himself. "That's impressive, naturally, but it doesn't speak to your skill at command. Or does the Warmaster class have other skills than just the one you demonstrated?"

"Many skills, yes. But mostly I see how things should go." She pointed at the sandbox. "With the attackers' greater numbers, the defenders shouldn't bunch up in front of the building—the fortress?—like that. They'll just be destroyed to no purpose, since I don't see relief forces anywhere nearby. Better for them to withdraw, pretend to flee, and then regroup *here* and *here* to turn that tactic on the attackers."

She hesitated. "Or, if it's the attackers you want to win, have them divide their forces, since they've got the numerical advantage, and be prepared for that rear assault I described. In fact, if they have archers, some of those troops should watch for attacks from the rear while the front troops use battering rams and ladders to breach the walls, protected by more archers."

She looked up. Everyone in the room was staring at her. Inside, she squirmed. It didn't matter that she was right; all these men were experienced military leaders, and maybe she'd challenged their wisdom. Probably they already knew all those tactics.

Finally, Ananyi cleared his throat. "Do you suggest these men run, like cowards?" he asked, pointing at the massed yellow soldiers.

"How is it cowardice to enact a different tactic?" Aderyn said. "It's not always about advancing. The point is to win at least cost of life, or am I wrong about that?"

"You are not wrong," Varoun said. "Does this display represent Adhiraj?"

"It does, commander," said a middle-aged man with thinning hair and a square jaw. "They anticipate battle will be joined sometime late tomorrow afternoon. We must dispatch forces to relieve them."

"There's no way to reach them in time," Chandar said. "The armies have engaged the enemy at various places, and we push them back, and yet the orcs continue to pour out of the Blighted Range like so many ants intent on the sugar bowl."

"It's past time we saw the map," Varoun said.

The middle-aged man and two others bustled around, removing the sandbox so carefully the figures didn't wobble. Chandar brought out a six-foot-long roll of paper and unrolled it on the table while Ananyi brought stones to weigh down the corners. Varoun regarded the map, while Aderyn watched the other men. They hovered anxiously, like mothers watching a child take its first steps—keeping their distance, but ready to leap in to prevent disaster.

Aderyn's system map hadn't yet expanded to include the Southlands, and she hadn't expected it to, but the map her father had given her back before she left Far Haven showed the Blighted Range and the land south of that. This map was nearly identical in shape but more detailed, showing cities, towns, and the red shading that indicated the high risk zone. The Blighted Range was entirely red.

Ananyi and the middle-aged man brought out boxes filled with small figurines and placed them all over the map. Most of them grouped near cities, though a few lone figures stood to Aderyn's eyes in random places in the middle of empty territory. When they finished, Chandar brought out more figures, these painted red and less detailed than the others. He arranged them in an irregular line between the edge of the Blighted Range and a city labeled ADHIRAJ that was due south, then put a couple of red figures to the sides of the line. Then he stepped back. None of the officers spoke, but again anxiety suffused the room in an almost palpable cloud.

Varoun studied the map in silence. Finally, he said, "Duke Simla failed to advance past the first round of tests. Did he return to Adhiraj?"

"Yes, and he has sent messages demanding we rush to support him," Chandar said. "As if we didn't understand the situation."

"This is not the time to squabble over precedence." Varoun's quiet voice didn't match the harshness of his words. He drew the black wand and tapped its tip against the tiny city of Adhiraj. "I have spoken to General Tamil at Adhiraj, who says the orcs will be upon them in less than twenty-four hours. What forces are these?" The tip of the wand shifted to point at a blue figure a few inches from Adhiraj.

"Colonel Sudiptar's," Ananyi said. "I dispatched his regiment three days ago." He sounded like he was bracing himself against Varoun attacking him.

Varoun didn't react. "I notice Colonel Sudiptar didn't join us."

Ananyi cleared his throat. "He said he couldn't be bothered to pay court when there are cities to defend."

Varoun raised his eyebrows. "That's not what he said."

Ananyi's eyes focused on a spot beyond Varoun's left ear. "No, commander, it was not, but—"

"Don't worry about it. I won't hold it against you this time." Varoun smiled, another of those tiny movements that Aderyn couldn't interpret. Either this Sudiptar was insubordinate, or he was forthright, and either way Aderyn didn't know if he was in trouble. She thought

Ananyi ought to be in trouble, if he had two colonels he couldn't control.

Varoun added, "I will meet with Colonel Sudiptar in the morning. For now, gentlemen—does this represent our best intelligence as to the position of the enemy?"

Chandar came to Varoun's side. "The orcs have an unexpected ability to spot our scouts, far more efficiently than before. Many of our people disappear, presumably killed—"

"Or captured," the middle-aged man said. "We can't discount the possibility that they've been forced to give information to the enemy."

"In either case, it's been difficult to establish the orc army's exact position, aside from their main body," Chandar said, glaring at the middle-aged man. "Or its full strength. If we had more scouts—"

"You know where the scouts disappear, though," Aderyn said. "That tells you where *some* orcs are, or were at the time."

All the men stared as if they'd forgotten she was there. "But that doesn't tell us the details," Chandar said.

"It's enough to give you the shape of the invasion," Aderyn persisted. "Anywhere a scout disappears is a place to look at more closely."

"That's true," Varoun said. "General Chandar, where are your forces?"

Chandar pointed at two figures southwest of Adhiraj, two inches from a city labeled SHANTOS. "These regiments are on the way to relieve the fighters at Adhiraj. One remains with the city."

"I think not." Varoun rested a finger against his lips. "You're to assemble twelve scout teams and their lieutenants to follow up on the missing scouts and what their absence means. Make sure each team can move quickly, and enlist extra spellslingers if necessary. Give command of the main army to your second and direct him to surround Shantos. If the worst happens at Adhiraj, the orcs will go there next. That's if they haven't already divided their forces for a secondary assault—Shantos is too close to the high-risk zone for us to be complacent about its defense."

Chandar was grinning. "Yes, commander."

"You can thank Aderyn for reminding me of why I promoted you in the first place, Pathseer. Find me those orcs." Varoun turned to the others. "General Ananyi, get your remaining regiments moving toward Adhiraj. General Rajman, take two regiments and return to Tielana to prepare for an attack there. Colonel Prasay, you and Colonel Mahir will move your regiments to defend Adhiraj, and General Deshen, the Home Guard is to continue fortifying Ikharatia."

All the officers nodded. Aderyn got the sense that they were all enormously relieved. Then the middle-aged man, Mahir, said, "What of Colonel Ishan's troops?"

"Ah, yes," Varoun said. "Where are they?"

Mahir pointed at a figure somewhat east of Adhiraj. "They haven't moved in a week, commander." He shot an accusing glance at Ananyi, who ignored him.

"General Ananyi, have you an explanation for why one of your regiments is insubordinate?" Varoun asked in a level tone. Oh, yes, Ananyi was in trouble. Having seen Varoun evict Ishan, Aderyn didn't give much hope for Ananyi's chances.

"Colonel Ishan claimed there was an outbreak of dysentery," Ananyi said. "He removed himself from the troops for his personal safety and stopped responding to communications. Tonight is the first I've seen him in over a week. I take responsibility for his failings, commander. I should have relieved him of command, but there isn't anyone to take his place."

"Noted. And that's no longer true." Varoun picked up the figure and set it down again. "Aderyn. You will take temporary command of Ishan's regiment, Raven Regiment. Bring those forces west as fast as possible. We will bring pressure to bear on both sides of the attacking forces, which means a near-simultaneous attack—you understand?"

"I do, commander." Nerves made her voice squeak, and in embarrassment, she cleared her throat and said, "Sorry. I understand. We'll set out at once—or maybe not tonight, it's getting late—"

Varoun twirled the black wand between his fingers. "This **<Wand of World Door>** will send you to anywhere I choose, but in the morning. There is still much to be done, and I have more instructions for you."

"Oh! All right. We'll be ready." Aderyn suspected Varoun had given her this command as... maybe not a test, because he knew her abilities, but what Owen referred to as “training wheels”? Something to let her orient herself and become used to the practicalities of command? She was too grateful for his consideration to feel insulted. Proving herself to others was the first step.

Chapter Nineteen

By the time Varoun finished instructing Aderyn, she'd completely lost track of time and felt she might burst with new knowledge. "I hope I don't forget any of that," she told Owen as they made their way back to the throne room, leaving Varoun to consult with the other officers.

"I'll remember as much as I can, and maybe together we'll keep hold of most of it. I know this was the plan, but the idea that you're in command of a small army is still stunning." Owen stopped Aderyn before she opened the door and took her in his arms. "You're not overwhelmed, are you?"

"Only by the sheer number of things I have to remember. Strangely, I feel confident about the rest." Aderyn put a hand around the back of his neck and pulled him close for a long, satisfying kiss. "I have you, and I have our friends, and if we could kill a Sarnok and a deep delver and win the Glory Games and destroy an evil dungeon, well, how much worse could a regiment of an army be?"

"You keep that in mind," Owen said, and kissed her in return.

The crowds had thinned substantially, and the throne room felt cooler. The king and queen were gone. "Oh," Aderyn exclaimed. "I'll have to send my apologies to the queen for not meeting with her tomorrow. We'll be with the army."

"Or you could *world door* back," Owen said. "There's no reason you have to be with the troops twenty-four hours a day."

"Really? That seems so… I don't know. Frivolous, maybe?"

Owen lowered his voice. "There's historical precedent in my world. Wellington was at the Duchess of Richmond's ball in Brussels the night before Waterloo and had to haul ass to the battlefield…" He took in Aderyn's confused expression and said, "Basically, officers in that war went to dances and parties in between battles. They didn't sleep rough like the soldiers, either. If near-instantaneous transport is a thing here, you can zoom all over the place and never be more than a few minutes' hop away from the front."

"Varoun sure seemed to think that's what he would do. But he has the wand."

"And you have Livia. I'm just saying, don't feel limited by geography and distance." Owen took her hand and led her toward where Weston stood, surrounded by men and women who weren't paying attention to him. Weston's shoulders were hunched, and he held a delicate glass filled with that pink bubbly stuff as if he wished he could crush it. He was glaring at nothing Aderyn could see.

"Weston? What's wrong?" she asked, pushing politely past a woman who glanced once at her and then took a second, longer look. To keep the woman from addressing her, Aderyn hurried on, "You look like you want to murder someone. Where's Livia?"

Weston scowled. "Over there, with her new friend," he snarled.

Aderyn looked where he indicated. Livia and Duke Kanan stood close together, talking and laughing as if they were the only ones in the room. Kanan's hand rested on Livia's shoulder, and occasionally she touched his arm, lightly, always in time with another laugh. Aderyn whipped around to stare at Weston. "What in *thunder* is going on?"

Weston's lip curled in another snarl, but he said nothing.

"It can't be serious," Owen said. "Livia's just being friendly." He didn't sound convinced.

"But—" Aderyn lowered her voice, conscious of the nearby woman who was almost certainly listening. "I know he's attracted to her, but she can't possibly—"

"Really?" Weston said sarcastically. "I guess I won't believe the evidence of my eyes, then." He drank down the bubbly drink like he wished it was hard liquor and headed for the door.

"I'll follow him," Owen said. "You go see what the hell Livia is thinking. And where's Isold? Is it bad that I really hope he got lucky and is warming some courtier's bed right now?" He hurried after Weston.

Aderyn searched for one of the serving men or women as she walked toward Livia and Kanan. All that planning and talking had made her thirsty. But no helpful servant bearing a glass of cool juice appeared, and she reached Livia's side feeling overwarm and parched. "Sorry to interrupt, but I was wondering if you'd seen Isold."

"Isold?" Livia sounded almost as if she didn't remember who that was. "No. Didn't he make a new friend?"

"I've been meeting with General Varoun and the other officers, so I haven't seen him. Are you enjoying yourself?/*What are you doing, flirting with Kanan?*" Aderyn had never used **[Secret Message]** with as much force before.

"It's a delightful party," Livia said, smiling at Kanan. "Kanan knows everyone here, and even better, he knows all the best gossip. I'm having such a good time."

"But—" In time Aderyn managed not to bring up Weston, who would be humiliated if she made him a figure of pity. "That's nice, I guess. Are you about ready to go? It's late, and we have somewhere to be tomorrow."

"It's not that late," Kanan said, running his hand over Livia's shoulder. "But if you feel the need to leave, General Aderyn, I will have my private carriage return Livia to her inn later."

Aderyn had never felt less inclined to leave her friend. Kanan looked at Livia like she was prey, and worse, Livia looked like she knew it and was happy to be the rabbit his hawk snatched up. Aderyn felt so ill it was just as well she hadn't found that drink. But she couldn't make Livia leave, and she couldn't blurt out that Livia was as good as married to Weston, and she certainly couldn't punch Kanan in the face for trying to ruin everything Aderyn and her friends cared about.

"Do you mind?/*Are you sure you know what you're doing?*" she asked desperately.

Livia glanced at her dismissively. "Don't worry about me."

Aderyn gave up. "Fine. Have fun. We're leaving Ikharatia in the morning, so don't stay up too late." She walked away without waiting for Livia's reply.

Owen and Weston were gone. Aderyn had never felt so alone in her life. She found a quiet corner and used **[Bonded Mind]**, hoping Owen was far enough away for a connection: *Did you leave?*

Almost immediately, the reply came: *I'm out front at the wagon.*

Relieved, Aderyn hurried to the exit, avoiding anyone who might want to talk to her. She didn't ask Owen if Weston was there; that might be too complex a question for **[Bonded Mind]**, however competent they were becoming at the skill.

She wasn't paying attention to those she passed, figuring that making eye contact might start a conversation, so she was startled when someone fell into step beside her. "I'm sorry, I—"

"No, I'm sorry," Isold said. "I'm afraid I've been hiding out here for the past hour."

Aderyn stopped, startled by his words. "Hiding? Why hiding? Isold, is something wrong?"

"Nothing you can help with, I fear." Isold wound his robe around both fists and tugged so the neckline sagged, an idle, frustrated gesture. "I don't understand it myself, so please don't ask me to explain. It's enough to say I didn't enjoy the attention I received."

"That seems so out of character for you. Is it that they're southerners?"

"Why would that matter?" Isold managed a smile. "If anything, I would expect to be more interested in people whose culture and attitudes are foreign. So many new things to discover. But... no. Let's just go, all right? And maybe if I sleep on it, things will become clear."

He walked on, and Aderyn hurried after him. Livia flirting with Kanan, Isold not flirting at all, Weston furious... if Owen suddenly declared he was giving up the Fated One quest to become a barman in Ikharatia, that would round out the evening nicely.

Weston and Owen sat at opposite ends of the covered wagon. Weston still looked thunderously angry. Owen gave Aderyn such a relieved look Aderyn's heart ached again, because that expression meant Weston hadn't been willing to talk it out. She climbed in after Isold. "Livia's returning later," she said, not looking Weston's way. "We can go."

Owen leaned forward to speak to the driver, who set the horses in motion. Aderyn settled next to Owen, who put his arm around her shoulders. The comforting gesture didn't soothe her as much as it usually did. Isold sat leaning forward, so drawn in on himself Aderyn couldn't imagine starting a conversation, and of course Weston looked like he never meant to speak to any of them ever again. It didn't feel like their team was breaking up—they'd been through too much together for one lousy night to do that—but if they couldn't talk to each other, maybe that was the path they were on.

"Weston," she began.

Weston's gaze flicked to her, his expression fierce, demanding her silence. Then, to her surprise, his gaze shot to the driver, whose back was to them and who didn't seem to be paying attention to anything but the horses. He gave a little negative shake of his head.

Aderyn watched the back of the driver's head for a few seconds. Then she said, "I'm glad tonight is over/*Are you faking anger?*" to Weston.

"You could say that," Weston said.

Aderyn subsided, though now curiosity took the place of unhappiness. If Weston was faking, that meant Livia had been, too, because Weston wasn't the type to placidly go along with his sweetheart making up to another man. Maybe it was her tiredness, but she couldn't imagine what the point of that game was. Whatever it was, it was something Weston didn't want to talk about in front of strangers, even one as oblivious as the driver. So Aderyn would have to exercise patience.

Exercising patience meant the short drive to the Jeweled Cuckoo Inn felt like it took an hour. Aderyn hopped down almost before the wagon came to a complete stop. "Let's meet in our room," she said over her shoulder. "Owen and I learned things you should know."

She slowed her pace so she wouldn't look ridiculous skipping up the stairs, but she still reached her door several paces ahead of Owen. Inside, she discovered the fan wasn't waving and the room was stiflingly hot. With a muttered oath, she opened the window, but it didn't help.

"Close it," Weston said. "I don't take chances." He reached past her and shut and latched the window. Owen, in the meantime, turned a wooden dial attached to a square ceramic plate set flush against the wall. Aderyn hadn't noticed it before, half hidden as it was behind a drape. The fan started flapping, slowly and then gaining speed until it sent a cooling breeze wafting through the room. Aderyn let out a deep sigh and sat on the end of the bed.

"Talk," she demanded. "What is going on? Livia was acting like she meant to sleep with Kanan, and you were acting like you couldn't stop her."

"'Acting' is the key word there," Weston said. He leaned against the wall and tilted his head back. "Kanan's attracted to Livia, and we thought we could make use of that. So Livia made up to him, and I played the jealous lover, and with luck he'll believe it."

"Okay, but why?" Owen said. "I mean, you were both believable, but I'm not sure what the point is."

"You weren't with Kanan except that one time near the beginning of the evening." Weston sounded so serious Aderyn's anxiety surged again. Weston was never serious about anything unless things were bad. "He made a point of staying close to Livia, and I'm embarrassed to say it took me a while to realize he wanted me gone so he could have her to himself. Anyway, I didn't like the way he talked about—well, everyone. He never said anything snide or derogatory, not explicitly, but he definitely resents Ruan not having gained command of the army."

"I'm not sure why that matters, either," Owen said. "Ruan didn't strike me as someone easily manipulated, so it's not like Kanan could run the army by telling Ruan what to do."

"That's why Livia and I decided on this. She was steering the conversation to find out what power the commander general has that isn't just the army. Something more subtle—though you were with Varoun, so maybe you already know." Weston grimaced. "This could all have been for nothing."

"We just talked tactics. And Varoun put me in command of a regiment. If there's anything more subtle, Varoun doesn't know about it." Aderyn twisted her robe around her finger idly, watching the colors shift as the fabric moved.

"There's more," Weston said. "Kanan dislikes Queen Devendra, and it's personal. Like she rejected his suit or something. Though it's not that, because I did a little digging of my own, and there wasn't any gossip about jilted lovers. The queen shows no interest in remarrying, which is probably for the best if that would muddy the succession issue." He began pacing from the door to the window and back, six measured steps in each direction.

"I'm afraid I learned nothing helpful," Isold said. "Unless an overview of courtship ritual and inheritance in Ikharatia is helpful. The queen can remarry and still keep her position, at least so long as she is regent, but her spouse retains his birth rank and has no claim on the throne, and any children of their union would not be princes or princesses. It's hard to see how a man of ambition would want to marry her, which means she may be doomed to loneliness."

"Trust you to find the most compassionate interpretation," Owen said. "So, Kanan wanted something non-obvious out of this contest, and he dislikes Devendra. And he's attracted to Livia and probably is the kind of guy who gets off on stealing other people's sweethearts. Nice guy."

"**[Improved Assess 3]** says Kanan's traits are 'determined, self-centered, driven, and generous,'" Aderyn said. "Which doesn't make him a villain by itself, but the first three traits, at least, are good qualities for someone who wants power."

The door opened, and Livia entered. She made straight for Weston and threw herself into his arms. "I know it was our plan, but I feel dirty," she murmured. "And like I should apologize to you."

"Dearest, you performed beautifully," Weston said, kissing her forehead and then her lips. "But I'll think twice before going with your suggestion we do that in future."

"That's bad, because I don't think it's over." Livia hugged him tightly and then stepped away. "I didn't do more than imply I'd be open to more advances, but I think I've committed myself to at least one more meeting. Which may be a good thing if we need to learn more."

"More about what?" Weston said. "I don't want you getting close to him if he's interested in pushing himself on you."

Livia shook her head. "It's not that," she said. "Kanan wants to be king."

Chapter Twenty

"Now, *that* makes sense," Owen said. "Controlling the army is historically a fast way to gain a throne, and if Kanan had any kind of control over Ruan, or could get rid of Ruan and justify taking charge of the army—"

"Slow down," Weston said. "How sure are you, Livia?"

"Maybe eighty percent sure," Livia said. "No. That's not accurate. I'm certain he wants to be king, but I'm less sure that he wants to take steps to ensure it. He might be all talk and no action. Which is why I think I should meet with him at least once more. If he has plans for a coup, we could be in danger."

"He'd need to get rid of Varoun at the least, because Varoun is loyal to Devendra and wouldn't hand over the army for the asking," Aderyn said, "and he'd have to get rid of us, because he can't assume we are opportunistic northerners who don't care who rules the Southlands. Do you know what kind of resources Kanan has, Livia? Adventurers in his pay, that sort of thing?"

Livia shrugged. "I don't know if he employs adventurers other than Ruan and Suveer, who are more like guests. But doesn't he have an army?"

"Tielana has a division of the army," Aderyn said. "All the dukes are required to maintain forces to defend their cities and to unite against a larger foe, like now. Kanan's is the second largest of those forces, with four regiments, but it's still small compared to the entire army. All those soldiers are adventurers, most of them low level, so few of them are a threat to us."

"Why is the army all adventurers?" Weston asked. "That seems like it would limit someone's adventuring possibilities. You couldn't go off on quests, for one."

"The Southlands face the threat of monster incursions often, though never on the scale the orcs represent." Owen leaned against the wall and crossed his arms over his chest. "Anyone here who accepts the Call can choose to join the army for a period of five years, during which time they receive training in working as a military team as well as increased opportunities to fight level-appropriate monsters. The kingdom also controls a number of dungeons reserved for the use of the army. It all adds up to soldiers advancing in level half again as fast as independent adventurers."

"Some of those soldiers stay with the army after their five years are up, and in this current crisis, there are also former soldiers who have reenlisted. So there are a number who are higher level," Aderyn said. "But I'm more worried about independent adventurers challenging us than Kanan sending an army to kill us. Ruan's weapons skill ranks are high, and with a Warmaster partner, he's as overpowered as Owen and would be a serious challenge."

"What, you don't think I can take that poser?" Owen said with a grin.

"A poser is someone who isn't as good as he claims. Ruan isn't that. And yes, I think you can take him, but it wouldn't be an easy fight." Aderyn sighed. "I hate to say it, but this isn't our responsibility."

"We can't let Kanan overthrow that little kid," Livia exclaimed. "Never mind that a succession crisis will destabilize the country right when it most needs stability, it's wrong to stand by and let a child be killed. Which is what it would mean."

"I know, but we have other responsibilities." Aderyn summed up Varoun's instructions, trying not to despair at how she'd already forgotten some. "If Adhiraj is overthrown, that gives the orcs the whole middle of the country they can move through freely to assault anywhere they please. Preventing that is more immediately important than stopping what might not actually be a coup."

"You're not saying our efforts were wasted, are you?" Weston said.

"No. It *is* important to know what kind of threat Kanan is, because we'll be prepared to defend against it. But doing anything more will have to wait. And I wish I didn't feel so crappy about saying that. I hate letting evil win, even in a small way."

Owen sat beside Aderyn and hugged her. "It's not letting evil win. There has to be something we can do, someone we can alert to the danger. You're supposed to meet with the queen tomorrow—maybe tell her?"

"I don't have enough evidence for you to be telling people," Livia said. "My surety is the kind that's enough for us, but anyone who doesn't know me personally will have a hard time taking it seriously. If I meet with Kanan again, maybe twice more, I'll have names and solid facts. He loves talking about how important and powerful he is, and what connections he has."

"Is that safe?" Isold said. "If he finds out you're digging for information and pretending your attraction to him... he's not the sort to think it's a funny joke when he's been humiliated. And what if things go too far, and he expects you to fall into bed with him? How far are you willing to take this, Livia?"

"It won't come to that." Livia's expression was determined. "I know how to fend off amorous advances, and like I said, I don't exactly have to dig because he gives information away like tossing bread crumbs to pigeons. I hate the idea of that little boy being in danger because Kanan is a greedy, power-hungry bastard. I'm willing to endure Kanan's attentions for a few days if it will help the king."

"Livia—" Weston sighed. "Aren't I supposed to be the idealistic one? Where's the cynical woman I fell in love with?"

"She's given precedence to the woman who has a soft spot when it comes to children," Livia said. She buried her face in Weston's shirt front for a few seconds, then raised her head and added, "If it helps, I didn't know that woman was in me until I saw that little boy sitting on the throne with his legs dangling. He's just a kid, Weston. All this nonsense about kingship is something the adults around him made up. I can't bear the thought of him suffering for that nonsense. And if pretending interest in Kanan will give me the opportunity to kick his noble dukeness in the balls someday, I'm for it."

Weston laughed and hugged Livia close. "I can't argue with that. But Aderyn's right that this isn't our immediate responsibility. What should we do?"

"I have to take official command of the army—Ishan's former regiment—in the morning," Aderyn said. "I need to know who my officers are and get them on my side. Hopefully, they'll be reasonable men—"

"No women?" Livia asked.

"Probably not. This army is heavily skewed toward the male population when it comes to its officers. But if they object to me, it could be on other grounds—it's not important now. I need to find out how things run, who's in charge of the smaller units, basically take command. Varoun gave me a quick lesson on army organization I hope I remember. Once that's settled, we—our regiment—starts moving west toward Adhiraj, which will be under siege when we arrive. We've got a few days' travel before that."

"But, as I was telling Aderyn, the five of us don't have to stay with the army," Owen said. "Aderyn will want to meet with the queen, and there's no reason you, Livia, can't spend some time with your new paramour and finesse a little more information out of him."

"That feels so strange," Isold said. "Breaking a siege is important and dangerous. It seems at odds with pleasant conversation and social subterfuge."

"Hold on," Livia said. "How are we getting from place to place? Are we talking about *world door*? Because you know it's much more difficult for me to open a *world door* anywhere that doesn't have stone to latch onto. And by 'difficult' I mean costly in terms of magical resources."

"Varoun has a <**Wand of World Door**> he will use to send us to the army. You'll only have to transport us back. But isn't that a skill you ought to develop? Not meaning to sound critical or anything, but you're the one who said your spells improve the way skills do, with use," Aderyn said.

"If we weren't fighting a war, it wouldn't matter," Livia said. "I could use up my resources experimenting, and we wouldn't be hurt by me running myself to my limit. But if I have to cast *world door* often, I won't be able to cast other spells. Are we not going to fight?"

"Ah," Aderyn said. "I hadn't thought about that. Well, for the days we're traveling, it won't matter so much, but when we arrive at Adhiraj —I guess we'll need to stay with the army at least the night before that so you can recover your resources. I'm sorry. I'm so used to you being able to cast whatever spell we need I forget they all take something out of you."

"I understand." Livia dismissed this with a wave. "All other considerations aside, I think it's important I practice *world door* so I refine my skills and see about bringing down the resource cost."

"I think we should invest in potions as well," Isold said. "Restoring Livia's magical energy via potion was key to defeating the deep delver, and while I don't think she should depend on those, they could be a valuable asset."

"I'm not going to get addicted," Livia scoffed. "But you're right about not depending on them. Assuming I'll have those potions to compensate for running through my reserves is a bad idea."

"You can get addicted to potions?" Owen said.

"Sure," Aderyn said. "My mother the Spiritsmith impressed on us kids the dangers of overusing certain potions, like physical enhancers or magic energy boosters. I know horror stories that would curl your hair. I'm still not sure how many of them were true and how many were the magical equivalent of 'don't walk in the forest at night or the bogles will eat you.'"

"So, dangerous if you're not careful."

"Like everything worth doing," Livia said. "And I'm always careful."

"Okay, if you're sure. Sounds like potion shopping needs to happen in the morning—except nobody in Ikharatia wakes up that early," Owen said with a groan. "Maybe we need to divide our efforts. Aderyn and I will go to the army first thing, Isold will shop for potions once the stores are open, and Livia will arrange a visit with Kanan, though my guess is he'll send you some kind of love note before you can contact him."

"And what will I do, fearless leader?" Weston said with a grin.

"Stalk around in public looking jealous and angry," Owen said. "Might as well sell the story as completely as possible. We'll meet back here in the evening to share information."

"What about me meeting the queen?" Aderyn asked.

"Queens always do the inviting, and I don't anticipate we'll be with the army more than a few hours. I predict there will be a royal summons waiting for you when we return." Owen frowned. "I know how we're getting to the army, but if Livia doesn't come with us, how do we get back?"

"I'm going to put that on Varoun. I hope he has some way to communicate, otherwise this will be an extremely complicated war." Aderyn leaned more comfortably into Owen. She suddenly felt exhausted. "And that's before we get to Suveer and his oddly irregular skill ranks."

"Irregular? You mean, like Jessemia was?" Isold said.

"Yes, exactly that." Aderyn summed up what she'd seen in Assessing Suveer and Ruan. "And Ruan kept me from talking to Suveer. He clearly doesn't want us to meet privately, and I don't know why."

"The most obvious reason is that Ruan knows Suveer is flawed as a Warmaster and Suveer doesn't," Weston said. "Ruan can't afford to let you be in a position to tell Suveer the truth."

"That's horrible," Aderyn said. "Ruan's his partner. What kind of awful person wants his partner to be less than his best? Especially since —" She paused. "Actually, all of Suveer's skills with high ranks were the kind that would benefit Ruan. All the paired skills, yes, but also things like **[Compel]** and **[Draw Fire]**."

"So you're saying Ruan arranged this," Owen said. "Encouraged Suveer to develop only the skills Ruan could get use from."

"I wasn't, but now I think I should." Aderyn shuddered. "That's even worse than my original idea that Ruan knows Suveer is weak and for whatever reason doesn't want him to know it. I was thinking it might even be protective, if Suveer has something wrong with him. Some mental or emotional problem."

"That's still possible," Isold said. "We shouldn't leap to conclusions.

All we know for sure is that Suveer is as crippled an adventurer as Jessemia was."

"Right. I need to talk to Suveer alone. I don't know how to do that, but there has to be a way to separate him from Ruan." Aderyn yawned. "I need sleep before I try to make any decisions. My brain is fuzzy."

"Sleep sounds great," Weston said. He glanced down at Livia, and his expression softened. "Sleep, or, you know, something sleep-adjacent."

"Take it to your own room," Owen said, grinning. "Good night, everyone."

When it was just her and Owen, Aderyn said, "I really am too tired to think, but I'm worried about Isold."

"He said practically nothing tonight, did you notice?" Owen removed his robe and pulled his shirt off over his head.

"I did. He told me he didn't enjoy having women come on to him at the party, and he didn't know why. And that he didn't think it was anything we could help with. Owen, I'm worried about him. It's not that I think he'll only be happy if he's having constant casual sex, it's that he seems down on himself for some reason. Like he doesn't like who he's become. Except he's the kindest person I know, and what could be wrong with that?"

"Then that can't be it," Owen said. "I don't know, maybe he *is* tired of casual sex. Maybe he's fallen in love with someone who doesn't love him. Maybe the pressure of pleasing a million different women has gotten to him."

"We haven't been anywhere long enough for him to fall in love, and I don't think he sees pleasing women as a hardship."

Owen shrugged. "I'm just saying there are ordinary reasons he might be feeling off his game. It doesn't have to be anything earthshattering."

"I guess you're right. I hate seeing him miserable, though."

Aderyn undressed and folded her gaudy clothes into the wardrobe. The room still felt too warm, so she lay on top of the thin blanket in her shift and drawers and took Owen's hand. "It's too hot to cuddle. Sorry."

"I feel the same way." Owen squeezed her hand lightly. "I'm having trouble remembering why we're doing all this. Being able to stop an orc invasion is important all on its own, not just because we have a quest. In fact, I feel sort of selfish caring about the **[Fated One's Destiny]** quest at all."

"I was thinking something like that myself." Idly, Aderyn brought up her Codex and focused on the **[Fated One's Destiny: Crush the Horde]** quest. The golden dot quivered and expanded into words.

An army of monstrous orcs has emerged from the Blighted Range, intent on conquering the southern human lands. Destroy their leaders and push the army back into the mountains. Recommended minimum party level for this quest is 17.

Victory conditions:
Death of ?
Death of ?
Death of ?
Death of ?
Death of ?
Orc army retreats

Reward: [75,000 XP] plus any XP gained through actions taken to complete the quest.

Aderyn gasped. "Owen, look at the quest."

Owen shifted beside her, then stilled so completely he might have frozen. "Since when are there victory conditions?"

"I bet knowing more about the war scenario opened up more information." Aderyn clutched Owen's hand tighter in excitement. "And that must mean only five orc leaders for us to defeat! I love knowing that. I was afraid it would be more like twenty."

"The system may be increasingly chatty with you, but I doubt it believes we can do the impossible." Owen rolled on his side to face her. "I agree. This feels more doable than the abstract 'destroy the leaders.' And it implies we'll gain more information, at the very least the names of the orcs we're meant to kill."

"Now I'm too filled with anticipation to sleep," Aderyn complained.

"Really?" Owen caressed her cheek. "Sounds like you need relaxing."

"Owen, it's so hot—"

Owen silenced her with a kiss that turned into several slow, passionate kisses. "You sure you care about that?"

"Not anymore," Aderyn said, and rolled him over to lie beneath her.

Chapter Twenty-One

The palm-sized oval hand mirror didn't look like anything special. Hair-fine scratches all over its silver frame gave it a matte finish that managed to look intentional rather than the result of years of wear. The mirror's surface, by contrast, had no flaws or cracks or even smudges. It was the kind of mirror someone might carry in a belt pouch if they didn't mind it getting dinged up by everything else they kept in a belt pouch. Perfectly ordinary.

Except the sockets.

Aderyn ran a finger along the curved socket at the top of the oval. It looked like someone had taken a bite out of the frame, but the groove inside was wide enough to fit a coin into. She turned the mirror over and examined the other socket, a round indentation that, again, someone could press a coin into. An abstract symbol, three curved lines and two dots, was etched into the indentation's center.

"And this will let me talk to you?" she asked Varoun.

"It's an improvement on a scrying mirror," Varoun said. "A two-way scrying mirror, to be precise. A <**Farspeaker**>."

"That's amazing," Weston said. "I've never heard of a magic item that could do that. What dungeon did it come from?"

"No dungeon. It was created by Spellcrafters in Ikharatia. They guard the secret of its construction more carefully than the king's treasure vault. Only they know how to make them, and only they know how to repair and maintain them."

"But someone could reverse engineer it, right? Um. I mean, study it and figure out how to make a new one?" Owen didn't show more than a moment's dismay at having said something that marked him as an otherworlder.

"I understand there are safeguards that prevent such an action. Reverse engineer, that's an odd phrase, but it's evocative." Varoun took the mirror from Aderyn. "I'll show you how to use it. It's a simple activation, but there are details you need to know."

He took a thick piece of folded cardboard from within his robe and opened it. Inside were round recesses cut to the size of a coin an inch and a half across, bigger than the biggest gold piece. Aderyn counted twenty recesses, but only twelve were filled, with coins too shiny to be real silver. Each coin had an abstract symbol engraved on its face, random lines and curves and dots. Varoun removed one from its recess and turned it over, revealing the back side was identical to the front.

"To attune the mirror to the person you wish to speak to, you insert the corresponding coin here." Varoun slid the coin into the slot at the top of the mirror. The mirror's surface immediately misted over with a thick fog that roiled and churned for a few seconds before disappearing.

Chandar's face appeared in the tiny oval. "Commander?"

"I'm just demonstrating the **<Farspeaker>** to General Aderyn," Varoun said. "Sorry to disturb. Please, carry on." He passed his hand flat across the surface of the mirror, right to left, and Chandar's image vanished.

Aderyn closed her mouth so she wasn't gaping in astonishment. "That's incredible."

"Does everyone in the Southlands have these?" Livia asked. She looked like she wished she could snatch the mirror out of Varoun's hand to look at it more closely.

"They're extremely expensive and of limited use." Varoun removed the coin from the slot and returned it to its recess in the card. "Each person must have their own mirror, and a token attuned to the other person's mirror... after about fifteen tokens, it becomes difficult to keep track. The Army uses most of the existing <**Farspeakers**>, and of course the king, or his regent, communicates with his dukes regularly."

He turned the mirror over and pressed the tip of his forefinger to the center of the recess on the mirror's back, holding it there for a count of five. When he removed his finger, a snap of blue-white electricity made a spiderweb across the space and vanished. In its place, a shiny coin appeared. It bore a symbol that matched the one etched on the recess. Varoun pried it out and slotted it into an empty recess in his coin card.

"The <**Farspeaker**> has the capacity to create five tokens attuned to it each day," he said. "This one will allow me to communicate with you. The device was formerly Ishan's <**Farspeaker**>, and of course I don't maintain connections with my generals' officers. It's too easy to jump the chain of command. But that means only I and General Ananyi can speak to you. You'll probably be grateful for that."

"What about me speaking to someone else? Don't I need a set of coins?"

"Of course." Varoun removed four coins from his card. "This one is mine. This one is for General Ananyi, who bears direct responsibility for your regiment. This is for General Chandar, and this one connects to General Rajman. I'm afraid I don't have one for General Tamil at Adhiraj just yet, but I will get that to you in a day or two." Varoun displayed each coin long enough for Aderyn to memorize the symbols. Chandar's was sort of shaped like a C, and Ananyi's looked a little like a lowercase A, which helped.

Varoun gave her a small pouch to put the coins in so she didn't have to dig through the <**Purse of Great Capacity**> to find them. "As I said, Colonel Ishan's regiment is part of the Ikharatia division, and you will coordinate with General Ananyi by keeping him informed of your movements, but you outrank him and he won't give you orders. I realize this is an unusual situation, but I have no one I can promote that wouldn't leave a hole somewhere else. So your command of the regiment will be for the extent of the Adhiraj siege, understand?"

"I do." Aderyn slipped the <**Farspeaker**> into the pouch with the coins. "And the other coins are because I'm second in command, right?"

"That's right. You'll need to be able to communicate with those generals as I do." Varoun suddenly smiled. "This is all very new to you, isn't it?"

"Of course! It's not like I've ever commanded an army before. I feel confident, if that helps. And I'm sure there are other officers who will know how a regiment works in practical terms." Aderyn glanced at Owen. "But, about my friends—"

"They'll make up their own team," Varoun said. "You recall what I taught you about army structure?"

"The fundamental unit is the platoon, which is six teams of six each," Aderyn said. "Or as close to six as possible, to make use of the system's benefits to adventuring teams. Three platoons make a company, three companies make a battalion, and two battalions make a regiment. And the platoons can be broken down into teams if necessary, based on their specializations." She remembered the words because Owen had been vocally surprised at how closely her world's military structure echoed his—or, rather, how much his world remembered from the prime world.

"Very good." Varoun managed not to sound condescending, though Aderyn thought, given the differences in their military experience, condescension might be justified. "I understand Warmasters and their partners share benefits from fighting as a pair, and with you being a member of a team, it's doubly sensible that your friends stay with you, directly under your command." He raised an eyebrow at Owen. "If you think you can handle that, Fated One."

"She tells us what to do in a fight all the time," Owen said. "I don't see how this is any different."

"That's the right attitude." Varoun saluted Aderyn in the gesture used by equals, first two fingers of the right hand touching the left shoulder. Aderyn returned it, feeling awkward. Maybe she wasn't as confident as she thought.

"One other thing," Varoun said. "We will need someone to take permanent command of this regiment. I want you to evaluate Majors Sahal and Kavish and make your recommendation as to who is ready for promotion. If you feel confident, go ahead and promote that person immediately. I have need of you elsewhere."

"All right, commander." *That* was intimidating, choosing a new leader for a large military unit. "I'll do my best."

"Then, if you're ready, I'll send you to join your regiment." Varoun pulled out the black wand. "Are you all going?"

"I'm staying behind," Weston said. "I have some moping to do."

Varoun gave him a puzzled look, but said nothing.

"It's just Owen and me this morning," Aderyn said quickly.

"We meet back at the inn this evening, all right?" Owen said.

Everyone nodded. Aderyn's eye was drawn to Isold, who hadn't said anything since breakfast. He didn't look despondent, just attentive, so maybe she was reading too much into his silence.

"Then we'll see you all later," Owen continued. "General, we're ready."

"I'd like to watch, if that's all right," Livia said. "I wondered if the **<Wand of World Door>** casts a spell that looks different from mine."

"It's no trouble. I don't need quiet or solitude." Varoun concentrated, then swished the wand in the familiar activation pattern. A rush of light that looked like flowing purple water shot from the wand's tip. The air shimmered and formed into an ebony arch through which wavering, hazy shapes were visible as if seen through deep water. "What do you think?"

"It's mostly the same, but much more refined than mine," Livia said, "though that could be because I'm inexperienced. I still say that's the most impressive magic item I've ever heard of. The **<Farspeaker>** is amazing, but I don't think you non-spellslingers appreciate how much raw magical power is bound up in that wand. Not needing to *scry* a location—that alone makes it extraordinary."

"It is precious to us, and I consider it an honor to be gifted its use." Varoun waved a hand in the *world door's* direction. "General?"

"Oh! Of course." Aderyn stepped through the black arch into the strange confines of *world door*. Livia was right that it was more refined than hers; the floor was only barely springy, and the walls were clear and sparkled like crystal on a bright morning instead of showing dim, shadowy shapes that unnerved Aderyn.

She focused on the end of the short tunnel. By this time, she'd experienced the spell often enough to be familiar with how the exit always felt like it didn't draw nearer no matter how many steps she took—and then she was through, stumbling at the abruptness. Behind her, the black oval disappeared with a snap like the crack of a whip.

World door had spat her out on a plain, so different from the humid forest of the war game Aderyn couldn't believe it was the same country. Tents surrounded her, drab canvas tents no taller than three feet that were dingy with mud and much use. Men and a few women dressed in gray uniforms stared at her with such astonishment her cheeks heated at the attention. She had no idea what to say. She settled for nodding politely, as there was no salute from a general to an ordinary soldier.

Another whipcrack behind her told her Owen had come through. She didn't turn around as he put a hand on her shoulder, but the gesture steadied her. Calmly, in a voice she hoped conveyed authority, she said, "I'm General Aderyn. Can someone direct me to Major Sahal or Major Kavish?"

Most of the soldiers took on the glassy-eyed look of someone Assessing another. One of the men said, "General, Major Sahal is on the perimeter, and Major Kavish is at the command tent. I can take you there."

"Thank you, um, soldier, I would appreciate that."

"It's 'private,'" Owen whispered in her ear. Aderyn nodded thanks. Here only five seconds and already she'd screwed up. With luck, this small slip of memory would be the worst thing she did today.

They walked through the camp following their guide. Everywhere they passed, soldiers stopped what they were doing to stand rigidly at attention. Aderyn stopped acknowledging them after the first ten. They clearly didn't expect her to give them special attention, and she was more interested in the camp. She didn't like what she saw. Dirty tents, that was nothing. The ground was muddy enough to make it clear they'd experienced several days of rain. But the ground was churned up in a way that suggested the camp had been there for more than a few days, and clutter surrounded several tents—clutter that made the camp look disorganized and ramshackle.

She saw the command tent well before they reached it. It was considerably taller than the other tents, and cleaner, with a canopy covering the entrance and a muddy rug in front of the tent flap that would probably put more mud on someone's boots than it removed. Her guide stopped to one side of the entrance and saluted. "General, sir. Er, ma'am," he said, not sounding embarrassed by his slip.

"That's all right," Aderyn said. She hadn't given any consideration to how she should be addressed, and now she was finally here, she discovered she didn't care. With Owen behind her, she pushed the flap aside and entered the command tent.

Four chairs surrounded a makeshift table at the center of the room, but none of them were occupied. A middle-aged man with a very dark complexion and no hair leaned back in a seat behind another table, this one narrower and made of thin boards that made it look flimsy. Since the man had his feet propped on the table, it couldn't be as flimsy as it looked, but when he jerked himself upright, Aderyn still expected the table to collapse.

"You're the northerner general," he said, his voice hoarse like he'd been crying, though his eyes were clear and dry. "It's about thundering time. Is it true Colonel Ishan has been demoted?"

"Not demoted, kicked out." Aderyn wished she knew what the official military term was. "He no longer has rank."

Kavish's eyes widened. He rubbed them like he didn't believe what he saw, as if Aderyn was somehow remarkable, then blinked rapidly. "Cashiered, was he? I thought he deserved discipline, but I didn't think... well."

"It wasn't that bad, but it was public. Ishan ran out of goodwill, and General Varoun decided to make an example of him," Owen said. Aderyn was increasingly grateful that Owen's knowledge about his own world's military translated to hers. She'd never heard the term "cashiered" before.

"I can't say I blame the commander," Kavish said. He blinked once more and straightened. "It doesn't matter. General, I and this regiment are yours to command."

Chapter Twenty-Two

"I expected more resistance," Aderyn whispered to Owen four hours later as they waited at the camp's outskirts for one of Raven Regiment's Windwardens to join them. There wasn't anyone close enough to overhear, probably, but Aderyn didn't want to take any chances. Letting on that she wasn't certain about her new command was the kind of thing that led to her troops losing confidence in her. Her troops. That was still a strange notion, but she was growing accustomed to it.

"I think Colonel Ishan's behavior lowered morale more than we realized." Owen kept his voice low as well. "Did you see how relieved Major Sahal was when you were introduced? Like he'd expected the worst."

"Yes, but I'm still young, female, and a northerner. None of that bothered them, and maybe it should have." Aderyn sighed. "I'm borrowing trouble, aren't I? I should be grateful it was so easy, because none of the rest of this will be."

"Right."

Aderyn surveyed her surroundings—not the camp, whose condition still disheartened her despite the renewed activity of soldiers cleaning up the messes and preparing to strike the tents, but the land beyond.

Thickets of trees to the north marked the beginnings of another forest, but in every other direction, plains extended to the horizon. The air was as muggy as always, and now that the sun was almost at its zenith, its rays beat down on Aderyn fiercely enough to make her wish for a hat, or a sunshade like she'd seen some people carry in Ikharatia. The air felt thick enough she imagined she could see it undulating in waves.

"I'm not built for this climate," she said. "Sweating would be a relief if there was a breeze. As it is, I just feel sticky. And the sun feels like it's beating on me with a hammer."

"You'll get used to it, I promise," Owen said. "I'll buy you a parasol."

"You don't think that will make me look unmilitary?"

"Remember Douglas MacArthur? He never cared what people thought. I'm sure he'd have carried a parasol if he'd thought of it. I bet the Philippines are as hot and humid as this. Look, there's the Windwarden. I'm glad Varoun had a plan for how we were getting back."

Major Kavish and Major Sahal were with the Windwarden, a thin, tall man named Kimay who looked so like a typical Windwarden it amused Aderyn. Apparently it didn't matter where you were born as far as stereotypes went. Major Sahal, on the other hand, didn't fit any stereotypes Aderyn knew about, though maybe she just didn't have expectations of what military officers should look like. He and Major Kavish were identical in build and height, though Sahal had a full head of curly black hair, and they were both Staffsworn, so maybe that was the stereotype.

Both majors saluted as they drew near, with Kimay following suit a second behind. "General, breaking camp is nearly finished, and we'll move out in the next half hour," Sahal said.

"Good. I'll be back tomorrow morning with another device so we can communicate." Aderyn tapped the pouch holding her **<Farspeaker>**. She hoped it was a promise she could keep, given how rare **<Farspeakers>** apparently were. If not, she was confident Varoun had a different solution.

"If there's a crisis, one of us will come to you," Kavish said, nodding at Kimay, who startled at the sudden attention as if he had been distracted by staring at Aderyn. She'd only met him once before now, and he'd stared at her then, too. He didn't have any of the self-confidence she associated with a level sixteen adventurer, which he had to be if he knew *world door*.

"The route is direct," Sahal added, "and we anticipate arriving at Adhiraj in three days. There's no way to shorten that time without exhausting everyone."

"I understand. Thank you both." Aderyn saluted the way Varoun had showed her and received their somewhat more formal salutes in return. "Veteran Kimay, please cast *world door* to Ikharatia."

Kimay nodded and raised both hands like he meant to take a box off a high shelf. Aderyn had reservations about calling anyone as diffident as Kimay "veteran," but that part of Varoun's instruction about military ranks had stuck. All soldiers serving their five years were called "private," as Owen had reminded her; soldiers who stayed on past five years or who reenlisted were "veteran;" platoon officers were "lieutenant" and company leaders "captain." She didn't remember all the types of teams aside from "slammers," the ones who did damage up close, but after two hours of talking to the majors and touring the camp, she felt better about her occasional missteps. Sahal and Kavish were helpful and not at all critical if she asked questions.

With a snap, a wooden circle appeared, the air within it rippling faster and more visibly than Aderyn had imagined the actual moisture-laden air doing. She thanked Kimay and entered the circle.

For the few seconds it took to traverse the *world door*, she imagined what she would do if Kimay was a traitor and this passage spat her out somewhere inhospitable. Nothing, of course. She was at his mercy. But it did get her thinking about whether there was a way to prove where a *world door* led to. Something to ask Livia.

That led her to worrying about what Livia was doing now. A messenger had delivered a note from Kanan to their inn that morning, asking Livia's presence at a private luncheon. Aderyn didn't think Livia was in any physical danger, and it wasn't as if *stone fist* wasn't an effective deterrent to unwanted attention, but it couldn't be easy for Livia to lie about being attracted to Kanan. But Livia had said, "This is how it's going to be. I'll learn what Kanan has in mind, and then it's over," and no one had argued, not even Weston, who had looked even less happy than Aderyn.

She stumbled as *world door* came to an end and caught herself. Kimay hadn't betrayed her; she was at the iron gate on the east side of the city. Neither of the guards reacted to her sudden appearance. Their stoic calm impressed Aderyn.

She waited for Owen to appear through his own wooden circle. Owen eyed the guards as if he, too, found their poise impressive. "I shouldn't bug them, but it's tempting," he said. "Are we going to find Varoun?"

"I thought about it, but I can tell him the regiment is moving just as well using the **<Farspeaker>**. In fact, I'm going to do that once we return to the inn. I want to see what Isold bought, and I'm worried about Weston."

Owen grabbed Aderyn's hand and brought her to a stop before she could take three steps. "We're getting a pedicab. No sense walking in this heat."

"You have such good ideas," Aderyn sighed.

Back at the Jeweled Cuckoo Inn, Aderyn spoke briefly to Varoun, then retied her hair so it left her neck bare and sponged down her face and neck with lukewarm water. Isold entered the room as she was standing beneath the ever-waving fan, letting its breeze cool her damp skin. "This weather does make one consider the benefits of near-nudity, doesn't it?" he said, and his wry tone of voice relieved her mind, it was so normal.

"I guess the sun would burn us red, so there's no winning solution, is there?" Aderyn replied.

"Too true." Isold seated himself on a chair near the window. "Owen went to roust Weston. I'm afraid his sulks and anger aren't as faked as we might hope."

And just like that, Aderyn's good mood evaporated. "I was afraid of that. I know he doesn't think Livia would ever be attracted to that man, but this still can't be easy on either of them."

"I believe he's worried about the possibility Kanan will realize he's being played. We don't know how dangerous Kanan is." Isold set his knapsack on his lap and began rummaging through it.

"Livia can take care of herself."

"There are many dangers that don't respond to being punched," Isold said. "Wait. What's this?"

He sounded so surprised Aderyn hurried to his side. "Did you find something?"

"Yes, and no." Isold withdrew a fat brass cylinder the length of his hand that tapered at one end. Aderyn recognized it as one of the strange writing implements they'd found in the Enchanterium, with four switches at the stubby end that controlled four different nibs. "I haven't looked at this since reaching level sixteen, and it seems my **[Identify Magic Items]** skill has grown enough to give me information about it." He turned it over in his fingers, examining it. "It's called a <**Draftsman's Pen**>."

"Wait!" Aderyn dug in her <**Purse of Great Capacity**> and pulled out the second one. "What does it do? We already know the black nib duplicates whatever was just written. And the white one didn't seem to do anything."

"The white nib writes in white ink on a dark surface, which is why it seemed to do nothing before," Isold explained. "The blue nib allows the user to write when the pen is immersed in liquid. And the red nib produces invisible ink, revealed by heat."

"Amazing." Aderyn reached for the basin filled with water, then hesitated. "What good is writing underwater? The paper would disintegrate."

"I believe it writes on any hard, flat surface," Isold said. "Try it."

Aderyn pushed the switch to extend the blue nib. It was fatter than the black and white ones, and dark blue ink pooled at its tip. She was sure the ink would wash away once she dipped the pen in the basin, but she lowered her hand into the water anyway and wrote her name across the bottom of the porcelain basin. Thick blue lines followed the moving nib, and Aderyn stared at her name, written in bold lines that looked as if they'd been tattooed on the basin.

"Hmm," Aderyn said. "Maybe I shouldn't have defaced this inn's property."

"We can afford to pay a little in the pursuit of knowledge," Isold said with a smile. "It's the invisible ink I'm most interested in. What a pity we didn't know to send this with Livia in case of emergency."

The door opened, and Owen entered, followed by Weston. Weston didn't look as angry or unhappy as Aderyn had feared, but he moved as if he expected to take a punch at any moment. "I don't want to talk about it," he told Aderyn. "Like I said to Owen, either this works or it doesn't, and all we can do is hope for the best. Though I scouted the location where Kanan asked Livia to meet him, and I'm going back there in a little while. Might as well skulk around like a jealous lover."

"And you'll be close in case the worst happens," Aderyn said.

"That's right." Weston spun the other chair around and straddled it backwards. "Give me some good news. How did things go with the army?"

"Surprisingly well. The majors are competent and they accepted my leadership with no argument. The camp is mostly recovered from dysentery and they were readying to march when we left. My overall impression is that Colonel Ishan is a posturing glory-hound who had a lot of genuine military successes under his belt, and he let that go to his head. Major Kavish wouldn't speak directly against him, but neither he nor Major Sahal concealed the fact that Ishan basically abandoned his post when the outbreak started. They seemed surprised that nothing worse had happened to the man than being stripped of his command."

"That surprised me too, honestly," Owen said. "It's so weird the things that are the same here as in my world, and the things that are different. Most of the ranks have the same names, though my world refined on them, but everything here strikes me as much less disciplined."

"Your world doesn't have soldiers who are adventurers," Aderyn pointed out. "The discipline you described wouldn't work here. Everyone's in it for experience, both individual and what they get from successfully winning a battle, and I'm not sure the promise of the latter is always enough to keep soldiers from haring off after the former."

"Is that why adventurers enlist in the army?" Isold asked. "The promise of experience?"

"Varoun says fighting a battle is like accepting a quest." Aderyn sat on the end of the bed, since the chairs were taken. "You get experience for the monsters you kill, but you get more experience from completing the battle 'quest.' It's how they keep discipline. Everyone has incentive to follow orders because they trust that those orders will result in a win."

"But that does mean the soldiers of your world are individualists, and in my world, the military trains that out of you," Owen said. "And now I think about it, it makes sense that your world does it this way. You need each soldier's initiative for the army to run smoothly."

Aderyn nodded. "I got the feeling that my regiment—oh, that still sounds strange!—that they had lost morale not just because of illness, but from Ishan not being a responsible leader. He certainly struck me as self-centered."

"If Ishan's behavior means the regiment is starved for responsible command, that benefits you, which is all I care about." Owen sat beside her.

"That's true. Anyway, each team has a specialty, and they get direction from their lieutenants, who receive orders from their captains, who take their orders from me—the majors are more administrative leaders, they take care of internal discipline and logistics—and I get my orders from Varoun. Except those orders are usually along the lines of 'relieve the siege at Adhiraj,' and the details are my business."

"Intimidating," Weston said.

"You'd think so, right? But really, it's reassuring that I don't have to run my strategy past someone else. Of course, that means I'm entirely responsible if it fails. But I do have to make sure the captains all know enough to execute the strategy without any hand-holding, and get information from the majors about regimental needs, *and* coordinate with the other colonels and generals about timing and so forth." Aderyn groaned. "I didn't think command would have so much talking involved."

"The higher the rank, the more the administration," Owen said.

"I'll be happier when I can see the enemy. That's got an obvious solution." Aderyn flopped back onto the bed and stared at the fan. "Isold, what did you get us?"

"Many, many potions," Isold said, "despite the poor exchange rate. Take a look."

Aderyn sat up and watched Isold remove several bundles of rolled-up leather. "Three magic energy potions for Livia, three **<Potions of Life>**, six of those weapon blanch oils we used against the deep delver, and four **<Potions of Strength>**."

He extracted a glass bulb whose cork was sealed so thoroughly with wax there was no way it could be opened in the heat of battle. Its contents roiled like pale gray storm clouds with flashes of lightning occasionally visible. "I also bought some of these **<Death Cloud>** potions. The bulb shatters on impact and frees a cloud that clings to the person or object it strikes."

"And kills them?" Weston asked.

"Sadly, no. But it does occlude that person's vision and hits them with an electrical attack. There are four." Isold put the bulb away and located another item, this one a metal tube with a cap instead of a cork. "And there were only two of these, but I felt inspired to take them anyway. The shopkeeper called them **<Zaps>** and said drinking one will *transport* the drinker instantly wherever the person is looking, with a range of one hundred yards. It's an intriguing idea."

"I like it," Owen said. "I'm not sure when we'd use it, given that Livia can cast *transport* far more efficiently, but it's the sort of thing that if you need it, you really need it."

"Precisely." Isold wrapped everything back up and stowed the rolls in the satchel.

A knock on the door brought Aderyn to her feet. When she opened it, a young woman barely in her teens stood there. Aderyn remembered seeing her around the inn. The girl bobbed a curtsey to Aderyn. "There's a message for you, miss, and one for the big man, but he's not in his room."

"Here," Weston said.

The girl handed Aderyn and Weston each a folded piece of paper and ran off. Aderyn's was folded in thirds and sealed, while Weston's was folded into uneven quarters. Aderyn broke the seal and scanned the contents. "It's the invitation from the queen, for a late luncheon at three this afternoon. That gives me something to do."

"You've got something to do now," Weston said. He held his unfolded paper crushed in one hand. "Livia's in trouble."

Chapter Twenty-Three

Weston explained as they hurried down the stairs. "We arranged a system in case Livia needed help," he said. "Code phrases for her to put in a message. This one means, 'I need you to get me out of this.'"

"Kanan can't have discovered the truth, or he wouldn't have let her send a message," Owen pointed out.

"Yes, and if she were in that much danger, we had a different plan. This one means Kanan started getting too friendly and she can't stop him without ruining our scheme." Weston sounded grim enough Aderyn didn't think highly of Kanan surviving an encounter with the giant Moonlighter unscathed.

"So, what will we do? Given that we can't reveal the scheme, either," Isold said.

They exited the inn, and Owen waved down a pedicab. "These only seat two. Somebody get another one. We'll figure something out on the way."

Aderyn sat beside Owen in their pedicab, feeling guilty at how resentful she was that the driver couldn't go faster. He was pedaling in this heat, which was more than Aderyn could do. To distract herself, she said, "I could say it's a military thing, and I need all my auxiliaries.

Kanan can't argue with that, and it's plausible. That I need Livia for *world door*."

"We don't even have to say that much." Owen's gaze was fixed on the driver's heaving back, and Aderyn thought he might be willing the driver to increase his speed, too. "Complicating a lie makes it more likely to be disbelieved. Stick with 'military emergency' and that's enough."

"True. I guess I'm worried it won't be enough."

The streets weren't busy at noon, which made Aderyn feel even guiltier that they were making the pedicab driver exert himself at the height of the day's heat. She reminded herself that pedicab drivers didn't earn much, and he probably welcomed their business during the slow part of his day, and got on with being grateful that there wasn't enough traffic to slow their progress.

Duke Kanan's residence looked just like all the other buildings: walls built of enormous pink-cream stones, narrow windows, high ceilings. It differed by being surrounded by a narrow strip of greenery, low bushes with fluffy emerald leaves between small trees with slim trunks. Its cool appearance and shade led Aderyn to speculate about how much work it took to keep the garden from overgrowing its bounds. In this climate, that seemed a likely possibility.

She and Owen waited on the sidewalk outside the mansion for Weston and Isold to arrive. When Weston alighted from his pedicab, he said, "You should say you need Livia for military business."

"That's what we decided, too." Aderyn waited for Isold to pay the pedicab driver, then led the way up the short walk to the front door. No guards waited there, but Aderyn didn't kid herself that made the mansion less defensible.

She pulled the bell rope and settled in to wait, making herself hold still rather than fidget with impatience and worry about what Livia might be dealing with. But instead the door opened immediately, revealing a guard wearing a blue and gold shirt beneath his leather armor. "Do you have an appointment with my lord?"

"I don't. I'm General Aderyn, and my business is with Duke Kanan's guest, the Earthbreaker Livia." Aderyn didn't even have to try to keep her voice steady. Now that the moment had come, she felt calm, and even without Assessing the guard she knew he was no threat to her no matter how intimidating he looked.

"His guest?" The guard looked surprised.

"Military business. Either send word that Livia is to join me immediately, or let me pass so I can carry the message myself." Aderyn captured the guard's gaze and held it so the man would feel her authority.

"I—come in." The guard still sounded confused, and Aderyn rated his competence a notch lower. "You can wait here while I summon, I mean while I ask my lord's guest to join you." He backed away from the door.

Aderyn didn't wait to press her advantage. She followed him into a wide, high-ceilinged room tiled on floor and ceiling in shades of blue and green that made it look cool and comfortable, though there was an actual cool breeze coming from somewhere. "I would also like to speak to Suveer," she said, inspired. "One Warmaster to another."

The guard actually bowed like Aderyn was a queen. "Yes, general. Please wait here." He opened one of the two doors opposite the entrance and disappeared past it.

"You really want to talk to Suveer now?" Weston exclaimed.

"I figure this is as good a time as any, especially since Ruan won't know about it to stop the meeting." Aderyn gave in to her fidgets and began pacing a line between the front door and the one the guard had left by. The floor tiles didn't make a pattern she could identify, but the randomness gave the floor the look of the ocean on a sunny day. The cool breeze relaxed her after the heat of the day. Too bad the inn didn't have this feature, though the fan was usually enough to keep her room from being unbearably hot.

It took forever before the door opened again. Aderyn stopped pacing. It had occurred to her during that waiting time, when none of them had spoken, that if Livia arrived first, they'd have to go without talking to Suveer or risk looking suspicious. To her relief, it was Suveer himself. He trudged forward and stopped about five feet from Aderyn, his head still bowed like he couldn't bear to meet her eyes.

When he didn't say anything, Aderyn said, "Hi, Suveer. It's good to see you again."

"I suppose," Suveer said. "Are you here to take over?"

"What?" Aderyn frowned. "Take over? Take over what?"

"Our position here," Suveer said. "That's what Ruan says."

"Um, no," Aderyn said. "I just want to talk to you. We might be the highest-level Warmasters in the world—don't you think that's interesting?"

Suveer shrugged. "I wouldn't be anything without Ruan. I'm not sure it's interesting to have a useless class."

Dumbfounded, Aderyn could only stare. "Useless? You have a partner, that's not—"

The door banged open again, and Ruan appeared. "Aderyn! I meant to send word. I don't know if you're available tomorrow night, but we were hoping to get together for that dinner we talked about." He put an arm around Suveer's shoulders. "Suveer, you've got to be exhausted, as hot as today is. How about you go upstairs?"

"It's practically freezing in here," Aderyn exclaimed. "I think you—"

The door banged open a third time, and Aderyn threw up her hands and said, "What now?"

"Sorry," Livia said. "I thought the situation was urgent, since I know you wouldn't pull me away from Kanan's company without a *good reason.*" She put emphasis on the last two words that pulled Aderyn back to the problem at hand.

"You're right," she said. "We should go. Military business. Ruan, dinner tomorrow will be fine. Suveer, thanks for talking to me." She turned on her heel and stalked out, not bothering to conceal her frustration. She was sure Ruan was laughing at how neatly he'd interfered in her attempt to get Suveer alone. Well, she wasn't giving up. Ruan was clearly controlling Suveer, and she meant to find out why.

"Back to the inn," she snapped when they were on the sidewalk again.

"Calm down, Aderyn," Owen said. "There's nothing more we can do about Suveer now."

"Didn't you hear? Suveer all but confirmed his brother is keeping him down. Why else would he believe Warmaster is a useless class?"

"I heard." Owen put an arm around her shoulders and hugged her. "We'll figure it out. But not right now. Livia needs us."

Aderyn finally looked directly at Livia. She stood alone, her back to Weston like she shunned him, but her mouth was pinched tight and her eyes were glassy with unshed tears. Remorse struck Aderyn, but she remembered in time that they were in front of Kanan's mansion where he or his servants might see, and as far as she knew, they still needed to keep up Livia's pretense. So she said, more calmly, "Sorry. Let's get back to the inn and I'll explain what military business we have next."

They rode back to the inn in a canopied wagon rather than pedicabs, but no one spoke, not even about banal topics like the weather. Aderyn kept an eye on Livia, who gradually relaxed until she no longer looked like she was going to have an emotional breakdown. It hurt to see Livia and Weston ignore each other, even though Aderyn knew it was fake. Even if this ruse produced results, Aderyn wasn't sure it was worth it.

Back at the inn, they gathered in Aderyn and Owen's room once more. Owen started to speak, but Aderyn's hand on his arm silenced him as Livia buried her face in Weston's broad chest and sobbed. That shocked Aderyn more than a screaming fit would have. Livia never cried, not in all the many times Weston had been badly injured, not even when *she* had been badly injured. Part of Aderyn felt she shouldn't witness this moment, but it was overridden by her knowledge that Livia needed their support more than she needed privacy.

When Livia's sobs dried up, Weston held her a few moments longer before saying, "Can you talk about it now?"

Livia nodded. She swiped an arm across her eyes. "I've never felt so helpless. I wasn't in any physical danger, but if I hadn't played for time—if you all hadn't arrived when you did—I either had to blow the whole game or..." She swallowed. "And I don't think I'd feel differently about Kanan if I was unattached. His attention feels like spiders crawling over my scalp, like it's something unsavory even though he never does anything weird."

"You don't have to continue," Weston said. "This knowledge isn't worth it."

"I agree." Livia drew in a deep breath. "He mentioned several names as being his allies and hinted that they agree it's time for a 'change in direction' for the Southlands. We can give those names to the queen, and that's it. The next time I go to Kanan, it's going to be so I can beat notions of usurpation out of his head."

"That's more like it," Owen said. "You're not weak. And you're not helpless."

"I know. I just felt trapped by this persona I made up. Now that I'm away from Kanan, I'm angry and in a mood to punch something. *Do* we have urgent military business? I could stand to kill a few dozen orcs right now." Livia smiled, and if it wasn't as firm a smile as usual, it was still a smile.

"We don't, sorry," Aderyn said. "In two days, we'll join the army in its march, and on the third day we'll reach Adhiraj and the fighting will start. For us, I mean. The city's already under siege."

"I guess I can survive that long," Livia said with a sigh.

"We have other things to worry about before that," Owen said. "Aderyn?"

"You're not going to believe this," Aderyn said. "Remember how Suveer has those strangely uneven skill ranks? I'm now sure Ruan is conspiring to keep them low. I don't know how he managed it, but Suveer believes the Warmaster class is useless even at level fifteen."

"That's insane. Why would a partner want that?" Livia sat in one of the chairs, but kept hold of Weston's hand. "How could he guarantee it wouldn't hurt him?"

"I—actually, I hadn't thought of that." Aderyn frowned.

"Suveer isn't a very strong personality," Owen said. "If Ruan could convince him that he was doing him a favor or something by partnering with him, he could get Suveer to go along with almost anything he proposed. Like telling him he didn't need to practice certain skills because they didn't benefit both of them—though really he'd mean they didn't benefit *Ruan*."

"This is all speculation, though it's solid enough I believe it," Isold said. "The point is that we don't know enough to do anything with it. And what's the goal? We can't boost Suveer's skill ranks."

"We can prove to him that Warmaster isn't a useless class," Aderyn said. "We can try to get him away from Ruan's control. I can't bear thinking that Suveer is wasting his potential. He might as well not be a Warmaster with a partner for all it benefits him."

"If we can think of that, you can bet Ruan has," Weston said. "You want to bet he comes up with a reason to cancel that dinner? He's worked so hard to keep Suveer away from Aderyn he has to know the danger to him."

"I wouldn't take that bet, dearest," Livia said.

"Neither would I," Owen said. "Let's forget about Ruan for now—no, I don't mean that, because now is the time to relax and let our subconscious minds work out a solution. Food, and a midday rest, and then Aderyn will meet with the queen and give her that list of names."

Livia brightened. "You're meeting her today? I'll write down everything I learned. Then maybe I won't feel so awful."

Weston gave her a one-armed hug. "You accomplished something important and protected the king. You should feel proud."

"Maybe when I don't feel quite so much like I nearly sacrificed my principles," Livia said. "And myself."

Chapter Twenty-Four

Aderyn emerged from the Jeweled Cuckoo Inn that afternoon anticipating hiring a pedicab to take her to the palace. Instead, she stopped short of walking into a carriage ornate with gilding and creamy white paint that glowed in the sunlight. Two horses much nicer than the ones she'd seen driving the people-wagons stood in the traces, tossing their manes restlessly as if they were impatient to move. A man dressed in the royal colors of dark gray and pale gold stood beside the carriage door and opened it when Aderyn appeared. "Madam general, your conveyance," he said in a tone grand enough to make Aderyn feel she ought to bow to him.

"Thank you," she said instead, and climbed without help up the two little metal steps and into the carriage. The luxury continued there, with thickly padded seats upholstered in golden velvet and glass windows instead of openings. Glass seemed like a mistake, given that it would heat the interior of the carriage to uncomfortable levels, but when the servant closed the door, a cold breeze began circulating, cooling the air until Aderyn was nearly uncomfortable for the opposite reason. The icy atmosphere reminded her that it was winter in the north. Heat and humidity aside, she wasn't sure she missed it.

She spent the journey to the palace not watching the people and buildings they passed, but mentally rehearsing what she'd tell the queen. She had Livia's list in her pocket, but she couldn't just burst out with "Duke Kanan is a traitor and dangerous." Even with her virtually nonexistent knowledge about nobility and royalty, she knew that was a mistake. She'd have to find a way to work around to the topic.

At the palace door, another servant dressed identically to the first, but female, bowed to her and said, "This way, madam general." Aderyn followed, trying again not to be intimidated. If a servant could cow her, what chance did she have against a queen?

The servant led her, not to one of the many sumptuous rooms, but outdoors again, to a grassy courtyard filled with trees and flowering bushes. The boldly-colored flowers weren't like anything Aderyn had seen in the north, with their fat, elongated petals that formed blossoms as big as Aderyn's head. Varying from yellow to deep crimson to a pink Aderyn would have sworn did not exist in nature, they emitted a sweet scent that indoors would have overpowered any gathering. Outdoors, with a breeze tossing the bushes, the smell came faintly and pleasantly to Aderyn's nose.

A striped blue and purple canopy at the center of the garden protected a square table Aderyn thought was too ornate for out-of-doors use, surrounded by similarly exquisite chairs with cushions in the royal colors. Queen Devendra sat behind a tea service big enough to cater to ten people, facing Aderyn. "Sit," she said. It wasn't a command, but Aderyn didn't hesitate.

She watched in silence as the queen poured tea for both of them. The canopy and the breeze combined to keep Aderyn from feeling overwarm, but she sweated anyway, mostly from nerves. She accepted her cup and sipped. It wasn't an herbal tea like she was used to, nor the black tea her grandfather Marrius liked; it was astringent and much stronger. She controlled a wince and set the cup down.

The queen poured a thin stream of milk into her cup and stirred it. "You've never had our tea before."

Aderyn blushed. "No, my lady."

"You can call me Devendra when it's just us. Hearing 'my lady' is tiresome from those I consider equals." Devendra pushed the jug of milk toward Aderyn. "Try that."

Aderyn added milk, stirred, and sipped again. "Oh, that's better," she said. "I mean—not that it was bad before, just unexpected."

"You should never apologize for your preferences," Devendra said. "And you must have seen how we in the south treat visitors. We consider them a gift and an opportunity to share what we have. No one here expects you to be southern in your tastes and habits."

"That's true, but for us, how we receive hospitality is as important as giving it is to you." Aderyn sipped again. The odd beverage was growing on her. "That includes not being dismissive of it, or rudely rejecting its gift."

"How interesting, that we are different and similar at the same time." Devendra set her cup down and sat back in her chair. "I have so many questions. I always wished to travel north, but my parents insisted it was too dangerous, and then I married Monesh and a northern journey truly was impossible. But I meant what I said last night. I am very curious about how there can be two real Fated Ones, and what it means that their quests don't interfere with each other."

"I don't know for sure. I was surprised to hear Ruan say he was following the Fated One quest chain, because he, um, acts like a typical fake Fated One."

"He sleeps around, yes." Devendra's expression soured. "I have heard complaints, not serious enough that I need to take action, but enough to make me dislike him. Go on."

"Well, anyway, my team accepted the **[Fated One's Destiny]** quest in Obsidian, and we've been fulfilling steps in the quest chain ever since. And Ruan doesn't have the same quests in his quest chain that we do, at least according to him. So we aren't both trying to defeat the orc horde. We've already had one encounter with a team racing to complete the same quest we were, and I never want to do that again."

Devendra nodded. "And the fact that Ruan is following the quest chain makes him a true Fated One... I'm afraid I still don't understand how there can be two of them."

Aderyn searched her memory for a way to explain it. "It's more that they're both runners of a race. Say there are a hundred people signed up to compete in a race. The first step is finding the track, and most of them don't. That means they can't win, but technically they're still part of the race. Those are the fake Fated Ones—they claim a title but don't do anything about it. The true Fated Ones are the ones who find the track and actually run, and only one of them can win. Owen and Ruan are both runners, and that means they both have the potential to become the actual Fated One and break the level cap. Obviously I think the winner should be Owen, but as far as the system is concerned—"

She stopped. Devendra said, "Yes?"

"I... it's nothing. Just a stray thought." It had occurred to her that she didn't know if the system did have a preference for who the Fated One should be. Suppose it cared about who won? Would that mean it was possible she and Owen and their friends were on a losing journey, if the system preferred Ruan?

"That's basically how it works, as far as we can tell. There's no rulebook about becoming the Fated One, and what we know comes from a lot of study and deduction," she concluded.

"Fascinating." Devendra tapped her finger against her lips thoughtfully. "I admit I'd rather Ruan not win. He'd be even more insufferable than he is now."

Aderyn laughed. "I agree. And—" She changed her mind about telling the queen her suspicions about Ruan keeping Suveer down in the instant before completing that sentence. "He even came on to me, despite knowing I'm married," she said instead.

"I wish I could say that surprised me." Devendra rang a small handbell near her left hand. When a servant joined them in response to the bell, Devendra said, "Please serve the meal now."

Aderyn had eaten lightly at noon, just enough to take the edge off her hunger—she was never going to adjust to Southlanders' ideas about when to eat—so the smells of cold roast chicken and savory pickles and hot parotta roused her appetite. She served herself, feeling renewed gratitude for the people who'd taught her southern dining habits, and ate in small bites, using Devendra as a guide.

"May I ask a question?" she said after a few minutes of silent eating. "Why was there no commanding general when I arrived? I was told none of the dukes could agree on precedence, but with the orcs invading, surely the need was too great to not act immediately?"

Devendra swallowed a bite of food and patted her lips with a napkin. "Traditionally, the king is the commander of the armies. With Colan being too young for the job, the natural next choice is one of the dukes. But they each rightly recognized that any duke who assumed that role gained tremendous power, and none of them liked the idea of that not being them. I agreed, but for selfish reasons."

"You didn't want any of the dukes in a position where he could usurp the throne," Aderyn said.

"Exactly. The army, or I should say the divisions of the army, have their own leaders and a measure of autonomy. I understand they worked out a plan of attack together. But none of those generals or their officers is the kind of soldier who is capable of seeing the big picture, by their own admission. That the history masters found not one, but two such is something of a miracle."

Aderyn blushed at the compliment. "I intend to prove your faith in me is justified."

"I hope so. I admit I like seeing a woman in command. If nothing else, you will shake assumptions, and the army could stand to have their assumptions shaken." Devendra smiled and pulled apart another round of parotta.

"Could the dukes have commanded, though?" Aderyn asked. "I heard that Duke Simla failed the first test. What if he'd become the commander back before you all agreed to let the history masters choose? Given that he lacked the skills."

"Monesh was no commander, either," Devendra said. "He delegated authority to his generals. I'm sure Simla would have done the same, just as Kanan intended to put Ruan in charge."

It was the perfect opportunity to lead up to Livia's information. Instead, Aderyn impulsively said, "You didn't love your husband, did you?"

Devendra fixed her with a stare Aderyn felt pierce a hole between her eyes. "Didn't I?"

"You didn't," Aderyn said. She might as well see this insulting line of conversation through to the end. "I'm sorry if it's rude to say. I find that sad."

"If you dare tell me I should have loved him—"

"No!" Aderyn exclaimed, aghast. "Of course not! I mean, it's sad you were married to someone you didn't like. I love my husband, and I can't imagine being united with someone else—someone I didn't love."

Devendra relaxed. "It was a political arrangement. My family has influence they were willing to use on Monesh's behalf, in exchange for certain monetary favors. And I liked the idea of being queen. I was probably too young to marry, only twenty-one—"

This time, Aderyn managed to control her self-conscious blush.

"And I didn't realize what you've already learned, that sharing a life without love becomes draining over time," Devendra concluded. "My children are excellent compensations, but I won't claim I was heartbroken over Monesh's death."

"My companion Isold told me you're unlikely to marry again, given inheritance law—is that true?"

"It is. I don't feel sad about that, either. Maybe it's just that Monesh only died five months ago, and I'm still enjoying my freedom, but I have no desire to remarry." Devendra shrugged. "Kanan would like to be my husband, but even if I loved him, which I definitely do not, I wouldn't elevate him to a position where he would be powerful enough to make the rest of the dukes nervous. It would be no different than if he commanded the armies."

Puzzled, Aderyn said, "He wants to marry you?"

"He's suggested as much. Very offhandedly, of course, so neither of us have to be embarrassed by my refusal."

Now Aderyn had far too many conversational options. She went with, "That's not what we heard. I don't like spreading gossip, Devendra, but I think this is something you should know. Whatever Kanan wants from you, it's not good, because he hates you."

Devendra recoiled. "*Hates* me? I've never seen a sign of that."

"I think he's a good liar, because—can I be honest with you? I had another reason for wanting to meet with you, not just to answer your questions about Fated Ones." Aderyn withdrew the folded paper from her pocket and handed it to the queen. "Kanan is plotting against you. This is a list of his supporters my friend Livia learned about from the man himself. She doesn't know when he'll strike, but she's convinced it will happen soon."

Devendra took the paper, but didn't open it. "And you have proof of this?"

Aderyn gestured. "That's all the proof we have, that and Livia's word. She went through a lot to gain that information, and she's the most honest and forthright person I know. And she doesn't want to see your little boy hurt."

"Colan." Devendra's jaw tensed with momentary anger. "Kanan would kill Colan to claim the throne, the bastard."

"That's what we believe. Look, I know it seems strange that northern adventurers would care enough about the fate of a country not their own to go out of their way to stop a coup, but we have a history of trying to do the right thing regardless of what we get out of it."

"I was wondering that, yes," Devendra said. She unfolded the paper, but didn't read it. "Thank you. For my son's life, I thank you."

"Not for the regency?" Aderyn asked.

Devendra smiled. "I'm sure you've guessed that if not for my duty to keep this country intact, I would take my children and find somewhere they can grow up without all this nonsense about kings and thrones. But I, too, try to do the right thing, and abdication would throw the Southlands into turmoil, particularly now that we are also at war with an outside enemy."

She stood, bringing the paper with her. "Forgive me for cutting our time short, but I believe this will not wait."

Aderyn rose as well. "I understand. Thank you for listening. I wasn't sure you'd believe me."

"Certain things about Kanan's behavior become clear now. Given that, and your evidence, I would be a fool not to take this threat seriously enough to investigate." Devendra rang the handbell again. "Good fortune, General Aderyn. I would like to speak with you again, sometime when there are no immediate crises hanging over us."

"I'd like that too. Thank you again."

The servant summoned by the bell took Aderyn back through the palace to a waiting carriage identical to the first, or maybe it was the same carriage. Aderyn was still too flustered to pay enough attention to figure it out. She hadn't thought beyond getting Devendra to believe her and take Kanan's threat seriously. Now she considered the ramifications.

Devendra was smart, and she had resources, but there was always an element of luck in any human endeavor, and suppose Kanan found out Devendra knew of his plot?

Aderyn leaned back and ran her fingers over the gold velvet. That was concerning, yes, but it wasn't anything she or her friends could affect. They'd done what they could, and the rest was out of their hands. Aderyn was sure Livia wouldn't want to rest until Kanan was eliminated as a threat, but Livia wasn't any better able to stop him than the rest of them. Time to focus on the reason they were here: fighting orcs, stopping an invasion, and fulfilling the **[Crush the Horde]** quest.

She checked the quest information again, in case it had become more detailed, but there was still only the list of question marks. Well, she hadn't actually expected a change, it just would have been nice.

At the inn, she ran up the stairs, eager to tell the others what had happened. Owen was alone in their room, and the look on his face, an expression of grim annoyance, made her say instead, "What's wrong?"

"Nothing, except Weston was right about Ruan." Owen handed her a folded piece of paper, not sealed, with her name scrawled loosely on the outside. "Read it. I already did, sorry."

Aderyn accepted the paper and opened it.

Aderyn, I'm afraid Duke Kanan demands my presence and Suveer's tomorrow evening—some event or other where he'll show us off as his prize guests. I'm afraid we'll have to reschedule dinner. Frustrating, I know, but I don't want to offend my patron, and dinner can happen anytime, right?

Ruan had signed his name as carelessly as he'd written Aderyn's. The scrawl looked so dismissive of her desires it infuriated her. "He's toying with me," she said. "He knows I want to talk to Suveer alone and he's doing this to taunt me."

"I could challenge him to a duel," Owen said.

"What good would that do?"

"It would make me feel better. Plus, I bet he's worth a lot of experience, and you know how I love experience." Owen put his arms around Aderyn. "We can't do anything about this now except figure out a way to get him away from Suveer. And that will have to wait on the siege."

"The siege. I'd almost forgotten." Aderyn returned his embrace. "Just a few more days, and we'll be at war. It feels so unreal."

"That won't last past your first encounter with the battlefield," Owen said. "It's more terrible than you can imagine."

"How do you know? You've never been to war."

"I've seen plenty of movies and read a lot of books. I can only imagine the real thing is worse." Owen hugged her closer. "I hope I'm wrong about that."

Aderyn sighed. "I hope our regiment makes a difference. I keep imagining monsters with cherry-red skin taking over Adhiraj so we're the ones beating impotently at the walls."

"In my world, orcs have green skin," Owen said.

"I've never seen an orc, so I have no idea," Aderyn said. "Green or red, let's hope they die easily."

Chapter Twenty-Five

Aderyn stayed well back from where Livia stood, holding the <**Soldier's Friend**> at arm's length. The bronze cube gleamed dully in the light from the nearest campfire, even farther back than Aderyn was. She heard soldiers moving around, and the clink of utensils against metal plates, but she chose not to make them uncomfortable by watching them. She'd already learned, during her many trips back and forth from the regiment to Ikharatia, that the soldiers found her intimidating. Whether that was her age, sex, or nationality, she didn't know. It might have been a combination of all three.

A horn sounded, and a whirlwind of motion surrounded Livia, tiny creatures whipping around her almost too fast to be identified as more than dark wind. The movement behind Aderyn stopped, and she heard a clank as someone dropped his tin plate on a stone. Inwardly, she cursed. She was so used to the <**Soldier's Friend**> she hadn't thought of its effect on soldiers who'd never seen anything like it. Camp had already been pitched when they arrived that evening, or she would have suggested using the sixth side of the bronze cube, the one that produced enough tents for an army. But that might have been even more terrifying. Reassuring the soldiers would only make their discomfort worse, so she gritted her teeth and resolved to handle setting up camp differently the following night.

The whirlwind vanished. In its place, three elegant white tents surrounded Livia, so different from the common grunt's tent they might as well have been completely different objects. That, Aderyn didn't mind. She'd already learned that the common soldier expected his leaders to have greater luxuries than he did. The common soldier didn't like that fact, but he accepted it, and Aderyn intended to trade on that acceptance.

She sat beside the campfire that burned merrily in its ring of stones, also summoned by the magic item. The ground wasn't muddy or damp where they'd positioned their camp, and she was grateful it hadn't rained recently. Major Kavish had said they were coming out of the rainy season, which only meant half the days in a week were wet as opposed to all of them. Aderyn had seen those rains, which were less showers than some heavenly spigot turned to full. She figured more rain fell in ten minutes here than in two hours back home.

Owen seated himself beside her and stretched out his legs, one at a time. "This feels surreal. Like, we're about to go into battle, but this night is so peaceful battle seems impossible."

"I agree." Aderyn accepted a plate of rice and meat sauce from one of the soldiers assigned to her personal service. *That*, to her, was surreal—that soldiers, some of them low-ranking officers, were at her beck and call. Major Sahal had assigned them and explained that they would take care of chores and cooking so she could put her energies toward command, and that made sense for General Aderyn. Aderyn the Warmaster adventurer didn't like the idea of someone else handling things she was capable of managing. But here, she was General Aderyn, so she shut up and took their service graciously.

She mixed rice and sauce and ate with her fingers. Parotta would have been nice, but when she'd asked Private Nandi about it—politely, so she wouldn't think it was a demand—the private had said the camp kitchen went into a wartime regimen the night before battle was joined, and while parotta wasn't difficult to fry, it did take longer to prepare than other foods.

Private Nandi had gone a long way toward reconciling Aderyn to her servants. Nandi, a level four Spellcrafter, was alert and quick to respond to Aderyn's requests, and she didn't need to have every detail explained to her. Now she presented herself at Aderyn's side and said, "Is there anything else, general?"

"We'll need someone to clear the dishes, and then I believe that's all for tonight." She took in the shallow bucket Nandi held, full of wet rags for cleaning up, and added, "Thank you for thinking of that, private."

"Of course, general." Nandi put the bucket near Aderyn and saluted. "I'll pitch my tent near yours tonight in case you need anything."

"Thank you."

Nandi saluted again and turned to speak in a low voice to the soldier who'd brought the food. After she'd walked away, Owen said, "She's quite the batman."

"What? You mean the man who dresses like a bat and fights crime? I told you I wasn't sure that would work. You were kidding me about him, right?"

Owen choked back a laugh. "Batman is a great superhero, and no, that's not what I meant. A batman in some armies is like a personal servant to an officer. He, or she, takes care of the officer's belongings and does chores just like Nandi."

"I don't know why your world insists on making up weird names for things. You could just say 'servant.'"

"Well, I think it had a more specific meaning once, but I don't know a lot about etymology—the history of how words develop. Your world doesn't have that concept." Owen scraped his fingers around the bottom of the shallow tin plate. "I'm grateful they don't expect us to dine on fine porcelain with silver utensils. I'd rather have this much solidarity with the troops."

"I need seconds," Weston said. He waved at the servant, who took his plate and hurried away. "Good, solid meals the night before something important are the best way to face an uncertain future."

"I'd rather have a glass of wine and a foot rub, thanks," Livia said.

"I can manage the foot rub. I don't think there's any wine in the camp. Have you noticed Southlanders aren't big drinkers?" Weston cleaned his hand off and tossed the soiled rag into an empty bucket nearby.

"I have. It's not bad, though if any of us were fond of liquor, it might be an issue. I like the bubbly pink juice." Aderyn scooped up the last of her meal and decided against licking the plate. She had an image to uphold, plus the taste of tin would ruin the taste of the rich meat sauce.

"Kanan likes his wine," Livia said. She didn't sound as if this was a difficult or painful memory. "It made it even easier to get information out of him, though I think he was more amorous because he was intoxicated."

Weston hugged her briefly. "You don't have to worry about him anymore."

"I know." Livia hugged him back. "And honestly, it wasn't all bad. He's a bastard, but he tells a good story. He's good at sharing gossip in a funny way—amusing enough that you don't at first realize how he's savaging the person he's talking about. And he knows a lot about Ikharatia and its history. That was interesting."

"Anything we might need to know?" Isold said.

"Probably not. The night of the party, I asked if he knew about local places or things adventurers might care about. You know, if we complete the **[Crush the Horde]** quest and have to level up here before moving on. He's not an adventurer, so he couldn't tell me about famous monsters, but we were in a group with some other nobles at one point that night, and one of those lords brought up a dungeon called the Ivory Palace. I didn't think it sounded dangerous with a name like that, and I said so."

She leaned back to let the servant hand a filled plate to Weston. Weston began mixing the rice and sauce, gingerly thanks to the steam still rising from the plate. "It sounds more like a holiday resort," he said.

"That's what I thought. But when I said that, everyone got very quiet, and they all stopped looking at Kanan like they were embarrassed. And Kanan laughed and said something like 'you'd think so, but beauty often conceals danger.' Then he changed the subject, which visibly relieved everyone else."

"Huh," Owen said. "Interesting. Makes me want to find out more about it."

Livia smiled. "So did I. When I wasn't digging for information about Kanan's possible coup, I asked him about it. I figured, if the subject was that sensitive, prying for details about it might conceal what I actually wanted to know."

"I'm curious," Isold said. "What did you learn?"

"It turned out Kanan wasn't at all reticent about it when we were in private. It's on a rock spur off the coast, a few miles east of Ikharatia, and it looks like a palace carved of ivory. It's really granite with marble facings tinted cream by magic, though the decorations are actual ivory." Livia sat forward like she meant to tell a great secret. "He wouldn't say what made it special, just that its beauty concealed a darker truth. And he said 'darker truth' like he was personally excited about it. That man is strange."

"Does ivory mean you have elephants in your world?" Owen asked in a low voice.

"I don't know what those are," Livia said. "Ivory comes from the tessobela, which is an enormous monster with four tusks as long as a human and a fat, flexible nose."

"The tusks can be harvested and used in Spellcrafting or construction," Isold said. "They emit a minor aura of protection that increases with the amount of tusk used in an item."

"Sounds more like an oliphaunt to me," Owen said. "Never mind. Go on, Livia."

"He didn't say much more than that. He implied he knew its secrets and implied even more that he had control of the dungeon, which seems unlikely. But as much as Kanan brags, he never claims to more than he actually is capable of, so it's possible his knowledge of the Ivory Palace's secrets gives him a way through it, or a way to defeat it easily." Livia sat back and leaned against Weston, who'd finished his meal and set the plate aside.

"It sounds interesting," Aderyn said. "Too bad we have a quest already."

"Yeah, we don't need to take on a mysterious dungeon, too," Owen said. "How about a song, Isold?"

"I—" Isold hesitated. "All right." He rose and ducked into his tent for his drum.

Aderyn and Owen exchanged glances. "I think we could use some music/*He's still not himself*," she said with **[Secret Message]**.

"That's true," Owen replied.

Isold resumed his seat and tested the sound of his drum. "Something cheerful, I think," he said, and beat the rhythm of the first line of "The Farmer's Wayward Daughter" before breaking into song. Aderyn tapped her toe to the music. She was aware of soldiers drifting toward the music, not approaching closely in case that was out of line, and wished the attention could help Isold regain his confidence. Surely he could see how his music affected people?

When the song ended, some of the soldiers clapped tentatively. Isold set the drum aside and said, "Come closer, and we'll sing together. This is a night for companionship." He sang again, a martial tune Aderyn didn't recognize. After a few measures, one or two other voices joined in, followed by more until everyone except the companions were singing heartily. It wasn't beautiful like Isold's voice—some of the soldiers couldn't carry a tune in a bucket full of molasses—but all together, the sound filled the night and pushed back the growing darkness.

At the end of that song, cheering and clapping resounded through their end of the camp, and soldiers called out suggestions for the next song. Isold chose "Away with the Army," one Aderyn had heard growing up in Far Haven even though no one there had ever joined an army. The rousing chorus of "we'll pack, and we'll track, and we'll break our backs/Away with the army, oh!" filled her with pleasure at being surrounded by comrades. Then she remembered that some of these soldiers wouldn't survive tomorrow's battle, and her good mood vanished.

Isold beckoned to a pretty young woman to join him. He whispered something in her ear, and she nodded. Aderyn's relief surged. That was more like it.

Isold shouted, "Everyone take a rest, and Suriya and I will sing for you." He began singing another song Aderyn recognized because she'd heard him perform it often, a melancholy tune about lost loves. At the end of the first verse, Suriya joined him, her pure soprano soaring over his tenor. How Isold had heard her through the din to know what she was capable of, Aderyn didn't know, but tears came to her eyes at how beautiful their mingled voices were.

No one spoke when the song came to an end, as if everyone recognized how fitting a tribute their silence was. Aderyn noticed several others wiping their eyes. Isold clasped Suriya's hand and smiled in thanks. Then he broke into something else, something raucous that had everyone laughing. Suriya sang along with that, too, and now that Aderyn knew what to listen for, she could hear her voice in harmony with Isold's.

They sang and laughed and wept until nearly midnight, when Aderyn said, "We'd better be off to our beds if we want to be any good to Adhiraj tomorrow." She watched Isold talk to Suriya, and again hope rose. But the two of them merely clasped hands once more, and Suriya left their campsite.

Aderyn kept her disappointment to herself until she was safely in her tent, when she said to Owen, "I thought for sure Isold had made a connection."

"Maybe she'll come back later," Owen said. "Maybe they both felt uncomfortable at having everyone watch her enter his tent."

"Maybe. But he didn't look at her the way he does a woman he intends to sleep with." Aderyn groaned. "And now I'm objectifying Isold, like he's nothing more than a sex-obsessed bard like they have in your world."

"It's not that he should have lots of sex, Aderyn. It's that he's acting out of character. Maybe this means he's changing, and he needs time to work through those changes."

"I don't think it's good for him to do it alone, though. I know we can't force him to talk, but maybe we need to bring up the subject so he knows he can."

Owen took Aderyn in his arms and held her close. "You're probably right. I trust your instincts about people. But now's not the time."

"I know." Aderyn sighed. "Let's sleep. Tomorrow will be unimaginable. Except to you, I guess, with your war movies. How is it all right for the movies to kill people for someone else's entertainment?"

"They don't. It's all acting, like in your theaters but a thousand times more realistic." Owen pulled Aderyn down to lie beside him.

"I wish I could see movies. But not the one with monsters in the ceiling," Aderyn said. "I have enough monsters in my life."

"And tomorrow, orcs," Owen said.

Chapter Twenty-Six

Someone clapped outside Aderyn's tent at just after dawn. "General, I have a package for you from Commander General Varoun," Nandi said.

"Just a minute," Aderyn replied. She dragged on her shirt and trousers—Nandi might be shocked to see her commanding officer in her underclothes—and pushed the tent flap aside. Nandi was fully dressed and wearing the typical soldier's armor, a hardened leather jerkin with matching vambraces and greaves, though to Aderyn's knowledge she wouldn't join the fight. She held a package wrapped in oiled paper and tied with string.

"General Varoun sends his compliments, and hopes this will be of use," Nandi said, extending the package to Aderyn.

"No other message?"

"No, general. Is there anything else I can do for you?"

"Thank you, no." Aderyn nodded in acknowledgement of Nandi's salute and returned inside.

Owen was sitting up in their bedroll. "What is it?"

"I have no idea. It's not too heavy and it bends like fabric." Aderyn picked at the knot with her nails until it loosened. Unfolding the paper, she touched the package's contents gingerly. "It is fabric—no, it's metal.

Chain links." The mesh was finer than any Aderyn had seen before. It wasn't visibly obvious as metal, but it was cool to the touch and too smooth for fabric.

She shook the thing out. It was a shirt, with a hem long enough to reach the middle of her thighs, and it shone like silver even in the dimness of the tent, like some unseen light struck it. "It's chainmail," Aderyn said. "But it weighs practically nothing for mail. It's about as heavy as a lined velvet cloak."

"Wow." Owen fingered the hem of the mail shirt. "You don't have dwarves in this world, do you?"

"I don't think so. Are they monsters?"

"Not usually. This looks like something out of a movie. Put it on, see if it fits."

The neck hole was barely big enough for her to fit her head through, but the shirt fit her just right, loose enough for movement but tight enough not to slip distractingly when she moved. It smelled of metal and oil and faintly of lavender, as if it really was an ordinary shirt that had sat in storage with fragrant herbs for a while. Aderyn bent and twisted. "It's comfortable. How did Varoun know? I didn't say anything about me still wearing the armor I bought months ago in Asylum."

"I didn't tell him, if that's what you're asking. But I did check around in Ikharatia for armor for you while you were in the history masters' test, and I didn't make a secret of it. The thought of Varoun prowling the armorers I went to is kind of ridiculous, but it's possible. Or maybe he's psychic."

"Psychic? Owen, do I have to smack you again for using other-worlder terms?"

Owen drew her swiftly into his embrace and kissed her deeply. "Wouldn't you rather this?"

"That's not going to work forever, you know."

Owen's lips met hers again, soft and enticing. He murmured between kisses, "Wanna bet?"

Aderyn gave up. "You really need to be careful—oh. *Ohhh.* How much time do we have before breakfast?"

Outside the tent, Weston shouted, "Everybody up! Time to eat! We have orcs to slaughter!"

Aderyn and Owen laughed. "None, it seems," Owen said. He began dressing. "That mail looks good on you. I hope it's as effective as its counterpart in my world."

"I hope I get a chance to find out," Aderyn said. "I'm ready for battle to begin."

Aderyn shouted, "Everyone stop!" Her voice boomed across the regiment thanks to **<Amplify Voice>**. Somewhat raggedly, all the soldiers came to a halt. Owen had thought their marching order looked weird, and had said something about columns and lines, but to Aderyn, the loose groupings of the teams into platoons made sense. The sunlight, diffused by the thick layer of high, yellowish clouds, cast no shadows anywhere. It was still bright enough to show the ready, determined, sometimes eager faces of the waiting soldiers.

She opened the Codex and read the relevant quest item.

You have accepted the battle quest [Break the Siege of Adhiraj].
You are authorized to extend this quest to others.
Continue? Y / N

Aderyn selected Y.

This quest is now available to anyone within [0.5 miles] of your current position.
Extend the quest? Y / N

Again, Aderyn touched the Y. She recalled what Varoun had explained and called out, "Accept the battle invitation!"

A ripple of movement went out from where she stood through the massed soldiers as one by one they gestured, mimicking her movements. Aderyn closed the Codex and waited. When she was sure everyone in the regiment had accepted the quest, she gestured to Kimay to cast *fly* on her and rose a few feet into the air. She felt no uncertainty at becoming the focus of several hundred eyes, though she still wasn't used to the gray uniform coat and gold sash.

"You have your instructions," she said. "General Rajman's Hawk and Ox regiments will attempt to draw some of the orc army away from the gates, at which point Raven Regiment will break the orc line so General Tamil's forces can leave the city and join the fight. Remember to press the attack when that happens so the Adhiraj regiments are free to move into position."

She drew in a deep breath. She might not feel uncertain, but she did feel foolish. She had no idea what to say to give the soldiers what Owen called a "pep talk." Clearing her throat, she added, "We're stronger fighters than a bunch of orcs who think all it takes to defeat humans is stand downwind and suffocate us with their stench." Laughter spread through the crowd. "Fight as one, fight with all your strength, and they don't stand a chance."

A roar rose up, shattering the air even more loudly than **<Amplify Voice>** had. Aderyn raised one fist high the way Owen had showed her and shouted back, "That's right! Make them fear us!" The shouting redoubled, and more fists punched the air as the soldiers picked up Aderyn's gesture.

Aderyn came back to earth. "I think that was enough. Was it enough?" she asked her friends.

"They're sufficiently motivated, and now it's a matter of getting them in place before that feeling wears off," Isold said.

"*Fly* lasts for several hours, right, Kimay? Then I can be a beacon when needed, and maybe get a good idea of how the battle goes."

"I wouldn't count on that," Owen said. "Battlefields are a mess even when the ground is mucky rather than dusty and dry. Everything I've read says it's hard to see anything that isn't right in front of you."

"And if you fly too high, you'll make yourself a target," Livia said.

"You make good points." Aderyn sighed. "All right. Kimay, stay with the rear forces. I've left a few teams to protect the low-level soldiers, and you should come to me if anything happens. Follow Isold's orders otherwise."

"I understand," Kimay said in his wispy tenor that left Aderyn conflicted again about his ability to remember, let alone carry out, his orders. Still, he was a level sixteen Windwarden, and that had to be worth something.

"I'm not sure leaving you behind is a good idea," Aderyn said to Isold. "What's that Owen always says about splitting the party?"

"Don't revisit your decision," Isold said. "Your point about the need to defend our lower-level soldiers is valid, and I am better equipped to deflect a horde, either with **[Shout]** or **[Cause Fear]**, than any of you."

"And this is the point of attack that would be most devastating if the enemy gets through," Aderyn said. "These newer recruits are no match for orcs twice their level. You're right, I shouldn't rethink my rational choices. It's extremely unlikely the orcs will come this way. It's just that we've never gone into battle missing one of us before."

"I promise not to make you regret it." Isold smiled. "Though I expect you all to return with tales of battle I can turn into a martial song."

Aderyn nodded. "Let's move. We have a few miles to cover." She settled her sword more comfortably to hang at her hip. The mystery weapon the kobolds had given her was still a mystery, since they hadn't found anyone to cast *heritage* and they hadn't been in a fight for it to manifest magical properties. Isold had said it wasn't terribly magical, but that there was something odd about it, so Aderyn still held out hope it would do something dramatic when she finally faced an enemy.

She walked instead of flying, surrounded by her friends and hundreds of soldiers. It didn't feel as strange as she expected. It was more like heading into the biggest monster fight of her life... which was exactly what it was. Excitement filled her. Maybe once she was there, once battle had been joined, she'd feel terrified or overwhelmed, but right now, she couldn't imagine anywhere else she'd rather be.

After about half an hour, the horizon grew fuzzy, as if something grew on the surface of the interminable plain. Aderyn didn't signal the army to slow or stop, but she did take out her **<Farspeaker>** and awkwardly insert General Rajman's coin into the socket as she walked. When the general's face appeared, she said, "We're nearing Adhiraj. How are things on your end?"

"We're nearly within range of our Archers' longbows," General Rajman said, sounding as clear as if he stood beside her. "The idea is to shoot the orcs until they get tired of being picked off and charge our position. That will be your signal to attack."

"Understood." Aderyn considered what else she wanted to know. "Can you see the orc army? Any idea how big it is?"

"Bigger than our combined forces, but they've encircled the city and that reduces the number we'll have to fight. Even so, I'd bet my men against those inhuman monsters any day."

Aderyn reflected on "men" and concluded Rajman was either one of those old-fashioned types who didn't consider women soldiers real soldiers, or he just liked the shorthand of saying "men." She decided to give him the benefit of the doubt. "I agree. I'll talk to you again once we're about to attack." She passed her hand over the mirror, and Rajman's image disappeared.

She put the magic item and the coin away and said, "Just a couple more miles. I'm so excited!"

"Excited about something bloody and dangerous?" Owen said.

"Something new and unexpected, too. I know, I'll probably change my mind after my first battle, but for now, I choose to be hopeful."

"You know what? So do I," Livia exclaimed. "I need something unequivocally evil I can punch without causing political repercussions. Let's do this!"

"If Livia is enthusiastic, I'm terrified," Weston said.

THE FUZZY SPOT ON THE HORIZON GREW AND SOLIDIFIED until it became a walled city surrounded by teeming movement. Catapults flung stones at the city in a way that suggested to Aderyn's Warmaster's vision were meant to intimidate rather than destroy, since when they hit the walls, they didn't appear to do damage. The sounds of crashing stone and splintering wood when a missile made it over the walls, however, made Aderyn cringe inwardly and want to walk faster.

Sweat dripped from her forehead and down her back, making the tunic beneath her mail cling uncomfortably to her body. She'd never been so aware of its texture before, the slight roughness rubbing her skin when the cloth shifted. Maybe battle would stop it driving her nearly mad.

After far too long, they came within sight of the orc army, and Aderyn signaled a stop. Teeming masses of movement filled the plain in front of the city gates and circled the walls, and distant cries of pain and terror came to her in waves as the wind gusted and fell again. She hoped her dismay wasn't obvious. There were so many of them—

She squeezed her eyes shut and cursed herself for foolishness. Then she Assessed the orc army.

Name: Orc Grunt [1352]

Type: Monstrosity

Power level range: 10-12

Attack(s): various weapons, preferably axe, bludgeon, short bow, or spear

Immune to: none

Resistant to: none

Vulnerable to: bright light, *daylight, sunburst*

Orcs are vicious, brutal killers who hate and resent humans for taking over territory they believe is rightfully theirs, namely, the entire world. Centuries ago, powerful adventurers drove them into the Blighted Range, where they've remained ever since—well, until now, obviously. They have their good qualities—they are devoted to each other, they are ferocious in battle, and they fight to defend the horde—but since they turn all those qualities toward eliminating humans, you probably don't see the positive there.

Grunts are the lowest-ranking members of the horde. They're strong but uninspired fighters who lack initiative in battle. Orc leaders don't do more than point them at the enemy and say "Kill." That's more than enough, as far as you're concerned.

Name: Orc Masher [1093]

Type: Monstrosity

Power level range: 11-13

Attack(s): various weapons, preferably axe, bludgeon, short bow, or spear

Immune to: none

Resistant to: none

Vulnerable to: bright light, *daylight, sunburst*

Another thing to remember about orcs is it takes a lot to make them flee. They're smart enough to realize that turning their backs on an enemy makes them vulnerable. When they do cut and run, it's generally because the horde has been reduced to more than half its original number or their leader has been killed.

Orc mashers are grunts who've survived enough battles to climb the ranks. They are more versatile fighters than grunts and more cunning as well, which ought to worry you—though you're cunning, too, so maybe it's a wash.

NAME: ORC ELITE [620]

Type: Monstrosity

Power level range: 12-14

Attack(s): various weapons, preferably axe, bludgeon, or two-handed sword, special

Immune to: none

Resistant to: bladed weapons, bludgeoning weapons

Vulnerable to: *daylight, sunburst*

Special attacks: ferocious might, fear aura

Speaking of orc leaders, orcs in general aren't big on military discipline or strategy. They tend to attack whatever's in front of them and pound on it until it stops moving. This means their leaders have to be powerful and charismatic to keep their people in line, and that eliminating an orc leader isn't a guarantee of victory.

Orc elites are the bridge between the ordinary grunts and mashers. They actually know something about fighting beyond bashing things and will use combat maneuvers against their enemies. Elites are terrifying to watch in battle and even more terrifying when it's you they're attacking. They attack with a

ferocity that can stun an opponent, and when they choose, they give off an aura that frightens nearby attackers. Elites are extremely dangerous, which means killing a lot of them intimidates the lesser orcs and makes them less capable. Not *in*capable, mind. Don't get cocky.

Name: Orc Elementalist [135]

Type: Monstrosity

Power level range: 10-13

Attack: spellslinging (special)

Immune to: none

Resistant to: none

Vulnerable to: *daylight, sunburst*

Special attacks: offensive spells

You've never encountered a monster that could cast spells before, have you? Orc elementalists draw their power from their connection to the natural world. They can't cast as wide a variety of spells as human spellslingers can, but don't think that makes them weak; they've learned ways to use their limitations to make themselves strong. Some elementalists have raw power the likes of which their human counterparts only dream of. Does that sound admiring? I suppose I admire them the way I admire a wasp: it's beautiful, deadly, and ultimately a blight on the world.

She couldn't think how to convey this information quickly to the soldiers. <**Amplify Voice**> had limits, and while they were all moving it would just make her speech unintelligible. Frustration at knowing so much when she wasn't in a position to share her knowledge filled her briefly. Then she remembered most of her soldiers had fought orcs before. They might not know the details **[Improved Assess 3]** revealed, but they wouldn't be caught off guard by the orcs' ferocity or refusal to back down.

She walked forward a few paces, with Owen trailing her. They were close enough to the battle that she could see the orcs nearest her as individuals and the rest as a shifting mass of bodies into which arrows periodically rained. "They can't possibly hold out long," she murmured, mostly to herself.

"It reminds me of Agincourt—of another battle, where the archers did the same to the enemy," Owen said, impressing Aderyn that for once he'd shown caution in referring to his otherworldly origins, especially since there wasn't anyone else around.

With a loud cry, the masses of orc warriors surged to the west, screaming out defiance against their tormentors. It was so sudden Aderyn only gaped for a few precious seconds. Then she shot into the air and shouted "They're moving! Everyone go! Go!"

It didn't feel like the kind of stirring battle cry that would be remembered by history, but it got the regiment moving. Aderyn dropped out of the sky to join her team, drew her sword, and charged.

Chapter Twenty-Seven

Aderyn's impression of a teeming mass of enemy bodies wasn't totally accurate. While most of the orcs had surged westward, there were still many surrounding the catapults, which continued to fling stones at the city walls, and several orcs with short bows shooting at what few defenders were visible.

One of the orc elites saw Aderyn's forces' approach. He bellowed something incoherent, and a number of orc warriors took up defensive stances around the siege weapons. More orcs surged into motion, rushing to meet the onslaught. Aderyn remembered in passing that they didn't know if any of these orcs was a leader the quest demanded they kill, but she was moving too fast to Assess individuals.

One *fireball* streaked from the orc ranks, then another. Screams, and the horrible rich smell of burning flesh, filled the air. The ground rumbled, shaking Aderyn as *thunderstomp* ripped the earth in both directions, knocking soldiers and orcs to the ground. Then the orcs closed on the human soldiers. Aderyn observed their appearance, their pasty greenish skin, their stringy hair or bald heads, their outthrust jaws with protruding lower fangs, their bulky muscled bodies wearing bits of badly-cured leather or furs that reeked of decaying flesh and sour sweat.

Then she was face to face with one of them and blocking the swing of his axe.

The dull metallic clank of the blow rang through her arms like steel on a bronze bell. She screamed a challenge, disengaged, and thrust with the mystery sword. The blade bit deep into the creature's side, and it howled in agony. Aderyn withdrew her sword with some effort as its flesh closed over the blade, pulling at it. She followed the blow with a slash to the guts. She was terrifyingly aware of the orc's size and its powerful muscles. It might be lower level than she, but she wasn't going to let it get in a hit if she could help it.

With another slash, she cut open its abdomen, releasing a stink of entrails. The orc clutched its belly and sagged to the ground.

Congratulations! You have defeated [Orc Grunt].
You have earned [4500 XP]

Beside her, Owen charged his opponent, using **[Overrun]** to knock the orc down and get himself into position for **[Outflank]**. Aderyn obeyed the skill's weird tug and closed with this new enemy. Another system notice appeared, but she was too busy parrying the orc's heavy blows to read it. Owen skewered it from behind, beneath its ribcage. As it dragged itself off his blade and spun to face the new threat, Aderyn followed up with a strike of her own. The orc shrieked and flung up an arm when it saw the brilliant light of the <**Sunsword**>. Owen took advantage of its distraction to impale it.

Congratulations! You have defeated [Orc Masher].
You have earned [5500 XP]

The press of the battle was too much for Aderyn to see anything beyond the next opponent, and the next. There was just her, and Owen, and the occasional thump of earth, rising above the screaming din, that said Livia was making good use of her spell *hungry pit*. Occasionally, Aderyn's vision tunneled, and she had to shake herself out of the focused state that left her open to being attacked by creatures she hadn't noticed. Her grip on the mystery sword was tight enough its leather wrapping felt melded to her hand, rough and smooth at the same time.

Small fires erupted here and there, filling the air with the smell of char and burning flesh, and to the sound of orcs howling was joined the screams of dying humans. Once, an overpowering wind that smelled bitterly of ash and blood engulfed her, pushing her back. She covered her face with her arm and pressed forward out of the whirlwind, killing the orc elementalist that had summoned it.

One after another, orcs fell before her. She knew her soldiers were progressing forward because of the bodies underfoot, some of them human, most of them not. The awareness of her fallen soldiers was distant, something to deal with later like the many system defeat notices. For now, there was only the fight.

After a while, tired and sweating and finding herself temporarily unopposed, she grabbed Owen's arm and shouted, "I'm going up to see what I can see. I'll be back soon."

Owen nodded. He looked as tired as she felt, with charcoal-red orc blood streaking the side of his face. Still, he saluted her with his sword and headed back into the fighting.

Disengaging, she shot into the air, not very high. The fighting really wasn't as fierce here. She and her neighboring teams had stumbled into the area surrounding one of the catapults and killed all its attendants. One of the teams, led by a lieutenant whose traditional red cap drew her eye, was engaged in disabling it by way of setting it on fire. It wasn't igniting easily despite three Flamecrafters battering it with **[Elemental Blast]**, and Aderyn smelled something pungent over the reek of the battlefield and guessed its wood had been treated with something to prevent what the soldiers meant to do. Some of the soldiers drew knives and attacked the tangles of ropes Aderyn couldn't make sense of. As the ropes began snapping, the catapult sagged, smoldered, and finally burst into flame.

Ahead and to the left, where the city gate stood, the two armies were nothing but masses of colors, greenish orc skin, the gray and gold of adventurer soldiers' uniforms, the occasional red dot of a lieutenant's cap. She flew in that direction. An arrow's ghostly form passed through her, and she dropped. She'd forgotten the archers. Another series of images, these of large stones flying through the air, forced her to dodge again. She needed to make herself less of a target.

Zipping away and keeping low to the crowd, she Assessed the city, not caring about the typical Assessment information of hospitality and spellslingers. She hoped for something more immediately useful.

Name: Adhiraj

Status: Fortified City

Government: Duke

Civilization Level: 14

Resources: Spiritsmith x18, Spellcrafter x17, Windwarden x20, Bonemender x21, Tidecaller x14, Flamecrafter x16; Level 12 crafters; Level 14 hospitality; Level 12 food supply

Adhiraj's position at the center of the Southlands makes it of key importance in the defense of the kingdom. All right, you knew that, but did you also know that its reinforced double wall means those small catapults don't stand a chance of breaking through? General Tamil has been watching, and the regiments are ready to move out as soon as your forces clear the area in front of the gate.

The area the Assessment referred to was nearly empty of fighters. Aderyn cast about frantically for a sign of some officer and got nothing. Frustrated, she called out with **[Amplify Voice]**, "Push them back! Clear the gate!"

She wasn't sure how useful those instructions were, since she doubted the soldiers saw the battle any more clearly than she had while she was on the ground. Her upper arm ached, and she touched it and her fingers came away bloody. She didn't remember being hit.

Swiftly, she flew up and over the wall, dodging the arrows of the defenders and attackers alike, waving her arms vigorously so the soldiers on the battlements would look more closely and realize she was human. "General Tamil," she panted when she alighted on the wall-walk. "Where is he?"

The Assessment was right; at least one full regiment waited at the gate. A Flamecrafter and an Earthbreaker stood at the head of the group, staring at the gate with the fixed expressions of two people using *clairvoyance* to look through the heavy banded oak. The other soldiers shifted restlessly, the rustle of cloth and the muted clank of weapons striking a neighbor's weapon unnaturally loud by comparison to the distant screams and shouts of battle.

Aderyn recognized General Tamil from the **<Farspeaker>**, though she'd only addressed him once after Varoun provided her with his token. The middle-aged general was wiry and hard as the oak of the gate. He greeted Aderyn absently. "You didn't need to risk yourself. The **<Farspeaker>** is enough."

"I was in the area." Aderyn wished she hadn't sounded so flippant. "We've almost cleared the gate, but I see you know that."

Tamil nodded. "Rajman says they are holding their own against the orc army, but only just. We will have to relieve them as soon as we're free."

"I'm going back now. We're prepared to move as soon as you leave the city." Aderyn saluted him and flew to the top of the wall. Once there, though, she changed her mind. The battle was moving along without her immediate direction, and she had other business to attend to.

Concealed behind the battlements so she didn't have to dodge the occasional arrow or elemental attack, she opened her Codex to look at the **[Fated One's Destiny: Crush the Horde]** quest.

An army of monstrous orcs has emerged from the Blighted Range, intent on conquering the southern human lands. Destroy their leaders and push the army back into the mountains. Recommended minimum party level for this quest is 17.

Victory conditions:
Death of ?
Death of heavily scarred, black-haired orc leader
Death of ?
Death of ?
Death of ?
Orc army retreats

Reward: [75,000 XP] plus any XP gained through actions taken to complete the quest.

Aderyn blinked. She focused on the new line. She didn't know what had happened to trigger this information. Maybe she'd seen this orc in passing. She wasn't sure it was totally helpful—how was she supposed to make out a single scarred, black-haired orc from thousands? For that matter, was there only one orc that met that description? Well, probably, or the system would have used a different description.

She decided to make a quick flight around the city walls to learn what other forces the orcs had. More catapults flung missiles at the walls, deafening Aderyn with the sharp crack of stone against stone. Since the missiles chipped the walls' surfaces but didn't do more damage than that, she tried to ignore the noise. Orc archers continued to shoot at anyone who showed themselves past the battlements. **[Improved Assess 3]** told her there were several hundred more orcs of various types surrounding the city, though not nearly so many as were attacking Rajman's forces near the gate. She told herself not to despair. The gate was nearly clear, she saw as she completed her circle, and soon—

The great oak gate creaked ponderously open, and soldiers streamed through the doorway. From Aderyn's position, the men and women looked like a current of gray and brown water surging toward and then over the pasty greenish orcs. To her Warmaster's vision, the current mingled with Aderyn's soldiers and then passed them, relieving weary troops. For a moment, the two tides met, and Aderyn imagined their collision as two inexorable forces under tremendous pressure, neither giving way.

Then, like a dam bursting, the orcs broke and ran. Exultant shouting filled the air, rising over the general din. The soldiers pursued the enemy, many of them stumbling over fallen bodies, but more of them taking advantage of the orcs turning their backs. Orcs staggered, fell, and hit the ground, sending up puffs of dry earth wherever they landed.

Aderyn flew in search of Owen, wishing her ranks in **[Spot]** were higher. She was much better with **[Awareness]**. More red caps caught her eye, scattered throughout the human troops. They served as visual markers to the movement of the army, not a perfect one, but enough to give her a sense of how the battle was going. Not all the soldiers pursued the orcs; many teams held their position, watching for a second onslaught against the now-undefended city.

Eventually, she found Owen near the catapult where she'd left him, fighting his way steadily forward. Two orcs engaged him, but he was fighting them both without sign of excessive exertion. Aderyn Assessed the orcs, watching the blue lines of **[Discern Weakness]** slide across their bodies. Their vulnerable spots were as expected, stomach, groin, throat, beneath the arms, and a flash of discomfort shot through her that these were the same weaknesses a human had. Maybe—but no, these monsters were merciless and hated humans, and compassion for them was completely out of line.

One of the orcs, the less wounded one, was gradually shifting to where if he was a Warmaster he could **[Outflank]** Owen. Even without that skill, it was a position that would endanger Owen. Instinctively, Aderyn focused on that orc. White light suddenly outlined it, faintly but clearly, and more lines of light extended in several directions from its body. Aderyn imagined grabbing the orc by the shoulders and shoving it away along one of those lines.

The orc slid backward as if its feet were greased, its next blow whiffing through the air without striking Owen. Aderyn dropped like a stone into the spot it had left. Her new skill **[Reposition]** was more effective and more dramatic than she'd imagined.

She shifted to **[Outflank]** the other orc, skewering it in the kidneys, then ducked as Owen's **<Sunsword>** cut its throat so deeply it nearly took the orc's head off. She ducked again to avoid the first orc's attack, though it was a wild swing that probably wouldn't have connected. Then Owen rushed the orc, **[Overrunning]** it and knocking it down. Its look of stunned surprise filled Aderyn's vision, driving her forward. Her next thrust and twist of the wrist disemboweled it.

Congratulations! You have defeated [Orc Masher].
You have earned [5700 XP]

"What was that?" Owen gasped.

"Reposition. Look out!"

Owen blocked the attack of another orc, who cringed away from the radiance of the <**Sunsword**> and then fled. "I think we've routed them," he said.

Aderyn looked around, but she still couldn't see anything past the immediate vicinity. It did look like the orcs were running, but she recalled the rest of the forces arrayed around the city and knew better. "The orc leader we have to kill is here somewhere. Scarred, with black hair."

"That could be anyone," Owen said. "Many of the orcs I fought were scarred. Looked ritualistic."

"Then—" Aderyn gestured to him to wait and flew to the top of the catapult, which stank of pitch and whatever pungent substance the orcs had treated it with. It smoldered dully now that the Flamecrafters' fire had nearly burned itself out. Sure enough, another mass of orcs approached from the south, coming around the side of Adhiraj. She Assessed the lot: five hundred and fifteen elites, seven hundred and eighty mashers, over a thousand grunts. The elementalists were scattered through the forces, and Aderyn thought that made it hard for **[Improved Assess 3]** to calculate their numbers, but about one hundred seemed right.

And, at the head of the orc army, someone different.

Name: Ornok

Type: Monstrosity (orc ravager)

Power level: 16

Attack(s): multiple weapons, bite, special

Immune to: none

Resistant to: bladed weapons, bludgeoning weapons, missile weapons

Vulnerable to: *daylight, sunburst*

Special attacks: fear

Orc ravagers rule the lesser castes through fear and strength. They serve as generals in the army, and among them, Ornok ranks high—second in command to its leader, Glasha, in fact. He is a powerful fighter, more powerful than you'd expect for his level—does that remind you of anyone?—and has taken many orc

lives as ordered by Glasha, who has his complete obedience. He's here because Glasha knows the strategic importance of Adhiraj, and he will not retreat until he's destroyed the city. Killing him won't break the siege, but it's a start.

Ornok possesses such an overwhelming physical presence he terrifies almost everyone he faces. In practical terms, this means attacks are less likely to hit and will do less damage if they do. Take him down, Aderyn, because he won't ever stop coming after the humans he hates.

Aderyn didn't stop to marvel at seeing her name written out by the system's message. "That one," she said, pointing at the scarred bulk with the stringy black hair caught up in a topknot. "He's our target."

Without hesitation, Owen ran to meet the oncoming horde and its terrible leader.

Chapter Twenty-Eight

Aderyn shot into the air again, heedless of the danger. The red-capped lieutenants and the soldiers they commanded moved to attack the orcs as if Owen's assault was a silent signal. Again, the tides shifted, the orcs flooding forward and lashing against the human troops. The onslaught was so fierce it pushed the humans back several paces, and the orcs shouted with fierce excitement.

But the humans rallied, and soon the tide flowed in the other direction. Aderyn, rapt in watching the pattern from above, was nearly impaled by a spear of sharp stone that lanced through the air aimed at her chest. She hurried to alight near Owen. Weston had joined him, and Livia was perceptible again only by the cries of her victims.

"The big one?" Weston gasped out, his voice hoarse from shouting. He buried one dagger to the hilt in the eye of his opponent. "The quest notice changed."

"The big one," Aderyn shouted.

"Livia!" Weston said. "We need a path cleared!"

Livia appeared by his side with a rush of displaced air. She chanted nonsense words, gesturing, and stomped one foot. The ground fractured and rose up as *thunderstomp* ripped through the crowd of orcs, knocking them to the ground in a single line that ended at Ornok.

Ornok swayed, but remained upright. He roared a challenge. Aderyn rushed after Owen, who ran without stumbling over the broken ground to close with Ornok.

Ornok strode forward, his enormous feet in hobnailed boots punching through the earth crust disrupted by *thunderstomp*. He was huge, half a head taller than the orc elites surrounding him, and his scars made patterns across his arms and face that almost looked like words. The stink of sweat and old cheese came off him in waves, sickening Aderyn. She slowed her steps. Her heart raced with fear rather than exertion. She saw as if with **[See It Coming]** the heavy, much-notched double blade of the axe Ornok spun in one hand embedded in Owen's chest. Screaming in terror, she ran forward and grabbed Owen's arm, pulling him back so his first strike missed.

"Aderyn!" Owen shouted. He twisted free of her grip and blocked the giant orc's blow. "You're going to get me killed!"

That woke her up. She retreated a few paces and then shouted in surprise as an orc elite lunged for her. Aderyn dodged the blow of its heavy club, but only barely. The orc bared its blackened teeth in a hideous grin. Aderyn's unnatural terror imposed by Ornok's fear aura faded. In its place, she felt a more natural fear that she was about to be cut down by orcs because she couldn't control herself. She snarled back at the orc and charged.

She lost track of Owen, lost track of everything as she fought her way through the crowd. Nothing mattered but the fight. The shouts and the clang of metal against metal filled her ears so she could barely think. The stink of blood nearly overwhelmed her, the coppery tang of human blood overwhelmed by the bitter charcoal smell of orc blood. Sweat dripped down the sides of her face, ignored so long as it didn't get in her eyes. She was nothing but an arm, wielding a sword, screaming defiance at the foe.

After a time, she found she was next to Livia, whose actual stone arm gleamed to match the glitter of the spell effect *stone fist* on her right arm. Anything Livia punched stayed down, either dead or incapacitated.

"*Daylight*," Aderyn gasped. "They're vulnerable to bright light. *Daylight* or *sunburst*."

Livia nodded. "Watch my back." She stepped away from the next orc fighter, leaving room for Aderyn to take her place, and threw back her head, chanting.

Brilliant light burst over the field, brighter than the sun, which was obscured by the overcast. Tremendous cries of pain filled the air, and many of the orcs cringed away from the light. Another cry went up, this one from human throats, as the soldiers shouted their exultation. Aderyn, on the ground, couldn't see the full effect, but she gutted the orc elite that went after Livia, and with her Warmaster's instincts felt rather than saw the shift that suggested the soldiers had pressed their advantage.

In that moment, she caught sight of Owen. Blood, both red and charcoal-crimson, matted his blond hair and smeared across the surface of his steel armor, but he and Ornok were still locked in combat. Aderyn fought her way to his side and then to behind Ornok, where the tug of **[Outflank]** took effect. Owen pressed the attack harder, but Ornok didn't look tired or even discomfited by the ferocity of Owen's strikes, regardless of how the sword shone with the brilliance of the sun.

Ornok's hardened leather armor deflected Aderyn's first slash, which thwacked across the leather like a whipcrack. Ornok didn't turn around to see what gnat had tried to bite him. His indifference infuriated Aderyn. She changed her grip slightly and thrust, aiming for the gap between his cuirass and the weird leather armor shaped like a rigid skirt that protected his rear and thighs. Again, her strike was deflected. Gritting her teeth, Aderyn struck low, aiming for the orc's leg tendons. She hoped he had tendons.

The mystery sword's edge bit deep into Ornok's calves, not deep enough to sever any tendons, but enough to make the orc bellow in pain and finally turn to see what was attacking him. The edge of his fear aura struck Aderyn again, this time faintly so shrugging it away was easy. She crouched in a fighting stance, her sword at the ready.

Ornok stared down at her. His lips curved in a cruel smile. Clearly, he found the idea of Aderyn being a threat amusing. He raised the double-bladed axe in what was sure to be a skull-cleaving blow if it landed. Aderyn readied herself to deflect it and hoped her sword wouldn't shatter.

From out of nowhere, a knife sailed through the air and impaled

Ornok through the throat just above where his cuirass ended. Ornok grabbed it and pulled it free, his smile vanishing. He snarled something and swung a great one-handed blow at Aderyn. Aderyn dodged the blow easily thanks to **[See It Coming]** and slashed at Ornok's armored chest. She couldn't pierce the armor, but Owen was nearby, and the point of her attack was to give him an opening.

Then Ornok bellowed in pain, his body arching to get away from the **<Sunsword>** buried to the hilt in his back. Aderyn backed away, out of reach of his spasms as he tried to reach the blade. Another thrown dagger took Ornok higher in the throat. The big orc jerked once more and then hit the ground with a meaty, wet thud, twitching a few times before lying still.

Congratulations! You have defeated [Ornok, Orc Leader].
You have earned [22,000 XP]

Aderyn shoved stray tendrils of hair out of her eyes before resuming her defensive stance. There were still orcs to kill.

Two orc mashers came to a halt near Ornok's body. They cried out in their guttural language, long, angry strings of incomprehensible words. Aderyn braced herself for their attack. Instead, the mashers backed away, then turned and ran. In moments, the entire orc army was in retreat. Aderyn stood over Ornok's body and watched, her mind foggy with exhaustion, as human soldiers pursued the enemy past the city.

Congratulations! You have completed the battle quest [Break the Siege of Adhiraj].
You have been awarded a battle bonus of [14,000 XP]

Livia and Weston joined Owen and Aderyn. Aderyn felt the tremendous weary letdown of a difficult fight won. "I should follow," she said, but she didn't move.

"You need to establish if the whole orc army fled when those did," Owen pointed out. "There might be stragglers."

Flying struck her as even more taxing than running, but Aderyn nodded and took to the skies, or tried to; instead of the light, airy feeling as her feet left the ground, she felt mired in the muck as if Livia's **[Earth to Mud]** skill trapped her. "I guess Kimay's spell wore off," she said. "We'd better get walking."

They hurried around the city to where they were within sight of the great gate. It hung open, but not as if it had been battered, so Aderyn didn't let herself freak out at the sight. Platoons milled about, if you could call orderly, intentional movement "milling." Some were destroying the remaining catapults, while others were sorting through the bodies. A few soldiers waved off the birds circling the battlefield. Aderyn focused on the nearest teams and felt ill.

"I forgot," she whispered. "I got so caught up in winning, I forgot not all of us would survive."

"There are way more dead orcs than dead humans," Owen said.

She rounded on him. "Is that supposed to make it better?"

"They chose to go, Aderyn." Owen didn't flinch at her anger. "They went in defense of their homes and families. Don't forget that."

Aderyn squeezed her eyes shut. "You're right. I just—we don't often fight creatures that leave our human companions dead, and there are so many... but you're right." She opened her eyes. "I need to communicate with Rajman. Would you all go on ahead? I think I need a little time alone first."

Owen hugged her close, putting a hand on the back of her head in a comforting gesture. "Understandable. We'll go see what we can do to help the others."

When her friends were gone, Aderyn pulled out the **<Farspeaker>**, but she didn't insert Rajman's coin. Instead, she surveyed the battlefield. Maybe she wasn't cut out to be a general, if this was her reaction to battle—this awful, gut-clenching heartache over those who wouldn't come back to their families. Or maybe that feeling meant she was exactly right for the job. She should talk to Varoun about it. But later.

Rajman, when his image appeared on the **<Farspeaker>**, showed signs of having been in the thick of the fighting, which made Aderyn wonder how disheveled she looked. "The orcs were routed completely," Rajman said. "My scouts indicate the area is clear, and the orc warriors were scattered rather than regrouping for a second assault."

"We killed their leader, Ornok."

"Killed their leader? Excellent. That ought to make them ineffective for now. Probably most of them will circle around and rejoin another of the orc armies, but they won't continue south because it would mean their slaughter." Rajman grinned like a mischievous child. "Congratulations on your first victory."

"We all had a part in it. But... thank you." His confident manner brushed some of her melancholy away.

She heard her name being shouted and saw Owen and Weston running toward her. In the next moment, Livia appeared at her side. "The rear forces were attacked," she exclaimed. "We have to go. Isold—"

"Sorry, general," Aderyn said, and cut the connection, making Rajman's face vanish. "Livia, that's not possible. Kimay would have brought word."

Livia shook her head. "I don't know about that. Nandi found us just now. She looks like ten miles of bad road and could barely speak."

A jolt of fear shook Aderyn to her core. She turned to run eastward, but Livia grabbed her with her stone hand and brought her to a halt. The slightly gritty feel of granite against her skin grounded her. "Right," she said as Owen and Weston stumbled to a halt in front of them. "*Transport.*"

With arms slung around each other's shoulders, they listened to the long, almost-intelligible syllables of *transport*, and in a rush and a jerk, they were among the few tents pitched where the rear forces waited. Aderyn gaped again. Smoke and scorch marks and blood splatter marred several of the tents, and the ground was churned up into mud that clung to her feet and spattered the rest of the tents. The smell of battle, the smoke and the coppery scent of blood, was fainter than around Adhiraj, but she felt sicker because it shouldn't have been here at all. Low cries of pain filled the air, not many, but enough to cut Aderyn to the heart.

"This wasn't supposed to happen," she murmured. "Where did the orcs come from? I thought we had them focused on us. Contained."

"Aderyn," Isold called out. The Herald trudged toward them, looking even more weary than Aderyn felt. "There weren't many orcs," he said more quietly when he neared them. "I believe they were fleeing the battle and stumbled on us by accident. I routed most of them, and our other defenders fought, but..." His voice trailed off. "Most of these soldiers were no match for even the lowest-level orc."

Aderyn surveyed the area. She saw no bodies, and the moaning came from inside the tents, but the absence of any movement horrified her as if the ground were carpeted with corpses. "Where's Kimay? Why didn't I hear about this?"

"Kimay went to find you, as ordered." Isold looked grim. "He was shot out of the sky by an orc elementalist. Stone shard through the eye. He died instantly."

"Kimay died." Aderyn's vision tunneled. "I told him to come to me, to bring me word if the worst happened." Her mind's eye insisted on throwing up images of Kimay alive, Kimay bloody, Kimay falling from the sky...

"Don't think like that," Weston said.

"He could have used *whispering wind* to communicate. I didn't even think of that. Instead—damn it. I knew he wasn't up to it. I should never have—"

Owen grabbed her by the shoulders and shook her. "Stop it," he said, his voice low and urgent. "Stop. If you're going to take on guilt for every soldier who dies carrying out your orders, I swear we're going back to the safe zone to retire."

Aderyn blinked. "What? Retire?"

"You are not to let this quest destroy you," Owen said. "Nothing is that important. Not even breaking the level cap. And I will do everything in my power to keep you from being eaten up by guilt. It's true, you made a mistake in giving too specific an order, and it cost Kimay his life. That's going to hurt for a long time. But this is war, Aderyn. He might have died a hundred other ways. You can't predict someone's fate, and you can't protect absolutely everyone. You know that. Don't take on more guilt than you can bear."

Aderyn's eyes felt too dry for tears. "I can't," she began, swallowed, and went on, "I think I can bear it. I have to bear it. But that feeling isn't going away any time soon." The memory of willowy Kimay casting *world door* struck her. He wouldn't cast any spell, ever again, and— She shoved the thought away. She could indulge in her grief and guilt later, in private.

Her hip warmed in the warning sign that someone wanted to address her via the <**Farspeaker**> that hung in its pouch there. She shouted down her immediate feeling that she couldn't bear any more bad news. It would be difficult for anything to be worse news than this.

She touched the shining mirrored surface with her forefinger, and Varoun's image appeared. "What's wrong?" Aderyn asked. Varoun's age-worn face looked haggard, like he'd seen nightmares he couldn't shake. Aderyn recalled her last thought and winced inwardly at the possibility she'd jinxed herself.

"I need you back in Ikharatia immediately," Varoun said. "You and your team. Put your regiment under the command of General Rajman for now—unless you've made a decision about promotions?"

"I have, but there hasn't been time to do anything about it. Sir, isn't there anything more you can tell me?"

Varoun shook his head, but in a gesture of helplessness rather than negation. "Queen Devendra has been kidnapped," he said. "I fear this is the beginning of a coup."

Chapter Twenty-Nine

Aderyn gasped. "Kidnapped?" She felt her friends gathering around, but shock kept her focused on Varoun's face.

"Thirty minutes ago, I received a message informing me that agents of Umed, the king of Durga, had sneaked into the palace intent on kidnapping the king. According to the queen's remaining attendant, Devendra fought to defend the king's escape and was taken herself after most of her attendants were slain."

"That's awful. You said a coup, though—wouldn't this be an act of war?"

Varoun shook his head. "As part of my defense against the orcs, I have men and women reporting on the state of affairs in Durga."

"You mean in case that kingdom attacks us while we're distracted by monsters."

"Yes." Varoun's expression was grim. "To my knowledge, Durga is not geared up for war against us. Its military might is aimed at defending itself should the orcs invade there next."

Aderyn remembered the map, how the high-risk zone cut the peninsula of Durga off from the rest of the continent. "How sure are you? If they're building their forces, couldn't that be turned to attacking this country too?"

"An attack by Durga would mean naval warfare. At the very least, a buildup of naval forces for conveying ground troops. There's been no such buildup."

Aderyn shook her head. "I'm still not sure I follow, sorry. I mean, I understand this is a ruse, but Queen Devendra really was kidnapped, right? Who could be behind that? I assume Kanan, obviously, but maybe he's too obvious. I still don't know anything about Southlander politics. Could it be anyone else?"

Varoun grimaced. "Only Kanan has the resources to pull something like this off. The primary witness, one of Queen Devendra's ladies-in-waiting, kept changing her story in ways that fit what she thought she wanted me to hear. I consider her extremely suggestible, and I believe Kanan primed her with her story."

"Primed her? You don't mean she's his patsy?" Owen said. "I mean, you know, someone working for him?" he amended as Varoun looked puzzled.

"She might be working for him, but it's more likely Kanan arranged for his false Durgan agents to leave her alive so she would be the one to spread the news she overheard from the 'kidnappers.' If the story came directly from him, suspicion would fall on him immediately." Varoun's sardonic tone said clearly he didn't think much of anyone who didn't suspect Kanan anyway.

"I assume Kanan has declared himself regent during this emergency," Isold said.

Varoun's grim expression soured further. "That's a correct assumption. He's done it as delicately as possible—claims that as the duke whose holdings are not in immediate danger, he is the only one who can spare the attention to protect the king 'in this time of crisis,' as he puts it."

"What can we do?" Livia said. "We can't let that bastard control that little kid. He'll wait until the furor over his usurpation dies down, and then Colan will have a tragic accident."

"We have time, as you suggest," Varoun said. "And we have the advantage that the queen is likely not dead."

"How is that even possible? She can ruin his power grab if she escapes captivity," Owen said.

"Right. She can't still be alive," Weston said.

But Varoun was shaking his head. "The queen has more power dead than alive. If her body turns up, that means Kanan's lies are exposed. Not to mention that murdering someone is much different from a mere kidnapping, and Kanan can't count on his people being so loyal as to not have qualms about taking that step. No, Kanan needs to confine her somewhere until he can solidify his power by killing the king. That gives us time to rescue her."

"Do you mean us?" Aderyn asked. "Because we're willing, but what about the war? Aren't we needed there?"

"You are, which is part of what infuriates me about Kanan's selfish power grab," Varoun said. "I cannot afford to lose any more commanders, and yet what I have in mind requires your particular skills, the five of you together. I have my informants searching a number of locations Kanan has access to where Queen Devendra might be imprisoned. Those informants, however, are not high level—none are more than level eight—and one of those locations is too dangerous for them."

"You mean the Ivory Palace, don't you?" Weston said.

"You've heard of it?"

"Kanan bragged about it to me," Livia said. "He claimed he had special knowledge that meant he could defeat it any time he wanted. I thought it was bravado, but that doesn't mean he wasn't right."

"For a non-classed noble, Kanan commands a surprising number of adventurers, and many of them have braved the Ivory Palace," Varoun said. "It's rumored that he gave them inside knowledge that made their victories possible. How he knows so much, I have no idea, since I know he's never entered it himself. But of all the places he might have trapped the queen, that is the one that is the most potentially dangerous, to Queen Devendra and to anyone who tries to rescue her."

"He might have imprisoned her there in the hope the dungeon would do his dirty work for him, right?" Aderyn's sick feeling returned. She knew nothing about the Ivory Palace, and immediately she imagined the worst.

"That is precisely my fear. Queen Devendra is a strong Tidecaller, but she is retired and only level seven, and the Ivory Palace reportedly holds many high-level dangers. If she is there, she has much less time than I originally thought. Will you go?"

"You don't even have to ask," Owen said.

"He's right," Aderyn added, "but what does this mean for the war?"

"With the siege of Adhiraj broken and the orcs there scattered, the next assault will be against Shantos," Varoun said. "You said you had a candidate for command of Colonel Ishan's former regiment?"

"Yes. Major Kavish and Major Sahal are both good commanders, but Sahal excels at logistics and I think it would be a mistake to promote him. He and Kavish work well together, and I don't think their working relationship will be disrupted by Kavish's promotion. And I was impressed by Kavish's initiative when the regiment was on the move. He took the lead in directing the platoons and handled a few disciplinary measures while I was gone. I suggest you promote Major Kavish to colonel—though maybe you want to evaluate him yourself first?"

"I trust your judgment." Varoun smiled, but on his haggard face the expression looked ghastly, not at all reassuring as he probably meant. "Colonel Kavish will take command of the regiment and help fortify Adhiraj against the orcs' return—they still need that city neutralized if they want to move freely through the Southlands. Have Kimay transport you to outside the Ivory Palace—"

Aderyn's throat closed up again. "Kimay is dead, sir."

Varoun cursed. "That's a terrible loss, and I hope it's not too heartless for me to say it also means more delays. I'm sorry to hear it. I will arrange for someone else to bring you back."

"We'll need to go to Ikharatia first," Owen said. "We have preparations to make."

"Very well. And, Aderyn, don't worry about leaving Raven Regiment. Your command there was always meant to be temporary. I can make up for your absence for a few days."

"You have a lot of faith in me and my friends if you expect this to take only a few days," Aderyn said.

"If it takes more than that, it might not matter," Varoun replied.

HALF AN HOUR LATER, THEY ENTERED THE EASTERN GATE OF the city. "Great," Livia said when they were all seated in one of the people-carrying wagons. "A difficult, mysterious dungeon, filled with who knows what kind of monsters and traps, and we're on a deadline."

"I'll Assess it when we get there, and that will give us an advantage." Aderyn stared down the street, willing the wagon to go faster.

"**[Improved Assess 3]** might not be enough. You know what we have to do." Livia was paler than usual, but her jaw was set in the firm expression that meant she'd made up her mind to do something impossible.

"Do what?"

"No," Owen said, grabbing Livia's shoulder and giving her a quick shake. "Absolutely not. You were nearly compromised the last time you pretended interest in Kanan. We're not that desperate."

"You heard Varoun," Livia said. "Kanan knows the secret of the Ivory Palace and he's given it to adventurers before. And I told you what I was willing to do for the sake of that little boy."

"I remember how you looked coming out of the duke's residence, Livia." Weston clasped her hand. "You said, never again. You pushed your luck the first time, and you know it."

"But it's my choice—"

"And if you have to sleep with him to get the information? No. I told you, we aren't desperate. We can defeat a stupid dungeon without you prostituting yourself." Owen sounded as firm as Weston.

"Please, Livia. We have other options." Aderyn took Livia's other hand and squeezed it.

Livia scowled, but her eyes were bright with tears. "I swear," she said in a low voice, "if Kanan makes another move against the kid, I will kill him myself."

"That's more like it," Owen said. "Now, how about you tell us again what you learned about the Ivory Palace? We'll use that and Aderyn's Assessment to give us a boost."

Livia nodded. "I know where it is, but I shouldn't use *world door* to get there, since I'll want all my magical reserves for the dungeon itself. That means half an hour, maybe an hour's walk down the coast. Oh, I forgot. Kanan mentioned it was sinking."

"Sinking? Do we have even less time than we thought?" Aderyn asked, alarmed.

"Not fast. It's sunk over the centuries, so there are submerged levels. I didn't think about us not being able to breathe." Livia got the intent look she wore when she was reviewing her spell list.

"We might not have to, if the queen is there. She'll have to breathe, too," Weston said.

"Even retired, Queen Devendra is a Tidecaller of high enough level she might have spells allowing her to breathe underwater," Isold said. "We can't make assumptions."

"Are there items, or spells, that will help us with that?" Owen asked.

"Spells, yes, but I only have *air bubble*, and that won't work for long." Livia scowled.

"There are items that will do what you suggest, such as **<Breath of Life Amulets>** or **<Gill-Lungs>**, but it will take time for us to locate them for sale. They may be more common here on the coast, but they are still rare," Isold said.

"We don't have time," Owen said. "We'll have to take our chances. Let's get out of these uniforms and head out. We'll need every advantage we can get."

Chapter Thirty

Twenty minutes later, they were on the coast road heading east. The sun's heat battered Aderyn's bare head, but the breeze coming off the ocean swept away the mugginess of the air and kept her from being completely miserable. Even so, she was grateful for the Southlander-style tunic and calf-length linen trousers she wore. She'd chosen them for how lightweight they were under her uniform coat, which she'd left behind at the inn, and they felt even better now.

"Does anyone know why we have ranks in **[Swim]** when I for one have never swum in anything bigger than a full-size tub?" she asked.

"I assume it's because it is a skill useful to adventurers, like **[Spot]** or **[Survival]**," Isold said. "A single rank is likely enough to keep someone from drowning. I have some small experience in swimming, but only enough for two ranks."

"I know how to swim," Owen said. "Most people where I come from learn how when they're kids, even if they don't live on a lake shore or near the ocean."

"What's the purpose?" Aderyn asked.

"Oh, we have swimming pools all over the place. I was a lifeguard for two summers at the community pool. Also, people like to vacation at the beach. Some people swim competitively." Owen looked out across the waves. "This shore wouldn't be appealing to swimmers or surfers, though. Too rocky, and the waves are choppy."

"I guess I don't see how swimming would be fun. All the stories talk about adventurers swimming across rivers to get away from monsters, or attacking sea monsters in their own element." Aderyn imagined propelling herself through the water like a dolphin. Maybe that was how swimming worked, that effortless glide with the water washing over you.

"Maybe we'll get the chance for you to discover the fun for yourself," Owen said.

They walked without speaking after that. Urgency propelled Aderyn faster until she felt the slightly dizzy sensation of too much exertion under too hot a sun. There was no sense exhausting herself when an unknown dungeon awaited them. So she made herself walk rapidly, but not too fast, and kept herself from going mad with worry by examining her surroundings.

The coastal road rose at least fifty feet above where the ocean lashed the land, high enough that even at high tide the road was in no danger of being washed out. The stony cliffside below the road sprouted shrubs here and there, tenacious plants and spindly trees whose trunks turned at right angles where they emerged from the land so they grew parallel to the slope. The phenomenon fascinated Aderyn. She promised herself that once this disaster was over, she'd find time to explore the shore.

Inland, to the left, the ground rose more gently, and trees with tall, straight trunks that didn't branch for eighty or a hundred feet up spread out across the land. Their foliage made a crazy quilt of a dozen shades of green, each tree's branches tangled with the next until it was impossible to see where each began and ended. The ground beneath would be permanently in shade, Aderyn guessed. Too bad the road didn't pass through that shady area, because cool breezes or no, the sun's punishing tropical rays made her sweat.

In another half an hour, Weston said, "That's it. Up ahead and to the right a bit. It's on a small headland, looks like. I was picturing something smaller based on Livia's information."

Livia squinted. "I don't see it yet."

"I do," Aderyn said, "or at least there's a shape out there that's too regular to be a rock formation. That means we're close enough for

[Improved Assess 3]." She slowed to a halt. "Let's see what it says before we get any closer."

She focused on the spot with her skill and read the Assessment aloud.

Name: The Ivory Palace

Type: Themed, large, victory condition B or D

Power Level: 17

Inhabitants: varying, including magical beasts, monstrosities, and vermin

Traps: see below

Reward: coin and mundane items worth a total of 2,983 gold at current rate of exchange; assorted minor and major magic items

The Ivory Palace was originally a secondary residence of the rulers of the Southlands, a lavish, lushly appointed summer home for when they needed to get away from their lavish, lushly appointed everyday home. Nothing says "privilege" like an ocean-side getaway, right? Rising coastal waters put an end to these excursions as the lower levels of the palace became submerged, but the inhabitants had plenty of warning and took all their valuable possessions with them. And that would have been the end of the story if other creatures hadn't taken over. Half a century after its abandonment, the Ivory Palace officially gained dungeon status.

The dangers of the palace are twofold. On the one hand, there are the upper levels, the ones still above water or only occasionally submerged. Those are the territory of the monstrous kaduvas, terrible shapeshifting half-mortal, half-demon creatures. Don't ask about the human half. You don't want to know. There are other monsters in those levels, most of them slaves or pets of the kaduvas, but trust me, they're not what you have to worry about.

The submerged levels offer the kind of threats you're imagining right now: aquatic monsters, animals or vermin altered by their proximity to the dungeon to be vicious killers, probably a giant squid. All right, definitely a giant squid. Victory condition B requires you to kill it on its home ground—or its home water,

more accurately. But to do this, you'll have to fight your way past the weresharks. They are the natural enemies of the kaduvas, but don't think that makes them your friends. Both groups of monstrosities lay traps for one another, but there's no reason they might not catch you instead, so beware.

However, there's another possible victory condition available to you thanks to Kanan's treachery. Victory condition D requires you to find Devendra and bring her out of the dungeon alive. I'll tell you right now this is the more dangerous option, as Devendra might be anywhere within the Ivory Palace, and who knows what you'll encounter along the way? But, since it's why you're here, I'll just wish you good luck. You'll need it.

Despite the Assessment's final sentences, reading all that calmed Aderyn. "It doesn't say it's impossible," she said, "and that's enough information to satisfy me for now."

"It's almost like it's a double dungeon," Owen said. "Too bad we can't get experience for it twice."

"Don't be too optimistic, you'll jinx us," Livia said.

"Maybe we can," Weston said. "Suppose we rescue the queen *and* kill the giant squid? Ow!" He rubbed his arm where Livia had smacked him lightly with her stone hand. "What was that for?"

"Excessive optimism again." Livia shook her head. "We haven't even come within actual sight of the place and already we're celebrating victory. We should assume the worst, and then we won't be caught off guard."

"Livia is right that we shouldn't anticipate a win before we've achieved it." Isold was staring into the distance as if he could bring the Ivory Palace into focus with his thoughts. "Confidence is important, but that can only take us so far."

"Fair point, Isold," Owen said. "Okay. Let's move on, but we should be thinking about ways to deal with the environment problem. We can't count on finding Devendra somewhere above water."

They walked faster now, still not fast enough for exhaustion to take its toll, but at a brisk pace that brought them within sight of the Ivory Palace in ten minutes and to its doors in another twenty. Except there weren't doors. Aderyn stood at the end of the short headland and gazed in dismay upon the smooth marble dome that rose some twenty feet above them.

"I don't get it," she said. "Where are the doors? The Assessment said the waters rose, and that made the palace uninhabitable, but this looks more like it slid off the headland into the water. It's even slightly tilted."

"I think I see," Isold said. "The Ivory Palace was carved out of the stone of the headland, top to bottom. I have no explanation for why it is tilted like that, but it has the look of a statue that needs the rap of a chisel to separate it from its marble block."

"That makes sense, once I look at it sideways." Owen tilted his head in emphasis. "And that explains the missing doors. Notice how the headland—the causeway, really—isn't smooth the way it would be if it was a road to the front door? I bet the Ivory Palace was originally accessed by boat, from the water. The doors are on the far side."

They all stared at the dome. "You mean, underwater on the far side?" Aderyn said. "In that case, we're screwed before we start, because we still don't have any way to breathe underwater."

"There's probably an upper entrance or something," Weston said. "I choose to believe the system would have mentioned it if going underwater was the only option. We can climb across the dome to the far side."

"I'll make holes for us to hang onto with *stone ladder*. That surface is too smooth." Livia cracked the knuckles of each hand. Her stone hand made a sound like pebbles striking a cliff wall.

"Oh, you can't—" Aderyn began, then blushed. "That was stupid. I was thinking, the palace is too beautiful to ruin with *stone ladder*, but of course Devendra's life is much more important."

"That's right. You keep thinking like that." Livia reached as high as she was able and punched a hole in the marble dome, just big enough for a booted foot to fit inside. Quickly, she made her way up the surface, pockmarking it with explosive cracks of stone and the pattering shower of expensive gravel.

One by one, they followed Livia to the top of the dome. It wasn't as slippery as Aderyn had imagined, being pitted and roughened by centuries of exposure to the elements, and once the curve wasn't steep, they were able to walk across the dome easily. Aderyn admired the view of the ocean, extending to the horizon in every direction except behind them, and the sight of Ikharatia, which was a scruff of colored roofs collected on the shore and dozens of white sails where ships stood at harbor.

"I wonder where the ships go," she mused. "There can't be that many that make the journey north. Do you suppose they travel along the shore to the other cities?"

"Tielana is the only other coastal city in the Southlands, but I imagine the trade is booming," Isold said.

"Well, they're beautiful. I'd almost want to risk the journey by sea, except *world door* saves so much time."

"Keep going," Livia said. An explosive pop and rattle of stone shards signaled that the Earthbreaker had reached the point where *stone ladder* was again necessary. "There's a terrace down there that must have been a balcony before the waters rose. It's not far, but the dome is steeper here."

The dome extended over the terrace, or balcony, with an overhang that meant they each had to drop a distance of about ten feet off the dome's curve. Aderyn landed lightly and without much of a stumble. She walked, not to the arched doorway, but to the balcony railing. It was of perfect, creamy ivory, with spindles carved to look like graceful maidens holding up the rail. She ran a finger along the rail, and a tingle shot through her, not unpleasant or painful, but definitely unexpected.

"The balcony railing and the door frame are saturated with magic," Livia said. She had her hands on her hips and was regarding the frame, which was also of ivory. "I'm concerned."

"Because it might be a forbiddance or something?" Owen said. "Zap us with twenty thousand volts when we walk through?"

"I don't know what a volt is, but twenty thousand of them can't be good." Livia chanted some nonsense words, and the ivory glittered like mica struck by sunlight. She swore under her breath. "*Dispel magic* doesn't work. That could be good if it means there's no hostile effect, or it could be bad if it's a hostile effect too powerful for me to remove."

"Ivory is imbued with protective magic that grows stronger the more ivory is used," Isold said. "If *dispel magic* didn't work, that suggests the magic is not an ongoing, active effect, but is instead passive."

"The rail didn't hurt me when I touched it," Aderyn volunteered. "But if there's a protection on the door, that makes me want to know who it's meant to protect against. Adventurers like us, or monsters?"

"Let's find out," Weston said. He strode to the doorway and stuck a hand through into the dark space beyond. Nothing happened other than the Moonlighter twitching in a full-body shiver. "Goosebumps. But the feeling is gone now."

"We can't hang around here forever. Let's take a chance." Owen walked past Weston and was swallowed up by the darkness. Aderyn bit back a cry of dismay when she realized Owen was still visible, just shadowy. She hurried after him. Her skin prickled with gooseflesh as if she had taken a dip in an icy bath, and then the moment passed, and she was inside the Ivory Palace.

Chapter Thirty-One

The dimness blinded her temporarily, so she grabbed Owen's hand to steady herself while her eyes adjusted. Gradually, the walls came into focus. Remnants of paint made pastel blotches on the walls, scoured and bleached by time and the elements. Years ago, they would have been brightly-colored murals, but now Aderyn couldn't make out their subjects or even where one began and the other left off. The room smelled damply of seawater and salt wind.

Above, the room's domed ceiling continued the theme of patchy, faded colors, though all the patches were pale blue. Aderyn guessed the ceiling might once have depicted the sky, possibly the night sky depending on how much of a toll the weather had taken on it. Tarnished brass lanterns hung from chains, their glass missing or shattered. There weren't enough of them to cast a bright light over the room back when they were intact, and Aderyn pictured a cool, dimly-lit patio overlooking the sea.

She left Owen's side and walked to where a doorway opened on a gallery that extended deeper into the palace. Grit and broken glass crunched under her boots. "I can't see far enough to know where this goes, but the corridor seems really long."

"So does this one," Weston said from across the room. He stood at another doorway diagonally opposite the first. "Which way, Aderyn?"

Aderyn fished the <**Wayfinder**> out of her <**Purse of Great Capacity**> and held it in her cupped hands. Her heart must be deeply engaged in wanting to find Devendra, because the orb's rings immediately whirred into life, and the spike warmed to bright rosy red. That was a good sign, but Aderyn pivoted slowly, sweeping the entire patio in the item's arc. There might be a secret door that was a more direct route to where Devendra was.

The orb's spike dimmed to pale pink as she turned, then, surprisingly, warmed to red again. "Weird," Aderyn said. She pointed the <**Wayfinder**> at the first door again, then back at the second. "They both show the same result. I've never seen this before."

"You're sure there's no difference?" Owen asked.

Aderyn nodded. "I've used the <**Wayfinder**> so often I've become familiar with its quirks. I can tell exactly the point at which it identifies the true path. This means both doors are equally likely to lead us where we need to go."

"Then it's up to us," Owen said. "Anyone have a preference?"

"There's a low sound like wind across a bottle top coming from this way," Weston said. "I don't know if we want to go toward potential danger, or away from it. Assuming noise means potential danger."

"Let's take this passage near me, and see where it goes. We can always come back and go the other way." Aderyn turned so she was facing the gallery again.

"Fair enough." Owen nodded. "Let's move."

In the illumination from Livia's *orbs of light*, the windowless gallery looked much the same as the patio, though the weathering wasn't as intense. The peeling, faded paint suggested more murals had once decorated the inside wall, possibly a single mural. It was impossible to tell, but Aderyn, examining the walls in between glances at the <**Wayfinder**>, liked to imagine one long story being told through pictures. The other wall, the one that formed the outer wall of the Ivory Palace, was blank white over grayish plaster. In all, it suggested visitors were meant to pay attention to the art, whatever it had been.

After only a minute, they came to a side corridor that branched deeper into the dungeon's interior. Aderyn swung the **<Wayfinder>** to aim at the new hall. "It's identical again," she said. "I don't understand. The **<Wayfinder>** can't be broken."

"It's coincidence," Owen said. "It just means there are equivalent paths all through this place. I say we leave this one for now and continue forward."

"Yes, we'll have something unexplored at our backs no matter which way we go." Weston gestured at the dark hallway ahead. "Let's not get sidetracked."

The rosy glow of the **<Wayfinder's>** spike intensified the closer they got to the end of the gallery. Aderyn told herself not to be excited. The odds of them finding Devendra immediately were vanishingly small. But suppose they got lucky?

The gallery came to an end at a door whose wood was swollen and puffy-looking. "More sea air," Owen said. "Is it locked?"

"No, nor trapped neither," Weston said. He rose from where he'd crouched to examine the lock. "And I don't hear anything beyond, though I'm not sure that means anything in a dungeon. It could be some monster concealing its presence."

"Stop being pessimistic. That's my job," Livia said. "Let's find out what's in there."

Owen pressed down on the handle. "It's stuck. Give me a hand."

Weston and Owen put their shoulders to the door and shoved, hard. With a creak and a groan of tortured, rusty metal, the door popped open, and the two men stumbled forward a few steps. Livia sent several orbs flying past before they recovered, but Aderyn said, "Look, there's already light!"

They stood in the doorway and stared in amazement. "It's a jungle," Aderyn said. "How can there be a jungle inside?"

"It's not actually a jungle," Weston said. "Just a lot of overgrown vines. I think this was some kind of giant terrarium before. Look at the tubs." He gestured around the perimeter of the room. Bathtub-sized pots filled with earth lined the walls, all of them overgrowing with big, bushy, fat-leaved plants or thick vines that clung to the wall as if glued there. Some of the vines were tall enough to reach the ceiling, which was higher than in the gallery.

More tubs clustered near the center of the room, these with shorter, spreading plants and vines whose tendrils curled in loose corkscrews across the tiled floor. The whole room smelled wet and green, not in a fresh way, but with a hint of decaying vegetation.

"The lights are magical," Livia said, pointing at the glowing glass circles embedded in the ceiling. The vines curved to avoid them. "I bet they're hot, too, like the ones in Gamboling Coil. It's amazing they still have enough magic to function after all this time."

"They must contribute to the warmth of this room, then," Isold said. "It's hotter here than outside."

Aderyn consulted the <**Wayfinder**> and pointed. "There's the door."

She took a step toward the door and came up short as something gripped her ankle. A vine curled around her boot, apparently loosely, but when she tried to move again, its grip tightened. "Great," she said, and Assessed the vine.

Name: Strangler Vine

Type: Plant

Power level: 8

Attack: special

Immune to: mind-affecting magic

Resistant to: elemental water damage

Vulnerable to: elemental fire damage, elemental cold damage, bladed weapons damage

Special attack: entangle, constrict, swallow whole

The strangler vine, despite what I said above, isn't really all that dangerous. It can't move fast, so it depends on sneaking up on prey, but that means avoiding it isn't too hard. Unless it's already grabbed you, in which case you could be in trouble. Strangler vines entangle their prey, looping around its body so they can squeeze it to death, then engulf the corpse like a snake swallowing a mouse whole. They prefer to attack sleeping creatures, but they'll go after anything that moves. In the time it takes you to read this, it's gotten even more of a grip on you, so I suggest drawing your sword before you lose the ability to.

Aderyn swiftly drew her sword. The strangler vine had tangled both her legs, but Aderyn swung and lopped off the vine a foot from where it entangled her.

Congratulations! You have defeated [Strangler Vine].
You have earned [2500 XP]

Aderyn silently cursed her distraction—though if she hadn't taken the time to Assess it, she wouldn't now know how to fight it. She kicked the dead vine off her legs as she summed up what she'd learned. "I don't think everything in here is a strangler vine," she began, Assessing the rest of the room. It lit with the brilliant blue lines of **[Discern Weakness]**, which shifted and intersected with each other to pinpoint dozens of strangler vines surrounding the team.

"Never mind," she boomed out with **[Amplify Voice]**. "They're all monsters. We need to fight our way to the exit and not worry about killing all of them."

All around her, the others were working their way across the room, surrounding Isold, whose mind control skills were useless against the strangler vines. The system defeat notices didn't happen as often as Aderyn thought they should, which told her lopping off tendrils wasn't enough to count as a defeat. Good thing they didn't count on gaining experience from them.

Livia spat out a series of unintelligible words, and three vines tore free of their pots and fell limply in coils at her feet. "That was a good one, right? Come on! I never come up with lines like that."

"What are you talking about?" Weston said. He slashed through a vine that wrapped around his foot.

"'I'll send shivers down your vine,' right? Like down your... you know, it's not as funny if I have to explain it." Livia gestured and chanted something else and uprooted more vines.

"Livia, sweetheart, you're babbling." Weston grunted and blocked the reaching tendril of another vine.

"I'm not babbling!"

"Wait a minute." Owen blocked a wrist-thick vine and slashed through another. "When did you say that?"

"When I cast *telekinesis*, of course." Livia shook free of the tendril coiling up her leg. "I've been thinking maybe I should get creative with my spellslinging, say something memorable. Make our easy fights more interesting."

"Livia, your spellslinging never sounds like anything but nonsense words—look out!" Aderyn lunged for a vine that threatened to wrap around Livia's throat from behind.

Livia gestured and spoke more unintelligible words. The tendril froze, quivering, at full extension, unmoving in a way that suggested it really wanted to be free to attack. "It does not. I admit, I usually don't get creative, because it's better to be fast than slow down to think of a clever pun or whatever, but it's hardly nonsense."

Aderyn chopped the frozen vine in half. "Let's save this discussion for when we're free, all right?"

They were within reach of the door finally, and Aderyn and Livia took up defensive positions while the men struggled to get the door, also swollen from long years' exposure to sea air, unstuck and open. It felt like much longer than half a minute before the door swung open and they all tumbled through. Isold slammed the door shut, trapping a vine tendril that waved in the air as if seeking prey before sagging in death. "That was bracing."

"I want to know why Livia thinks we understand her spellslinging," Owen said. "Do you mean all this time you've been saying ordinary words?"

"Of course." Livia rubbed a streak of sap off on her trousers. "It's not like there's a special spellslinger language."

"I swear we didn't know," Weston said. "It always sounds like it's close to being real words, but we can't understand it at all. Right?"

Livia gazed at the others, who all nodded in agreement. "Thunderation. You're serious." She started laughing. "It's taken us sixteen levels to realize this. I wonder if there's anything else we don't know about each other's abilities."

"Let's hope it's nothing important, if there is," Owen said. "And the odds are in our favor there. Aderyn?"

"There's only one way to go," Aderyn said, retrieving the **<Wayfinder>** from her purse and holding it where the others could see. "Down this hall."

The new hall went only a short distance before turning left. After a short distance, they came to another door. Weston examined it and shook his head to indicate it was unlocked and free of traps. It opened easily, and Aderyn started to follow Owen through the door, but he came to an abrupt halt and she bumped into him. His shoulders tensed in anticipation of a fight, and she looked past him to see what had startled him.

The room reminded Aderyn of her father's fighting studio, except that the weapons in racks against the walls were real and not wooden. A man holding a sword in an attack position, facing off against a straw-stuffed wooden practice dummy, stood as still as Owen, his gaze fixed on him. A second, longer look told Aderyn this wasn't a man—the creature had the head of a panther, black and sleek and with a pronounced muzzle from which the tips of fangs protruded, and its hands, while humanoid, were covered in silky black fur. It wore a loose, knee-length robe that tied shut in front, and its legs were as furry as its hands and ended in feet with three clawed toes.

Aderyn came to her senses and Assessed it.

Name: Kaduva [1]

Type: Demon

Power level: 16

Attack: sword, claw x2, special

Immune to: none

Resistant to: mind-affecting attacks

Vulnerable to: dispelling magic

Special abilities: shapeshifting, night vision

Special attack: compelling gaze

Kaduvas are monstrous creatures created when human men have sex with demon females. Incapable of surviving for long in the demon void but disdainful of their mortal halves, they are forced to live in the human world, where most of them isolate themselves where humans won't find them. They're powerful fighters, but they're outnumbered by their enemies, and being a powerful fighter does you no good against a determined mob.

Kaduvas are capable of changing shape to something small and quick that can evade capture, enabling the kaduva to sneak

up on an enemy and take it by surprise. In their humanoid form, they have the appearance of fur-covered men and women with the heads of panthers and hands with retractable claws. They fight to the death and rejoice in killing humans. I don't need to tell you how dangerous they are.

Owen was as still as the monster, not moving even when Aderyn shoved past him. "Kaduva!" Aderyn shouted. She stepped in front of Owen, blocking his line of sight to the kaduva's compelling gaze.

The kaduva took a step back. Then it raised its sword and charged.

Chapter Thirty-Two

Owen blinked and shuddered as if waking from a bad dream. Aderyn ducked out of his way as he shouted a challenge and raced to meet the monster. He brought the **<Sunsword>** up to meet the kaduva's blade, and the creature vanished. Its sword hit the tile floor with a dull ringing sound before the kaduva's empty robe fluttered down to cover it. A small black cat streaked away, heading for one of the room's other doors.

"Stop it!" Aderyn shouted. "It will warn the others!"

Weston flung a knife at the fleeing kaduva. The cat dodged to one side—directly into the path of Weston's second knife, which impaled the creature at the base of its neck. The kaduva jerked in a full-body spasm and then slid a few inches, limp and unmoving, before coming to a halt in front of the door. Its cat body twitched, and in its place appeared the humanoid form of the kaduva, sprawled naked on the tiles and clearly dead.

Congratulations! You have defeated [Kaduva].
You have earned [20,000 XP]

Owen and Aderyn approached it slowly, moving to either side of the body. “What’s this?” Aderyn said. Weston’s knife had severed a strip of leather that had circled the kaduva’s neck. Aderyn wormed the thing out from beneath the body and held it up. An ornate brass buckle about the size of a ten-gold piece ornamented the leather strap. A second buckle, smaller and plainer, dangled from one of the cut ends. “This little buckle is what held the collar on, but what’s this gaudy thing?”

“It is a <**Breath of Life Amulet**>, meant to allow the user to breathe underwater for a time. I can’t imagine why this creature has one.” Isold took the collar from Aderyn and slid the amulet off the strap. “Or why he wore the amulet in such a way that it would always be next to his body, regardless of his shape.”

“The dungeon Assessment said the kaduvas were mortal enemies of the weresharks,” Aderyn said. “If this lets someone breathe underwater, the kaduvas could fight the weresharks in their own territory.”

“So, you’re saying there could be more of these amulets,” Owen said.

“If you mean we should go hunting kaduvas until we collect five amulets, you’re mad. You didn’t see what the system said about them. They’re the same level as us, and if we run into a large group of them, we could be in trouble.”

“If Devendra’s not on this level, we need to be able to access the submerged areas.” Owen gestured at the amulet. “That looks like our best chance. But I agree that we shouldn’t take on the kaduvas all at once. We need a better plan.”

“I have an idea,” Weston said. “Aderyn, try using the <**Wayfinder**> to locate more kaduvas.”

Aderyn stared at him. “Did you not hear what I said about large groups of them?”

“I did. What’s more, it occurs to me that just because the <**Wayfinder**> points to your heart’s desire doesn’t mean we have to follow it. We can identify where the kaduvas are and circle around the other way, see if we can isolate one or two.”

“Oh.” Aderyn considered this. “You’re right. It could work that way.”

She focused on the kaduva at her feet and willed the <**Wayfinder**> to locate her heart’s desire. It took more than a minute, but then warmed up when it pointed at the door the kaduva had tried to reach. "I guess that was obvious. I think it knows the kaduvas aren't really my heart's desire."

"We have to try," Owen reminded her. "There are two other doors. Let's see where they lead."

When Aderyn turned her back on the direction the **<Wayfinder>** indicated, the orb cooled and dimmed immediately. "I guess it isn't so easy to make it work against its fundamental purpose. You don't suppose it will get upset if I keep forcing it?"

"Magic items, in general, don't have will or intelligence to become upset," Isold said. "But I understand your concern. It feels unnatural, I imagine."

"Yes." Aderyn resolved to only use the **<Wayfinder>** in reverse, so to speak, at crucial decision points. She knew it was irrational, but she couldn't help imagining it refusing to work at all.

The **<Wayfinder>** warmed again when she faced the left-hand door, not as much as before, but still visibly different. "Not that way," Aderyn said. "I guess we try this one." She pointed at the right-hand door.

The door opened on an empty room that held nothing but a tattered, moldy rug covering floorboards that showed traces of old varnish. "Don't step on it," Owen warned. "It might be alive."

Aderyn Assessed it. "It's just a rug. Still, it's disgusting and it smells bad. I wouldn't want to track that everywhere I go."

"The thing I like about this room is there are no kaduvas," Weston said. He was already examining the room's other door, which was metal instead of wood, hammered brass tarnished with age. "I want to fight them on our terms, which means an ambush if we can manage it. This door's clean."

The door swung open on a short corridor, at the end of which sunlight was visible. Aderyn took a few involuntary steps toward the light before stopping herself. "We've barely been in this place ten minutes and already it's getting to me."

"Let's see where the light comes from." Owen started down the hall. "It might just be more of those growth lights."

But the hall ended at a room with one curved wall lined with windows taking up two of its sides. The frames were all that was left; all the glass was missing, and a strong sea breeze blew constantly through the empty space, moaning and whistling by turns.

"Another beautiful view," Livia said.

"And an open door," Weston said. "More specifically, it's been wrenched off its hinges." He pointed at the upper door frame, where corroded metal hinges twisted out of true sagged. "The door is gone."

"That's unsettling." Owen looked through the doorway. "The next room is full of rubbish. Broken furniture, that sort of thing. Like storage."

Aderyn consulted the **<Wayfinder>**. "It doesn't show anything if I try to locate the kaduvas, but when I focus on Devendra, it points that way."

Owen shrugged and walked through the door. The others followed him.

Broken furniture lay in tall heaps here and there throughout the room, leaving plenty of space for the friends to walk between. The windowless room was dark except for the light coming through from the next room, so Livia chanted and tossed a dozen *orbs of light* into the air. They cast moving shadows over the furniture, unsettling Aderyn so she slowed, examining her surroundings for creatures. "Maybe I should try—"

A wild chittering noise erupted from all around them. Gray figures the size of large cats emerged from the heaps of furniture, climbing as high as they could and then clinging to the walls and shrieking at a pitch that made Aderyn want to cover her ears. Instead, she Assessed them.

Name: Meddler Monkey [9]
Type: Magical beast
Power level: 12
Attack: claw x2, bite, missile attack, special
Immune to: none
Resistant to: none
Vulnerable to: none
Special attack: disease

Meddler monkeys like to mess with people. They have a low-level empathic skill that tells them what the best way to mess

with an individual is: stealing items, destroying belongings, flinging shit, that sort of thing. They're enough of a nuisance adventurers often wrongly assume they're nothing more than that. However, they are tenacious fighters whose bite and claws carry disease, and they have the kind of accurate aim Deadeyes dream of. Don't let them hit you with their missiles. No, they won't do damage, but I guarantee their idea of appropriate ammunition isn't something you want to be in contact with.

"Their bite and claws are diseased, so don't let them get you!" she shouted. "And they fling—oh, gross!" **[See It Coming]** warned her well in advance of the turd one of the monkeys hurled at her face. She ducked away, right into the path of another monkey that leaped at her, clawing her hair. It plucked the <**Wayfinder**> out of her hand and leaped for freedom.

With a shriek of mingled outrage and fear, Aderyn grabbed its long, disturbingly motile tail and kept it from going farther. They tussled over the orb, Aderyn grunting with effort, the monkey hissing and spitting, until the monster clawed Aderyn's hand, drawing blood and startling her into loosening her grip. With a cry of exultation, the meddler monkey leaped to one of the piles of furniture and climbed one-handed to the top, where it settled to admire its prize.

"Oh, that does it," Aderyn snarled. She ignored the sounds of fighting going on around her, Isold's song, the sound of Livia chanting, and focused on the thief. White light outlined it, with lines of light extending from its body indicating possible ways she might **[Reposition]** the little monster. Aderyn imagined grabbing the meddler monkey around its waist and pulling it along the line that ended near her feet.

The monkey shrieked in surprise as its body abruptly slid down the pile of furniture to land next to Aderyn. She was ready for it. As it came to a halt, she thrust with her sword, impaling the creature. The monkey's shriek became agonized, sounding like a baby's cry, but Aderyn wasn't fooled. She drove the blade deeper. The monkey's grip on the <**Wayfinder**> loosened, and as it sagged in death, the orb fell from its hand and rolled a short distance away. Aderyn pounced on it and dropped it securely into the <**Purse of Great Capacity**>.

Congratulations! You have defeated [Meddler Monkey].
You have earned [8250 XP]

She became aware that other system defeat notices had popped up while she was fighting with the thief, but the fighting seemed to be over. Mostly. A few meddler monkeys had retreated out of reach and were flinging their disgusting missiles at her friends. She rubbed the claw marks on her hand. The deep scratches stung painfully.

"Isold," she began.

"One moment," Isold said. He lifted his flute to his lips and played a soothing, soporific melody. The meddler monkeys lowered their arms and let the turds they were holding fall. With eyes half-lidded, they swayed as if falling asleep on their feet. Then they collapsed, some of them falling to the floor, one sinking into sleep in a precarious position atop the broken remains of a wardrobe.

"Let's finish them," Owen said.

When the final monkey was dead, Isold said, "What was—Aderyn, you're injured."

"Yes, and I'm worried about what kind of disease I'm dealing with," Aderyn replied.

Isold brought out the **<Healing Stone>** and ran it over Aderyn's right hand. The green glow illuminated her from within, revealing the shadows of her bones. When he removed the stone, the claw marks were entirely gone. "I don't know if you contracted a disease from the scratch. If so, the stone still might not have healed it."

"Why wouldn't it?" Aderyn flexed her hand. She didn't feel ill.

"Because the stone heals injury, and I'm not sure it recognizes disease as an injury." Isold put the stone away. "We have no choice but to wait and see, I'm afraid. I'm sorry I don't have a better answer."

Aderyn shivered. "No, I'm fine," she said when Owen exclaimed. "That was nerves, not fever. At worst, we have the **<Potion of Life>**, and that heals everything, right?"

"Right." Owen hugged her. "Let's see where that door leads." He nodded at another open doorway. "I'm guessing if there were more of the meddler monkeys, they'd have been drawn to the fight, but there might be some other threat, so let's be more than usually careful."

The doorway led to a short, dark corridor, wide and high-ceilinged, that almost immediately turned right. As they followed Livia's lights down the hall, around more right-hand turns, Livia said, "We're going in a spiral. And it's not getting any smaller."

"What do you mean?" Weston asked.

"I mean a spiral gets smaller the closer you get to the center. These halls aren't getting shorter. And it's not going up or down, because the floor isn't slanted. I think something's wrong." Livia stopped and gestured so her lights spread out, illuminating all of them and the hall ten feet ahead and behind.

"A trap," Owen said.

Aderyn was already Assessing the hall they stood in. Green fire leaped up to trace the outlines of the walls and floor and ceiling.

Name: Eternity Trap

Power Level: 15

This trap creates an endless loop of corridors that begins where it ends, locking its victims within the loop and sealing itself off when triggered. It can be breached from the outside easily, but from the inside it's a different story. Don't overthink this.

Aderyn read this aloud. She idly scratched her itching right hand. "There has to be some way out. Not an easy one, but the system didn't say it was impossible. And I don't know what 'don't overthink this' means." The itching got worse the more she scratched.

"We have to do *some* thinking about it," Livia said. "I have *greater dispel magic*, and Isold has **[Break Enchantment]**. We can start with those."

The itching was becoming unbearable. Aderyn rubbed the back of her hand roughly against her trousers, then tried using the stones of the wall. This far into the palace, the weather hadn't gotten to them, and the smooth plaster facing gave her no relief. "I don't," she began, looked at her hand, and shrieked.

Gray fur sprouted where the meddler monkey's claws had struck. The skin around the fur was red and oozed from wet, broken blisters popped open by Aderyn's scratching. Owen grabbed Aderyn's hand, carefully not touching the wounds. "Isold!"

Isold took the **<Healing Stone>** from his belt pouch. His hands were blurry, Aderyn noticed, shivering around the edges like her vision was fogged. Then they were blurry because she was shaking so hard her hand jerked out of Owen's hold. Owen caught her as her knees folded, but his arms around her were all she felt. She couldn't tell anymore if she was upright or lying down. Her hand burned with an invisible flame that spread up past her wrist to her elbow and then to her shoulder. She cried out in pain, and the fire swept over her whole body, and she closed her eyes and let the agony take her.

Chapter Thirty-Three

In her dream, she swam like a dolphin through murky waters, following the glints of light that made a path through the dimness. The path rose and fell, curving and turning, reminding her of the path in the Repository the <**Wayfinder**> had guided her along. Then, with a jerk, she was back in the Repository, staring at the orb while simultaneously watching the colored balls of light that were the witnesses. Her dreaming brain knew this was impossible, and that awareness brought her near the surface of the dreaming world. Voices became audible though not intelligible, the speakers mumbling as if they were the ones underwater.

She strained to see in the increasing darkness. She was convinced if she could see the speakers, she could understand them, and in her dreamlike urgency understanding them was the key to waking. Just as she realized it was dark because her eyes were closed, her eyelids fluttered open. Blurriness obscured her vision. The air was the color of deep night, punctuated by fuzzy white discs. She blinked rapidly to clear her eyes, and slowly the charcoal air and the spots of brightness resolved into walls and Livia's *orbs of light*.

Her throat was too dry for speech, so she swallowed several times until she could croak out, "I need water."

The ground beneath her shifted, and she realized she was half lying in someone's lap. Above her, Owen said, "Can you sit? Here." He pressed the mouth of a waterskin to her lips, and she drank thirstily. It didn't take much to satisfy her before she pushed the waterskin away. Owen shifted again. "It's all right. You're going to be fine."

"What happened? Am I diseased?"

Owen didn't say anything.

Panic bubbled up inside her. "Owen, tell me the truth. What happened?"

"We gave you the **<Potion of Life>**," Owen said, drawing her into his embrace. "It did something, we're not sure what because we don't know what all the meddler monkey disease effects are. At least it kept you from dying. But..." He took her right hand and raised it to where she could see it.

Aderyn let out a sharp cry and snatched her hand from Owen's grasp. The entire back of her hand and past her wrist was covered with fine gray fur. "I'm turning into—"

"No, you aren't," Isold said firmly. "This is temporary, I'm certain. It's not like in Sorrowvale where the touch of the stone statues nearly turned Livia to stone. The **<Healing Stone>** repaired the physical damage before the disease could take full effect, and the **<Potion of Life>** kept the disease from spreading."

"But—" The pressure of too many thoughts kept Aderyn from speaking any of them. "I don't want to go through life like this!"

"Aderyn, it's going to be fine. The, um, effect has already retreated some. It used to be farther up your arm." Owen hugged her more tightly. "How do you feel otherwise? Any other symptoms?"

Aderyn wished she was a Bonemender to Assess her body's condition. She had to settle for flexing her limbs and evaluating her internal organs' condition, comparing them to her normal state. "I feel fine. Invigorated, the way a **<Potion of Life>** leaves you. It's just..." She shuddered. "It feels like something's been implanted in me that's waiting its time to burst out."

"Good thing you've never seen *Alien*," Owen said. He helped her stand and steadied her when she wobbled. "You're sure you're all right?"

"Just a little shaky. It's already passed." She looked around. "I'm guessing we haven't solved the **[Eternity Trap]** yet."

"Your dramatic collapse was a distraction," Livia said.

"I can imagine." Aderyn let out a deep breath. "All right. I need something else to think about. What next?"

"I tried to locate the spot where the trap triggers. It isn't visible—or, rather, it's a long line rather than a single spot. It runs along the base of the wall, all the way to both corners." Livia scowled. "I don't know what effect *greater dispel magic* will have on it."

"That's not going to destroy the magic on our gear, is it?" Owen asked.

"No. Oh, you mean—this isn't like in the Lonely Tor, where I couldn't find the center of the trap. Then, I would have cast the spell as an effect on the whole area. Here, I can see the trap structure, more or less, so I have something for the spell to aim at." Livia bent to press the fingers of her stone hand against the line where the inner wall met the floor and muttered something unintelligible. A flash of green light flickered around her fingers and streaked along the line until it reached the corners.

Livia straightened. "There's still magic there. I can't tell—crap. It didn't work. We would have seen the system notice."

Aderyn hurried to the end of the corridor. "Did we come this way? I'm all turned around now."

"That was the way we were going," Isold said. "Let me try **[Break Enchantment]**."

He flattened both palms against the wall above where Livia had crouched and closed his eyes. "I see something," he said, his voice quiet. "A string, tangled and glowing with magic. I believe untangling it is a matter of finding a loose end."

No one spoke. Aderyn scratched her hairy wrist idly and was cheered when clumps of loose gray hairs clung to her fingertips. The silence stretched out for a few minutes before Isold stood upright and said, "I don't think there's an end. At least, I've reached the limit of how long I can keep the skill effect going. After a time, **[Break Enchantment]** simply slips away from me."

"Like a moebius strip, then," Owen said. "There's no beginning or end—fitting for something called an **[Eternity Trap]**. We're going to have to get creative."

Aderyn Assessed the trap and read the system message aloud again. "There has to be a way out. The system would have said otherwise."

"I have an idea. Everyone stay here," Weston said. He walked to the end of the hall and turned the corner. "Can you still hear me?"

"We can," Livia said. "What do you have in mind?"

"Just wait." Weston started whistling a cheery tune that struck Aderyn as completely inappropriate for their situation. The sound grew fainter, but never entirely died away. Then it became louder, and soon Weston appeared again, strolling around the corner in the direction they'd originally come. "I was wondering what sort of shape the trap has," he said. "Seems like it's a closed loop. I figured there was a chance it just kept going and going, so I walked a full four turns and came upon you all from behind. That may not make it infinite. We could just be trapped in a loop."

"Is that important?" Aderyn asked.

Weston shrugged. "I have no idea. But the more we know about the trap, the easier it will be to find a way out."

"So it should work both ways," Owen said. He walked back the way they'd come, and after about a minute returned from the other direction. "It does. What can we do with that?"

"Why is it in a circle?" Livia said. "Why not an endless straight hallway?"

"Good question," Isold said. "It suggests there are limits on the trap. Spatial limits. That is, there is a world outside this corridor, and—" He snapped his fingers. "Aderyn, what about **[Spot Weakness]**?"

"Oh!" Aderyn focused on the outer wall. She was used to seeing blue spots of light indicating where the weak spots were in a building or object, and it disappointed her that nothing appeared, not even the faint lines where the stones of the wall were piled atop each other. Discouraged, she tried the inner wall anyway.

A zigzag pattern of pulsing blue lights blazed across the wall.

"I see it!" Aderyn dug through the **<Knapsack of Plenty>**, searching for a **<Write-All>**. Even drained of magic, the writing implement had a sharp, wide tip. She dragged the **<Write-All>** across the plaster, scoring it deeply as she traced lines connecting the blue dots. When she was finished, she stepped back to examine her work. "Hah. Somebody has a sense of humor."

Owen traced the lines with his fingers. "It's shaped like a door. Is that real, or was it your instincts?"

"Both, I think. Livia?"

Livia wound up and punched the wall with her stone left fist. The plaster shivered and cracked, and chunks of it scattered across the hall. "Hmm," Livia said, examining the dent she'd made in the granite beneath the plaster. "I think I need more muscle." She cast the spell *stone fist*, making her left fist glitter with an aura of power. Taking a solid stance, she punched again. Stones cracked into gravel as she shattered a hole through the wall.

A strong smell of seawater drifted through the hole. Livia punched again and again until the hole matched the door outline and was big enough for even Weston to fit through. Livia stuck her head through the hole. "It goes down."

You have received [19,500 XP] for defeating the [Eternity Trap]. Well done.

A chill ran down Aderyn's spine. "I wonder if this is the secret Kanan knows. If it's the way his adventurers can pass freely through the Ivory Palace."

"You mean, something that lets them avoid the trap?" Owen's brow furrowed. "What I want to know is how soon the trap resets. We might want to come back another way."

"It's not impossible that this is a secret of the Ivory Palace," Isold said. "But my map shows that we are far from the entrance, and I doubt the second exit from the patio could have led here. There must be other routes down, which suggests that there are other secrets we should be alert for."

"I'll go you one further, Aderyn," Livia said. "I'd bet Kanan is the one who set this trap, or at any rate had one of his tame adventurers set it. It's the kind of nasty thing I expect from him. But Owen is right that the trap might reset soon, and I don't want to waste resources breaking through more walls. There's a ladder below us—I say we use it."

The space beyond the hole was a stone chimney or well descending into darkness. The ladder was actually a series of rusting iron rungs set into the unfinished stone wall. They weren't as unstable as Aderyn feared, and although the friends' passage made flakes of orange rust shake free, the rungs didn't move.

"I find it difficult to believe this was original to the Ivory Palace," Isold said. "It's not the sort of stairs wealthy people put up with. It might have been an access stair for servants, for maintenance."

"So we missed the actual stairs," Weston said. "Not that it matters, since it's likely the kaduvas control that territory. They would need to guard it against enemies making an assault."

Owen, in the lead, leaped down the five feet between the last rung and the floor. "Wet. There's about two inches of seawater covering the floor. I bet this place is more submerged at high tide—there's water marks on the stones at about neck high."

"Not to panic anyone, but do we have any idea when high tide is?" Aderyn asked.

"No clue, except that it looks like the tide is coming in, based on this movement." Owen backed away to let Aderyn hop down. "I don't see a door, do you?"

Aderyn used **[Spot Weakness]** again, turning in a slow circle to examine the whole round chamber. Owen was right about the tide; dark marks on the paler stones showed the limits of how far the water rose. She stopped, facing the wall opposite the ladder. "There's a door there. I think it's an actual door and not a shape."

Weston was already prowling around the wall Aderyn indicated, searching for a trigger. "There," he said, pressing in on a stone that looked like all the others. With a groan and the sound of stone grating on stone, a section of wall moved inward and then slid to one side, revealing an unlit corridor.

Aderyn stared into the darkness. Nothing moved. "Livia?"

"Just a moment. I don't want to announce our presence until Weston finds the mechanism to open the door from the other side." Livia prodded Weston. "You *were* going to do that, right?"

Weston jumped. "Of course. I wasn't at all gazing into the darkness and imagining what horrors might be at the other end of this hall." He stepped out of the narrow room and felt around the walls. "It's right here. I think it's concealed, just not from me at my level. Sometimes it's hard to tell how things look to non-Moonlighters."

"But you can access it again," Owen said.

"Yes. Easily."

"Then let's see where this hall takes us." Owen nodded at Livia.

In a low voice, Livia chanted and gestured, sending little balls of light flying slowly down the corridor. Now that Aderyn knew Livia's perception of her spellslinging wasn't the same as hers, she paid closer attention. She still couldn't comprehend Livia's words, but she recognized the *orb of light* spell always used the same nonsense words.

"Do you make up new words every time?" she asked.

"To cast spells? Not for the ones I use frequently. It takes too much time to be creative. *Orb of light* is always 'light up my world,' for example."

Aderyn shook her head in wonder. "I still can't believe it."

"Neither can I." Livia cast one more *orb of light*. "And the corridor ahead looks empty. Let's see what kind of trouble we're getting ourselves into."

Chapter Thirty-Four

Darker marks on the walls, and exposed stone, showed where the tide flowed in. Above the tide marks, the walls were as patchy with peeling plaster as they had been on the level above. The floor underfoot squelched as they walked, suggesting water-logged carpet. But when Weston voiced this opinion, Owen said, "How likely is it that there's still carpet here after centuries of decay and tides?"

Aderyn made a face. "Now I really don't want to look too closely at what we're walking on."

"It's probably just sediment," Livia said. "Washed in by the tide."

"A sensible guess, but the feeling is still unsettling," Isold said.

"Yeah, let's not think about it." Owen slowed. "The high water marks are only about three feet high here. I think we might be going uphill, given how the palace was tilted."

"There's a door. Let me take a look." Weston moved to the front of the group and examined the lock. He stilled. "I hear the sounds of fighting. Weapons on weapons. It's not in the next room, but could be just beyond that."

"We can take advantage of that," Aderyn said. "Like we did that time against the waspnettles. Wait for one side to defeat the other, then attack the winners while they're weakened."

"That assumes they're both our enemies," Isold said. "Suppose we're not the only adventurers in the dungeon?"

"I can cast *invisibility* on all of us, and we can get closer to see what the situation is." Livia cracked her knuckles.

"Good plan," Owen said. "Everybody group up."

Weston unlocked the door and opened it. The sounds of combat were audible to everyone now. They huddled close together, not close enough to impede Livia's spellslinging, and Livia muttered a string of nonsense syllables. The air around them thickened like clear jelly, spreading outward from Livia until it covered all of them.

"The area the spell affects is bigger than I remember," Livia said in a low voice. "I think we can spread out a little. Just pay attention to where the air ripples, and don't step outside that." She extinguished all the *orbs of light*. "Just in case."

As Owen opened the door wider, Aderyn's heart beat faster. Despite Weston's assurances, the battle sounded like it was in the room with them. A dim light shone through an open doorway, enough to illuminate the room so they didn't stumble and make enough noise to make *mass invisibility* pointless. Figures moved beyond the doorway, shoving each other in near silence, the only noises grunts and whistles and eerie clicks like giant insect legs clacking.

Owen approached the doorway, and Aderyn followed him, breathing shallowly to avoid inhaling the stink of decay, bitter and thick on the air. For a moment, the situation struck her as absurd: they were sneaking up on a battle, their furtive movements completely at odds with the frenetic fighting. Then the moment passed, and she focused on the room beyond to Assess the fight.

Name: Kaduva [2]
Type: Demon
Power level: 16
Attack: sword, claw x2, special
Immune to: none
Resistant to: mind-affecting attacks
Vulnerable to: dispelling magic
Special abilities: shapeshifting, night vision
Special attack: compelling gaze

They can see in the dark. How much good do you think invisibility will do you?

NAME: WERESHARK [3]

Type: Monstrosity
Power level: 15
Attack: spear OR bite, special
Immune to: none
Resistant to: bladed weapons damage
Vulnerable to: sunlight and related spells
Special ability: night vision
Special attacks: shred, frenzy

You haven't encountered a were-creature before, have you? Weresharks were bred by spellslingers, centuries ago, in an attempt to create humans that could not only survive in the ocean, but do battle with the monsters that live there. It was as stupid an idea as it sounds, given that sharks are as efficient predators as humans, and the two natures reinforced each other into what became vicious and terrible killers.

You're wondering about the special abilities. *Shred* is what happens when in shark form they bite their prey and hang on, tearing flesh with all those razor-sharp teeth. *Frenzy* is triggered by the smell or taste of blood, sending the wereshark into a rage that increases its ability to do damage and stops it caring about pain. This doesn't mean the damage it takes is reduced, just that it can fight through its injuries right up until it drops dead.

Don't give up, though! Weresharks live in darkness, and while they can see in the dark, their vision is poor and easily compromised by bright light. A wereshark can only remain in humanoid form, or stay out of the water, for one hour. You're clever—maybe you can make use of that.

Aderyn blinked away the Assessment text and observed what **[Discern Weakness]** told her. Blue lights shone at the kaduvas' eyes, throats, and lower bellies, though the latter were haloed in red to indicate protection. The weresharks' weaknesses were their eyes and abdomens, though again their stomachs shone with reddish light over the blue. She whispered this to her companions, adding, "I can't tell who's winning."

The nearest kaduva's feline ears swiveled back. Its lips peeled back in a snarl, and it howled, a sound more like a wolf's cry than a cat's yowl. The sound brought the combat to a halt. The kaduva hissed. Its wereshark opponent lowered its spear. Both creatures turned slowly to face the doorway. Aderyn swallowed nervously. For a moment, she met the kaduva's gaze before remembering the system's caution and looking at the wereshark instead. It looked more human than the kaduva, though its forehead sloped far back, its skin was grayish-white and hairless, and its nose wasn't more than a couple of elongated holes in the middle of its face.

And its solid black eyes, glistening like drops of black blood, clearly saw her.

"They see us!" Aderyn shouted. "Livia, *daylight*!"

All the remaining combatants, weresharks and kaduvas alike, lunged for the doorway, weapons raised. Aderyn dodged to the side and back a few steps, shouting for Owen to do the same and turn the doorway into a bottleneck. Then the brilliant light of noon exploded over the room. Cries of pain, howls and that strange chittering noise, filled the air.

"Now!" Owen called out, and lunged for the kaduva in front, the enemy nearest him. Aderyn, unable to get behind the creature for **[Outflank]**, searched for another opening. **[Reposition]** would be stupid, since pulling one creature into the room would leave a space for another one to attack. Weston was fighting the wereshark, whose spear was unexpectedly effective against his sword. With an effort, Aderyn used **[Compel]** to force the wereshark to target her. The wereshark's broad mouth spread wider in a smile. Clearly it thought her a better target. Aderyn didn't care. **[Compel]** had been a distraction.

The wereshark raised its spear for a finishing thrust, and Weston's knife buried hilt-deep in its eye. It threw its head back and let out a loud clacking, chittering roar, exposing its throat for Weston to slit.

Congratulations! You have defeated [Wereshark].
You have earned [17,025 XP]

Almost immediately, another system notice appeared.

Congratulations! You have defeated [Kaduva].
You have earned [20,000 XP]

Aderyn moved closer to Owen. "They're going to rush us!" She didn't know what about the purposeful movement beyond the doorway told her this, but then her prediction came true as two weresharks and the last kaduva lunged through the doorway, bowling Weston over and shoving Aderyn. She regained her balance in time to block the attack of a wereshark's spear. Then the tug of **[Outflank]** seized her. The wereshark jerked and spun around to face Owen, whose **[Sunsword]** made it flinch, but not enough to stop its attack.

Aderyn thrust low, striking the wereshark a blow near its spine. It rang through her bones like striking oak, the blade not penetrating as deeply as Aderyn expected. The wereshark ignored it and bore down on Owen. Owen aimed, not at the wereshark's flesh, but at its spear. Aderyn's momentary fear for him vanished as the **[Sunsword]** sheared through the shaft and continued its arc to cut off the monster's hand.

Without hesitating, Owen drove the blade into the wereshark's belly. The wereshark didn't seem to notice this, either. It struck with its truncated spear at Owen's face. Owen dodged and shoved the blade in harder. "Aderyn!"

Aderyn focused on the line of yellow light that **[Discern Weakness]** revealed as the wereshark's current target. With a groan of effort, she wrenched the wereshark's focus to herself with **[Compel]**.

The wereshark spun to face her. Owen kept his grip on his sword. The blade bit deeper, slicing through the wereshark's belly as it disemboweled itself. Aderyn stepped out of reach of its flailing weapon. For a moment, she remembered *frenzy* and pictured the wereshark dragging its bloody, dismembered body back together to keep fighting. Then the creature's gleaming black eyes filmed over, and it dropped, unmoving.

The system defeat message overlapped a second one. Only the kaduva remained. Aderyn, bent over and breathing heavily, heard scuffling noises that didn't seem like fighting. She dragged herself upright and covered her mouth to hold back a scream.

Livia was backed into a corner, muttering the words of a spell. The last kaduva had Isold in its grip, its claws poised to tear out Isold's throat, but all its muscles were tense and unmoving. Isold's gaze was fixed on the kaduva, his body rigid like the monster's.

"Don't!" Aderyn exclaimed when Weston approached the pair. "If you break the impasse, the kaduva might be faster than you and it will kill Isold."

"We can't do nothing," Weston said.

"Livia is—"

Livia was sweating and pale, but her voice was strong. It rose until the words of her spell sounded like a command. With a final shout, she pointed at the kaduva in an imperious gesture that so clearly was a dismissal Aderyn nearly turned to leave.

The kaduva's rigid body convulsed, its extended claws drawing thin lines of blood down Isold's neck from a series of shallow cuts before it released him. It convulsed again, and again, each time drawing further in on itself until it curled into a ball.

"What spell is that?" Aderyn asked, impressed and horrified at once.

At every place it folded in on itself, blood-red light leaked from the kaduva's body, an unhealthy light like the glow of some abyss leading to the demon void. A terrible keening sound came from nowhere, the sound of a wind sharp enough to cut flesh. The red light deepened. The kaduva convulsed again, flinging its arms and legs wide. Something long and thin the color of a fresh wound dragged itself free of the monster's chest with a horrific screech and vanished. The kaduva went limp in the perfect stillness of death.

Congratulations! You have defeated [Kaduva].
You have earned [20,000 XP]

Livia's harsh breathing became audible. "*Dismissal,*" she rasped. "It's for dismissing demons, but your Assessment said kaduvas were vulnerable to it. When it turned out to take forever to cast, I was sure we were both dead, but I didn't have any other spells that wouldn't hurt Isold."

"I appreciate that," Isold said from where he sat on the ground. He touched the bloody scratches and winced. "I knew they were resistant to mind-affecting skills, but it went for Livia and I didn't have time for anything else."

"It's fine," Owen said. "Livia, are you all right?"

"Sure." Livia stared at the kaduva's body. "I've never used *dismissal* before. Never had a reason to. That was dramatic."

"'Dramatic' is an understatement," Weston said. He put an arm around Livia's shoulders. "You're not feeling any regrets, are you? Because that kaduva would have killed Isold and torn you apart afterward."

Livia shook her head. "No, I was reflecting on how glad I am we haven't fought demons before this. And how glad I am I took that spell on a whim. Let's see what we can take off these monsters, all right?"

Between the monsters the team had killed and the ones who'd died in the battle before that, there turned out to be five kaduvas and seven weresharks. All the kaduvas wore leather collars with **<Breath of Life Amulets>** attached, making Owen say, "Well, that's a relief. I didn't actually want to hunt these guys. Talk about risky." Aside from their swords, which were sharp but pitted with rust in places, the kaduvas had no gear. All of them wore the same loose wraparound robes the first one had.

The weresharks puzzled Aderyn. Each one wore short leather pants with large, bulging pockets sewn into them. When she gingerly investigated the contents of one, she let out a gasp. "Look at this!"

The others gathered around to look at the enormous sapphire she held. "I think they're a scavenging party," she said. "If only because I can't imagine why warriors might think they need to carry gems into battle—or is it magical?"

"Not magical," Livia said, "but very, very pretty. And valuable. Let's see what else they have."

Between the seven weresharks, the friends found a total of fifty-eight gold coins of various denominations, seven loose gemstones, and a golden necklace set with rubies the size of Aderyn's thumbnail. "Only gold," she mused. "I guess it's the one precious metal that doesn't tarnish."

"I wish I knew where they'd found the stuff," Weston groused. "If there's a treasure chamber here—"

"The system said the owners took all their valuables with them when they abandoned the Ivory Palace, remember?" Livia dropped her handful of coin and gems into Aderyn's **<Knapsack of Plenty>**. "It's more likely they looted the bodies of fallen adventurers."

"Which makes me wonder why we haven't seen anything like that," Owen said. "If adventurers who die here aren't disposed of when the dungeon resets, we should have come across bodies ourselves."

"I say we don't worry about that," Weston said, "and worry instead about not becoming bodies. Also, the tide is coming in, and even though we have the amulets now, we ought to explore the non-submerged part of the dungeon first."

"You make a good point," Owen said. "Does everyone have a **<Breath of Life Amulet>**? Then let's move on."

Chapter Thirty-Five

Wearing the <**Breath of Life Amulet**> on a leather strap around her neck felt strange to Aderyn. It wasn't just the sensation of it touching her throat, it was the memory of seeing the kaduvas wear it that way that left her with the sensation of having done more than kill the monsters. The feeling was foolish, and she ignored it as best she could, but every time she turned her head and the amulet shifted, the memory returned.

To distract herself, she focused on the <**Wayfinder**>, willing it to lead her to Devendra. The path was clearer than it had been on the level above, with no more of the strange identical possibilities, but that didn't relieve her mind. The magic item knew not to point directly at her heart's desire, ignoring obstacles like walls, but Aderyn didn't think it was aware of other hazards, like monsters. Though none of them had been seriously injured in the last fight, Aderyn didn't kid herself that that meant weresharks and kaduvas were easy prey, especially since they'd joined forces to attack her and her friends. The idea of finding Devendra and sneaking away with no more combats had increasing appeal.

There were no more hallways, just room after room opening directly on each other, empty except for the rising tide waters. They found no adventurer bodies, either, for which Aderyn was grateful. At the end of one long row of high-ceilinged chambers, they found stairs going up, or the remains of stairs. Owen regarded the piles of rubble burying the steps and said, "We could get out this way if we had to."

"It would use most of my resources to clear the steps and use *stone ladder* to get across the collapsed section." Livia prodded one large rectangular stone with her toe. Its edges were rounded from centuries of erosion. "So it couldn't be an emergency exit. Besides, we haven't found the queen yet. It's too soon to make exit plans."

"I know. This place is getting to me. It feels like it's waiting its moment to collapse." Owen turned away from the stairs. "Where next?"

Aderyn crossed to the hall leading away from the stairs. "I've lost track of direction. Are we going south, or west?"

"West," Isold said. "That is, the new hallway leads west."

"Then we've circled around to the cliffside again, right, Isold? I mean, if Livia tunneled through this wall, she'd reach the cliff."

"That is correct." Isold's eyes glazed over the way they did when he studied his system map. "Does the **<Wayfinder>** still point in that direction?"

"Yes, and it gives me hope, because the water level hasn't increased for the last several minutes. If Devendra is near, maybe we won't need the amulets." The **<Wayfinder>** continued to glow warm red as Aderyn faced the hallway.

"I haven't heard anything that might be a monster," Weston said. "And I'm not going to say anything optimistic about that so Livia won't smack me again."

"So wise," Livia said.

The glow from Livia's magic lights seemed to decrease as they walked down the hall, with the ambient light mysteriously increasing, but then they turned a corner and discovered the hall was open to the outdoors and the light came from the sun. A long row of windows, their glass long missing, looked out over the waves that lapped a few feet below their sills. The light had the warm, rosy quality of sunset, and when Aderyn stopped to get her bearings, she saw the headlands to the west outlined with golden light. The water between the headland and the Ivory Palace was cast in shadow, giving the ever-shifting waves an eerie appearance.

"We're headed back downhill again," Weston said.

Aderyn set off walking again. "Nothing we can do about that. But we are getting closer! And there's a door up ahead." She rubbed her arm again and wiped the last of the gray monkey hairs off on her trousers. Her arm looked perfectly whole.

The wooden door showed evidence of water damage, but only to chest height. It also swung freely open, swishing through the pool of ankle-deep water. Though Aderyn's boots were waterproof, they weren't meant for constant immersion, and her feet had grown cold with all the trekking through seawater. She wriggled her toes to no effect.

Owen held up a hand for silence. "I thought I heard someone talking."

They all stilled. Weston leaned forward, tilting his head. "It sounds like a conversation, but it's too quiet or too far away for me to make out words."

"We need to be careful, then. If it's other adventurers, we can't assume they're friendly." Owen stepped through the doorway, with Aderyn close behind.

The room beyond was too small for more than three of them to fit at once. Another door opposite the first, this one firmly closed, took some effort to get open. "Feels like an airlock," Owen muttered. "Like the decontamination chamber in the Enchanterium."

Aderyn closed her hand tightly on the **<Wayfinder's>** spikes, letting their dull pressure distract her from the feeling of being trapped in a tiny room with no exit. When Weston finally forced the unlocked door open, she stumbled past him despite Owen's whispered warning. Her feet splashed across the wooden floor to a railing, where she stopped and stared at her surroundings.

This room, too, was open to the elements, though some of its windows retained their glass. Aderyn gaped in wonder at the high ceiling, tall enough to reach the first level and covered in thick green vines that trailed down the walls to conceal them completely. Immediately, she Assessed the vines, but they were just plants. Every wall and most of the windows were adorned by greenery. The water level was high enough to submerge what had once been a balcony, and the room reeked of salt and brine.

"I don't get it," she said. "Those aren't sea plants. How do they survive?" She pointed at the dangling ends of the vines, which were withered and gray-green, and then at a point two feet higher, where the vines were green and healthy.

Weston grabbed her shoulder. "Shhh. I hear voices again. They're closer, but they aren't any clearer."

Isold tilted his head back, surveying the distant ceiling. "I see movement, and color. Birds."

Aderyn looked where he pointed. Birds clustered on the upper branches, shifting occasionally and making the leaves shake. They didn't seem to notice her and her friends, or maybe they just didn't care, but she Assessed them anyway.

Name: Chattering Pakshi

Type: Magical beast

Power level: 10

Attack: claw x2, bite, special

Immune to: sonic damage

Resistant to: none

Vulnerable to: none

Special attack: dissonant cry

Chattering pakshis are fierce fighters whose beautiful plumage makes a lot of adventurers discount their sharp talons and beaks capable of snapping arm-thick branches, or arms, in half. Despite this, they aren't aggressive except when they're defending themselves or their nests. Some adventurers, mainly Pathseers and Heralds, have tamed them to become fighting companions, but I warn you, it took them weeks or months, so don't go cherishing images of sending them flying into battle on your behalf.

You may have already noticed the reason for their name, which is that their song sounds like human speech on the verge of being intelligible. Don't get distracted trying to make it out, because it never will make sense. In addition to their immunity to

sonic damage, chattering pakshis can emit a dissonant cry, which is a sonic attack that disorients the hearers as well as causing damage. This attack can only happen when they're in flight, so keeping them grounded if you intend to fight them is key. You're not going to fight them, are you? Because that would be a serious waste of your resources.

"Wow," Owen said when Aderyn finished reading. "The system sure has strong opinions sometimes."

"I'm not sure we needed the warning," Weston said. "It's not like we go around indiscriminately killing things. We're not that hard up for experience."

"I choose to see it as the system taking an interest," Isold said, "and in that respect, any advice is good advice. What I wish we knew is what the chattering pakshis consider aggressive behavior. Staying away from their nests is obvious, but what if their idea of a threat isn't the same as ours?"

"They're up there, and we're down here," Livia said. "We don't need to climb, do we?" Her tone of voice said clearly what she thought of that possibility.

"I think we need to go the other way," Owen said. He leaned over the railing. "There's no floor there. This atrium keeps going down—I bet it goes all the way to what used to be ground level."

Aderyn joined him at the railing. The water sloshing over her feet was clear enough to show the wooden floor of the former balcony she stood on, but past the railing, the water was darker, obviously deeper than the few inches it was where she stood. "We knew the lower level was submerged. This is as good a place as any to reach it."

"Then I guess we just jump in," Owen said. He climbed over the railing.

Aderyn grabbed his arm. "What, just like that? You forget none of the rest of us have swum much before. And we don't know how the **<Breath of Life Amulets>** work."

"When submerged, a **<Breath of Life Amulet>** alters the wearer's body to take in oxygen from water rather than air," Isold said. He ran his finger along the surface of the amulet he wore. "There is a moment of disorientation when the change occurs, but then breathing underwater is as natural as we're breathing here now."

"What, like we take water into our lungs?" Owen exclaimed.

"I think so. My **[Identify Magic Items]** skill isn't high enough for more than the most essential information about these amulets. There is another moment of disorientation when the wearer leaves the water, which backs up my guess. The effect lasts for only three hours, after which the amulet requires ten minutes to recharge, so we should take care how far we go."

Owen climbed back over the railing. "Maybe we should think this through first."

"We have to go down if we want to rescue Devendra," Weston said. "Let's see how it works." He leaped over the railing and plunged into the water, submerging instantly.

"Weston!" Livia shouted.

Above, the chattering pakshis' conversation grew louder and more discordant, and a few birds took to the air. Aderyn spared them a single glance before fixing her gaze on Weston's indistinct shape in the murky water. Weston thrashed for a moment, roiling the water's surface. Then he went still. Livia shouted his name again and started to climb over the railing.

Isold grabbed her. "Look. He's moving."

Weston's arms and legs twitched. He kicked a couple of times, propelling himself across the pool. Then he dove out of sight, making all of them exclaim. In the next moment, his head broke the surface, and he thrashed again, coughing wildly.

"Grab him!" Owen said. "The amulet is still partly submerged."

Livia shouted something that made the remaining chattering pakshis fly from their branches. An invisible force grabbed Weston and hauled him out of the water to land with a splash on the balcony. Livia held him steady while he coughed up water that sprayed across the floor. "All right," he said, gasping, "I didn't exactly think that through. I forgot the amulet might still be underwater even if my head wasn't."

"Stop being stupid," Livia demanded. "I don't want—" She swallowed. "Just cut it out, all right?"

Weston gathered her into his arms. "I'm sorry, dearest. There's a fine line between daring and reckless, and I just crossed it. Thank you for rescuing me." He coughed once more. "Let's see what I can tell you that will make it worthwhile."

"We know we need to get out of the water quickly," Owen said. "What else?"

Weston squeezed water out of his long hair. "I thought I could hold my breath for a bit before the amulet took effect, but it forced water into my lungs immediately. That felt like drowning, but it lasted only a second, not long enough to make me panic. It was worse coming out, because my body was still trying to breathe water even though my head had surfaced."

"What about swimming? Was that hard?" Aderyn asked.

"Surprisingly, no. I guess three ranks has some use." Weston's breathing had returned to normal. "But I didn't make much progress despite kicking and waving my arms as hard as I could. Diving was easier. We're going to need to be careful about the fights we get into down there, because I have no illusions about my ability to outswim a wereshark."

"I've got ten ranks in **[Swim]** and I wouldn't try it either," Owen said. "It sounds like there's a lot we'll have to learn as we go."

"There's more." Weston scrubbed at his eyes. "The salt water burns. I couldn't bear to open my eyes. That's going to be a problem."

"Crap. You're right. I forgot. Last time I was at the coast, I had goggles." Owen frowned. "And the **<Cat's Eye Goggles>** aren't the right kind."

"I think I can do something about that, and about being able to keep track of time." Livia dug out her pocket watch and held it out flat on her palm. With a few nonsense words, a shimmering field sprang up around it that smelled strongly of violets. "*Air bubble* is thicker the smaller it is. At this size, at my level, it's impermeable, and water won't reach the watch."

"Amazing," Weston said. "So we can do that for ourselves? Surround our heads with an air bubble so the water won't get in and we can breathe?"

"We'd suffocate on the waste air we exhale," Livia said. "But I can cover the tops of our heads with that impermeable barrier, like a cap pulled down to the bridge of your nose." She pressed two fingers to Weston's face below his eyes and spoke a few quick words. The same shimmering, violet-scented field spread quickly from her fingers to cover Weston's eyes and the crown of his head. Weston shook vigorously, but the "cap" didn't move at all.

"How does it feel?" Isold asked.

"Like a band stretched around my head, but not painfully," Weston said. He rapped on the field with his knuckles, and the shimmering became concentrated at the spot where he knocked and rippled outward from it.

"That's pretty damn cool," Owen said.

Livia repeated the gesture and words on herself. "So, we can go forward for an hour and a half before we have to turn back or find another source of air. And *orb of light* works anywhere, so no worries about not being able to see."

"What about not being able to hear?" Isold said. "It occurs to me that I may be useless down there if the sound of my music or sonic attacks can't be heard."

"I read somewhere that sound travels better through water," Owen said. "But my experience playing underwater tag at the community pool tells me that understanding speech underwater is hard. We'll have trouble communicating."

"There's no way around that," Aderyn said. "Even **[Secret Message]** depends on being heard. The only communication we have that doesn't require speech is **[Bonded Mind]**, and that has its own problems." She snapped her fingers. "I forgot! We *do* have a way to communicate. The **<Draftsman's Pen>**!"

"What's that?"

She'd forgotten only she and Isold had been present when Isold identified the mystery pen from the Enchanterium. "It's that pen that does four things. In addition to duplicating a line, it writes in white on dark surfaces, writes in invisible ink—and writes underwater."

"Invisible ink?" Weston exclaimed. "Hold on, why didn't I know about this?"

"We learned its abilities the day Livia had to be rescued from Kanan's palace," Isold said. "That pushed everything else out of my mind." He rummaged in his knapsack until he came up with the fat brass cylinder. "We have two of these. It will be awkward, but when communication is necessary, we have options." He stuck the <**Draftsman's Pen**> into his belt.

"Then we'll worry about overcoming the communication problem when it happens," Owen said. "Are we ready?"

"We should hide anything that will be ruined by immersion," Livia said. "Our magic items are fine, but things like rations will dissolve."

"And boots," Owen said. "Swimming is easier when you're barefoot."

Aderyn pulled off her boots and stockings and wiggled her cold toes. She contemplated the pool, which looked colder now she knew she'd have to swim in it. She cinched the top of the <**Knapsack of Plenty**> shut and tied a double knot in the strings of the <**Purse of Great Capacity**>. Both were watertight, as she'd learned from experimentation. The possibility of either of those items, much bigger on the inside, filling and filling with water had been an early concern. She tucked her <**Draftsman's Pen**> into her waistband and gripped the <**Wayfinder**> in her left hand. She had no doubt it would work underwater.

Weston held some of the vines away from the wall, exposing a section with patchy plaster over solid stone. Livia pressed her hands to the stone and moved her fingers like she was kneading dough. The stone moved like clay beneath her hands. Livia sculpted the stone until she had a good-sized cavity, deep and wide. Weston arranged their gear inside and shifted the vines until they covered the cavity so well Aderyn couldn't tell where it was, and she'd watched him the whole time.

Once everyone wore a shimmering cap like Weston's, they lined up along the railing. Owen flexed his bare toes. "You ready?" he asked Aderyn.

Aderyn nodded. "But I think we should have light first."

"Good idea," Livia said. She tossed *orbs of light* into the pool like crumbs to fish. They sank beneath the surface of the pool and glimmered like stars fallen to earth. Again, the chattering pakshis' conversation grew louder.

Aderyn glanced up. A few of the birds circled high above, and as she watched, they descended in a great spiral centered on the pool. "They're so beautiful," she exclaimed.

Owen was perched on the railing and offered her a hand up. "Let's admire them later."

Aderyn climbed up. The birds were almost close enough to touch. One of them swooped low over the pool. With a snap, its beak opened, and it swallowed one of the floating lights.

Livia cried out, "No, don't—"

A dull boom sounded through the room, and the chattering pakshi's beak flashed with light from within. The bird let out a squawk that echoed across the surface of the water, shrill and discordant, and then dropped like a stone into the pool, limp and dead.

Congratulations! You have defeated [Chattering Pakshi].
You have earned [4025 XP]

The air was suddenly full of rippling light that made the walls tilt and shiver. Pain flashed across Aderyn's skull, dizzying her. She flung out her arms for balance, leaned over to stay upright against the tilting surface, and fell. As she sank beneath the water, she heard more dissonant cries, and Owen shouting, "Everybody in!" Bodies struck the water all around her, and then she submerged.

The cold shocked through her, and she gasped in surprise, then gagged as water rushed into her lungs. For a moment, her head felt swollen to twice its size and her chest ached with cold and pressure. She thrashed, convulsing helplessly. Then the moment passed, and she drew in a grateful breath—except it wasn't air she was breathing, it was water. The strange sensation of fluid in her lungs combined with how easy it was to breathe brought her to a stop. She floated peacefully, taking in the feeling of weightlessness. It was different from *fly*, which had given her control over her body's movement but hadn't taken away her sense of weight; floating in water was more like levitation, complete with her sense that she didn't know how to move.

That brought her to her senses. She lifted her arms, which pushed water aside and shifted her a few inches in the opposite direction. Heartened, she tried kicking. That moved her faster.

Something grabbed her from behind. She shrieked, a garbled, incoherent sound, and thrashed to get free. The person's grip tightened, and as she twisted around, she discovered it was Owen. He said something that, combined with his lips' movement, she made out as "Sorry." Aderyn nodded. Owen released her and pointed. Weston and Livia floated nearby, and Isold rose to join them. Livia gestured, and the *orbs of light* coursed through the water to surround them, seeming not at all bothered by flying through liquid instead of air.

Owen gestured, then dove, kicking smoothly to propel himself. Aderyn flailed a bit before getting her limbs oriented. The others were already moving, so she kicked hard and followed them, trailed by lights.

Chapter Thirty-Six

Despite the light Livia carried with her, Aderyn couldn't see more than about ten feet around her. Beyond that, the water was nearly opaque, blue and pearly from the glow of the *orbs of light*. She'd expected the shimmering of the *air bubble* to blind her, but the closer it got to her face, the less the shimmer was visible, and all she saw was a ripple in the water.

The sensation of floating in space, unmoving, filled her with awe, as if they'd ascended into the sky instead. More *orbs of light* appeared as they descended, spreading out so the nearest wall was visible. Waving tendrils of seaweed clung to its stones, dark green in the magical light. Aderyn wished she could investigate, but she'd already fallen behind and had to kick hard to catch up with her friends.

Ahead, Weston rolled to face her and beckoned to her. Aderyn thrashed her arms and legs and gained on him, not by much. Swimming was harder than she'd imagined. Her vision of sailing effortlessly like a dolphin through the water vanished.

She realized her vision was clearing at the same moment she caught up to the others, which only happened because they'd stopped moving. In the distance, great empty arches revealed where the windows had once been, and schools of fish, silver-dull in the light, flashed in and out of the openings. The light from outside was dim, and Aderyn recalled that they'd seen the setting sun. Her gratitude for Livia's magic increased.

Isold swam downward, more gracefully than Aderyn had, and waved a hand at the ground. The floor was covered with corals that, unlike the fish, were extravagantly colored: orange, red, purple. More seaweed grew in the spaces between the corals, its dark green striping the brighter colors and making them even more brilliant by contrast. Larger fish swam past, none of them bigger than two feet long, some of them as colorful as the corals. Aderyn had never seen anything like it, not even in pictures.

She watched one of the fish, round and flat-bodied like a dish with trailing fins, brighter blue than she'd imagined existing in nature. It wove in and out between the pillars of a red coral. She was about to point it out to Owen when the coral moved. Faster than Aderyn could react, it sucked the blue fish into its tubular body, the mouth of the tube expanding to take in the whole fish at once.

Aderyn let out a cry the water garbled. The others surrounded her immediately, with Owen grabbing her hand. Aderyn shook her head to mean she was unharmed. "Stay away from the corals," she said. Belatedly, she Assessed them.

Name: Carnivorous Coral

Type: Formless

Power level: 15

Attack: special

Immune to: elemental damage fire

Resistant to: bladed weapons damage

Vulnerable to: bludgeoning damage

Special attacks: engulf, contact poison

There's not much to say about carnivorous corals, since they're not more sophisticated than what I said above. They range in size from a few inches to two feet across, and they can engulf creatures half again their size. Their surfaces are abrasive, easily removing skin, and while the scrapes seem minor, the poison coating the corals' surface causes painful, itchy rashes that don't heal except by magic. However, their hard exoskeletons are brittle

and can be smashed easily, and they can't get up and walk around. That's for the best. Imagine a city overrun by carnivorous corals!

Aderyn stopped reading aloud when it became clear no one could make out what she was saying. Finally, she got everyone's attention, pointed at the corals, and shouted, "Dangerous. Stay away."

She had to repeat herself three times before she felt confident they understood. Owen swam upward a few strokes and pointed at Aderyn's left hand. She kicked her way to his side and extended the **<Wayfinder>** at arm's length. She kept a firmer grip on it than usual, conscious of how hard it would be to retrieve it if it fell into the coral bed.

As she expected, when she focused her desire to find Devendra on it, the orb warmed immediately and began spinning exactly as it did when it wasn't submerged. She turned, reveling in the floating feeling, until the **<Wayfinder>** pointed in the direction of the missing windows. Owen was watching it, too, and nodded. He swam as gracefully as the dolphin Aderyn had imagined in that direction, followed by Weston and Livia.

Aderyn tried to join them, but immediately discovered it was impossible to get anywhere without using her arms. She tried holding the **<Wayfinder>** with one hand and swimming with the other. That was better, but still slow.

Beside her, Isold grabbed her by the back of her belt and hauled her upward. The surprise nearly made her lose her grip on the orb. She realized she'd sunk too low and was almost in range of being attacked by the carnivorous corals, and another shock of fear pulsed through her. She kicked and moved her one arm rapidly to help Isold tow her higher. She was starting to understand how swimming worked, kicking her legs rapidly to propel her forward and waving her arms to guide her movement. It was the timing she didn't understand yet. Frustrated, she tried waving her arm in a different direction and was cheered to feel her movement speed up.

The others had returned and surrounded her and Isold. Owen looked concerned. He said something Aderyn made out eventually as "try something different." Then the grip of *telekinesis* wrapped around her waist, and she shot forward a few feet. Livia brought her to a halt and swam to where Aderyn could see her. Aderyn nodded. She focused on the <**Wayfinder**> again, holding it away from her body where the others could see it. After some milling around for position, they set off again, this time with Aderyn at the center of their group.

Telekinesis didn't immobilize her, and Aderyn kept kicking, more to (she hoped) increase her **[Swim]** ranks than because it helped Livia's spell. She divided her attention between the orb and her surroundings. They swam through a wide hall, staying near its ceiling to avoid patches of carnivorous coral. Nothing remained of the plaster that once covered the stone; the walls were bare, and the edges of the stones were rounded, the cracks between them visible. Sea plants grew within some of the cracks, widening them, but the walls seemed solid and not in danger of collapse.

They passed through rooms as bare and decrepit as the hall and from there to more halls, with the <**Wayfinder**> gradually brightening. When the orb darkened unexpectedly, Aderyn shouted, "Stop! Stop!"

She turned slowly, her gaze fixed on the orb, until it regained its bright color. When she looked up, she saw only a wall covered with trailing green seaweed. She Assessed it, but saw nothing, not even a line of text identifying the seaweed. She waved at it and said, "Secret door?"

Weston didn't have any trouble understanding her. He swam to the wall and searched through the seaweed for a few seconds. Then he began dragging great armfuls of the stuff off the wall, letting them drift down until they draped across the stones of the floor and a nearby pink coral that didn't react. Soon, a hole in the wall became visible. It was easily five feet across and wide enough for a human to fit through without trouble.

Weston held up a hand to say "stay there" and ducked into the hole, followed by a few of Livia's hastily conjured lights. He returned almost immediately and swam to Owen's side. With his lips close to Owen's ear, he said a few words that were indistinct to Aderyn. He moved to each of them, finally speaking into Aderyn's ear in muffled but intelligible words. "It's a tunnel. Turns out of sight immediately."

Aderyn nodded. Weston released his steadying grip on her shoulders and turned to Owen. Owen gestured, swimming to the tunnel entrance to take the lead. *Telekinesis* moved Aderyn forward into the tunnel behind him.

She saw no more worked stone, just the raw sides of the cliff they had to be under now. The tunnel turned at random, making curves like a snake's, but always headed inward, deeper beneath the land. Aderyn didn't know why the knowledge that they were deep underground in a tunnel with a low ceiling didn't frighten her the way being in small spaces usually did. Swimming, or even being propelled through the water, felt so peaceful she couldn't imagine being afraid. She reminded herself not to be so relaxed she wasn't alert to danger.

After several minutes of swimming, the *orbs of light* shone on a dark wall blocking the tunnel. Everyone looked at the **<Wayfinder>**, which continued to glow a bright cherry red. Then Owen swam forward and touched the wall. It shifted like a curtain. Owen grabbed a handful of seaweed and was about to pull it free when Aderyn shouted at him to stop. Quickly, she Assessed the wall, hoping she was right that **[Discern Weakness]** and **[Improved Assess 3]** worked through this kind of obstacle.

Her Assessment showed nothing. Reflecting that this was exactly the result she didn't want, she swam forward and parted the curtain of seaweed and tried again. Still nothing. She yanked on the seaweed, which resisted her first pull before giving way when she pulled harder. Soon everyone was tearing seaweed away from the exit. When the tunnel mouth was clear, Livia sent more *orbs of light* into the space beyond.

Light filled the small cave, revealing bare stone and a few plants clinging to the floor. It hadn't started small, based on the height of its ceiling; a rock fall had collapsed one half of the cave. Not a recent rock fall, Aderyn guessed, based on the number of large plants growing on and around the stones.

Owen gestured to all of them to form up around him. He pointed at the **<Wayfinder>**. Aderyn waved the orb at the rock fall, then awkwardly swam toward it. Its glow brightened as she neared the pile of stone. That made no sense. The **<Wayfinder>** knew, or whatever you called how a magic item worked, not to point at a path that was blocked. It shouldn't have led them there.

She swam to the wall beside the heap of stones and flicked the blue switch on the **<Draftsman's Pen>**. Writing on the rough surface was difficult, and the ink skipped and pooled as she dragged the pen over the stone, so she wrote only MUST BE A WAY THROUGH OR WF WOULDN'T BRING US HERE.

Livia swam away from the group and laid a hand on a large stone protruding from the rock fall. She held up a hand in a "wait" gesture. Shaking out her arms, she dove forward, into the pile, disappearing from sight in an instant as the stone shaped itself around her body. Weston grunted and twitched like he wanted to follow her, but he stayed put.

It was about five minutes, Aderyn guessed, before Livia returned. She didn't say anything, just handed her watch in its impermeable shell to Weston. She leaned close to say something into his ear. Then she returned to float near the pile of rocks and took her usual solid stance when shaping stone. Since she was still floating, it didn't look nearly as solid as usual. Livia clasped her stone hand over her flesh-and-blood hand and let out a garbled shout. The pile shifted, stone grinding on stone until the room echoed with the weird, discordant underwater noise.

Aderyn, watching the roof warily, shouted as well when the roof sagged and traces of rock dust drifted through the water. Livia stopped her spellslinging and turned her attention to the roof. She swam up and laid her stone left hand against its surface so from Aderyn's perspective she looked like she was holding the roof up with one hand. Then she swam back down to where she could stand atop the pile of rubble and began chanting. Slowly, a stone near the top slid away from the pile and drifted to lie on the cave floor as lightly as if it weighed nothing. The roof didn't move.

Livia rejoined them and held out a hand to Aderyn, who gave her the <**Draftsman's Pen**>. She wrote WILL TAKE TIME BUT CAN DO. WATCH THE TIME.

Owen gestured for the pen. He wrote COULD GO AROUND BUT MIGHT TAKE LONGER. BEST HERE? The question mark was jagged but clear.

Aderyn nodded. The <**Wayfinder**> always found the shortest route, and that was what they needed now that time was their enemy. She returned the pen to her waistband as Livia swam back to the top of the rock fall.

Livia continued to move stones into piles around the circumference of the cave. Time passed. Aderyn was too nervous to be bored at having no part in Livia's plan. She swam to where she could look at the watch Weston held, but without knowing when they'd entered the water, the time it showed meant nothing to her. Weston clearly knew, because he paid Aderyn no attention even though he hated people reading things over his shoulder. He barely moved as he floated near the rock fall.

Owen swam back and forth near the entrance. Aderyn hadn't even considered they might need to worry about being attacked. The tunnel had felt abandoned, between the seaweed curtains and the lack of carnivorous corals, but that didn't mean they were safe. Isold swam between piles of stone, searching for something. Eventually he picked up a fist-sized stone and tapped it lightly against one of the rocks that had a flatter surface than the others. He struck the stone harder, and a rhythm emerged, a hollow beat that sounded like it came from deep underground. Aderyn felt instantly stronger and more competent.

The **[Inspire Courage]** drumbeat worked on Livia, too, based on how the stones flew away from the blockage faster and more efficiently. Soon, a gap showed at the top of the pile, jagged like something had taken a bite out of the wall. Aderyn clenched her fist, willing Livia to move faster even though that was a bad idea if it meant collapsing the room. The gap gradually widened. Soon, it was large enough for Livia to fit her hand through. Then her arm. Finally, Livia flung one last stone away, revealing a gap big enough for a person to squeeze through.

Livia ducked to swim through the gap. Weston grabbed her foot and pulled her back. He showed her the watch and tapped the *air bubble* shell. Livia grimaced. She held up both hands with all ten fingers splayed wide, then lowered one hand and flexed the fingers of her other hand again. Aderyn's terror that they had only fifteen minutes to get to safety faded when she remembered Weston wouldn't have let Livia cut it that close, and she meant they had fifteen minutes before they had to turn back.

Owen nodded. He slid through the gap and waved a hand for the others to join him. Aderyn swallowed her doubts and followed him.

The room beyond was part of the Ivory Palace, not more unfinished tunnels. Fish swam in and out through holes where stones in the wall were missing. Aderyn's heart lurched when she saw a humanoid figure apparently waiting for them. But it was a body, stripped of its flesh to the bone, its clothing in tatters. Isold examined it and shook his head—no way to tell how the person had died, only that it had been there for a while.

The remains of two doors opened off the chamber. Aderyn used the **<Wayfinder>** to determine their path lay through the westernmost door. "Now what?" she said, exaggerating her lip movements to make her meaning clearer.

Livia held up ten fingers, then two more. Owen grimaced. He gestured at the gap and waited for the rest of them to pass back through into the cave before following. Then he led the way through the tunnel and up the shaft of the atrium to just below the surface of the water. If the chattering pakshis were still alert and angry, Aderyn heard no sign of it.

Owen maneuvered himself around to beneath the remnants of the balcony. He grabbed the balcony edge and, with one fluid movement, hauled himself out of the water. Aderyn watched helplessly as he thrashed for a moment, convulsing as he coughed water out of his lungs. Then he pulled himself all the way out and lay flat on the balcony, extending both hands to Aderyn.

She gripped his wrists securely and kicked to propel herself upward as he pulled. When her head broke water, the sensation of having lungs full of the stuff struck her like a mallet to the chest, and she coughed desperately to empty her lungs. It was worse than entering the water had been, and her chest hurt terribly after the water was gone and she could breathe air normally again. She lay on the balcony beside Owen and sucked in air, closing her eyes. The way she felt, she didn't care if a chattering pakshi tore into her.

Splashes indicated everyone was leaving the pool. Weston said, "I don't know whether we succeeded or not. That feels like failure."

"Breaking through the rock fall took most of our time," Livia said, sounding winded. "When we go back, we'll be able to move faster."

"I am thinking, though," Isold said, "that we have no idea where we can find air along that route. If it takes too long to find Devendra—"

"Let's not worry about that now," Owen said. "Livia, I bet you're close to the end of your reserves."

"Not too close, but close enough I don't want to get in any fights," Livia said. "Let's rest, and tackle this in the morning."

"We don't have much choice," Owen said. "This is the worst part, knowing that time is passing and not being able to do anything about it."

Aderyn clasped his hand, but said nothing. With Devendra in who knew what kind of danger, Weston was right—it felt like failure.

Chapter Thirty-Seven

Weston wedged the door they'd come in by shut. "The atrium is accessible from above, but the birds will give us warning if anyone approaches from there. And anyone coming through that door is going to make more noise than a chattering pakshi. I think this is as safe as anywhere to rest."

Livia rummaged through the cache in the wall and came up with some wrapped packets. "Tomorrow, I want to use the **<Wand of Epic Bounty>**. We're going to need every advantage. For tonight, let's eat up the stuff we can't take underwater. I don't want to assume we'll return this way, so don't leave anything you care about."

"I like my boots," Weston groused.

"Then put them in Aderyn's knapsack."

"Let's not do that," Aderyn protested. "No offense, Weston, but our boots are all pretty ripe after a hard battle and wading over I don't know what kind of growths flourish in this environment. Suppose we ruin something important?"

"I'll buy you new boots if it comes to that, dearest." Livia patted his cheek fondly. "Have some of these crackers. They're crunchy, but they don't leave your mouth feeling dry."

Aderyn ate grapes and crackers and shelled almonds and beef jerky and washed it all down with cold water produced by Livia. Despite being soaking wet, she wasn't cold. The temperature didn't drop much after sunset in the Southlands, and for the first time, she felt comfortably cool, though the discomfort of wet clothes and hair balanced that feeling out.

The chattering pakshis stopped "talking" once it was full dark. Nobody asked Livia to cast *orb of light*. If Aderyn squinted, she could see the floating body of the bird that had swallowed one of the orbs. She hated remembering its accidental death, though who could have known the birds were drawn to moving lights?

When she finished eating, she settled near Owen with the knapsack under her head and stared into the darkness until she fell asleep. Her dreams were fragmented slivers of real memories, people she'd met and places she'd been, only every memory was overlaid with a sense of fear regardless of who or what it was. When Owen woke her for her turn at watch, she rose gratefully and accepted the **<Cat's Eye Goggles>** he pressed into her hand.

Even with the goggles in place, there wasn't much to see: walls covered with vines that thankfully didn't move or try to strangle her, the open ocean whose waves crashed against the walls below where she paced, the barely visible bodies of chattering pakshis as they shifted and muttered unintelligibly in sleep. No moon shone over the endlessly moving black ocean, and Aderyn counted back and realized it was nearly new. That meant even if it had risen, which she thought wouldn't happen for a few hours, its thin crescent wouldn't provide enough light to be useful. Aderyn's gratitude for the **<Cat's Eye Goggles>** increased.

She paced quietly between the door and the outer wall, occasionally stopping to look out across the ocean. No lights indicated where Ikharatia was. She and her friends might as well be the only people in the world. That was a depressing thought. She made herself go over plans for the morning, though that was pointless when they knew nothing about what lay beyond that little room, and finally woke Weston and returned the goggles to him before falling into an untroubled sleep until sunrise.

They all stared at the little jar labeled BRICEN'S MIRACLE MEALS after Livia conjured it with the <**Wand of Epic Bounty**>. Finally, Owen picked it up and passed around the pills it contained. One pill was left when they'd all received one, and Owen sealed it into the jar and handed the jar to Aderyn. "I have no idea what happens to the ones we don't use," he said, "but we should hang onto it for as long as possible. Maybe Devendra can use it."

Jumping into the pool was easier now Aderyn knew what to expect, and the transition from breathing air to breathing water barely registered. Livia waited until they descended a few feet to cast *orbs of light*. The corals were as beautiful as ever, and for the first time Aderyn considered whether that was on purpose, to draw prey to them. Did fish see colors?

They made better time on this journey, and only fifteen minutes after entering the water, they floated in front of the heap of stones with the gap at the top. Aderyn went first, using **[Improved Assess 3]** to see if anything had taken up residence in the room beyond while they were gone. The room was still empty except for the skeleton. Livia confirmed it wasn't carrying anything useful and magical, and Weston forced the westernmost door open.

Beyond, a hallway identical to the ones they'd seen before extended a short distance and turned left. Corals clung to the floor, one of them snatching a tiny fish out of—it wasn't midair, obviously, but Aderyn didn't have another word for how the fish was swimming placidly just inches from the carnivorous coral that extended itself to suck the fish into its maw. She kicked herself higher above the floor, just in case.

With Weston in the lead searching for traps, they proceeded as rapidly as caution allowed, which wasn't very. Aderyn, once more propelled by *telekinesis*, glanced occasionally at the <**Wayfinder**> in between watching her surroundings. Livia's magic orbs cast a bluish light on the walls and floor, which Aderyn found remarkable, given that the lights were a warm yellow-white. Water was clear rather than blue, but maybe it was true that a lot of water all in one place had a blue tint.

After that turn, the hall went on a very long way. Now they saw lanterns fixed to the walls at intervals, corroded and with their glass missing. Fish swam in and out of the empty lanterns, some of which were covered in seaweed that drifted lazily in the currents made by the friends' swimming bodies. The lanterns gave the halls an eerie look that reminded Aderyn of Owen's tales of that one movie with monsters in the ceiling. She occasionally Assessed the area around them, particularly above, but no warnings emerged.

They came to an intersection, and Aderyn directed them to the right. Another long hall, more destroyed lanterns, more creepy silence. When the hall ended at an enormous room, Aderyn's relief at leaving the eerie halls behind propelled her forward too rapidly, ignoring the tug of *telekinesis*.

Something big and bulky reared up in front of her, and she scrambled to back up, Assessing as she did.

Name: Statue of Mahandrum

Type: Forged

Power Level: 13

Attack: trident, net, special

Immune to: mind-affecting skills and spells

Resistant to: bladed weapon damage

Vulnerable to: elemental electrical damage, bludgeoning damage

Special attack: howling thunder

Relax, Aderyn, it's broken. Completely inert. A good Spellcrafter could make it run again, if you could convince one to come all the way down here.

She became aware of the others shouting. "It's fine," she gasped. "Not a threat." She repeated herself twice more, then floated toward it.

She caught sight of motion out of the corner of her eye, something speeding toward her from her left. With a garbled shriek, she kicked and flailed to get out of the path of the attacker. She saw a sleek, white body made pearly by Livia's lights, saw rows of serrated, vicious teeth, then those teeth closed on her bare foot and tore gashes in her flesh. She screamed again and fumbled her sword free, stabbing desperately at the thing. It held on, its teeth digging deeper as it worried her like a dog with a bone.

Suddenly Owen was there, his <**Sunsword**> bright as daylight thrusting at the shark's face. It released Aderyn and dove to get away from the blade. Owen followed it. Aderyn blinked away tears she was sure were a bad idea within the *air bubble* and Assessed the creature.

Name: Wereshark [5]

Type: Monstrosity

Power level: 15

Attack: spear OR bite, special

Immune to: none

Resistant to: bladed weapons damage

Vulnerable to: sunlight and related spells

Special ability: night vision, heat vision

Special attacks: shred, frenzy

You know how *shred* feels now. With blood in the water, *frenzy* is inevitable.

Don't wonder now why your first Assess didn't see them. You don't have time for introspection.

Trailing blood, Aderyn rolled to Assess the far side of the room and nearly wept again when no system messages appeared. Her foot burned hot agony all through her leg, but she kicked with the unwounded one, trying to follow Owen. With five weresharks to fight, he would need the help of **[Outflank]**.

But Owen moved faster than she did, and just as she realized **[Keep Pace]** wasn't working, he struck at the wereshark who'd injured her, driving the <**Sunsword**> into the monster's side. Aderyn flailed harder, but with both hands full and only one working leg, she barely made any progress.

Something loomed in front of her, startling her. It was Isold, waving the <**Wand of Healing**> in her face. Aderyn drew her legs in, raising them to where Isold could grab her knee and steady her injured foot. The green light that dribbled from the wand's tip didn't dissipate in the water, instead flowing in a coherent stream to wrap around her foot. The pain eased, then disappeared, and Aderyn flexed her healed foot and nodded thanks.

Isold nodded back. He put the wand away and rolled backward, pointing himself at one of the weresharks. Aderyn swam clumsily after him, cursing inwardly. She was going to be useless in this fight if she couldn't keep up.

She searched the room to see where everyone was. Weston and Livia were back to back fighting a wereshark that rushed past, snapping at them, then turned in a sharp circle and darted at them again. Its body was marked with dark bruises and a couple of long slashes, showing where *stone fist* and Weston's blade had found their mark. Isold had captured the attention of another wereshark and, as Aderyn watched, that shark swam after one of its companions, tearing into the unsuspecting victim thanks to **[Coercion]**. She didn't at first see Owen, but when she swam around the enormous statue, she discovered he was still fighting the one that had injured Aderyn. That left—

Aderyn got her sword up in time to deflect a blow from the remaining wereshark. It was smaller and more agile than the others and surged smoothly upward, away from her blade so Aderyn didn't do more than score a line along its belly. She kicked until she faced the wereshark again. It had turned smoothly and was swimming back toward her, slowly and with such deliberation it unnerved her. She hated the way the water dragged at her sword when she moved it, like trying to slice through mud. She changed her grip slightly and prepared to thrust instead.

When it was ten feet away, the wereshark sped up, accelerating. **[See It Coming]** showed Aderyn its intent to ram her. She held her position, her heart racing, until it was almost on her. Then she rolled onto her back, letting it speed over and past her, and thrust.

The mystery sword impaled the wereshark below its throat. Aderyn held tight as the wereshark's momentum carried it forward, dragging the blade from its throat through its stomach so it disemboweled itself. Black blood made a huge cloud in the water, and Aderyn kicked to dive lower. Breathing the blood seemed like a really bad idea.

Congratulations! You have defeated [Wereshark].
You have earned [17,025 XP]

Another, identical system message appeared seconds later. Aderyn swam as fast as she could manage toward Owen, who came to meet her.

The <**Sunsword's**> light cast sharp-edged shadows across his face and her arms. Owen gripped her shoulder briefly, his gaze searching her body for signs of injury. "I'm fine," Aderyn said, mouthing the words exaggeratedly.

Owen nodded. He grabbed her upper left arm and towed her after him, back around the statue. Aderyn held her sword close to her body where the water wouldn't drag at it and kicked her legs to assist. Two weresharks still fought each other, biting and thrashing and slamming against each other's bodies. Isold hovered nearby, ready to use **[Coercion]** again. Owen dragged Aderyn past that fight to where Livia and Weston battled. Aderyn screamed as the wereshark bore down on Livia, who brought her stone left arm in front of her face to deflect the blow.

The wereshark's jaws closed on Livia's arm, grinding hard enough to tear flesh—if there had been any to tear. It made that odd clacking noise Aderyn remembered from the first wereshark fight and drifted away, stunned. Tiny slivers of serrated teeth floated through the water. Before it recovered, Weston straddled it from behind and slammed his dagger through one beady black eye. The wereshark convulsed and fell limp.

Congratulations! You have defeated [Wereshark].
You have earned [17,025 XP]

Aderyn heard Isold shouting something that sounded like a warning. She turned just in time for **[See It Coming]** to warn her to drop out of the way of a wereshark slamming into her. Another system defeat notice appeared, which confused her—the wereshark was clearly still alive—but she was too busy trying to orient herself to worry about it.

The wereshark was already out of reach, and Aderyn thought it might be fleeing, but then it turned around at the far edge of Aderyn's vision and swam back in their direction. She made herself think tactically. It was far too fast and maneuverable for **[Outflank]** to be effective. Swords were of limited use even if the wereshark weren't resistant to bladed weapons. And it was in a frenzy, so it wasn't likely to respond to Isold's **[Cause Fear]** skill, though that would give the friends an advantage.

Owen and Weston were maneuvering to take the monster from

both sides. Livia had assumed the stance she took when she prepared to deliver a beating. The shark was closing fast. Aderyn Assessed it again, noted the yellow ball of light that said it meant to attack Weston, and in the last second before it struck him, she used **[Compel]** to force the wereshark to go after her instead.

The wereshark's smooth advance turned into a jerky, spasmodic twist, and in its momentary disorientation, Owen, Weston, and Livia all struck at once. Aderyn kicked herself out of its reach and switched its target to Isold. Again, the wereshark flailed in confusion, and again, the friends attacked. If the wereshark had emotions, Aderyn had no way to read them in its fathomless black eyes and permanent smile, but she liked to imagine it was confused and afraid. It struggled free of its attackers. Then it turned to flee.

Livia shouted something. The floor tiles cracked, and with a rumble, tentacles of stony earth shot out of the exposed ground to entangle the wereshark, immobilizing it. The wereshark made that horrible chittering clacking sound again until Weston silenced it forever with **[To the Heart]**.

Congratulations! You have defeated [Wereshark].
You have earned [17,025 XP]

Aderyn swam after the others to the base of the statue. Owen extended a hand for the **[Draftsman's Pen]**, started to write on the stone plinth, then apparently thought better of defacing it and wrote on an uncracked floor tile instead. SHOULD HAVE BEEN HARDER

Aderyn had thought it was plenty hard, but when she considered that she had been the only one seriously injured—a glance at the team roster showed everyone's health to be nearly full—she had to admit Owen was right. The **<Wand of Epic Bounty>** had probably kept her from losing her foot, but it couldn't do anything to make the weresharks easier to kill.

DON'T KNOW WHAT IT MEANS, Owen continued. SHOULD BE CAREFUL

He gave the pen back to Aderyn and gestured for them to follow him. Aderyn took one last look around with Assess and saw nothing dangerous. Now she considered what the system had said about the failure of **[Improved Assess 3]** to notice the wereshark. It had come from the side, and she'd used Assess ahead of her. So its effect was limited to line of sight, perhaps? It was a good warning. Making assumptions was the fast way to getting killed—or, in her case, losing a foot.

Chapter Thirty-Eight

Aderyn swam upward, skirting the inert Forged. Her initial impulse to hurry along died when she got a better look at the creature. The statue was of a naked man five times the size of a human, wielding a similarly-sized trident and dragging an enormous net behind him. Aderyn's amazement that the net had survived all these centuries underwater diminished when she realized the mesh was made of corroded iron made to look like rope. She swam all the way around it, admiring its construction. Even the greenish-white patina that covered it couldn't obscure how beautiful it had been when it had been new and functional.

Owen shouted something, and she jerked in surprise and fear, expecting enemies **[Improved Assess 3]** had missed, before realizing he wasn't in danger, he just wanted her attention. She swam to his side, proud of not needing Livia to tow her. Owen gestured at the walls. The room was round, Aderyn realized, with a domed ceiling and several exits, most of them leading to the open ocean. She held the **<Wayfinder>** in both hands and focused on finding Devendra.

Another shout startled her into looking up. Weston and Isold, swimming near the ceiling, were gesturing frantically for her and Owen and Livia to join them. Aderyn Assessed the area, but got only her friends' Codex information. Curious, she swam after Owen. When she drew nearer, she realized why Weston and Isold were so excited. The water's surface ended well below the top of the dome.

As soon as she neared them, Weston removed the <**Breath of Life Amulet**> and kicked his way above the surface. His thrashing stilled, and his feet moved slowly but unceasingly, keeping him in place. Then he submerged and put the amulet back on. Without being asked, Isold handed him the <**Draftsman's Pen**>, and Weston swam to the nearest flat surface and wrote rapidly.

BIG AIR RESERVE BUT NOT HUGE

BIGGER AT LOW TIDE I THINK

EMERGENCY USE TO RECHARGE AMULETS

Owen waved at him to hand over the pen. USE NOW?

Weston shook his head. WASTE OF THE TIME WE HAVE. COME BACK IF NEEDED

Owen nodded. ADERYN, WHERE NOW?

Aderyn focused on the <**Wayfinder**> and turned in a slow circle, then pointed. Owen swam away, faster than the rest of them could follow, and returned when they had only reached the base of the Forged statue. He jerked his head in the direction Aderyn had indicated and mouthed "Doorway."

They swam low across the floor, which was clear of corals but bore signs of wear. Stones lay scattered across the black and white tiles, some of which were cracked or missing. Occasional plants grew from the cracks where grout was missing, but they weren't big enough to conceal anything dangerous. Aderyn Assessed the space anyway. Fish swam alone or in schools around the base of the Forged statue. It was all so placid it put Aderyn's nerves on edge. This was exactly the time for an ambush.

The <**Wayfinder**> directed her to an arched doorway next to another opening that led to the ocean. Aderyn took a moment to examine that one, but Livia's lights didn't extend far enough to reveal anything but that the sea floor was covered with thick grasses that moved like the water was a stiff wind. The doorway they wanted was just inside the palace. Beyond it was another hall, wider than the previous ones, with smaller doorways piercing it on the inner side. Aderyn Assessed each room as they came to it, just in case. Still nothing.

"I'm starting—" she began, heard the garbled sound of her own voice, and decided not to babble when she might make her friends think it was something important.

The hall made a few sharp turns and ended at a door, or what remained of a door after centuries of immersion. Weston listened for a minute, then examined the door all over for traps, and eventually signaled that it was clear. When he pushed on the latch, it fell off and hit the tiled floor with a dull clunk. Everyone froze. Finally, Weston took hold of the door and wrenched it off its hinges, setting it to one side.

Aderyn pushed past Weston to float in the doorway, Assessing the room. With the system's warning still ringing in memory, she was careful to do more than one Assessment, turning so her field of vision covered the entire room.

To her surprise, a system message appeared.

Name: Devendra

Level: 7

Class: Tidecaller (retired)

Aderyn blinked and surveyed the room with her natural vision. It was empty except for a cage of iron bars, five feet tall and about the same wide, which was also empty. The cage bars were free of rust, showing it wasn't original to the Ivory Palace. "She's not here," she said.

"What?" Owen said, pointing at his ear to indicate he didn't understand.

Aderyn shook her head and held up a hand requesting patience. The system notice had appeared when she was facing the iron cage. She tried again, using Skill Assess, and another system notice appeared. Aderyn had never Assessed Devendra's skills before, but what she read seemed reasonable for a level seven Tidecaller. But there still wasn't anyone there.

She gestured to Livia, pointing at the nearest *orb of light* and then at the corner where the cage was. More lights popped into existence, illuminating that area. Most of the floor tiles were gone, and the ones that remained were cracked, with plants growing out of the cracks. There were corals, the ordinary kind, not carnivorous, and masses of tall sea grass growing out of the bare earth.

Something moved within the grasses behind the cage. Aderyn slowed her approach and Assessed again.

Name: Devendra

Level: 7

Class: Tidecaller (retired)

Whatever was there was small, no more than two feet across, with a sleek body that glimmered in the magic light. "Devendra?" Aderyn said.

A fish emerged from the grasses, dark gray and silver where the light hit it. For a moment, its outline was clear, and then the water rippled with an effect like heat haze around it. In the next moment, Devendra floated in front of Aderyn. She stretched her arms and flexed her fingers. "It's you," she said. Her voice was as clear as if she wasn't underwater. "Why you?"

"We came—that is, Varoun sent us," Aderyn said. "Wait, let me—" She reached for the **<Draftsman's Pen>**.

"Varoun did?" Devendra sounded as if she'd understood Aderyn's waterlogged words. "Then Kanan has been defeated."

Owen spoke at length, words Aderyn could make out just well enough to know he was explaining the situation. Devendra's frown deepened.

"And my children?" she asked.

All of them spoke at once, reassuring the queen, who only barely relaxed. "Then you can help me return, and I will see to Kanan's overthrow myself," she said. "He took me by surprise, murdered my handmaidens, locked me in here—" She gestured at the cage. "I have a spell that lets me take the shapes of certain aquatic creatures, and the sea bass is small enough to fit between the bars, but the wereshark guards are too many, and they're intelligent enough to recognize there is something unusual about what is otherwise an ordinary fish."

Weston said, "We took... clear now... respawn," which Aderyn understood to mean they should leave before the weresharks respawned.

Owen asked Aderyn for the pen. On the wall, he wrote, DEVENDRA SHOULD STAY IN HUMAN FORM. CIRCLE UP AROUND HER

Aderyn returned the pen to her waistband. She wished she could put the **<Wayfinder>** away, but it was still a bad idea to open the **<Purse of Great Capacity>** underwater, and her linen trousers didn't have pockets. She gripped it tightly in one hand and patted the mystery sword to make sure it was securely fastened.

With Owen and Weston in the lead and Devendra in the center of their group, they returned the way they'd come. Aderyn continued to Assess the rooms they passed, visions of hidden enemies filling her imagination—though now that she'd seen Devendra's shapeshifting spell, her imagination expanded to include harmless-seeming fish transforming into monsters.

They reached the statue room, and Owen and Weston sped up. Aderyn called out to them to slow down, but then *telekinesis* gripped her and she began to catch up. Belatedly, she thought to Assess the room. Again, the system message about the Forged statue appeared.

And so did something else.

Name: Wereshark [3]

Type: Monstrosity

Power level: 15

Attack: spear OR bite, special

Immune to: none

Resistant to: bladed weapons damage

Vulnerable to: sunlight and related spells

Special ability: night vision, heat vision

Special attacks: shred, frenzy

Kanan knows the secret of the Ivory Palace, and now, so do you. A lightning-fast respawn rate means you can't take anything for granted.

Aderyn screamed, "They've respawned already! Devendra, tell them!"

"What?" Devendra said, turning to face Aderyn.

Aderyn pushed past her and grabbed Owen's shoulder. "They're already back!" she said. "We have to fight!"

She scanned the rest of the room, Assessing, and terror struck. More weresharks. A group of two to the right. Another group of two coming up behind. "Isold!" she shouted, waving at the ones behind.

Isold twisted around to face the oncoming weresharks and let out a howl that underwater sounded even more terrifying and strange than it usually did. The two weresharks thrashed to turn around and flee. Two system defeat notices popped up, but Aderyn was watching the other pair of weresharks and didn't feel much relieved.

As one, the weresharks attacked. Aderyn was barely aware of Devendra resuming her fish shape and hoped it would make the queen less of a target. She drew her sword and took a defensive stance. Her lesser mobility meant the best thing she could do was wait for them to come to her. Beyond, Weston and Owen were fighting all three weresharks at once, while Livia fought one with her fists and Isold sang in a low voice that sounded like waves crashing on the shore. The wereshark he faced drifted before him, perfectly still. Then it convulsed, thrashing as if it couldn't breathe. Something snapped, and instead of a shark, a humanoid figure wielding a short spear floated before Isold. The wereshark shook itself like a dog shedding water and lunged for Isold.

Aderyn swam without thinking how awkward she was at it and put herself in front of Isold just as the wereshark reached him. The monster gripped its spear and thrust at Aderyn's midsection. Though **[See It Coming]** warned her of the blow, the water made her move too slowly, and the spear tore a gash in her side. Aderyn ignored the burning pain and drew her sword.

Isold's song changed to something higher pitched. The wereshark lowered its spear, and Aderyn lunged at its stomach, impaling it. Its high-pitched, chittering scream drew the attention of another wereshark, who rushed past Weston, slamming him out of the way, and swam at Aderyn. Controlling her fear, Aderyn ignored the monster in favor of finishing the wounded wereshark in humanoid form. Black blood billowed in the water the second wereshark swam through.

Aderyn kicked and swam backwards just fast enough to avoid the wereshark's frenzied lunge. Her side burned painfully, too painfully for her to ignore, but she raised her sword to a defensive position anyway. The wereshark rushed her, biting and thrashing in its maddened thirst for her blood. Aderyn fended it off, but only just. Its onslaught forced her slowly backward.

She shrieked as she bumped into something that grabbed her shoulders. Isold said something unintelligible in her ear and pressed the **<Healing Stone>** to her wounded side. The shark veered away from the ethereal green light that shone from within Aderyn's flesh. Aderyn kept her guard up. She wasn't yet healed when the shark recovered and flew at her again—but her thrust missed, and Isold cried out in pain as the shark struck him instead, its jaws fastening on his shoulder.

Aderyn screamed and stabbed the wereshark in its side. It didn't let go of Isold. Desperate, Aderyn grabbed the fuzzy ball of yellow light that connected Isold to the wereshark and with **[Compel]** dragged it to herself. She couldn't kill the wereshark on her own, but she could stop Isold from dying at the monster's teeth.

The light didn't move. Pulling on it felt like trying to break a chunk of rock off a boulder. Aderyn tried again, with the same results. Isold's struggles were weaker now, and the team roster that was always at the edge of her vision showed his health bar sinking fast. Aderyn screamed in fury and stabbed the wereshark, cursing the water that dragged at her blade and slowed her attack.

Behind her, Devendra shouted a string of nonsense words, and the water around the wereshark roiled, slowly at first, then with thousands of bubbles that flowed over its body in streams. Aderyn held her next strike, puzzled. She realized the bubbles outlined a translucent humanoid form straddling the wereshark's back above the dorsal fin just as the figure's nearly invisible fingers reached into the shark's mouth and pried its jaws apart. Aderyn dropped her sword and grabbed Isold, dragging him out of reach.

The shark thrashed, trying to get at the thing riding it and ignoring the humans entirely. Aderyn heard Isold mumbling something. When she watched his lips, she understood he was asking about the **<Healing Stone>**. A flash of fear shot through her as she realized it had fallen out of his hand. She dove, for once not thinking about how slow she swam, and searched the floor. Why couldn't it have been a giant ruby instead of an ordinary-looking river stone?

She passed her sword and swept it up just as two overlapping system defeat notices appeared in her vision. She couldn't spare the attention to see which weresharks were dead. If the **<Healing Stone>** was lost, their chances of survival dropped significantly.

Her gaze passed over it before her brain identified the smooth oval stone that was out of place amid all the jagged rocks scattered across the floor. She snatched it up and waved it at Isold. Isold floated unmoving below the wereshark that was still fighting its watery opponent. Aderyn focused on the team roster. Isold wasn't dead, but it was a close thing. And Aderyn didn't know how to use the **<Healing Stone>**.

Another system defeat notice appeared. Aderyn ignored that one too and swam to Isold's side, patting him all over in search of the **<Wand of Healing>**. Before she found it, Owen grabbed her and shouted, "We have to get out of here!"

Aderyn nodded. One wereshark remained, but it was the one Devendra's summoned creature rode, and Aderyn was just fine with not getting experience for killing it so long as they all survived to enjoy the experience they had received.

Livia's *telekinesis* wrapped around Isold, dragging him, and Aderyn swam after them. Swimming was easier than it had been, though some of her proficiency was probably mortal terror. She was able to swim and use **[Improved Assess 3]** at the same time, at least.

Which was why she was the one to scream the warning.

"Five more weresharks ahead!" she shouted. "Devendra—"

"There are five weresharks in our path," Devendra said, her clear voice ringing out through the vast room. "Make for the open ocean!"

Owen turned and swam ahead, aiming for one of the openings that had probably been an enormous window centuries ago. He said something Aderyn couldn't understand, but Devendra replied, "We are not far from the shore. It's the best exit, regardless."

Aderyn flapped her free arm awkwardly to point herself after Owen. She didn't get far before Owen backed and slowed, and **[Improved Assess 3]** revealed four more weresharks between them and freedom. The weresharks approached slowly, and it didn't take **[Read Body Language]** for Aderyn to recognize their satisfaction at having the friends cornered.

Aderyn madly reviewed her mental map—not an actual system map, but what she remembered of their surroundings. They couldn't go forward, they couldn't go up—

"Back to the hall!" she shouted. "All the way back to that room—

they can't fit inside!" She swam away without waiting for her friends as Devendra repeated her words. She might be improved at **[Swim]**, but she still wasn't fast.

Owen overtook her seconds later. They all swam at top speed, with Livia towing the unconscious Isold, down the hall and back into the room where Devendra had been imprisoned. Aderyn didn't hear the sounds of anything following them. The hall was wider than she remembered, easily wide enough for a wereshark, so if they didn't reach that room in time—

She shot through the gap where the rotted door had been and didn't stop going until she hit the opposite wall. Breathing heavily, she put her back to the wall and stared at the opening. Surely it wasn't wide enough for a wereshark? Her heart sank when she remembered their enemies didn't have to stay in shark form, and a humanoid monster would fit through just fine.

Livia chanted something and waved her hand as if lifting something. With a rumble, stone rose up to fill the gap, closing it off entirely. She summoned a few more lights, and they all stared at one another as if looking for reassurance that they were safe.

Finally, Owen said, "Rest... figure it... later."

Aderyn had hoped she was the only one who realized they were trapped, though that was irrational. She closed her eyes and sagged against the wall. Figure it out later. That was more optimistic than she was prepared to be.

Chapter Thirty-Nine

She heard Livia say Isold's name and jerked upright. How could she have forgotten Isold? A glance at the team roster showed his health bar was lower than before.

She rushed to his side. Livia had taken the <**Wand of Healing**> from the sheath along Isold's leg and was concentrating on it. The problem of what to do if the one who usually did the healing was the one who needed to be healed had come up before, and they'd all learned to activate a wand, but Livia was the most experienced. Aderyn hovered, hoping Isold's wounds weren't so serious only a <**Potion of Life**> could restore him. Drinking potions underwater was impossible, her mother had repeatedly told her children, along with horror stories of what happened if you tried.

The wand's tip glowed with green phosphorescence, and a trail of light unrolled toward Isold's mangled shoulder. It coiled around the many jagged wounds and settled into them, quivering like bright green jelly. Aderyn watched the team roster rather than the healing, her hands clenched as she willed Isold's health bar to rise. Slowly, the fat blue line grew. After a few seconds, Isold stirred.

"Hold still," Owen said.

Isold's health was at half when the phosphorescence faded and died.

Livia handed him the wand without comment, and they all waited while he used the <**Healing Stone**> to restore himself to full. "What did I miss?" he finally said.

"We ran," Owen said bluntly. "Too many—" He rolled his eyes and gestured for the <**Draftsman's Pen**>. TOO MANY TO FIGHT. THEY JUST KEPT COMING. AND WITHOUT THE MIRACLE MEAL, YOU'D BE DEAD. ANYBODY ELSE INJURED?

Isold pointed at Aderyn's still-injured side. He drew the wand again and gestured to her to lift her shirt and shift on that side.

OWEN AND I WERE BATTERED BY THE WERESHARKS, Weston wrote. BIG BRUISES NOT SERIOUS

Isold shifted the wand to his left hand and withdrew his own pen from his belt. I PREFER NONE OF US TO BE AT LESS THAN TOP CONDITION. DO WE HAVE TO FIGHT THAT BATTLE AGAIN?

"What are you doing?" Devendra asked, peering curiously at Isold's pen. "Clever solution, but I have a better one." She murmured something unintelligible and drew a line across Isold's throat.

Isold swallowed. Then he said, in clear words, "What a remarkable spell. Thank you."

Devendra repeated the spell for each of them. To Aderyn, it felt as if ice water numbed her vocal cords briefly before warming them to a pleasant throb. "I never knew how much I like speaking," she said.

"I am just vain enough to like the sound of my unhindered voice," Isold said with a smile. "Not to mention I suspect my vocal skills are less effective when muted by water. But now, what do we face out there? Did we not kill them all?"

"Yes, what in thunder is going on?" Livia demanded. "Is this another of Kanan's tricks?"

"It's the secret of the Ivory Palace," Aderyn said. "The respawn rate is a matter of minutes. I think it's faster the deeper you get. And it looks like, if we clear a space, it respawns more enemies each time. First, there were five weresharks, then seven, then nine—the pattern might be coincidence, but I'm sure the number will always increase."

"I studied that room when I first tried to make my escape," Devendra said. "There were originally six weresharks, but one swam away after a while. It's possible not all of them will remain. If we can wait them out—"

"We're on a timer, your majesty," Owen said. "Unless you can cast a spell that lets us breathe underwater the way you are?"

Devendra shook her head. "At my level, I can only cast the spell on myself, though it lasts a very long time."

Owen stared at the rock wall Livia had conjured to block the gap. "Bulling through didn't work," he said. "We need another plan. Thoughts?"

"The walls are stone," Weston said. "Livia can make openings anywhere. We could create our own path through the Ivory Palace and then she can tunnel through the cliff to the surface."

"Going through means facing the same problem as going back, though," Livia said. "He's right, but who knows how many weresharks patrol the rest of this level? And the more we defeat, the more the difficulty increases."

"The <**Wayfinder**> won't help, either, because it doesn't know what enemies there are to steer us around them," Aderyn said.

"There's got to be an alternative," Owen insisted. "What about *transport*? *World door*?"

"I don't have enough resources now for more than three castings of *world door*. That would leave half of us here to drown. Even if my magical energy levels are at full, I can still only manage five *world door* spells, and that uses everything I have. We didn't come all this way to leave someone behind. But *transport*... let me think about it." Livia squeezed her eyes shut and rubbed her face. "*Transport*... six of us... from here to... no, it won't work. At my level, I could *transport* myself from here to a mile down the coast road, and transport myself and one other person from here to right around where that causeway to the palace begins."

"That sounds ideal, dearest," Weston said.

"Except it's not five trips, it's nine, and at my current reserves I could only manage six of those before rendering myself unconscious." Livia counted on her fingers. "And—never mind the details, but basically it takes even more out of me to *transport* an increasing number of people. Even fully refreshed, I don't think I could manage it."

Owen frowned. "What about *transporting* us back to the atrium? That at least gets us past the weresharks."

"I can try," Livia said. "But I'd be helpless afterward, and if my calculations are wrong, somebody gets left behind. And we'd still have to fight our way past more weresharks and the kaduvas, all of whom have respawned at greater numbers by now."

"This is ridiculous," Aderyn exclaimed. "We are not going to die here. Even if it means fighting a dozen weresharks, we are getting out." She scanned the walls with **[Spot Weakness]**. It was probably pointless, since Livia could break through anywhere, but she needed something to do that wasn't falling deeper into despair.

The walls bore only traces of plaster over thick, oblong stones that fit so tightly together Aderyn could barely see the grout. She turned slowly and then jerked in surprise. "There's a secret door!"

The others all clustered around her as she swam to touch the blue lighted outline **[Spot Weakness]** revealed. Weston immediately set to searching. "You're right. It's really hard to detect, too. I don't think anyone's opened it in centuries."

Livia grabbed Weston's hand before he could do anything else. "Wait a moment. Let me see what's on the other side. No sense walking in on a room full of weresharks." She faced the wall, and her eyes filmed over with the bright blue of *clairvoyance*. "There's enough light coming from somewhere above that I can make out a short hall that ends in stairs going up. And there's no water."

"No water?" Owen said. "How is that possible?"

"If it was sealed before the Ivory Palace submerged, there's no reason that space might not be airtight." Isold ran a hand over the stones. "The question is, how can we reach it without flooding the chamber?"

"That depends on how high those stairs go," Owen said. "If we open this door and fill the room beyond with water, the water will only rise as far as the overall water level. Suppose those stairs lead to the second or first level? It could be a fast way out of here."

"I know what to do," Livia said. "I'll use **[Pass Through Stone]** to get in there without opening the door and then see how far the stairs go."

"That's incredibly dangerous," Weston protested. "What if you run into more kaduvas or weresharks, or something else we don't know to expect because we haven't seen it yet?"

Livia chanted something and waved a hand to indicate all of her, and vanished. "I'll be careful," she said. "Exploring only. Besides, I'm the sensible one."

"How much time do we have?" Owen asked.

"You probably should have asked me that before I made my watch invisible," Livia said with a chuckle. "Less than an hour. More than enough time for reconnaissance." The water moved, and then the surface of the secret door rippled as Livia passed through it.

No one spoke for a while. Finally, Devendra said, "How sure are you that my children are safe?"

"I won't lie to you, your majesty—" Owen began.

"Just Devendra."

"All right. I won't lie to you, Devendra, we don't know what's happening at the palace. Varoun told us Kanan is behaving as if this is all a tragic incident he blames on the king of Durga. That means he can't afford to let anything happen to Colan, because that would be too big a coincidence. So unless something else changes, your children are safe."

Devendra's expression was grim. "Kanan will pay for this. I will not tolerate threats to my son. I will have to make an example of him."

"You'll have to get in line behind Livia," Weston said. "She swore to kill him herself if he did anything to your son."

"I don't understand why it matters to her. You're all foreigners." Devendra stared at the secret door as if she could see Livia through it.

"Livia feels strongly about protecting children," Aderyn said, "and she has a personal hatred of Kanan. And we all believe in doing the right thing."

The wall rippled again, and Livia appeared, shedding *invisibility* like taking off a cloak. "The stairs lead all the way to the second level," she said. "It's not anywhere we've been before. Isold, what's above us?"

Isold's eyes unfocused. "You're right, we haven't explored that part of the palace, and in fact, we passed it without seeing any doors that would lead that way. It must be a secret annex."

"It looks like it might have been a suite originally. There's a water closet and everything." Livia sounded excited. "And all of it is above the water line."

"Then we go," Owen said. "Weston, get that door open."

Weston was already feeling around for the unlocking mechanism. "Stand back so the water doesn't sweep you away."

With a stony clunk and a scrape, a section of wall swung inward. Aderyn grabbed Owen's arm as water rushed past, tugging at her despite her obedience to Weston's instructions. When the flood abated to the barest movement, Owen drew Aderyn with him through the door.

The short hallway had the look of something that had been well sealed off. Though the plaster was cracked in places, none of it had fallen, and the colors it was painted with, green and blue and purple like an underwater fantasy, hadn't faded. Aderyn and Owen swam up the stairs to where the water made a faintly blue ceiling overhead. As one, they removed the **<Breath of Life Amulets>** and surged out of the water to lie on the exposed stairs, coughing up seawater until they could breathe air freely.

Aderyn crawled up another dozen steps to get out of the way of the others coming up behind. She drew in breaths of waterlogged air and tried to blink away the fogginess across her vision. Touching the *air bubble* over her face revealed that it was the source of the fogginess. Tentatively, she worked her fingers beneath its edge and pulled the thing backwards off her head. It evaporated seconds later.

One by one, the others emerged from the water and hacked and coughed to clear their lungs. Devendra walked up the steps as casually as if she were in her own home. If she felt strange going from breathing water to breathing air, she didn't show it. She spoke a few nonsense words, and water rushed off her in a cascade until her clothes and hair were dry. Aderyn, still dripping, gaped.

Devendra noticed her amazement and smiled. "Here, let me help." She repeated what to Aderyn sounded like the same nonsense words, then turned to do the same for Owen. Aderyn's skin tingled with the sensation of a force gently dragging at her body in every direction. Water sluiced off her, running in little streams back down the stairs as if eager to rejoin the ocean. After only a minute, she was completely dry.

"I didn't realize I was uncomfortable until I wasn't anymore," she said. "Thank you."

"It's my pleasure," Devendra said. She continued casting the spell until everyone was dry.

Livia was already halfway up the stairs from where the water lapped at the steps. "Come on. You all have to see this."

Aderyn followed Livia, her curiosity roused. The stairs made a right-angle turn and continued up to a wooden door that wasn't as weather-ravaged as the others. It also was unlocked, as Livia demonstrated by opening it.

Aderyn gaped. The room beyond looked untouched by time, the walls uncracked and the lanterns attached to them barely tarnished. Brightly-colored murals covered two of the walls, depicting an underwater scene of the ocean floor covered with sea grasses and corals. On one wall, the artist had painted a submerged building like a giant gazebo, with a golden statue of a robed woman wearing a crown at its center. Painted fish swam in and out of the gazebo's pillars.

Weston disappeared through the room's only other door. He returned a minute later, saying, "There are two more rooms in this suite. No furniture, so I don't know what they were for, but they've all got murals like these. My guess is this used to be the royal suite."

"This is all from before my time," Devendra said, tracing the lines of the golden statue painting with one finger. "Your guess is likely, though. Members of the royal family often stayed here, according to history, and it was an uncertain time, in which they faced many threats. I can imagine them being security minded."

"I didn't see any way to access the rest of the level from here, so I assume there's another secret door." Weston stood with his hands on his hips surveying the room. "We can worry about that once we've rested."

"Maybe that's what we should do," Aderyn said. "Find out where the secret door lets out, and work our way back to the entrance from here."

Owen sat with his back to the wall, facing the mural. "It might not be any better, but it might also not be any worse than facing the were-sharks. Plus, we'd be on our own turf. I'm tired from all the swimming. Not as much as I'd be without the Miracle Meal, but still."

"We should sleep," Livia said. "Even if I can't get us out of here when my reserves are full, I'll still have more magical oomph for fighting our way through whatever kaduvas and weresharks have respawned up here."

Aderyn opened her mouth to agree, but a yawn emerged instead. "It's not like things will get worse."

"Don't say things like that," Livia moaned. "You know that's like an invitation for the system to make our lives harder."

"I don't think the system does that. It's not malicious."

"No, but after everything it's said to you, you can't tell me it doesn't have a warped sense of what's good for you." Livia sat heavily and leaned against Weston's shoulder.

Aderyn thought about this as she joined Owen, who tugged on her arm to indicate she could lay her head in his lap. He was right; swimming had tired her out to the point that all her muscles felt on the verge of soreness. She yawned again. The system didn't torment them; even the evil dungeon Sorrowvale hadn't been part of the system, or so Aderyn felt. It gave them extra challenges because Owen was the Fated One, secret quests and more monsters and the like, but it didn't give them help or advantages in overcoming those challenges. And yet Aderyn couldn't help thinking that the warm, casual comments that were increasingly part of her Assessments reflected the system's interest in seeing them succeed.

It was getting harder to keep her thoughts coherent. She squirmed around to get more comfortable. Her hip felt hot, like she'd sat too close to a fire. It took her fuzzy brain a moment to remember the **<Farspeaker>** and another moment to realize someone was trying to speak to her. She shot upright and snatched the magic item free, pressing a finger to the shining surface.

Varoun's face appeared in the mirror, and Aderyn had another moment of disorientation, because he looked as haggard and distressed as he had the last time he'd contacted her. "What's wrong?" she asked.

"Have you located the queen?" Varoun demanded.

"Yes. We're figuring out a way to return now."

Varoun visibly relaxed. "Excellent. You need to return at once. Kanan just declared himself king."

Chapter Forty

"*What?*" Devendra snatched the **<Farspeaker>** from Aderyn's grasp. "Varoun, where are my children?"

Varoun's eyes widened. "Your majesty—"

"Never mind that. Are my children safe?"

"Yes, your majesty," Varoun said. "Yes. One of their attendants discovered Kanan's plan and got them out of the palace before Kanan took control. They are in the army encampment now. I promise you they are as safe as we can make them."

"Kanan captured the palace?" Aderyn said. "How did he justify that?"

Varoun's gaze shifted to Aderyn, who was looking over Devendra's shoulder. "Half an hour ago Kanan announced that messengers from Umed, King of Durga, brought word that they have killed the queen. In light of the current crisis, Kanan declared a regency is unstable, and to defend against the orcs and Durga, the Southlands need a strong ruler. Meaning himself, of course."

"But that's ridiculous," Owen said. "Is Umed the sort of fool who would start a war when another one is already raging?"

"He is not any sort of fool, and Kanan's power grab is blatantly obvious." Varoun spoke in precise, bitter words. "But Duke Simla of

Adhiraj backs him, which means it is not as simple as ordering the army to remove Kanan from power. Even with Janesh supporting the queen, and myself by extension, that only means civil war. We need the queen's presence here to pull Kanan's teeth."

"I can *world door* her back to the city," Livia said.

"Just the queen? Not the rest of you?"

"It's beyond my resources." Livia sounded as if the admission hurt her physically.

Varoun shook his head. "Don't do that. Kanan's forces are watching all the gates, and without you to defend her, you would only be sending her to her death. Can you send her to the army encampment, outside Ikharatia?"

Livia closed her eyes and cursed. "No stone. I'm not skilled enough."

"Then you will have to escort her overland," Varoun said. "How soon can you return?"

Owen gestured to Aderyn to give him the **<Farspeaker>**. "Soon. We'll be as fast as we can. But even Kanan can't act quickly, can he? It's not as if he can consolidate power in a matter of hours."

"He has already struck at Janesh's forces, calling them traitors to the true king." Varoun's bitterness showed how he felt about that. "The longer it takes us to confirm his illegitimacy and restore the queen, the more lives will be lost. We cannot afford any delay."

"But—" Aderyn began.

"Understood," Owen said. "We'll do this quickly. Is there anything else?"

"I choose to be grateful that the queen isn't actually dead, or imprisoned elsewhere. We have a chance." Varoun inclined his head, and his image vanished.

"Owen, we can't get out of here quickly. You shouldn't have given Varoun false hope," Aderyn said.

"We can't get out of here quickly *and* safely," Owen corrected her. "We now have incentive to figure out the shortest, fastest route out of the Ivory Palace. Which means risk. But I don't think we dare do anything else."

"No," Devendra said, rounding on him in fury. "You'll send me back to the palace immediately."

"Devendra, that's suicide," Weston said.

"Do I look like I care, Moonlighter?" Devendra's face was flushed with anger. "I have given everything for this kingdom. Kanan needs a lesson in what that means."

"I'm not going to do that," Livia said. "If you're killed, Kanan wins. That's unacceptable."

"I don't care." Her words were weak this time, and she looked away from meeting Livia's eyes.

"You do care. You want to live to see your children again."

Devendra sighed. "It does not sit well with me, waiting."

"We have that in common." Livia smiled. "Owen, how do we solve this?"

"The only way we can. We go straight through." Owen stared into the distance, though Aderyn didn't think he was reading the Codex or looking at his map. "We have three choices. One. We find our way back the way we came, through this level and the one above. That's got to be the longer route, but it's known territory and it's not underwater. The disadvantage is that the kaduvas are even more deadly enemies than the weresharks, and if they respawn even close to as fast, we could be overwhelmed. I consider this our last resort."

"We could use the <**Wayfinder**> in reverse again, to steer us away from where enemies are," Aderyn offered. "But that would slow us down even more."

"We should keep that in mind, thanks. The second option is to try to get past the weresharks and head for the open ocean. That's a much shorter route, but the number of enemies is greater and we won't be able to avoid them by going around. Also, we'll be at a disadvantage swimming."

"Those seem like the only two options to me, Owen," Weston said.

"The third option is the riskiest and least likely," Owen said. "We use the <**Wayfinder**> to locate a different path out of here, one we're not yet aware of. It knows the most direct route to Aderyn's heart's desire, and if there's a third path, a shorter one, the <**Wayfinder**> will find it. The trouble there is how it doesn't recognize enemies or traps in the way. The shortest path might be the most dangerous. But if it gets us out of here quickly, it could be worth it."

Isold opened his knapsack and removed several bundles of leather. "Now that we're above water, we have more options," he said, unrolling the bundles and revealing glass vials and bulbs. "Five boosts to speed, which will affect us whether we swim or walk. That should put us on a more even footing, so to speak, against the weresharks, if we go that route. They enhance our movement as well as our reaction time."

Aderyn crowded around with the others. She picked up a prism filled with goopy purple liquid that glittered. "Will the weapon enhancers work underwater, or will they just wash off?"

"They don't wash off, though it's possible they don't last as long in an underwater environment, with the constant friction of the water wearing the coating down," Isold replied. "Unfortunately, we have to decide between speed and strength."

"That's right, drinking both makes you violently ill," Aderyn said. "I know that for a fact and not from my mother's horror stories. My brother Nollan—never mind, I'll tell you later."

"Speed, definitely," Owen declared. "And Livia has the magical energy boosters. I thought those shouldn't be consumed unless the spellslinger is almost out of her reserves."

Livia was already uncorking the bulb of thick red liquid. "Guess we'll find out," she said, and swigged its contents down. Aderyn watched breathlessly, but Livia just made a face like she'd bitten a lemon. "Feels strange, but I'm also fully rejuvenated. Fire and thunder, but I hate this. If I had just another month's worth of practice with *world door*—"

"Don't beat yourself up," Owen said. "We'll get through this. Any other buffs available?"

"That depends on which way we go," Isold said. "If we return to the submerged level, the <**Zaps**> and the <**Potions of Life**> will be useless to us."

"Then let's roll the dice and see where the <**Wayfinder**> takes us." Owen gripped Aderyn's shoulder. "Go for it."

Aderyn held the orb in both cupped hands and closed her eyes. In all the time she'd had the magic item, she'd never felt so passionate about getting a response as now. She focused on her heart's desire, hoping it wasn't too complicated: find the shortest way back to the surface. Other thoughts intruded, other desires, like finding the safest way, or finding the way that would meet their needs in the long run, and she shut them out. Without singleness of mind and hope, the <**Wayfinder**> responded sluggishly or not at all.

She let her desire flood through her until she tingled all over with urgency, then opened her eyes. She was facing north, and the <**Wayfinder**> glowed the pale pink that said it was working but hadn't latched on to her desire yet. Slowly, she turned, keeping her gaze fixed on the largest spike. The color deepened and warmed almost immediately, but Aderyn didn't look to see what it indicated, instead continuing to turn until she'd made a complete circle and confirmed its first reaction. Then she oriented herself on the spot the <**Wayfinder**> was most attracted to.

The <**Wayfinder**> pointed back at the stairs they'd come up by.

Momentarily disheartened, Aderyn saw the rosy glow dwindle and focused again on her desire. She hadn't realized how much she didn't want to return to the ocean. Swimming was tiring, and slow, and fighting underwater was a slog. She reminded herself that the magic item wanted her out of the water as quickly as possible. All right, it didn't have the awareness to want anything, but thinking of it as her ally in escaping the Ivory Palace gave her confidence.

"So, that eliminates one possibility," Owen said. "Let's make our preparations. Devendra, how long will that speak underwater spell last?"

"Twenty-four hours," Devendra said. "What is my role in this plan?"

"Keep up with us, and don't get hurt." Owen accepted a prism of thick, glittering purple ooze from Isold. "Can you cast spells when you're in fish shape? No? Don't endanger yourself for the sake of joining in the fight, then. If the worst happens, we'll fight to protect your escape, and you get yourself to Varoun's encampment as fast as possible."

Devendra didn't look as if she liked this answer, but she nodded.

"Let's go to just above the waterline to do this. Maximize the effect," Owen said. "And—I know this is probably the most dangerous thing we've ever done. But we've defeated challenges we were just as sure would kill us, and I have faith in our ability to outthink this dungeon. Are you with me?"

"More fighting, less talking," Livia said with a grin.

They gathered on the steps where the seawater lapped. Owen, Aderyn, and Weston poured the purple oozing liquid over their blades. Owen's <**Sunsword**> gave off a purple-tinged light that sucked at Aderyn's vision every time she glanced at it for more than a few seconds. Her mystery sword, on the other hand, didn't do anything unusual. It still looked like a normal sword, its only oddity how worn the hilt and quillons were compared to the shining, rust-free blade that might have been forged yesterday. Idly, Aderyn watched the purple potion soak into the steel and considered where she might find someone to cast *heritage*. Even if that spell didn't reveal some secret magical abilities, it would be fun to know who the sword had belonged to once.

She drank down the yellow potion, which tasted disgustingly of lemon and soap, taking her back to her childhood and Borrus's dare that had ended with her licking a big bar of lye soap and then throwing up. The memory was strong enough to make her gag, and she didn't at first feel any other effects. Then a rush of jittering energy surged through her. She recalled running the obstacle course to audition for the Glory Games, how she'd stood poised at the starting line with every nerve in her body alight with anticipation. This felt a hundred times better.

She made a few passes with her sword. Her muscles sang with energy, and the blade whipped past faster than anything she'd managed before. "This is great!"

"The effects last for three hours," Isold said. "If things go well, that should be more than enough to see us through."

"It's time," Owen said. "Aderyn, you and I go first."

There was room on the stairs for two of them to go side by side. With *air bubble* once again protecting her eyes, Aderyn sheathed her sword and dove awkwardly into the water. She gave herself a few seconds for her body to become used to breathing seawater and focused once more on the <**Wayfinder**>. Since they were still on the stairs, there was only one way to go, but its quick response cheered her. She swam, more easily than before—she wished she'd thought to check her Advancement to see if her **[Swim]** ranks were higher—down the stairs and around the corner into the room they'd sheltered in. She had a moment's fear that it would be full of weresharks, but the rock barrier still filled the doorway.

She swam around the room, watching the rosy glow deepen and fade. "This way," she said finally, and then looked up. The <**Wayfinder**> pointed at a blank wall.

Weston examined the wall. "Another secret door. Weird."

"I'll look," Livia said. Her eyes turned blue from *clairvoyance*. She stiffened. "More weresharks. Only three that I can see, because the room is big. But it's in the opposite direction from the statue room, and there's only two exits. One small, one large. I don't know what that means, tactically."

"Draw a picture," Aderyn suggested.

She studied the outline Livia produced with the <**Draftsman's Pen**>, using her imagination to translate it into real walls and doorways and compare it to what they'd seen so far. "Isold, am I right that both exits lead away from the statue room?"

"You are." Isold tapped the smaller door on the picture. "This is the opposite side. As to the larger door, anything beyond it is parallel to the statue room. We didn't pass anything that would connect the two."

"So while the rapid respawn is still a problem, we don't have to worry about reinforcements coming the old-fashioned way. Weston, which way does this secret door open?"

"Toward us. And it's going to make enough noise to ruin any surprise attack."

"I have a spell that will create an area of silence around the door," Devendra said. "Will that help?"

"Absolutely," Weston said, grinning. "I love that idea."

"So long as it doesn't catch me in the effect," Livia said.

"Silence. Yes. And I think we should try *invisibility*." Aderyn thought back to the fight when the weresharks and kaduvas fought as one against the friends. "The last time, we made noise that drew their attention, and it was the kaduva who heard us and warned the weresharks. I think *invisibility* will be effective if we're also silent."

"Then here's what I think," Owen said. "We get inside and do our best to sneak around them. Aderyn, you concentrate on finding the way out. Let's hope it's one of those two doorways and not a secret one Livia will have to waste energy pummeling. If we have to fight, make it a defensive battle if possible and keep moving to the exit. We don't care about experience, we just want to avoid triggering the respawn effect. Once we know which exit, we head that way and evaluate our next steps. Got it?"

"It's dark in there, and I can't use *orb of light*. The <**Wayfinder**> light is dim and small enough it will go unnoticed, but *orb of light* isn't hidden by *invisibility*," Livia said. "We'll need to stay close together."

"That means I should sheathe the <**Sunsword**>," Owen groused. "What a waste of a good potion."

"We shouldn't count on them not seeing us at all," Aderyn said. "I'm confident *invisibility* will work if we don't draw their attention some other way, but that's not the same as one hundred percent certainty. What's the plan for if we're revealed?"

"I'll cast *sunburst* once they see us," Livia said. "It will weaken them, but I'm more interested in disorienting them so their attacks are less effective. And there won't be any problems with visibility after that."

"Great idea." Owen's eyes met Aderyn's. "Anything else? Then—good luck, everyone."

Livia cast *mass invisibility*, making the water ripple and thicken like clear jelly. She backed away, and Devendra spoke three words that sounded almost like a mother admonishing her noisy children. They had no apparent effect, but when Weston swam to the secret door and rapped on the stone with his knuckles, no sound emerged. Weston's grin showed clearly that he thought this was the best trick ever. Aderyn wasn't sure Weston, who already moved like a cat and had to concentrate to make sound when he walked, needed a magical boost to his natural sneakiness.

Livia extinguished the *orbs of light,* leaving them in near-total darkness. The door swung silently inward, revealing another dark, seemingly endless space. Aderyn, eyeing the thickened effect on the water around Livia, put herself in position next to the Earthbreaker. Being in the lead was better for the <**Wayfinder**>, but she couldn't watch it and the *invisibility* effect at the same time. She swam next to Livia as Livia passed through the secret door.

In the darkness, Aderyn couldn't tell how large the room was or where the weresharks swam, and disorientation struck briefly, the feeling that she was suspended in a vast, empty, weightless space surrounded by invisible enemies. In the next moment, her eyes adjusted, and she realized the room wasn't completely lightless. Faint glowing patches of luminescent growth clung to the walls and floor. Aderyn closed her eyes briefly and then held the **<Wayfinder>** in front of her. The orb's central spike reddened immediately. They were close to an exit.

She opened her mouth to speak, but stopped herself before she could stupidly announce their presence to their enemies. Instead, she tapped Livia's arm and swam to the right. Her memory of Livia's picture suggested the **<Wayfinder>** was leading her toward the bigger exit, and instinct told her to hug the walls rather than swim into the open.

Her speed-enhanced reflexes and muscles screamed at her to swim faster, but she controlled the urge, which would put her ahead of her friends and out of reach of *invisibility*. The magic orb continued to glow deeper red, and after a while she stopped paying close attention to Livia and focused entirely on its direction. Livia would grab her if she ventured too far ahead.

Motion in her peripheral vision drew her gaze. She stopped swimming, her heart in her throat, as a wereshark swam past and then over their little group. More terror struck, the fear that the wereshark would pass through the *invisibility* effect and realize something was wrong. But it didn't slow or turn, and after a few seconds, it had disappeared into the dimness.

Aderyn waited for her heartrate to slow before continuing on. Ahead, something big and dark loomed, bigger than a wereshark and more geometrical in shape. Aderyn hadn't pictured the larger exit to be this large, easily twenty feet tall and wide. There were no doors, just this huge square hole in the wall ahead.

Someone behind Aderyn turned rapidly, the wake of their movement buffeting Aderyn with its speed. "They're agitated," Owen whispered, pointing. "Something's caught their attention. Maybe us."

Aderyn looked where he pointed. She saw nothing but pale blurs of movement that might be wereshark bodies swimming rapidly in circles. Then one of the blurs broke free of the cluster and headed their way.

"Don't move," Owen whispered. "If it hasn't seen us, we shouldn't give ourselves away."

Aderyn clutched the <**Wayfinder**> close, barely feeling the dull pressure of the spikes against her flesh. The wereshark continued to approach. It seemed to be headed straight for them. Aderyn controlled her panic and examined it, not for Assessment but to analyze its behavior. It swam rapidly but not as fast as she knew it was capable of, at a measured pace rather than the swift speed of something hunting prey. She was convinced it didn't see them, but if it kept on its trajectory, that wouldn't stay true for long.

The wereshark neared the edge of the *invisibility* effect. Aderyn held her breath. It would be a close thing, but even if it brushed against the effect, *invisibility* wasn't tangible despite its appearance. It would have to pass entirely within it to perceive the hidden humans.

Owen, floating nearby, had his hand on the basket hilt of the inactive <**Sunsword**>. Weston held his sword in one hand and a dagger in the other. Isold gripped Devendra by the shoulder as if holding her back. All of them watched the approaching wereshark.

The wereshark's pace slowed. It turned and swam in the other direction. Then it let out an eerie, chittering howl and dove at them. This time, there was no question about what it saw.

"That's it," Owen said. "Livia!"

Livia chanted and threw her arms wide. Glorious sunlight burst over the room, brightening it to noonday at midsummer in an instant. The wereshark cringed, then resumed its course, but more slowly. Ahead, an enormous square space marked the entrance to another room.

"The door," Aderyn said. "Follow me, go for the door!"

She swam for the exit and nearly tumbled over herself as her body responded far more rapidly than she expected. It took a moment for her to right herself, and by the time she did, Livia had caught her up with *telekinesis* and given her a shove in the right direction. Behind her, she heard more of the hideous calls of the weresharks. Not turning to look at how close their pursuers were was torture, but she reminded herself that slowing for any reason could be fatal and kept going.

Ahead, Owen had reached the gaping doorway and paused to wait for the others. The **[Sunsword]** shone nearly as bright as day. Aderyn, near the back, cursed silently at her slowness even with the magical boost.

Light from *sunburst* and the <**Sunsword**> revealed another, larger room beyond the great doorway rather than the open ocean she'd hoped for. Carnivorous corals grew along the floor just inside the doorway, and she saw skittering movement beyond that made her think of spiders.

She was about to Assess the room when more movement loomed beyond Owen, dark and lithe and ponderous all at once. Two enormous eyes blinked open. And a dozen tentacles clung to the edges of the doorway as an enormous squid with a beak as tall as Owen pulled itself through the opening and bore down on him.

Chapter Forty-One

"O*wen!*" Aderyn shrieked, letting **[Amplify Voice]** fill the room. It no longer mattered who heard them. "Watch out!" She didn't stop swimming. Her rational brain shut down her fear response and brought up **[Improved Assess 3]**.

Name: Devouring Horror

Type: Abomination

Power level: 18

Attack: tentacles x4, bite, special

Immune to: elemental water damage, elemental electrical damage

Resistant to: bludgeoning damage

Vulnerable to: bladed weapons damage, elemental fire damage

Special attacks: constrict, electric shock, concealment

Normally, giant squid live in the deep ocean and prey on anything smaller than them, which is practically everything. You wouldn't want to meet the creature giant squid are afraid of—but I digress. This giant squid, named Devouring Horror by the weresharks, lives under the Ivory Palace. The weresharks act as its servants and guards, venerating it as the source of their power. It's not true, but weresharks aren't bright, so the fact that

Devouring Horror, well, devours them on occasion hasn't changed their opinion.

Devouring Horror can produce an ink blast that conceals itself, and its two tentacles can *constrict* anyone they wrap around. I don't need to elaborate on that, do I? More concerning is that it can deliver an electrical attack through contact with its body—constriction, or a bite. It's the equivalent of being struck by lightning, so don't get bitten or grabbed. I mean it.

The good news is that killing Devouring Horror demoralizes its wereshark servants into not pursuing prey. You are really, really close to escaping, Aderyn. Don't give up.

Owen half turned, then jerked in surprise. He sped away from the giant squid, which still moved ponderously in his direction. Aderyn swam to meet him, shouting instructions as she went. "Don't let its tentacles grab you, and avoid its bite! Bludgeoning damage is less effective, it's vulnerable to swords, and if we can kill it—"

"Are you crazy? That thing is huge!" Owen shouted. "Let's see if we can avoid it—maybe it will eat the sharks instead."

Aderyn shook her head. The weresharks were almost on them, swimming in a way that suggested herding sheep to the shearer, if the shearer meant to crush and devour them. "Killing it will weaken the weresharks! Follow me!"

She swam toward the giant squid, whose tentacles lashed out in a lazy way she could have avoided even without **[See It Coming]** and the speed enhancer. "Ignore the weresharks—focus on killing the squid—its death will make them flee!"

"Got it," Owen said. "We need to draw it out so we can **[Outflank]** it!" He sped away, shooting rapidly through the water as if he was a dolphin, and dove past the tentacles and arms to strike at Devouring Horror's swollen mantle. The giant squid let out a squeal that sounded like a pig being slaughtered and lashed out with its tentacles. Owen avoided them, but only just, and continued to make his way around to the monster's far side. Weston took advantage of Devouring Horror's distraction and swam at its enormous eyes. Devouring Horror clacked its beak at Weston, sending pressure waves through the water and knocking him back before his sword could connect.

Aderyn swam, dodging tentacles with **[See It Coming]**, and waited for the strange pull that said **[Outflank]** was in effect. Behind her, Isold sang a soporific melody, and she risked a glance over her shoulder. Five weresharks swam a frightening pattern around Isold and Livia, but in the next moment, they slowed and came to a stop, drifting in sleep. Aderyn's elation died when the first defeat notices appeared. Of course. She'd read some sharks had to keep moving or they'd drown. Isold had given the team a moment's respite, but the next wave would return in greater numbers. By his look of chagrin, Isold seemed to realize that, and his **[Inspire Courage]** song rang out next instead.

Another group of sharks—**[Improved Assess 3]** told her three more—raced at Livia and Aderyn from the other side, out of range of Isold's **[Sleep]**. Livia met the first two with a shout and pummeled one with *stone fist*. Aderyn kicked to get out of the path of the third and was thrilled when the maneuver worked. She felt effortlessly light and able to swim faster than ever.

"Aderyn!" Owen shouted.

Aderyn dodged the shark's next attack. "Coming!" She dodged again, frustrated at the shark's interference with the battle she wanted to join, fighting Devouring Horror with Owen. **[Outflank]** wouldn't protect her back against a wereshark's teeth.

The creature slowed. Then it swam past her, not in a direct line as before, but swerving back and forth as if hunting for something it had lost. Someone grabbed her arm, making her shriek in surprise. "It's **[Suggestion]**," Isold said. "They don't stop moving, but I have to affect them one at a time. Go!"

Aderyn flipped backward and swam toward Devouring Horror. Owen was out of sight, but she felt the tug of **[Outflank]** and it reassured her that he wasn't dead. She took a moment for **[Discern Weakness]** to pick out the giant squid's vulnerable spots, and her heart sank when only two appeared—right over its enormous eyes with their weird pupils. She told herself to be grateful there wasn't a red haze of weapon resistance over its body and thrust at the eye nearest. Her blow missed, but Devouring Horror turned away, its tentacles lashing out at something behind her, its arms flailing. Weston, some feet away, dove at the elongated mantle.

He didn't see the tentacle that lashed out and wrapped itself around his body, trapping his left arm against his chest and squeezing.

Weston shouted a strangled cry of pain and beat at the tentacle with his sword. The weapon moved sluggishly through the water, weakening his blows. Aderyn raced toward him and joined in attacking. The tentacle might be vulnerable to bladed weapon damage, but the monster's skin was still thick and rubbery, and their blows made little impact.

Suddenly, the tip of Devouring Horror's mantle lit up with blue luminescence that reminded Aderyn of *clairvoyance*. Lines of light sped from the tip down its mantle and through its head and streaked down every tentacle and arm. Weston screamed and convulsed as the electrical shock speared through him. Aderyn screamed in tandem with him. It seemed forever before he stopped thrashing and hung limp and lifeless in Devouring Horror's grip.

Aderyn reflexively checked the team roster. Weston wasn't dead, but his health bar had dropped to less than a quarter of its length. He also didn't seem to be breathing. Aderyn slammed her sword against the tentacle, which didn't release him. Madly, she looked around for Livia. *Loose bonds* might help. But Livia was still fighting the two weresharks and hadn't noticed.

Loose bonds—Aderyn remembered something about the spell, or something better than the spell... With a shout, she sheathed her sword and grabbed the **<Rod of Unfettering>** from where it hung from her belt. She'd carried it long enough she'd almost stopped feeling it.

The ebony rod carved to look like a short length of chain felt smooth and warm against her skin. She aimed it at Weston and cracked it like a whip. It flexed once like a real chain before becoming inert once more. Devouring Horror let out another terrible cry as its tentacle loosened and then whipped away, apparently out of the monster's control. Weston, still inert, began sinking.

Aderyn put away the rod and grabbed her friend. "Isold!" Even with water buoying him up, Weston was too bulky for her to manage. All she could do was keep him from falling into the carnivorous coral bed below. He still wasn't breathing, and Aderyn was afraid his heart had stopped as well.

Then Isold was there, and between them they dragged Weston away from danger. "Go," Isold said, bringing out the <**Healing Stone**>. Aderyn swam back to where Owen fought the giant squid alone. A system message appeared as she passed Livia, who looked grim at having killed another of the sharks. Aderyn ignored her own growing feeling of despair. There was nothing left to them but pressing forward.

The light from Owen's <**Sunsword**> seemed to hurt Devouring Horror's eyes, because it bobbed and ducked away from the brilliance. Once more, Aderyn got into position for **[Outflank]**. Then she screamed a warning. "Owen, they're coming up behind you! More weresharks!"

Owen thrust again and scored a hit on the monster with **[Anatomist]** that went deep into an earlier wound, then dropped to swim beneath Devouring Horror. The giant squid lashed out at the seven weresharks approaching from behind. Six of them avoided its tentacles. The seventh let out a chittering cry that cut off as Devouring Horror wrapped a tentacle around it and dragged it to its mouth, biting it in half with its enormous beak. Black wereshark blood filled the water, and the remaining six sped up, intent on tearing into Owen and Aderyn.

Behind them, Livia chanted something soothing, completely at odds with her normal spellslinger speech. The oncoming wereshark horde slowed until they were drifting forward, barely twitching their fins to keep going. "*Mass daze*," Livia said. "I took a chance—watch out!"

Owen grabbed Aderyn and sped downward. Devouring Horror's bloody beak snapped close enough Aderyn again felt the rush of waves buffeting her. Owen thrust at the soft flesh behind the beak and connected solidly, sending more blood, this even darker than the weresharks', flowing in a thin stream that didn't dissipate in the water.

Devouring Horror gathered its tentacles close. It convulsed, and for a second, Aderyn thought Owen had killed it. Instead, a jet of black ink shot from its body, billowing into a cloud that engulfed Owen, Aderyn, and Devouring Horror itself. Aderyn froze. She felt Devouring Horror shift as it swam away, but she could see nothing, not even her hand in front of her face, not even the light of the <**Sunsword**>. She waited for the system defeat notice. If Devouring Horror fled, that counted as a defeat just the way enemies fleeing **[Cause Fear]** were defeated.

Nothing appeared. The realization that the monster was regrouping infuriated Aderyn. Anger scoured away the last of her fear. The kingdom was in danger, and this stupid monster stood in the way of them doing something about it.

Aderyn Assessed the blackness, and two blue points of light glowed with **[Discern Weakness]**. Without a second thought, she swam at them. Distantly, she knew it was madness. She couldn't see the tentacles for **[See It Coming]** to protect her, Owen didn't know where she was to provide **[Outflank]**, but she was so angry she didn't care about anything except sinking her blade deep into the monster's huge eye.

Just as she realized Devouring Horror might be able to see through its own ink, she reached the blue light. With a shout of defiance, she thrust, impaling the spot and letting her momentum drive the blade deeper.

Devouring Horror screamed and recoiled, nearly taking Aderyn's mystery sword with it. It shook with convulsions that gradually weakened until they were barely more than tremors. Finally, it floated motionless, and Aderyn once again felt alone in the blackness.

Congratulations! You have defeated [Devouring Horror].
You have earned [42,000 XP]

Congratulations! You have completed the quest [Defeat the Ivory Palace].
You have been awarded [30,000 XP]

"Aderyn! Where are you?"

"I'm here, Owen. Keep talking." Aderyn swam toward the sound of his voice until she bumped into him. Owen put an arm around her waist, and together they swam out of the ink cloud.

The only weresharks remaining were dead. Aderyn's momentary excitement vanished when she saw Isold and Livia crouched near a motionless body lying in a patch of sea grass. Devendra, in human form again, drifted nearby. Owen beat Aderyn to Weston's side.

"He's still alive," she said. "What's wrong?"

"His heart's not beating," Isold said. "The <**Healing Stone**> can't do anything about that. We need the <**Potion of Life**>, but that won't work underwater, especially when he's unconscious."

"Back up," Owen said. "Aderyn, brace yourself against me." He pressed his hands against Weston's chest and pushed hard, over and over again, quick pulses like the beat of a heart. Every blow made him bounce away from Weston, so Aderyn leaned against his back and held him in place as best she could.

"What are you doing?" Livia demanded. "You're going to hurt him more!"

"I learned CPR as part of my lifeguard training," Owen said. "Never thought I'd do it underwater." He stopped pounding Weston's chest and covered the man's mouth with his. Weston's chest rose and fell as Owen breathed into his lungs. "Damn it," Owen said, resuming his chest pounding. "Come on, Weston, come on—"

Weston drew in a deep breath and coughed long and hard, exactly as if he was breathing air instead of water. Livia cried out and shoved Owen aside, throwing her arms around Weston and hugging him tightly. Weston's arms slowly rose to encircle her. "That hurt," he murmured. "Did we win?"

"We did," Owen said. "And now we have to haul ass out of here, except I don't know where to go."

"Those other weresharks had to come from somewhere," Aderyn said. "Hang on."

The <**Wayfinder**> warmed immediately, almost eagerly. Aderyn chastised herself for once more attributing human emotion to a metal object and turned until she had a heading. "This way. I don't know how long those weresharks will stay scared off, and who knows how long it will take Devouring Horror to respawn?"

The ink cloud had dissipated, leaving the water murky but clear enough to see through. Livia cast *sunburst* again anyway when they passed into the room Aderyn thought was Devouring Horror's actual lair. The sunlight filled the room with its radiance, illuminating skittering creatures Aderyn's Assessment identified as dire crabs. The crabs ignored the humans, continuing their endless sideways movement across the uneven rubble of the floor—or what at first glance appeared to be rubble. The brilliant light sparkled over what lay on the floor:

gems and jewelry and assorted gold coins heaped in careless piles. "That's why the weresharks had that loot," she exclaimed. "It's tribute."

"I notice it didn't stop the monster from eating one of them," Owen remarked. "Keep going. We don't have time to loot."

"But—" Weston complained.

"Shut up and swim," Livia ordered him. "We're getting out of here with our lives. That's better than loot."

Weston didn't look like he agreed, but he only cast a regretful glance at the treasure and continued to swim.

The <**Wayfinder**> led, not to a doorway, but to a rough hole low in a wall Isold said was on the far side from the statue room. Aderyn didn't like it. By her mental map, they were heading deeper beneath the Ivory Palace. But she trusted her magic item, so she kept swimming.

The hole was the opening to a narrow tunnel barely big enough for a human and much too small for a wereshark in shark form. Aderyn hated small tunnels. She'd never realized she was claustrophobic until they'd explored the Lonely Tor. Small spaces weren't always the problem; it was small spaces underneath a mountain of earth and stone waiting to crush her that terrified her, and the Ivory Palace was definitely that. She kept her gaze focused on the <**Wayfinder**> and swam until she abruptly emerged from the tunnel—into the open ocean.

Gasping in relief, she clutched the orb to her chest and waited for the others to arrive. Owen didn't stop; he continued swimming, rising upward until he broke the surface of the water some thirty feet above. Aderyn swam after him and dragged herself onto dry land. She coughed up seawater until she was wrung out and exhausted, then lay back and stared up at the clouds. A thin, high overcast yellowed the sky, but she didn't think she'd ever seen anything so beautiful.

Congratulations! You have completed the quest [Free Queen Devendra].
You have been awarded [35,000 XP]

Welcome to Level Seventeen

"We should move," Owen said, but he didn't put his words into action. All around them, their friends lay along the rocky shore. Devendra alone was on her feet, casting the spell that would wick all the water from her clothes and body.

"Get up," she said, in a hard, flat voice that brought Aderyn to her senses. "We have no time to waste."

Aderyn got to her feet and shivered as Devendra's drying spell took effect. "Where are we? I mean, in relation to Ikharatia?"

"We are on the far side of the Ivory Palace from the city," Isold said with a glance at his system map. "The east side. At the bottom of the hill that leads to the causeway.

Devendra immediately set off for the hill. Owen grabbed her hand and brought her to a halt. "Let's see if we can shorten that journey," he said. "Livia?"

"If I do, I won't be any use in fighting Kanan," Livia said bitterly. "And there's no thundering way I'm sitting that one out."

"Then I guess we start walking," Owen said.

He didn't say *and hope we're not too late*, but Aderyn was sure they were all thinking it.

Chapter Forty-Two

An hour later, with Ikharatia looming ahead, Aderyn lifted her gaze from the <**Wayfinder**> and saw a sea of canvas tents spread out in front of the city gate. The thin overcast had become heavy clouds promising rain, and the weird pre-storm light seemed to weigh down the tent roofs. Her fear that they would arrive to find themselves in the middle of a pitched battle vanished, replaced by worry that everything was far too quiet and peaceful. Varoun had made it sound like war was imminent.

"The way they're spread out, it looks like Varoun is the one besieging the city," Owen said. "If they're at a stalemate, it's probably not too late."

Devendra broke into a run and was restrained by Livia's hand grasping her wrist. "I won't waste time," Devendra said.

"You'll exhaust yourself for no reason," Livia said. "I know it's hard, but we need information."

"The <**Wayfinder**> knows where Varoun is," Aderyn said, gesturing with the metal orb. "We can hurry a little."

The camp was eerily silent, with only a few soldiers striding rapidly through in the manner of people on important business. Aderyn wasn't sure what to make of that, but it worried her. She led the way between the tents to a larger one near the center of the encampment. It looked exactly like the command tent she'd had as general over Raven Regiment. Owen always said armies thrived on uniformity, but Aderyn hadn't thought that extended to its tents.

Soldiers standing at guard in front of the tent flap moved to intercept her when she was fifteen feet away, but they stood down almost immediately. Aderyn hoped this meant she was known to the soldiers and not that they were intimidated by high-level adventurers. The last thing the army needed was for some of its soldiers to cower before others.

The tent's interior was identical, too, down to the musty, somewhat mildewy smell. Varoun and Janesh stood at a makeshift table that canted on the uneven ground. They looked up from the map spread across it when Aderyn and her friends entered. Varoun's relief when he saw Devendra behind them was palpable. "Your majesty. I'm so glad to see you. Now we can end this farce."

"Where are Colan and Rila?" Devendra demanded.

"This way, Devendra," Janesh said. He put his arm around the queen's waist and hustled her out of the tent.

Aderyn turned to follow, but Varoun said, "General Aderyn, I need your insight." The use of her military title reminded her of the skills that mattered here. And it wasn't as if Devendra needed the team to be present when she reunited with her children.

She put the **<Wayfinder>** in her purse and joined Varoun at the table. She frowned. "This is a map of the Southlands. What about defeating Kanan?"

"We are currently in a standoff," Varoun said. "News of an orc assault on Shantos came just minutes ago, while we were awaiting Kanan's response to our latest demand that he surrender. The resolution of his treachery is paramount, but there's only so much we can do."

"You said proving Devendra is still alive will stop Kanan's power grab," Owen said. "What does that look like? If there's a battle going on, it won't be safe to parade her around in front of the troops."

Varoun shook his head. "We have other ways of passing the word. At the moment, Simla hasn't committed any of his regiments, citing the need to defend Adhiraj against orcs. I believe his support of Kanan is opportunistic, and he'll pretend he was concerned for the kingdom when he learns Devendra is alive and reaffirm his loyalty. He's not what we have to worry about. The real problem is that Kanan's regiments from Tielana clashed with Ikharatia's defenders twenty minutes ago."

"How many fighters—soldiers—do we have here?" Aderyn asked.

"Most of Ikharatia's regiments are dispersed to Shantos and Adhiraj. One remained here, along with the Home Guard." Varoun's scowl deepened. "Obviously no one thought we would have to defend against treachery. We are outnumbered—not substantially, but still at a disadvantage."

"And Kanan won't stop regardless of Devendra's presence," Owen said. "He's committed now. He'll have to kill the entire royal family and solidify his power."

"That's right," Aderyn said. "Up until now he could pretend he was acting for the good of the kingdom, but once it came to a battle, he became a traitor."

"And this is a battle we have to win," Varoun said. "Win quickly, too, unless we want the kingdom overrun by orcs."

"So what do *we* do?" Aderyn said. "It's not like I can lead troops now, because they already have leaders. But we're not going to sit back and wait for the battle to be over."

Varoun regarded her steadily. "You're still willing to risk yourselves for a country that isn't even yours?"

"We have a history of doing the right thing even when it doesn't benefit us," Owen said. "Which I realize sounds hopelessly stuck up. It's just who we are."

"Though we do like experience," Livia said.

"And riches," Weston said. "Let me tell you about the gold we left behind... all right, that story can wait," he added when Livia glared at him.

"What I intend could get you all killed," Varoun said. "But you're level sixteen—"

"Seventeen," Livia said. Aderyn had totally forgotten the level up notice.

"Well." Varoun thought about this for a moment. "Let's say I believe you have a chance of succeeding, and a much better chance of surviving than anyone else in a position to do this."

"You want us to go after Kanan," Owen said.

"Is it that obvious?"

Owen shrugged. "I don't know about obvious, but I assume taking him out will make his generals think twice about continuing with a battle. Particularly if they want any chance at not being called traitors. They might be able to claim they were just following orders, but if they go on fighting, that avenue is closed to them."

"Very clever." Varoun smiled. "It seems Aderyn isn't the only one gifted with strategic insight."

"I just read a lot." Owen cleared his throat. "And on that note, what can you tell us that our Warmaster can make use of?"

Varoun rolled up the map and tossed it into a brass-bound chest lying open nearby, revealing the table top covered with sheets of loose paper, some of them blank, others scrawled on haphazardly. He found a charcoal pencil and sketched on one of the blank sheets. "The armies clashed north of the city, closer than I'd like, but nothing we can do about that. At last report, the Home Guard was holding the line while Blackbuck Regiment came in from the east."

"Is Blackbuck moving to reinforce the Home Guard?" Aderyn asked, drawing an imaginary line of movement across the paper.

"That's the intent, yes. They face strong opposition from Tielana's regiments, Tiger and Snake."

Someone clapped outside the tent door. "Commander general? I have a message from Colonel Manoj."

Varoun strode rapidly to the tent door. "That's the commander of Blackbuck. Excuse me a moment."

He pushed back the flap and spoke quietly to the woman standing there. Her higher-pitched voice was faint, but still audible as she said, "No, commander, he was very clear." Varoun spoke again, still too low to hear. "Understood, commander," the woman said, and sped away.

Varoun returned to the table, saying, "Blackbuck has pushed Tiger back enough that they have nearly joined forces with the Home Guard. But I can deal with that later." He tapped the paper where he'd marked a five-pointed star. "We believe Kanan abandoned the palace and is now with Snake Regiment. I need him captured."

"Not dead?" Livia said. The intensity in her voice, the suppressed outrage, frightened Aderyn. "It's no less than he deserves."

Varoun seemed to hear it, too. He turned his attention on Livia. "It's war. Death happens. But for the sake of the kingdom, Kanan must be made an example of. That means a trial and a just execution."

"That's fair," Aderyn said. "It's more important that everyone sees what happens to someone who tries to take control of the kingdom, for Colan's sake. Otherwise someone else might try this in the future. We don't want Colan to be hurt, right?" She didn't address Livia directly, but she watched her friend out of the corner of her vision. Livia's jaw was set hard as rock, and she wasn't looking at anyone, but she nodded once.

"So, is there some better strategy for reaching Kanan, who is presumably in the middle of his army, than just plowing through that army?" Owen asked.

"I was hoping you could devise a solution," Varoun said. "I believe *transport* and *world door* are out of the question?"

Livia cleared her throat. "Even when I'm fully rested, five castings of *world door* will leave me unable to fight and potentially render me unconscious. *Transport* is possible. I can't guarantee I'll be able to put us right where Kanan is, but with *scry,* I can get us close."

"And *scry* can show us the tactical situation for improving on our plan," Aderyn said. "To be clear, we're to go in, grab Kanan, and bring him here?"

"You make it sound so simple," Varoun said with a smile. "I leave the details to you. Apprehend Kanan, make sure his generals know it, and return safely."

"Then I guess we get started," Aderyn said.

"Thank you, general. Please excuse me—and if there's anything I can provide, let me know." Varoun tapped the **<Farspeaker>** he wore at his hip and left the tent.

No one spoke for a few seconds. Aderyn gathered her thoughts. Time to be a Warmaster. "Livia, can you *scry* the area?"

"I'm not irrational," Livia said. "I know I shouldn't kill Kanan. Varoun had a good point."

Weston cleared his throat. "Livia, I know he hurt you. But your desire for revenge is hurting you more. I don't understand—"

"No. You don't," Livia said, her voice hard and flat and shutting down Weston completely. "I'll deal with this. Let's worry about getting the bastard, all right?"

Aderyn, watching Weston, thought she'd never seen anyone look so completely devastated, like his world was ending. She felt deeply disturbed herself at not having realized how badly Kanan had rattled her friend. True, Livia tended toward what Owen referred to as "dark" behavior, but this went beyond her usual grim satisfaction at seeing evil people get what was coming to them and into pleasure in hurting others. "Livia—" she began.

"I said I'll deal with it," Livia snapped. She withdrew her scrying mirror from her knapsack and spoke a few short, curt words that made its surface shine like a stray beam of light had struck it. Livia tilted the mirror one way and then the other. "There," she said.

The others crowded around. The mirror showed Kanan, his handsome face twisted in shouting at someone who wasn't visible in the oval. Fortunately, *scry* didn't transmit sound, or his raging fury would have echoed through the tent.

"Let's back up," Livia murmured. The view expanded, revealing the woman—an adventurer, not a soldier, based on her clothing—getting a tongue lashing from the duke, and a handful of other adventurers watching, and one man in soldier's gray and a sash of office standing nearby. Then dingy white canvas filled the mirror. "Farther," Livia said. Like they were a bird flying higher, the scene spread out before them: tents pitched in the orderly fashion Aderyn expected, a few men and women moving between them, some adventurers, most soldiers. She didn't see the battle anywhere.

Livia grunted. "It's enough. I can't get us as close as I'd like."

"I thought you could *transport* anywhere you can see," Isold said.

"*Transport* is in some ways like *world door*," Livia explained. "With *world door*, the farther you want to get from a city or even a building, the more practice you need, even with *scry*. *Transport* works like—look, it's not important now. If he was in a building, I could drop us on his thunderblasted head. As it is, we'll be thirty feet from his tent when we appear."

"That's still plenty close," Owen said. "But it looks like he's got bodyguards, or something. And I didn't see Ruan or Suveer."

"Is that good, or bad?" Isold said.

"No idea," Owen said. "It could mean we'll end up fighting them when we've exhausted ourselves taking out the bodyguards, or maybe we'll avoid them entirely, damn it. I really did want to beat him senseless."

"And you criticized *me* for being bloodthirsty," Livia said bitterly.

"Hey, it's not at all the same," Owen exclaimed.

"*Stop,*" Aderyn said. "Stop it! We're about to go into danger, against who knows what kind of other adventurers of possibly high level. We can't fight each other, too!"

Owen subsided. Livia still looked angry. Aderyn went on, "It doesn't matter what our personal motivations are. We have a task—"

A system message appeared.

A new quest is available: [Defeat the Usurper]
Capture Kanan and return him alive to Devendra for trial and execution.
Accept? Y / N

Aderyn gaped. "All right, we have a quest. We're not going to succeed at the quest unless we can set aside those personal motivations. If we can't do that, I'll go right now to Varoun and tell him he'll need to find someone else."

Owen let out a deep breath. "No. You're right. Ruan isn't important." He gestured to accept the new quest. Aderyn touched the Y and then set it as her primary quest. Maybe the system would be inclined to give her help if it was her main focus.

Beside her, Livia gestured as well. She looked less angry than before, but Aderyn's instincts told her not to push her friend. Livia's stubbornness usually meant she succeeded when others gave up, but right now, Aderyn feared it was a hindrance—and that same stubbornness was likely to lead to her getting angry again if she felt badgered. Aderyn couldn't think of a solution, so she fell back on hoping for the best.

"The speed enhancement will continue to affect us for a little more than an hour," Isold said. "That means we still can't take advantage of the strength enhancement."

Livia took out another of the bulbs of red liquid. Aderyn, alarmed, forgot her earlier reservations and said, "Livia, it's too soon."

"I'm down to less than half of my magical reserves. That's not dangerous." Livia pulled the cork with her teeth, spat it at the wall, and drank down the contents before anyone else could protest. This time, she not only grimaced, she shuddered, and when she opened her eyes, it took her a while to focus on Aderyn, who watched her in alarm.

"Livia," Aderyn said, "you shouldn't drink too many of those too quickly."

"I know what I'm doing, Aderyn," Livia said. "Trust me. I'm not stupid."

Aderyn couldn't protest any further. "All right. You—all right." She picked up Varoun's charcoal pencil and drew a square with an eight-pointed star inside on a sheet of paper. "Kanan is here. There were—did anyone else count who was in the tent with Kanan?"

"Did you not Assess them?" Owen asked.

"**[Improved Assess 3]** doesn't work unless I'm physically within sight of someone or something. *Scry* doesn't count. I saw eight. Weston?"

"That's what I counted," Weston said. His voice was quiet and completely lacking in his usual enthusiasm, and Aderyn's heart sank. He and Livia needed to talk, but there just wasn't time—but if Livia's rejection of him affected Weston's ability to focus, it could be dangerous for him, maybe for all of them. Aderyn wanted to scream.

She settled for saying, "So, eight of Kanan's adventurers for hire. They're not soldiers, so they could be a fairly high level. Given how Kanan treated Ruan, I'm guessing no more than level fifteen, but we shouldn't rely on that. The other soldier is one of Kanan's generals. We want to leave him alive."

"Why? If he's a soldier, he has a class, and he could be high enough level to be a threat," Owen said.

"Because we want someone to witness Kanan's capture and tell the army to stand down. Right?" Aderyn waited for Owen to acknowledge her point, then continued. "Then there's the soldiers and adventurers moving through the camp. We can't stop to fight them, not only because it's a waste of our time and resources, but because the noise of fighting will warn Kanan and he'll be prepared for our attack on his tent. So we're going to see how fast that speed enhancement makes us. Livia, did you see enough for us to arrive within sight of the tent door?"

"Sure," Livia said, sounding almost like herself. "And I'll *burrow* beneath the tent so we can attack from two directions at once."

"That's a great idea." Aderyn heard herself being too enthusiastic, knew she was trying to compensate for Weston's discouragement, and made herself shut up.

"I am already faster than the rest of you," Isold said. "If I use **[Sleep]** on those inside the tent before you attack, I may be able to reduce their numbers."

"Oh!" Now Aderyn felt genuinely enthusiastic. "Why not make all of them fall asleep? It worked on the weresharks."

"Weresharks are stupid, and **[Sleep]** is less effective the more intelligent a creature, or human, is. We can't count on my skill rendering everyone unconscious. But it's worth trying."

"I agree. It's a good opening move." Aderyn drew more tents around the central one, recalling what she'd seen in the *scrying* mirror. "Livia, is this right?"

"Looks right to me." Livia tapped a spot south of the central tent. "We'll arrive here."

"Then the only other thing is how to capture Kanan alive," Aderyn said. "He's non-classed, so he's not a fighter, but I don't think that makes him harmless."

"He's the type who'd carry a poisoned dagger on the off chance he might need it," Livia said, with such finality Aderyn again wanted to cry. "We need to be wary."

"I hate to say this, but maybe we need to worry about defeating his bodyguards and then see what happens," Owen said.

"Hmm." Aderyn considered possibilities with her Warmaster's instincts. "We need to give him a chance to surrender. It's possible some of those bodyguards aren't fanatical about giving their lives to protect him. If we can do this without killing anyone—"

"You can't be serious," Livia said. "He's not going to surrender. And that will just give them time to prepare to attack."

"That's possible. But if Isold has already put some of them to sleep, it may make the others reconsider their allegiance. And all I have in mind is asking for his surrender, not getting into a conversation that really will give him and his people an advantage." Aderyn gave the sketch one final look, though she'd committed it to memory. "Anything else?"

She watched Livia, hoping her friend might say something to break the tension, some apology or explanation. Livia just said, "Everyone huddle up."

"And good luck," Isold said.

Livia chanted the long rolling syllables of *transport*, and with a crack of thunder, they were elsewhere.

Chapter Forty-Three

Rain pattered across Aderyn's bowed head, a hard, driving, unexpectedly cold rain. She backed away from her team's huddle and swiftly looked around. Tents surrounded them, aligned just the way they'd been on her sketch. Thirty feet away in a straight line from where they stood was the large command tent, its door flap hanging slightly open.

Two soldiers in gray flanked the door, beneath the canopy that had concealed them from *scry*. Their wide eyes and stunned expressions were almost comical, but what Aderyn cared about was that their weapons weren't at the ready. Only a few other people were visible between the nearby tents, two soldiers and three adventurers, all of them equally caught off guard.

With an incoherent shout, Livia disappeared into the ground, kicking up earth and small stones as she *burrowed* out of sight. "Go!" Owen exclaimed, and the rest of them ran for the command tent.

They hadn't run on their return to Ikharatia, not wanting to exhaust themselves, so Aderyn didn't expect the exhilarating feeling the potion of speed gave her of almost flying across the ground, her feet barely touching earth before sending her sprinting off again. **[Keep**

Pace] accelerated her faster still. She controlled a silly shout of excitement and concentrated on their goal.

Isold was out in front as expected. When he was ten feet away from the tent, and the soldiers had just begun to react to their oncoming menace, he let out a howl that made the men drop their weapons and bolt in fear. Aderyn hoped **[Cause Fear]** didn't work on people who were within earshot but out of sight of Isold. Terrified enemy adventurers trapped in a tent might complicate a fight.

Isold put on speed for his last few running steps to the tent. With one hand, he flung the door flap open and held it to one side. As Weston, Owen, and Aderyn approached, he sang a melody of slow, soporific notes that made Aderyn think of lullabies and falling asleep in front of a warm fire. She could well imagine the effect on their enemies.

Then Weston and Owen charged past Isold into the tent. Aderyn was half a step behind her partner. Before anyone came close enough for combat, Aderyn shouted with **[Amplify Voice]**, "Kanan! Surrender now, and everyone lives!"

She followed this with a quick Assessment of the tent, ignoring names in favor of swiftly checking classes and levels. Three people lay asleep on the floor, one next to the door and the other two in a back corner. One of the sleeping men was Kanan's general. The remaining six were a mix of martial classes, two Swordsworn, one Staffsworn, a Deadeye, a Swifthands, and a Lone Wolf. None of them were higher than level thirteen, which still made them a challenge but not an impossible one. Ruan and Suveer weren't there.

Her gaze finally landed on Kanan. He didn't look angry, or afraid, just triumphant. "Devendra's lap dogs," he said dismissively. "You have no reason to involve yourselves in this conflict. I can pay—"

Aderyn rolled her eyes. "Attack!" she shouted.

As if waiting for her command, Livia burst through the ground and landed in a solid stance near the door, and Weston and Owen charged the Staffsworn and the Lone Wolf. With Isold's battle music ringing in her ears, Aderyn worked her way around to **[Outflank]** the Lone Wolf. She heard Livia chant the familiar nonsense words that invoked *stone fist*, but then the Swifthands was in her face, kicking and punching.

Aderyn dodged every blow with even greater ease than usual and rejoiced in the woman's expression of mingled rage and bewilderment.

Congratulations! You have defeated [Boyan the Lone Wolf]. You have earned [7500 XP]

Relief that Owen had defeated his opponent without her help sent a surge of energy through Aderyn. She swept the mystery sword from its scabbard and advanced on the Swifthands. This felt incredible, like being swept away in a deadly dance, and she forgot her initial reservations about the possible innocence of these bodyguards in her excitement.

Which was when she saw the Deadeye aim a hand crossbow at Weston's unprotected back.

"Weston! Watch out!" she screamed.

Time suddenly slowed to a crawl as the crossbow continued to rise. Distantly, Aderyn heard Livia spit out a couple of caustic syllables. A sickly greenish-yellow ray sprang from her finger and shot across the room, narrowly missing Weston and striking the Deadeye in the face.

A hiss and the stink of acid filled the air. The Deadeye screamed. He dropped the crossbow and clawed at his face. Aderyn watched, horrified, as the acid ate away flesh down to the bones of his skull and his fingers where they touched the stuff. The Deadeye's screams grew weaker. He collapsed to his knees, then fell in a lifeless heap, his exposed skull pitted like something years dead.

Congratulations! You have defeated [Hollis the Deadeye]. You have earned [9250 XP]

Aderyn let out a cry of pain as her moment of distraction left her open for the Swifthands to strike her shoulder with the edge of her hand. Her left side went numb. The Swifthands smiled fiercely and pressed the attack. Aderyn jerked out of the fugue witnessing that horror had put her in. She ducked the next blow, dodged a kick aimed at her stomach, and drove her sword through the woman's heart.

Congratulations! You have defeated [Deseri the Swifthands]. You have earned [8850 XP]

Aderyn shoved the body off her blade and ran to where Livia crouched on the floor, her eyes wide, her breathing so rapid Aderyn didn't know how she hadn't passed out. "Livia, get up," she urged. "It's not over."

"Did you see that?" Livia's voice was faint. "I didn't know it would do that."

Aderyn slapped her. "Snap out of it! Livia—"

"I know what to do," Livia said in that same dull voice. She got to her feet, brushing aside Aderyn's assistance, and, ignoring the combat happening all around her, walked to where Kanan pressed against the back wall of the tent. Dread filled Aderyn, and she moved to intercept Livia, but a Swordsworn got in her way. She fought desperately, not for fear of her life, but to stop Livia before she did something she wouldn't be able to come back from.

"Livia!" she shouted. "Livia, don't!"

The speed enhancement gave her enough time between blocking and delivering blows that she could see, as if in a series of still images, Kanan and Livia facing off. Kanan's lips moved with words inaudible over the clamor of the fight and the hollow rattling of rain on canvas. Livia took her familiar solid stance and began speaking. Kanan smiled cruelly and laughed. The laughter stopped as Livia's words grew loud enough to be audible. Aderyn blocked another blow, then another, trying to force her opponent back so she could disengage and stop Livia killing Kanan.

Livia's spellslinging always sounded like the words were on the verge of intelligibility, but this time, that was even more true than usual. The individual words were nonsense, but Aderyn felt she understood Livia's meaning. It sounded as if her friend was urging Kanan to do something vital, something that would change the outcome of this fight. Near Kanan, the general stirred and sat up, blinking away the effects of **[Sleep]**.

An extraordinary sound filled the air, like a bubble of something thick and goopy bursting, *glorp*. Kanan let out a cry, not of pain or fear but of astonishment, and vanished. In her surprise, Aderyn missed a block and hissed as the Swordsworn's off-hand dagger plunged into her left side, high on her chest. Since that was the side that was numb still from the Swifthands' attack, it felt more like being punched than being stabbed. She backed up a step for a better attack position.

"Hey!" Livia shouted. She bent and picked up something small that she held high above her head. "Aderyn, get their attention!"

"*Everybody stop!*" Aderyn shouted with **[Amplify Voice]**, though she was still mystified.

To her astonishment, it worked. People paused where they were and turned to look at Livia. Aderyn focused on what she held, something white that quivered and kicked with its long hind legs as it struggled vainly to free itself.

A rabbit.

"Listen up!" Livia shouted. Her voice was hoarse, like the spell had torn up her throat on its way out, but she stood firm. "This is what I did to your boss. Anybody else want to join him? No? Then throw down your weapons and get on the ground. *Now.*"

Silence. Then the air filled with the pattering and thud of weapons hitting earth, louder than the rain, followed by the sound of three people dropping to their knees. The general continued to stare slack-jawed at the struggling rabbit.

Aderyn gaped. "Livia," she said, "how did you..."

"You may have forgotten about leveling to seventeen, but I sure as thunder didn't," Livia said, lowering her arm with the rabbit Kanan still held firmly by the scruff of his neck. To Aderyn, the rabbit looked a little blurry around the edges, but when she blinked, the effect was gone. "My new eighth level spell. *Greater polymorph.* He's perfectly safe and completely incapable of leading troops."

Her knees wobbled, and suddenly she was on the ground, too. Weston dove to catch her. She clung to him with her free hand and whispered, so quietly Aderyn almost couldn't hear, "I think I've gone too far."

Aderyn was sure she wasn't talking about her magical resources.

ADERYN WALKED AROUND GATHERING WEAPONS WHILE Owen and Isold secured Kanan's bodyguards. Her left arm wasn't working right, but it wasn't until Owen exclaimed, "Isold, Aderyn's wounded!" that she remembered being stabbed.

"Good thing that Swifthands made my side numb so I didn't feel the pain, right?" she said, trying for a light tone.

"You bled heavily, and it's a wonder you're not unconscious," Isold said, sounding grim. "That numbness might have killed you."

"Oh," Aderyn said, feeling stupid. He was right. But with Livia nearly incapacitating herself, and Kanan's transformation and capture, and above all that Deadeye's face being eaten away by acid, part of her had wanted something not to be entirely awful.

Owen hugged her when Isold finished healing her. "That was both better and worse a battle than I expected. I got lucky killing that Lone Wolf. And I was trying to reach you so we could fight the Swordsworn together when Livia did that..." He shook his head. "I thought for sure she was going to kill him regardless of what we'd agreed."

"Me too. I hope—"

"Hope what?"

"I hope *greater polymorph* is enough. To satisfy her, I mean. I don't like what she's become."

Owen nodded. "To be honest, though, I don't think she likes it either," he said.

Aderyn followed the line of his gaze to where Livia and Weston sat close together, talking quietly. The sack containing rabbit-Kanan bulged and thrashed beside them. Weston brushed the hair back from Livia's face and kissed her forehead, and Livia clung to him, not weeping, but without the terrible anguished look she'd worn after killing the Deadeye.

Beyond them, Kanan's general sat on a low stool. His eyes were fixed on the sack. Impulsively, Aderyn moved to join him. "Are you ready to call your troops off?"

"She turned him into a rabbit," the general said in a low, dull voice.

It was the voice of someone who had seen too many terrible things in too short a time.

Aderyn grabbed him under the arm and hauled him up. She thought surprise brought him to his feet, because he outweighed her by at least forty pounds. "Get out there and call your troops off," she said. "Do it now, or I'll make sure you hang for treason."

"Don't let her turn me into a rabbit," the general said.

Owen grabbed his shoulder and marched him to the door. "She won't if you act quickly. Get out of here, and be glad she has mercy."

The general ran.

"I don't think Livia has enough magic left to turn anyone into anything," Aderyn said quietly to Owen.

"He doesn't need to know that." Owen pointed at the **<Farspeaker>**. "Shouldn't you communicate with Varoun?"

"Oh!" She really was feeling muzzy to have forgotten that. She fished the coin out of the little pouch and slotted it into the **<Farspeaker>**, then waited for Varoun's image to appear. "Commander, Kanan has been, um, neutralized, that's a good word for it. We will bring him to you as soon as we can."

"That was fast," Varoun said, sounding startled. "We haven't seen any change in the fighting."

"One of his generals was present for his capture, and we sent him to have his men stand down. I don't know how long that will take. I've only been in one battle, but that taught me communication is sometimes slow."

"Too true, general." Varoun turned his head and said, "It's almost over, your majesty."

Aderyn heard Devendra's voice, though the queen was far enough from Varoun that Aderyn could only make out the words "traitor" and "stand trial." Varoun turned back to Aderyn. "He *is* alive, yes?"

"Definitely alive," Aderyn said. "We'll tell you the details when we arrive. For now—"

"Livia can't manage *transport*," Weston said. "We'll have to walk back."

"It will be a while before we return. I don't want to fight our way through—well, I guess they're still sort of enemy lines. You know what I mean."

"Take care, Aderyn. And... thank you." Varoun's image vanished.

Weston was helping Livia to her feet. Aderyn glanced warily at the sack. "Is he going to turn back soon?"

"He's not going to turn back at all unless someone uses another *greater polymorph* spell," Livia said. Her voice was still hoarse, but stronger than before. "And that won't be me until I've rested. No more potions." She smiled grimly. "And here I thought I was safe because I wouldn't get addicted. Those are hard on the body."

Aderyn couldn't think of anything to say that wasn't *I told you so.* She met Weston's eyes, pleading. Weston said, "You want to tell them what you told me?"

"Not really," Livia said. "All right, that was poor humor. I mean I've been stupid and I hate admitting that. I just—" She swallowed. "Kanan made me feel weak and helpless, and I couldn't stop remembering it. And I thought, if I could turn that on him, kill him or humiliate him or both, I'd stop feeling that way. But all it did was make me hard and cruel. I never want to be that."

"Don't be afraid to admit that to your friends," Owen said. "We've all done things we regret. If we held those weaknesses against each other, this team would disintegrate."

"And, not to heap more misery on you, but speaking of disintegrate," Isold said.

Livia winced. "I took that spell when I achieved my last elemental affinity, for acid. That was the first time I ever used it. It was the only spell I had that's faster than a crossbow bolt, and that Deadeye was going to shoot Weston. I feel torn up inside because I don't regret saving Weston's life, but the sight of that man with his face eaten away, and the *smell*..." She shook her head. "I'm never using that spell again. Not even on the evilest, most terrifying monster we face."

Aderyn hugged Livia. "Do you feel better now?"

"I feel like I chose the right path," Livia said. Then she smiled, a weak but cheerful expression. "I admit, turning Kanan into a bunny was deeply satisfying. Even though he's not aware of his condition."

"Because bunnies are too cute to kill?" Weston teased.

"Don't laugh. That was part of the decision." Livia's smile vanished. "I let anger take over for far too long, and I'm afraid, even now, I'll be too weak to do the right thing. So anything I can do to stop myself until I regain my inner strength, I'll do it."

"You have more willpower than anyone I know," Aderyn said. "I'm betting on you coming out on top."

"My confidence isn't what it used to be, so I'll lean on yours." Livia took a step away from Aderyn and wobbled. Weston caught her elbow, then put his arm around her waist to steady her. "And I'll lean on Weston in a more literal sense. Can we get out of here? I really want to dump Kanan on someone else and then sleep for a thousand years."

"I guess we start walking," Owen said. "Again. Can I get in on that sleeping for a thousand years action? I'm ready to lay down being responsible for a while."

"Just one more task, and we can do that," Aderyn said.

WHEN THEY WALKED INTO VAROUN'S COMMAND TENT, Devendra was there, with Rila in her arms and Colan standing close beside her with his fists wound into her skirt. Janesh sat across from the command table, looking exhausted. "I've been back and forth a dozen times from each army's command, arranging things, explaining things... can I just say how grateful I am not to be the commander general?"

"It is a thankless task," Varoun said, straight-faced.

Devendra surveyed their group. "You said you captured Kanan. Where is he?"

Owen held up the sack he carried. "Livia subdued him with *greater polymorph*. I'm afraid he's stuck this way until tomorrow. Can somebody get us a cage?"

Devendra frowned, puzzled. "Excuse me?"

Owen untied the sack and held it open. Kanan burst free and leaped frantically around the tent until Weston caught him and held him securely by the scruff of the neck. Colan's face lit with pleasure. "A bunny!" he exclaimed. "Can I keep it?"

Devendra exchanged glances with Livia. Livia let out a deep breath. "You don't know how tempting that is, your majesty," she told Colan. "Maybe, if your mother says it's all right, you and I can find you another bunny to play with. This one has a different destiny."

Colan's eyes widened. "Can bunnies have destinies?"

"Some of them do." Livia knelt in front of the boy. "Just like you."

Colan made a face. "I don't want to be king. I want to be an adventurer like you."

"I suppose we'll have to see," Devendra said.

Varoun had left the tent while they were talking, and now he returned, followed by a soldier bearing a rough cage made from breaking off a few slats of a small crate. Weston deposited the rabbit into the cage, and all five of the team watched closely as the soldier nailed it shut.

Congratulations! You have completed the quest [Defeat the Usurper].
You have been awarded [15,000 XP]

Unexpected relief hit Aderyn at the sight of the system message. Why it felt so good when it wasn't a **[Fated One's Destiny]** quest, could even be considered to have been a distraction, she didn't know. Then she watched Colan badger his mother to let him have a bunny for a pet. All right, maybe it wasn't such a mystery, after all.

Chapter Forty-Four

The letter from the palace came at eleven o'clock the following day, when Aderyn and Owen were eating a late breakfast. Aderyn read the words silently, then folded the paper along its original creases and set it aside. "Devendra invites us to be present for Kanan's trial this afternoon. I'm not sure I want to, but as Varoun's second in command, I probably should. Do you think the rest of you need to go?"

"Let me see that." Owen read the letter as well. "To me, it sounds like she made the offer to our team as a formality. Honestly, I don't want to be involved in Southlander politics any more than we already are. And it's not like our presence will change matters. Kanan's guilty by any standard."

"I'll write a response. Though I ought to let Livia know, since she has to turn Kanan human again. Where *is* she, anyway? I haven't seen her or Weston since yesterday."

Owen grinned. "Well, they did have some reconciling to do."

"Yes, but for twenty-four hours? I... all right, I suppose it's not impossible. But that doesn't explain where Isold is."

"Unless he's got his mojo back, and is entertaining a bevy of young ladies elsewhere." Owen waggled his eyebrows suggestively.

"Owen, not everything is about sex."

"That's not what you said this morning."

Aderyn blushed, recalling how she'd woken that morning and how late they'd been to breakfast. "Yes, true, but really—"

Isold entered the dining room. Aderyn blushed harder, as if she'd made sexually loaded implications to his face. Isold waved to catch the attention of one of the serving men and joined Aderyn and Owen. "I was wearier than I realized," he said. "I believe I slept for more than fourteen hours."

"That was the most physically exhausting dungeon we've ever faced," Owen said. "Sleeping late is natural."

"I know I needed it, because—" He leaned back for the server to put a plate in front of him and set down a basket of fresh parotta and bowls of rice and sauce. "Because I normally feel out of sorts when I oversleep. Now I just feel hungry." He heaped his plate with food and dug in.

"Devendra sent word of Kanan's trial." Aderyn flapped the folded letter at him. "We were saying we don't think the rest of us should go."

Isold swallowed a large mouthful of food. "I agree. Our presence there could be considered inflammatory, as we are still outsiders and technically interfered in Southlander matters someone native should have done."

"I hadn't considered that, but you're right." Owen picked up a round of parotta and idly peeled strips off it, popping them one at a time into his mouth.

"The only thing I want from Kanan is to find out where Ruan and Suveer are," Aderyn groused. "I can totally see Ruan being opportunistic and leaving when he thought Kanan was going to lose, except nobody knew that would happen right up until Livia turned him into a bunny."

"Are we talking about Kanan?" Livia asked. She and Weston stood in the doorway, hands clasped. "Because I'm done thinking about him. For real this time."

"We were talking about Ruan being a selfish jerk," Owen said. "Come have breakfast."

"We ate already," Weston said, smiling. "In Asylum."

Everyone stopped eating to stare. "Asylum?" Aderyn said. "How—"

"I used *world door* to take us there first thing this morning," Livia said. Her smile was just as wide as Weston's. "I needed Weston to meet my family. It's my father's custom that he gives his approval to his children's marriages."

Owen dropped the remnants of his parotta. "Are you *married*?"

Livia and Weston's smiles became positively blinding. "I came to a lot of realizations in the past twenty-four hours," Livia said. "And one of those is that I've been waiting for a perfect moment that will never come. So I asked him, and he said yes, and..." Her smile became mischievous. "My mother loves him. My father wanted to argue, but—"

"I swear I don't mean to be intimidating, but someone my size, well, it's surprising how many fights I *don't* get into," Weston said. He put his arm around Livia's waist and spun her around, making her laugh.

"Congratulations," Isold said, clapping Weston on the shoulder. "It was a long time coming."

Aderyn hugged Livia, who hugged her back. "Now we just—" She stopped, her face flaming again, and couldn't look at Isold. Hopefully she'd shut up before she actually said anything insulting.

Isold smiled ruefully. "I understand," he said. "I haven't been myself recently, have I?"

"I really didn't mean to imply—I mean, Isold, it's not like you have to have sex, or be married," Aderyn babbled. "We just want you to be happy."

"Funny you should put it that way," Isold said. "I haven't wanted to share my troubles, because they are personal, but you are my closest friends, and, well..." He sighed. "In truth, I was afraid to say anything because I'm afraid my recent contemplations make me sound like the most self-centered man alive."

"That would be impossible," Owen said. "And you know we won't judge you even if that's true."

"I know." Isold gestured for Weston and Livia to sit. "I have always been fond of women, and my enjoyment of sex is well known. I took pleasure in charming the women I met and giving *them* pleasure—sometimes to the extent of feeling prideful of my skills. But that's not what disturbed me recently. Owen, you recall the place where we purchased our nobles' finery?"

Owen nodded.

"The shop owner was exceptionally lovely, and she responded to my mild flirtation in a way that said she would be open to more. In my imagination, I saw our flirtation expanding to a greater intimacy. I pictured the ways I would court her, the ways I would show her how beautiful I found her. I saw us consummating that intimacy. I saw the end of that consummation, and leaving her satisfied and pleased with our time together. And in that moment, I felt nothing but emptiness."

Isold's eyes were distant, as if he was reading his Codex, but Aderyn was sure he didn't see anything just then. "I didn't know what to make of that revelation—whether I no longer enjoyed sex, or whether I was tired of encounters that went nowhere, or even if I was simply in need of a change. It took many days of contemplation for me to realize the truth."

"What truth?" Aderyn couldn't help asking. She was sure he didn't need prompting to continue, but he looked so remote she wanted to make even the smallest connection with him.

Isold focused on her. "The truth that for years, I have put others' needs ahead of my own. In every sexual encounter I've ever had, my desire was for my partner's pleasure. Of course I enjoyed them as well, but most of my enjoyment was in satisfying the woman I slept with. And because that's a good thing, it never occurred to me that I was denying myself what *I* enjoyed." He shook his head. "As I said, hopelessly self-centered, to complain that my happiness is derived from the wrong source."

"No, I get it," Owen said. "Your heart was never engaged, just your body."

"That's well put." Isold's eyes again unfocused. "I have no regrets about the life I've lived. I like to think the women I've been intimate with are the better for our liaisons. But I'm now in a position of not having any idea what I want from those liaisons. And until I discover that, I have no desire to sleep with anyone."

"That doesn't make you sound terrible," Weston said. "Sex is powerful. You shouldn't feel obligated to have sex if it doesn't satisfy you."

"Which is why I am concerned that my denial of my own needs goes farther than sex," Isold said. "When I realized the truth, I didn't feel relieved, I felt guilty. As if I did have a duty, and my needs didn't matter. Which I know intellectually isn't true, but my heart isn't convinced."

Aderyn squeezed Isold's hand. "You are the kindest person I know. You need to be kind to yourself now."

Isold's brow furrowed. "I hadn't seen it that way."

"She's right," Livia said. "You want to help people—well, you're a person, too. There's no reason you should treat yourself poorly."

Isold smiled. "And now I know I was wrong to keep this secret for so long. Thank you all. Your perspective makes a difference. I don't know what I'll end up becoming, but now I'm convinced it won't be something terrible."

"I'm telling you, that would be impossible," Owen said, "unless you've been concealing your true nature all this time."

"Yes, you're acting like you're going to go on a destructive rampage," Livia said. "You can leave that to me."

"Livia," Aderyn said, alarmed.

"Sorry," Livia said. "I guess I'm still disturbed by killing that Deadeye. I didn't mean to sound so flippant."

Weston hugged her. "You don't ever have to use that spell again, dearest."

"I know. But I feel burdened by the knowledge of it." Livia's eyes were red with incipient tears. "So I'm going to do something about it."

"What?" Aderyn asked.

"*Acid ray* is a seventh level spell. I only get five of those, and it hurts all of us for me to have a useless one. So I'm going to replace it." Livia's voice was firm. "It's a difficult process, and it takes time, but in the end, I'll have something I'm not afraid to use."

"I can't imagine anyone more capable of taking on a difficult challenge than you," Weston said.

Livia nodded. "That's because I have the best team in the world. I can't do this alone."

Aderyn gripped her hand. "None of us can."

THAT AFTERNOON, ADERYN AND LIVIA RODE TO THE PALACE in a pedicab. Livia was quiet, and Aderyn guessed that despite her earlier words, she was thinking about Kanan. But then Livia said, "Being married feels strange. Good, but still—I mean, nothing's changed for us, and everything's changed as well."

"That's how I feel. And I love that everyone who Assesses me knows I'm united with someone. Owen says in his world, in the place where he comes from, people exchange rings they wear on their left hands to show they're married. But that's not nearly as satisfying as **[Unite]**."

"My parents were so surprised, but that makes sense. I've been gone for only a few months, and I show up with a giant Moonlighter in tow and announce we're getting married. *And* I'm level seventeen. That stopped them thinking I was a dilettante who never would amount to anything." Livia grinned. "I can't wait for them to meet the rest of you someday. And for you to kick my father's ass at Wall. Don't think I've forgotten."

"Your family is strange," Aderyn said with a laugh.

The palace guards ushered them in, and one of the women stationed inside said, "General Aderyn, please come with me." She indicated Livia should come along as well. Aderyn couldn't help wondering if the woman knew Livia was responsible for Kanan's current state. Probably not, or she'd have been more respectful. Livia didn't look like she minded being in Aderyn's entourage.

Aderyn had never been to the throne room and didn't know what to expect. Her experience with royalty other than Devendra to date had been in her parents' fanciful books about pretend kingdoms. This room was smaller than the place where Varoun had been invested as commander general, and chairs all occupied by nobles lined the walls flanking the throne. Aderyn had thought the thrones from before were grand, but this one had a back easily fifteen feet tall and appeared to be made of solid gold. Colan sat with his legs dangling, fidgeting and shifting his bottom like the seat was painfully hard.

Beside him, Devendra stood instead of sitting. She acknowledged Aderyn and Livia's entrance and beckoned to them to join her. "Bring in the prisoner," she called out.

Soon, two guards carried in the cage containing the rabbit. The nobles seated near the throne muttered quietly. Aderyn couldn't tell if they knew Kanan had been transformed or if they were just ready for the trial to be over. One of the guards broke open the crate and removed Kanan, holding him at arm's length as he struggled. He was blurry in Aderyn's vision the way he had been in the tent, like he was surrounded by a gauzy veil, but the guard's hand was clear and without distortion. Aderyn blinked away the effect and focused on Livia.

Livia took a position facing Kanan and began to speak. Again, Aderyn had the strange sensation of nearly understanding what Livia said. Again the *glorp* sound filled the air, and suddenly it was Kanan struggling in the guard's grip. Kanan tore himself free, then froze. He stared at the queen, then at Livia. "What magic did you use on me, bitch?" he said.

"Kanan, you stand accused of high treason against the kingdom," Devendra said coolly. "Have you anything to say in your defense?"

Kanan's gaze turned to Colan, who flinched. Livia's hands clenched, and she took a step toward Kanan before controlling herself. Kanan drew himself erect and said, "This is a sham. You've already made up your mind."

"You're right," Devendra said. "This kingdom will not endure a challenge to the king's person or his rule. I ask again, how do you defend yourself?"

"I will be a better king than you," Kanan spat at Devendra. "Your selfish grasp of the throne will destroy the Southlands. We need a strong ruler, not a child puppet whose mother pulls his strings."

"I am certain you know all about selfishness," Devendra said. "For the final time, what have you to say to defend yourself?"

Kanan glared at her in silence.

"The prisoner has failed to make a compelling case for his actions," Devendra said. "King Colan, what say you?"

Colan looked up at his mother, his eyes wide. "I—" He swallowed. "I declare the, um, prisoner is guilty of treason. High treason," he corrected himself as Devendra nudged him. "The penalty is death."

"Take him away," Devendra said. "The execution will be carried out at high noon tomorrow. Let everyone see the results of attacking the king."

Kanan didn't resist. He held his head high as the guards marched him out of the room.

Aderyn felt dizzy. Surely that hadn't taken long enough? Kanan was evil, and he'd imprisoned Devendra and tried to kill a child, but deciding to take a man's life shouldn't be so abrupt, should it? Aderyn was grateful she wasn't responsible for the Southlander government.

"Colan, I want you to go back to your room with Anagha so I can talk to these ladies. Aderyn, Livia, walk with me," Devendra said. She exited the room by the main doors, and Livia and Aderyn followed her.

They walked through the palace until they reached the courtyard where Aderyn had first met with Devendra. Today, no tea tray or food lay on the table, and no servants were present. Devendra waved a hand tiredly. "Have a seat."

Aderyn and Livia sat as Devendra sank into her chair. The queen looked exhausted, and Aderyn said, "Are you all right?"

"It has been a tumultuous few days," Devendra said. "And the difficulties aren't over. Orcs still assault Shantos, and General Varoun tells me he will need your presence at the front soon. But at least this one thing is done. Kanan will never threaten my son again, and anyone else considering such an action will think twice before attempting it. Does that satisfy you?"

"I don't want vengeance anymore," Livia said. "But I agree it's justice."

"I'm not sure of that, but a mother will do anything to protect her children." Devendra smiled. "Perhaps someday you'll know that personally."

"Are you worried about Ruan taking revenge? Kanan was his sponsor, after all." Aderyn didn't like thinking about Ruan being free to carry out some unknown plan of the former duke's.

Devendra leaned back in her chair and interlaced her fingers in her lap. "Ruan and Suveer left the duke's employ some hours before I was captured, after a spectacular argument. No one knows why they parted company, but some of those here in the palace believe they disagreed with Kanan over his proposed usurpation. I don't see it, myself, but I don't have a high opinion of Ruan or his morals. More likely Ruan believed Kanan would fail, leaving Ruan guilty of treason. At any rate, they are gone, and I hope never to see them again."

"Same here," Aderyn said.

Devendra sighed. "Kanan was right about one thing: having a child king has weakened the Southlands. I made poor decisions because I was motivated by Colan's safety, not by what the kingdom needs. But I see no way around that."

Livia sat up straight. "That's not true," she said. "You do have an idea. You just hate it."

"What idea?" Aderyn said.

Devendra eyed Livia. "You're more insightful than you seem, Earthbreaker. You're right. I intend for Colan to abdicate."

"But you can't," Aderyn exclaimed. "The confusion and turmoil surrounding the transfer of power, even if it's peaceful—and then, who would you choose? Wasn't the point of the College choosing the commander general that all the dukes didn't want one of them taking power? That says none of them will be acceptable as king."

"I did not say I would do it immediately," Devendra said. "I intend to find a suitable candidate and prepare the kingdom to accept him or her. And if I can't, then Colan will simply have to endure. But my dream is to take my children far from here so Colan can't be a rallying point for someone interested in challenging the new ruler years from now. And I will not see him destroyed by the machinations of others."

She looked so fierce Aderyn's next protest died on her lips. In the silence, Livia said, "You're more responsible than I would be. I'd take Colan and Rila and be on the next ship out of here, and to thunderation with the consequences. But I honor you for your faithfulness."

"As I honor you for your silence," Devendra said. "I don't need to tell you to speak of this to no one but your team members." She smiled wryly. "I won't bother requiring you not to tell them. Such a caution wouldn't work, I'm sure."

"Then why did you tell us?" Aderyn asked.

"Because you risked your lives for my son's sake." Devendra again looked fierce. "Your care for the Southlands isn't tied up in tradition or expectations, but in your sense of doing what's right. When the time comes, I may call on your support." She rose and bowed low. "Thank you. For everything."

Aderyn couldn't think of anything to say. She bowed in return. "You're welcome."

"And take care of the kid," Livia added.

That evening, the five friends gathered in Aderyn and Owen's room, lounging in chairs or on the bed. Aderyn had eaten well at dinner and now felt disinclined to move. There was only one thing she had the energy to manage. She whispered, "Advancement."

Name: Aderyn

∞ Jacob Owen Lindberg

Level: 17

Class: Warmaster

<u>Skills</u>: Bluff (16), Climb (13), Conversation (15), Intimidate (11), Sense Truth (17), Survival (9), Swim (3), Knowledge: Monsters (17), Knowledge: World Lore (9), Knowledge: Demons (2), Unite

<u>Class Skills:</u> Improved Assess 3 (29), Awareness (20), Knowledge: Geography (15), Spot (17), Discern Weakness (28), Dodge (18), Improvised Distraction (17), Outflank (22), Draw Fire (13), Keep Pace (20), Amplify Voice (18), See It Coming (24), Basic Weapon Proficiency (Swords) (15), Read Body Language (16), Basic Map Access (7), Compel (10), Spot Weakness (8), Secret Message (5), Bonded Mind (7), Sense Ambush (3), Reposition (4), Truesight (1)

[Truesight]? She focused on the last skill.

[Truesight]: Grants the ability to detect the existence of visual falsehoods, including illusions, transformations, and magical disguises. Higher ranks in this skill allow the user to see more powerful illusions, as well as to perceive what truth lies beneath them.

Aderyn's breath caught. That might explain the strange gauzy effect she'd seen when Kanan was in rabbit form. She sat up and looked wildly around the room, realized nobody there could create an illusion for her to test the skill on, and flopped back onto the bed.

"Something wrong, Aderyn?" Owen's voice was a little distant, and he, too, was reading his Codex. "Hey, can you tell me what **[Combat Momentum]** means?"

Aderyn Assessed him and focused on his newest skill. "It means the more rapidly you hit opponents, the greater the damage you do. Right now, if your blows come two seconds apart or less, the damage continues to build until you miss or slow down. And as you gain ranks, that period increases, so you have more time to take advantage of it."

Owen whistled. "It's like filling a reservoir of power. I can't imagine what skills I have left to gain, that one is so powerful."

"I don't have anything nearly as dramatic, but my **[Evasion]** skill has an upgrade. I think it becomes the equivalent of **[See It Coming]**," Weston said. "I like it."

"I'm not sure about this one," Livia said. "It's called **[Counter-spell]** and it lets me use magical energy to turn a spell back on its user. But when do we ever face enemy spellslingers?"

"Orcs have spellslingers. Elementalists," Aderyn said. "We'll probably face more of them in future. Sounds like that skill appeared just in time."

"Well, just in case it's not useful, in addition to *greater polymorph* I also chose a seventh-level spell called *summon earth elemental*. It's like that water creature Devendra summoned to get the wereshark off Isold, but made of earth or stone. It doesn't do much damage by comparison to us, but the important thing is that if it and I are both connected to the earth, I can deliver certain spells through it." Livia grinned. "Imagine *thunderstomp* coming from two directions at once."

"I love this plan," Weston said. "What about you, Isold?"

Isold was smiling a funny little half-smile like he'd heard a joke no one else got. "Let me see if I can show you." He rose from his chair and whistled two notes. His whole body rippled, and in his place stood Owen.

Exclamations of surprise filled the room. The real Owen leaped up and put himself in front of the disguised Isold, peering at his face. "It's not a perfect copy, but it's damn close," he declared.

To Aderyn, Isold's false shape seemed shrouded in mist. "Now I know how **[Truesight]** works," she exclaimed. "I can tell Isold's disguise isn't true, but I still see Owen instead of him."

Isold took a step back from Owen, and the disguise shredded like old cloth and disappeared. "It's called **[Mimic]**, and it's limited to people I can either see or people whose appearance I know well. I can think of any number of uses, especially as my skill ranks grow."

"Sounds like something I'd appreciate," Weston said. "I have a **[Disguise]** skill I never use. We're not that kind of adventuring team, I guess."

"And now that we've established what our new abilities are," Owen said, "it's time we talk about the future."

In silence, each of them opened the Codex and looked at the **[Fated One's Destiny: Crush the Horde]** quest.

An army of monstrous orcs has emerged from the Blighted Range, intent on conquering the southern human lands. Destroy their leaders and push the army back into the mountains. Recommended minimum party level for this quest is 17.

Victory conditions:
Death of Glasha, orc commander general
ACHIEVED Death of Ornok, second in command
Death of ?
Death of ?
Death of ?
Destruction of Charnel Keep
Orc army retreats

Reward: [75,000 XP] plus any XP gained through actions taken to complete the quest.

"When did we learn their commander's name?" Livia said.

"It was in my Assessment of Ornok," Aderyn said. "I'm sure the system considers that knowledge enough to update the quest. But—Charnel Keep? What is Charnel Keep?"

"Can't you find out?" Owen said.

Aderyn blinked. "Of course. I was startled." She focused on that line.

Charnel Keep is the main orc stronghold, located within the Blighted Range. It is considered a dungeon for quest purposes. You'll need to approach it physically for more information. Saying more would be against the rules. You understand.

Aderyn *didn't* understand, but she didn't care. "It's a dungeon that's also the primary orc stronghold. I'd be more discouraged if I hadn't already half expected this quest to take us into the Blighted Range. We're not so lucky that all the orc leaders we have to kill will come to us."

"You're right, it doesn't matter that the system added to the quest," Owen said. "We've come this far and we're not stopping now."

"Tomorrow morning I'll meet with Varoun and tell him about Charnel Keep," Aderyn said. "Maybe he doesn't know. The fact that the orcs have an important stronghold is valuable information. And then we'll make a new plan. The fighting is still heavy around Shantos."

"Yeah," Livia said distantly. "Plenty of orcs for us to kill."

"Is something wrong?" Weston asked.

Livia shook her head as if coming out of a daze. "I don't know. I just got this premonition that what comes next will be the kind of unexpected we don't know how to prepare for. But that's stupid. We can handle anything."

"That's the kind of optimistic thing you always punch me for saying," Weston said.

"I'm all right with a small jinx," Livia said. "And probably it's nothing. Just superstition."

"Just superstition," Aderyn repeated, but a chill had gone up her spine at Livia's words. The memory of seeing the words Charnel Keep appear in the quest notice wouldn't leave her. A surprise dungeon added to their quest conditions? She was sure Livia was right about one thing: whatever came next would be unexpected.

Appendix: Character Sheets

NOTE: These character sheets represent the status of the companions at the end of the book, which means it reveals everything the companions learn about their skills throughout the story. If you haven't finished the book, don't read this unless you don't mind spoilers!

Name: Aderyn

∞ Jacob Owen Lindberg

Level: 17

Class: Warmaster

<u>Skills</u>: Bluff (16), Climb (13), Conversation (15), Intimidate (11), Sense Truth (17), Survival (9), Swim (3), Knowledge: Monsters (17), Knowledge: World Lore (9), Knowledge: Demons (2), Unite

<u>Class Skills:</u> Improved Assess 3 (29), Awareness (20), Knowledge: Geography (15), Spot (17), *Discern Weakness (28),* Dodge (18), Improvised Distraction (17), *Outflank* (22), Draw Fire (13), *Keep Pace* (20), Amplify Voice (18), See It Coming (24), Basic Weapon Proficiency (Swords) (15), *Read Body Language* (16), Basic Map Access (7), Compel (10), Spot Weakness (8), Secret

Message (5), *Bonded Mind* (7), Sense Ambush (3), Reposition (4), Truesight (1)

*italics are paired skills with partner

Name: Jacob Owen Lindberg

∞ Aderyn

Class: Swordsworn

Level: 17

Skills: Assess (13), Awareness (17), Climb (13), Conversation (15), Sense Truth (14), Spot (13), Survival (9), Swim (13), Knowledge: Demons (2), Unite

Class Skills: Superior Weapon Proficiency (29), Advanced Armor Proficiency (22), Knowledge: Monsters (14), *Exploit Weakness* (28), Dodge (18), Parry (18), Improved Bluff (17), *Outflank* (22), Trip (7), *Keep Pace* (20), Disarm (8), Intimidate (15), Charge (8), Two-Weapon Fighting (12), *Read Body Language* (16), Basic Map Access (7), Overrun (7), Shatter Confidence (3), *Bonded Mind* (7), Weapon Mastery (longsword), Anatomist (6), Combat Momentum (0)

*italics are paired skills with Warmaster

Name: Weston

∞ Livia

Class: Moonlighter

Level: 17

Skills: Assess (15), Climb (16), Conversation (14), Intimidate (12), Survival (9), Swim (6), Knowledge: Social (15), Knowledge: Demons (2), Unite

Class Skills: Pick Locks (18), Advanced Sneak Attack (17), Superior Weapons Proficiency (15), Advanced Armor Proficiency (15), Improved Detect Traps (19), Disable Traps (17), Improved Spot (21), Awareness (17), Dodge (18), Stealth (20), Improved Bluff (15), Dirty Fighting (12), To the Heart (18), Hide (11), Improved Thrown Weapons Proficiency (12), Disguise (3), Hide in Plain Sight (7), Improved Evasion (9), Basic Map Access (7),

Escape Artist (5), Unarmed Combat (3), Improvised Weapon (3), Glibness (2), Improved Sense Truth (15)

Name: Isold

Class: Herald

Level: 17

<u>Skills</u>: Assess (12), Awareness (17), Bluff (12), Climb (8), Conversation (10), Intimidate (6), Sense Truth (18), Spot (16), Survival (9), Swim (5), Knowledge: Demons (3)

<u>Class Skills</u>: Perform (singing) (21); Knowledge: Magic (15); Knowledge: Monsters (16); Knowledge: History (14); Knowledge: Social (12); Knowledge: World Lore (15); Identify Magic Items (17); Charm (18); Distraction (13); Improved Map Access (17); Inspire Courage (16); Fascination (12); Persuasion (11); Perform (drum) (13); Suggestion (11); Resist Magic (8); Shout (6); Hypnotize (11); Find Object (5); Coercion (5); Break Enchantment (6); Perform (flute) (4); Cause Fear (4); Sleep, Mass (2); Mimic (0)

Name: Livia

∞ Weston

Class: Earthbreaker

Level: 17

<u>Skills</u>: Assess (8), Awareness (10), Bluff (9), Climb (5), Conversation (11), Intimidate (15), Sense Truth (12), Spot (13), Survival (9), Swim (6), Knowledge: Demons (2), Unite

<u>Elemental Powers</u>: Earth, stone, acid

<u>Class Skills:</u> Knowledge: Magic (17), Elemental Blast (earth spray, shower of small stones, rain of large stones, stone sphere shrapnel) (15), Earth to Mud/Mud to Earth (10), Mage Armor (shifting stone slabs) (11), Excavate (10), Summon Elemental Hammer (5), Basic Map Access (7), Tremorsense (7), Sculpt Earth/Stone (6), Speak with Stone (3), Pass Through Stone (3), Counterspell (0)

Spell List

0-level spells: Daze; Drench; Light; Telekinesis, minor; Mending; Freezing Ray, minor; Root, Spark

1st Level spells

Air Bubble; Break; Force Shield; Grease; Heat Metal (slow); Loose Bonds; Mudball; Sunder Weapon; Thunder Punch

2nd Level spells

Create Pit; Dust Cloud; Earth's Endurance; Thunderstomp; Mirror Image; Mud Minion; Improved Mending; Protection from Fire, Mass (big earth dome); Skip

3rd Level spells

Iron Spike Attack; Thunderstomp, Greater (directed); Clairvoyance; Dispel Magic; Immobilize; Telekinesis, Greater; Daylight

4th Level spells

Stone Ladder; Stone Sphere; Transport, Minor; Invisibility (self); Earth Glide; Stone Fist; Daze, Mass

5th Level spells

Hungry Pit; Dismissal of Demons; Scry; Lighten Object; Darkvision; Passwall; Burrow

6th Level spells

Move earth, major; Stoneskin, Mass; Invisibility, Mass; Dispel Magic, greater; Truthspeak

7th Level spells

Immobilize, greater; Sunburst; Reverse gravity, localized; Acid ray; Summon large earth elemental

8th Level Spells

World door; Greater Polymorph

Acknowledgments

I gratefully acknowledge the insights of JR Handley, who shared his experiences of being in combat in support of the events of Chapters Twenty-Seven and Twenty-Eight. The real thing far outstrips my ability to convey it. JR, thank you for your service.

Sherwood Smith recommended some excellent books on the principles of combat strategy and leadership that I found invaluable, *The Face of Battle* by John Keegan and *Command in War* by Martin van Creveld. All mistakes, screw-ups, and inventions for the sake of story remain mine alone.

And now a special message...

Did you enjoy this book? Want more LitRPG adventure goodness? Then the LitRPG Books Facebook group is for you! Find new recommendations, connect with fellow readers, and more!

About the Author

In addition to the Warmaster series, Melissa McShane is the author of many fantasy novels, including the novels of Tremontane, the first of which is *Servant of the Crown;* The Extraordinaries series, beginning with *Burning Bright;* and *The Book of Secrets,* first book in The Last Oracle series.

While her home remains in the mountains out West, she currently lives in Kerala, India, with her husband and two rambunctious Persian cats who believe they own the house. She wrote reviews and critical essays for many years before turning to fiction, which is much more fun than anyone ought to be allowed to have.

You can visit her at her website

www.melissamcshanewrites.com

for more information on other books and upcoming releases.

To subscribe to her newsletter, which is published monthly, visit **www.melissamcshanewrites.com/contact-me-2/join-my-mailing-list**

ALSO BY MELISSA MCSHANE

WARMASTER

Warmaster 1: Dungeon Spiteful

Warmaster 2: Winter's Peril

Warmaster 3: Gamboling Coil

Warmaster 4: Sorrowvale

Warmaster 5: The Glory Games

Warmaster 6: The Lonely Tor

Warmaster 7: The Ivory Palace

Warmaster 8: Charnel Keep (forthcoming)

Warmaster 9: Stormwatch Citadel (forthcoming)

Warmaster 10: Winterforge (forthcoming)

THE BOOKS OF THE DARK GODDESS

Silver and Shadow

Missing by Moonlight

Shades of the Past

Path of the Paladin

Bright Moon Deception

Black Wings' Shadow (forthcoming)

THE LAST ORACLE

The Book of Secrets

The Book of Peril

The Book of Mayhem

The Book of Lies

The Book of Betrayal

The Book of Havoc

The Book of Harmony

The Book of War

The Book of Destiny

THE LIVING ORACLE

Hidden Realm

Hidden Enemy

Hidden Pursuit

THE EXTRAORDINARIES

Burning Bright

Wondering Sight

Abounding Might

Whispering Twilight

Liberating Fight

Beguiling Birthright

Soaring Flight

Discerning Insight

THE NOVELS OF TREMONTANE

Pretender to the Crown

Guardian of the Crown

Champion of the Crown

Ally of the Crown

Stranger to the Crown

Scholar of the Crown

Servant of the Crown

Exile of the Crown

Rider of the Crown

Agent of the Crown

Voyager of the Crown

Tales of the Crown

COMPANY OF STRANGERS

Company of Strangers

Stone of Inheritance

Mortal Rites

Shifting Loyalties

Sands of Memory

Call of Wizardry

THE DRAGONS OF MOTHER STONE

Spark the Fire

Faith in Flames

Ember in Shadow

Skies Will Burn

THE CONVERGENCE TRILOGY

The Summoned Mage

The Wandering Mage

The Unconquered Mage

THE BOOKS OF DALANINE

The Smoke-Scented Girl

The God-Touched Man

Emissary

Warts and All: The Deluxe Expanded Edition

The View from Castle Always

Winter Across Worlds: A Holiday Collection

www.ingramcontent.com/pod-product-compliance
Lightning Source LLC
Chambersburg PA
CBHW051443260626
47162CB00001B/220

* 9 7 8 1 9 6 4 5 4 5 1 6 5 *